MW01093639

Temptation TRAILS

A SMALL-TOWN ROMANCE

CLAIRE KINGSLEY

Always Have LLC

Published by Always Have, LLC

Edited by Michelle Fewer

Cover design by Lori Jackson

ISBN: 978-1-959809-16-6

www.clairekingsleybooks.com

❀ Created with Vellum

For all the delightful women who immediately raised their hands when I asked for volunteers to be un-alived in this book.

And for the real Jasmine. You're welcome?

About this book

He's hunting a killer so she won't be next.

Single dad Garrett Haven doesn't have time for dating. With a
teenage son and a high-stakes job in law enforcement, he has
enough on his plate.

Besides, he risked his heart once. He has no intention of
doing it again.

Until he meets her.

Harper Tilburn brought her passion for baking to the
small town of Tilikum to take over her aunt's bakery.
Anything else will have to wait, at least until her bad luck
curse runs out.

Her dating hiatus is essential, and she's sticking to it.

Until she meets him.

The sparks that fly between Garrett and Harper are instan-
taneous—their attraction undeniable. And suddenly, the practical, responsible sheriff's deputy is throwing caution to the
wind, boldly pursuing Harper, determined to make her his.

But when the cold case Garrett is investigating takes a
chilling turn, he fears the perpetrator will strike again—and
Harper will be his target.

With his career—and his life—on the line, he'll sacrifice everything to protect the people he loves, and catch a killer before it's too late.

Author's note: a buttoned-up sheriff's deputy gets thoroughly unbuttoned by a sweet as sugar baker. A hero who falls hard and fast, a heroine you'll root for, a teenage son who will steal your heart, page turning suspense with a shocking twist, and heartwarming found family vibes with a big HEA.

Temptation Trails can be read as a stand-alone.

CHAPTER 1

Garrett

THE TRAIL WAS CLEAR. Tire tracks ran through the bed of pine needles, leaving a depression in the ground. It wasn't a road, but someone had driven that way recently.

The spring air was warm and I could feel a bead of sweat drip down my back as I hiked up the low hill. We'd received a call from a hiker who'd come across a car in the woods, well away from any roads or parking. It had seemed suspicious, so he'd reported it. Unfortunately, he hadn't taken pictures or given us the license plate number, so I wasn't sure what I was going to find.

It was suspicious, the hiker had been right about that. There was no good reason for a car to be out there.

Plenty of bad ones, though.

Cresting the hill, I saw it. A silver Hyundai sedan. It had seen better days, although at a glance it was hard to tell if that was due to how long it had been at its current location or to normal wear and tear. Probably a bit of both. There were rust spots on the trunk and around the bottom of the doors, and a few minor dents.

After confirming no one was inside, I keyed my mic to check in with Brenna in dispatch.

"Squad seven."

"Go ahead, squad seven," Brenna replied.

"Found the car. Looks abandoned."

"I'll run the plate and see if we hit on anything."

"10-4."

I gave her the license plate number and pulled out my flashlight to look underneath the car while I waited.

"Winner, winner, chicken dinner," she said a moment later. "Silver Hyundai sedan, reported stolen from a residence in Echo Creek a week ago."

Echo Creek was a town about thirty minutes away, just outside my agency's jurisdiction. "You want to let the PD down there know we found it?"

"I'm on it."

"10-4."

I walked slowly around the car, looking for anything that might give us information as to why it was there. Through the windows, I could see a mess of garbage. A greasy pizza box sat on the passenger's seat and the floor was strewn with wrappers, bags, and empty bottles.

There were three backpacks and a duffel bag in the back seat, all of which appeared full. That was a big red flag. Unless the car's owner had been packing for a trip, those bags were probably full of contraband.

It was typical. Criminals generally stole cars for several reasons. Reselling, parting them out, joyriding, or using them as getaway vehicles or as a means to commit other crimes. Based on what I was seeing, my first instinct was that the car had been used in a string of other thefts, then abandoned.

I wouldn't normally have been the responding officer for this type of call, but my role in the department had recently changed. I was still a deputy, but I was also a part-time detective. We were a small agency, without the resources for a fully staffed detective bureau. That meant I was still on patrol a lot, and, unlike detectives on cop shows, often still in uniform.

But it was giving me the opportunity to do more investigative work. And it meant fewer graveyard shifts, which was a big win considering I was a single dad.

I glanced at the time. If this call hadn't come in, I'd have been off duty in about ten minutes. That would have given me just enough time to go home and make sure Owen had done his homework, get us both a quick bite to eat, then head out to the Timberbeast Tavern.

Unfortunately, I had a date tonight.

How I'd let my aunt Louise talk me into a blind date, I had no idea. She inexplicably took credit for the fact that two of my brothers, Josiah and Zachary, had both gotten married earlier that year. She hadn't orchestrated either of those relationships, but try telling her that. And, as Aunt Louise was notorious for her questionable matchmaking efforts, I never said yes when she tried to set me up with someone.

But for some reason, when she'd started bugging me about letting her set me up with someone named Harper, I'd caved.

Now I had all the regrets. I didn't want to date. Not only did I not have time, I had no desire for another relationship. Been there, done that, got the divorce decree. The only good thing that had come out of my horrible mistake of a marriage had been my son. But parenting a fourteen-year-old boy on my own while working in law enforcement was the equivalent of about five full-time jobs. I couldn't handle dating on top of that.

And I didn't want to.

Harper and I had texted back and forth enough to make plans, but I didn't know anything about her. And it was anyone's guess if I could trust Aunt Louise's description.

Out of a sense of duty, or maybe it was just manners, I texted Harper to let her know I was going to be late.

I pocketed my phone and went back to my search. The trunk was empty, but the bags in the back seat were stuffed with a random assortment of items—cell phones, other electronics, watches, prescription drug bottles, and a handful of wallets.

I had a strong feeling I already knew who'd stolen the car. It wouldn't have been the first time this guy had jacked someone's ride and dumped it—after committing multiple other crimes.

Trent Jones.

Every agency has people we all know. Frequent fliers, we call them. They're in and out of the system, often for the same crimes. Trent Jones was one of them.

He had the dubious distinction of being my very first arrest. He'd gone to prison after that, but he was probably on the streets again.

One way to find out. I keyed my mic to ask Brenna. "Squad seven."

"Go ahead, squad seven."

"Can you find out if Trent Jones is still incarcerated?"

"What'd you find?"

"Nothing specific yet, but this looks a lot like him. We've got bags of contraband in the back seat and someone apparently decided to have a pizza in the middle of their crime spree."

She chuckled. "That's lovely. Hang on a second."

I walked a few feet away while I waited for Brenna to report back. Whoever had dumped the car had left at least some of what they'd stolen. That meant they were probably planning to come back for it.

Had the suspect been there when the hiker found the car? Maybe he'd taken off and that was why he'd left stuff behind.

There was a trail to the east and another to the south, both of which would make reasonable getaway routes back to civilization.

Which way did you go?

A metallic glint on the ground caught my eye. It was

about ten feet behind the car, in a spot where the pine needles and other debris had been churned up by the wheels. I took a few pictures with my phone, then put on one of my gloves and crouched to take a closer look.

I picked up a dirty silver bracelet. It had a curved plate with writing engraved on it and the chain connecting the two sides was broken. I wiped off enough of the dirt and squinted so I could read it.

The outside said, *be kind*, but on the inside the sentence finished with, *of a bitch sometimes*.

Okay, that was funny.

It didn't appear to have anything to do with the stolen car. If I had to guess, it had been out there for a while. Years, maybe. The tires had disturbed the forest debris enough to dig it up.

Probably didn't mean anything, but I put it in a plastic bag and tucked it in my pocket. Just in case.

"Squad seven," Brenna said over dispatch.

"Go ahead, Bren."

"He's out. Released two months ago."

"Thanks."

Didn't prove it was him, but he was the first guy I wanted to talk to.

"Can we get impound out there?" she asked. "Obviously someone drove the car there, but that doesn't mean a tow truck can make it."

"They'll make it. There isn't a road, but it's pretty clear. Trees are sparse."

"Got it."

There wasn't much more for me to do at the scene. The car would be impounded and the evidence processed. I needed to get back to the office and connect with my counterpart in Echo Creek to find out if they had any leads already.

Plus, I had that date. I could still make it. And that was the right thing to do. Whether or not I wanted to go, I was a man of my word. I wasn't going to stand her up.

The hair on the back of my neck stood on end and I paused. Had I heard something? My instincts lit up. Something—or someone—was nearby.

There was plenty of wildlife in those woods. It could have been any number of things. But my gut was telling me it was our suspect, coming for what was in those bags.

I took a few slow steps in the direction of the noise, scanning the area for movement.

A man poked his head out from behind a tree and his eyes widened when he saw me.

I was right. Trent Jones. I would have known his face anywhere.

"Stop," I called out. "Show me your hands."

He was close enough, I could see the flash of anger cross his features. I knew him, and he clearly remembered me.

I had a feeling I was not on his list of favorite people.

His hands went up and he stepped out from behind the tree.

"What are you doing out here, Trent?"

"Haven," he spat.

He was going to run. You didn't have to do this job long to learn the signs. He shifted his body weight and his right shoulder drew back, as if he were about to spin around.

"Don't do it, Trent."

Too late. He spun and took off running.

I keyed my mic. "Suspect fleeing the scene. In pursuit on foot." And I took off after him.

The terrain was fairly clear, without a lot of underbrush. We darted past the trees, kicking up dust and pine needles in our wake. He was a decade older than me, but he'd just done time—probably in prison shape—and I was carrying at least twenty pounds of gear.

But he was not getting away.

Sweat broke out on my forehead as I ran. Where the hell did he think he was going? There wasn't anything out there. Nowhere to hide or take shelter. He was heading toward one of the hiking trails, but that wasn't going to help.

Did he actually think he was going to outrun me?

"You're making this worse, buddy," I called out in between breaths.

He glanced over his shoulder and ran harder.

The ground rose in a small incline and I started to close the gap between us. His pace slowed; he was probably getting tired. I was sweating, and my legs burned with effort, but I knew I had him. I just had to keep pushing.

Finally, I got close enough to grab him. I took him to the ground, earning myself a face-full of dirt in the process. He thrashed around, trying to squirm away, and threw a punch at me. That missed but his second connected, glancing off my jaw.

I didn't hit back, just got control of his arms. He kicked at me, grunting with rage, but I had him. I rolled him onto his front and pinned him down.

"Fuck you, Haven," he growled as I cuffed him and hauled him to his feet.

I could have lectured him about the fact that he was the one who'd—allegedly—committed a string of crimes. And he was the one who'd run when I told him to stop. But I knew it wouldn't do any good.

"You're a piece of shit," he said.

"This isn't personal. I'm just doing my job."

He glared at me, hatred burning in his eyes.

I checked in with dispatch, letting them know I'd apprehended a suspect. Dirt and pine needles stuck to his clothes but that was his problem. After brushing myself off, I grabbed his arm so I could lead him back to where I'd left my car.

This is going to be a fun hike.

Shit. Harper. I wasn't just going to be late, I wasn't going to make it at all. Bringing in a suspect was great, but it meant a hell of a lot more work.

Fortunately, Trent didn't seem interested in chatting as we hiked out of the woods. And he didn't try to run again, either. Getting him off the streets again was a big win. He'd been caught for property crimes numerous times, but I wondered if he was guilty of more. My instincts weren't evidence, but the way he habitually resisted arrest showed he had a violent streak.

I made a mental note to cross check any unsolved assault or murder cases that also included property crimes, just in case there were more serious charges Trent needed to face.

By the time I got him back to the sheriff's office and booked him in a holding cell, I was hopelessly late. I called Owen and told him to make do with a sandwich for dinner and I'd get home when I could. Then I texted Harper to apologize. She'd probably been sitting at the Timberbeast waiting for me.

I felt bad about that, but I also had a job to do. Besides, it was for the best. I didn't want to start dating anyway.

CHAPTER 2

Harper

MY DATE WAS LATE. Because of course he was. That was my luck.

The Timberbeast Tavern might have seemed like an odd choice for a blind date, but I appreciated the casual atmosphere. The walls were decorated with vintage logging photos, old business signs, and rusty timber tools. The floor was sticky and my stool was a little wobbly, but the whole vibe made it feel like there wasn't any pressure. We could have a drink, chat a little, and see if we hit it off.

I was new in town, so it seemed like a good idea to get out and meet someone.

Or it had seemed like a good idea when my aunt Doris had talked me into it earlier that week. Her friend Louise had a nephew named Garrett, and she and Doris had set us up.

More specifically, they had gushed about all the amazing qualities Garrett supposedly possessed. Which made me wonder how badly they were exaggerating. Handsome, loyal, protective, kind, good job, stable, generous, helpful… They'd gone on and on. Louise had added ample and well-endowed with obvious winks.

I didn't buy it. Nobody is that perfect. Although if he were half as great as they claimed, he was certainly worth meeting.

Even worth breaking my self-imposed dating ban.

"Can I get you anything?" the bartender asked, his voice a low rumble.

He was the most intimidating bartender I'd ever seen in person. He was huge, tall, and barrel chested. He had a bushy beard and the sleeves on his red and black buffalo plaid flannel were rolled up to the elbows, revealing thick, hairy arms.

"No. I mean, not yet. I won't just sit here taking up your stool all night and not buy anything. That would be rude." I was babbling. "Maybe just a water for now?"

He didn't seem bothered by my rambling. Just slid a coaster with the Timberbeast Tavern logo on it across the bar, then poured an ice water and set it on the coaster.

"Thanks."

No answer. Just a chin tip.

"I'm new in town, so I thought, why not agree to a blind date?" I had no idea why I was talking to him. By his slightly puzzled expression, he didn't know either. "Do you know my aunt Doris? Doris Tilburn? She owns Angel Cakes Bakery."

With a grunt, he nodded.

"She's not as young as she used to be. Turns out she was having health problems and barely keeping up with the bakery. But did she tell anyone? No, she didn't, not until she was almost too behind to catch up. When I got here, she had a wedding cake due that very day. Thankfully I was able to finish and get it to the reception on time."

He blinked but his expression didn't change.

"Sugar cookies," I mumbled. "Sorry, I'm rambling. But Angel Cakes is still open, so I guess that's the good news."

"You're the new baker?"

"Yep."

"You make good cookies."

I smiled. "Thanks."

He nodded again and walked away.

I probably shouldn't have started babbling at him like that. But I was anxious. Not because of the blind date. Well, yes because of the blind date, but not for the reasons you'd think. I was a little bit nervous about meeting someone new, but mostly I was nervous because of the curse.

I know, *curse* sounds so dramatic. And I'm not usually a dramatic person, but in this case, I had reason to be.

A little over six years ago, I'd broken a mirror.

Most people scoffed when I told them about the curse, especially my always-practical mother and sister. But I knew it was real. Seven years bad luck for this girl, and I had the unlucky list to prove it.

Lost keys, cars with dead batteries, flat tires on the highway—I'd lost count of how many nails I'd run over—spilled coffee on brand new clothes, dropped eggs, misplaced mail, packages returned to sender for absolutely no reason. If there was a puddle, I'd step in it. A trip hazard, I'd trip over it. Most incidents were mere annoyances, a few were worse.

The curse was why I'd banned myself from dating. As much as I would have loved to meet a great guy, fall in love, get married, and start a family—let's not talk about how much my ovaries ached every time I saw anything baby related—the curse kept screwing things up.

For six years, every time I met someone with even the slightest hint of potential, something would go wrong. At least, something would go wrong *for me*.

Shortly after I'd broken the mirror, I'd gone out with a great guy. Handsome, smart, funny. We'd totally hit it off, made plans to see each other again. The very next day, he was offered a huge promotion. In Singapore. Needless to say, our one date hadn't been magical enough to get him to turn that down.

Then there was the guy who got an offer for his dream job

right after our second date. It took him to the east coast and we hadn't been dating long enough to try to make it work. Another guy ghosted me after what I'd thought had been a nice first date. Turned out, something in our conversation had inspired him to quit his job and follow his dream of moving to Costa Rica. Nice for him, but boo for me.

The curse was relentless.

I'd had my share of bad dates, too. A friend had set me up with her cousin once. She'd told me he was artistic. Turned out, he was perpetually unemployed and looking for a sugar mama to support him. Another guy I'd met at the bakery where I'd worked had seemed nice, until I found out he didn't believe in commitment and insisted all his relationships remain "open."

Um, no. Not my jam.

At some point, I'd realized what was happening. The mirror curse was sabotaging me. So I'd decided to wait until it was over. Then I could start dating again and at least have a chance at finding the one.

I checked my phone. Garrett had texted, letting me know he was probably going to be late. It had come in a while ago. How had I missed that?

Mirror curse.

Maybe agreeing to the date had been a mistake. I'd talked myself into it, hoping the new setting would make a difference. After coming to Tilikum to help Doris with Angel Cakes, I'd quickly realized it either needed to become a permanent situation, or she'd have to close. She had one other baker and an awesome employee who helped with the front counter, but no one to take charge.

She'd instilled in me my love of baking as a little girl. And had given me the courage to pursue it as a career, despite my mother's misgivings.

And by misgivings, I mean lectures about how I was

selling myself short and wasting all my potential on a silly hobby.

In any case, I owed a lot to Doris. So I'd quit my job and moved to Tilikum to take over Angel Cakes Bakery.

I'd been hoping the curse wouldn't follow me. And at first, I thought it hadn't. Things at the bakery were going well now that I was there full-time. I'd found a cute rental house. Moving had been a lot of work—as moving always is—but nothing major had gone wrong. There were a box or two that had disappeared into thin air, but considering the mirror curse could have done much worse, I hoped it might be on its last leg.

But sitting alone at the Timberbeast Tavern, waiting for a blind date who was late, made me wonder if I'd been wrong.

I knew from Aunt Doris that Garrett was a deputy with the local sheriff's office. Man in uniform certainly had appeal. I also knew he had a son, which was a little bit intimidating, although not a deal breaker by any stretch.

But what was the curse up to? Giving him a flat tire? Stirring up trouble with his son?

Or maybe he didn't want to come at all and he was looking for an excuse to stand me up. If his aunt Louise had been as pushy about this as Doris, he might have given in under duress and had all the regrets.

I traced my finger through the condensation on the outside of my glass and sighed.

"You sure you don't want a drink?" the bartender asked.

"I should have known better," I said, half-aware that I hadn't answered his simple and direct question. "I banned myself from dating for good reason. I have another seven months. Less than a year. I couldn't have waited?"

He just watched me, his heavy brow furrowed with confusion or concern—or maybe both.

"Pathetic, right? I know. I'm thirty-one and spent most of my twenties being chased by a bad luck curse. And now, here

I am, in a new town, rambling on to a bartender who probably thinks I'm the weirdest girl he's ever met while waiting for a blind date who probably isn't going to show."

My phone buzzed. It was Garrett again.

So sorry. I can't make it. Something came up at work.

I held up my phone. "See? Told you."

He hesitated for a second, then grabbed a shot glass from under the bar. He poured a shot of whiskey and slid it over to me. "On me."

Despite hating whiskey, I sighed again and swallowed the shot. I winced as it went down. "Thanks."

He tossed a fresh Timberbeast Tavern coaster toward me. "Take one home if you want."

I picked it up. It had the name of the bar with a cartoon lumberjack with a thick beard and big hairy arms. It was cute. Kinda looked like the bartender.

Yep, a date had been a mistake. I felt bad for Garrett. He had no idea he'd been caught in my bad luck curse.

Then again, maybe it was a good for him, bad for me situation. Maybe he'd just solved a huge case and all his career dreams were about to come true.

Meanwhile, I was banning myself from dating. Again.

Seven more months. That was all I had left. The bad luck curse would be over, and I could move on.

Besides, I was starting a new life in a new place, and my bad luck was sure to show up in all sorts of ways. I had a feeling I was going to have my hands full enough as it was.

There'd be time for dating again. But that time was not now.

CHAPTER 3

Harper

THERE WERE few things that smelled as good as freshly baked bread. Sugar cookies were one of them, and both scents mingled in the bakery kitchen as I worked.

Horatio had already been in to bake the day's batch of fresh bread. Although Angel Cakes specialized in cakes, cupcakes, and cookies, Aunt Doris had wanted to expand our offerings to include bread and dinner rolls. That wasn't my specialty, so I was glad Doris had brought him on. He was a bread-baking genius.

I scooped more cookie dough onto a large baking sheet. This batch was very much an experiment and I wondered if customers would be willing to give them a try. I'd been dabbling with grain-free baking—I know, it sounds strange—and the snickerdoodles didn't have an ounce of wheat flour.

Tilikum didn't have a lot of options for people who were gluten free or just watching their carbohydrate intake, so I'd been refining this recipe for the last several days, hoping to find one that tasted as good as it smelled. I had a feeling I'd finally nailed it.

With its stainless-steel counters and appliances, four ovens, and plenty of shelves to keep everything organized, the bakery kitchen was a dream to work in. The walls were white with a scalloped pink border near the ceiling and the large island provided ample workspace. The motif carried into the front, with an exposed brick wall painted white and the same scalloped pink border. Wooden shelves displayed bagged treats to go, as well as the bread and rolls, and there were a few café tables with chairs, usually used for cake tastings.

But the crown jewel was the pastry case.

Every day, we filled it with a new selection of delicious creations. Our specialties were cupcakes and cookies, but we also dabbled with brownies, cake pops, and other treats. The classics were always popular—sugar cookies, chocolate chip, peanut butter, oatmeal raisin. I liked to offer seasonal specialties as well. It was spring, so we had strawberry cream cheese and lemon blueberry cupcakes, as well as frosted sugar cookies shaped like tulips.

I put the cookies into the oven and set two timers. I didn't trust just one. Such was life when it was ruled by your bad luck.

The back door opened and my aunt Doris walked in. She greeted me with a warm smile and I was pleased to see she was looking energetic. Retirement seemed to be helping her recover.

"Morning!" Her voice was cheerful, but when she didn't trade her beige knit cardigan for an apron, I knew she wasn't there to work.

"Morning, Doris." I tightened my low ponytail and adjusted the wide floral headband I wore to keep my long, blond hair out of my face. "How are you feeling?"

"Fine, more or less." She knocked her knuckles against a door frame. "Knock on wood."

I tapped a knuckle on a wooden cutting board in solidarity.

"What smells so good? Cinnamon?"

"Snickerdoodles."

"That will be a nice addition. We haven't offered them in a while."

I hesitated. "These are grain free."

She raised her eyebrows, adding a few creases to her lined forehead. "Oh, honey. That can't taste good."

"Trust me. They will. I've been working on this recipe and I think I have it down."

She made a noncommittal noise and I knew she wasn't sure if she believed me. Doris had a hard time with change.

I glanced at the timers. "A few more minutes and you can try one. If you hate it, I'll toss them all."

But I'd keep trying to get the recipe right. I was determined.

She scooted a stool to the stainless-steel island in the center of the room and sat. "Fair enough. You have good instincts, I should trust you. So…" Her tone changed, taking on a conspiratorial note. "How was your date?"

"Oh, it was great." I didn't bother to keep the sarcasm out of my voice. "I hung out by myself at the tavern, which was almost empty by the way, so I couldn't hide or pretend I wasn't pathetically waiting for a guy who was clearly going to stand me up. I babbled at the bartender so much, he gave me a free shot of whiskey, probably to get me to be quiet. Then Garrett didn't show. Said something came up at work."

Her mouth dropped open and she wrinkled her nose, as if in disgust. "That won't do." She started digging through her enormous red handbag. "I need to call Louise."

"It's okay, I'm not mad about it. It's probably not even his fault."

"What do you mean? He stood you up, of course that's his fault."

I shook my head soberly. "No. It was my bad luck."

Gasping, Doris froze with her hand still in her bag. "Oh, no."

"Oh, yes. That has to be it. I've had too many good things in a row, it was bound to happen."

"That dratted mirror." She gave up her search for whatever she'd been looking for. Her phone, presumably. "It'll get you every time."

"I know." I nodded slowly. "It always finds me."

Aunt Doris was the only person in my life who believed in my bad luck streak. Which wasn't too surprising. I'd probably gotten my superstitious nature from her. I certainly hadn't gotten it from my mom. She was far too practical—a very literal thinker. So was my older sister. I was the odd one in the family. The creative one. The weirdo with funny habits and rituals that no one else seemed to understand.

Except Aunt Doris. Like me, she'd been the odd one in her family. Odd enough to leave her family decades ago when she'd moved to Tilikum, a small town in the central Washington Cascades, and opened a bakery. Coming from a family of scientists, doctors, and at least one psychologist, choosing the life of a small-town baker had seemed downright radical.

Growing up, I'd spent time with her whenever I could. Despite having two children, my mom hadn't married either of our fathers, shouldering the burdens of single motherhood and a busy career as a research scientist. Doris didn't have children of her own, and had often made the drive to Tacoma to pick us up and taken us to stay with her in her quaint small town. It gave my mom a break and gave me my deep love of baking.

And probably my propensity to toss salt over my shoulder, always knock on wood, and never, ever walk beneath a ladder.

One of the timers caught my eye. It had stopped dead with one minute and twenty-seven seconds left.

And that was why I always set two.

"Anyway," I said as I peeked into the oven to check the cookies. "Don't worry about Louise or the date. It was for the best. I shouldn't be dating until I'm sure the mirror curse is over."

"And you shouldn't be dating Garrett Haven at all. Standing you up on the first date is a red flag in my book."

"True." I put on two oven mitts and took out the cookies. They looked perfect—slightly browned with crisp edges. I set the baking sheet on the island and the scent of cinnamon and sugar wafted into the air.

"They do look pretty," Doris said. "And they smell good."

I tilted my head to regard my handiwork. They were perfectly uniform, just the right size and shape. "Let's hope they taste as good as they look."

"Doris?" a voice called from the front of the bakery. "Are you back there?"

"That sounds like Louise." Doris eased her way off the stool. "Her nose must have been itching."

"I thought it was ears burning."

"I think it's the nose. Itchy nose, someone is talking about you. Coming, Louise!"

Doris disappeared to the front and came back a moment later, ushering her friend Louise Haven into the kitchen. Louise wore a lavender velour track suit—I'd never seen her in anything else, although the colors varied—and her gray hair was in a loose bun at the nape of her neck. She was roughly my aunt's age, but until about six or seven years ago, their friendship had been strictly clandestine. Doris had been friends with the Bailey family, the former rivals to the Havens.

Growing up, the feud had been a huge thing in Tilikum. Certain restaurants and stores had been forbidden to me and my sister Holly, like the Copper Kettle Diner and Home Slice Pizza. Holly had always declared it to be stupid, but I'd taken it very seriously. You didn't mess with feuds.

Although nothing bad seemed to have happened to Doris or Louise on account of their secret friendship.

In any case, it was all in the past. And thank goodness for that, because Home Slice had the best margherita pizza I'd ever tasted.

And Doris and Louise could openly be friends.

"Oh good, you're both here." Louise set her purse on the island and fixed her gaze on me. A knowing smile curved the corners of her mouth. "How did it go?"

"He stood her up," Doris cut in before I could reply, her tone clipped. "Of course it isn't your fault, and I'm not blaming you, but he is your nephew. The boy needs a talking-to."

"He's a grown man," I said. "I don't think anyone needs to talk to him."

"He did what?" Louise's voice was filled with shock.

Doris gestured toward me. "Stood her up. He left her sitting at the Timberbeast all alone. Rocco gave her a free drink."

Louise clutched her hands to her chest. "Scandalous. I hope no one was there to see it."

"I think there were a couple of people there, plus the bartender guy," I said. "Is that Rocco? The name fits."

"You know how word gets around." Doris shook her head sadly. "If something like this happens again, her reputation will be in serious jeopardy."

"My reputation?"

Louise clicked her tongue. "We can't have that."

"What is this, Victorian England? How is my reputation going to be ruined?"

Doris blinked, as if just remembering I was standing there. "I don't mean that sort of reputation. I just mean that people might begin to assume you're…"

"I'm what?"

"Unlucky," Louise said with a definitive nod.

"Shh." Doris put a finger to her lips. "Don't use that word in front of her."

I sighed. "I'm not that fragile. And I am unlucky. You know this about me."

Louise produced a small notebook from her purse and thumbed through the pages. "I was going to consider Luke as a backup if things with Garrett didn't work out, but now I'm not so sure. No offense, dear, but he's unlucky enough as it is, at least when it comes to love."

"He isn't with Jill again, is he?" Doris asked.

"Oh my stars, no." Louise waved that off. "Heaven forbid."

"Didn't you set them up in the first place?"

"Twice, but who's counting?" Louise smiled, her voice sounding more chipper. "Of course, the second time I didn't recall they'd dated before. And Jill has a way of hiding her… let's say her *eccentricities*."

Doris leaned toward me and lowered her voice to a conspiratorial whisper. "She's a bit batty, if you know what I mean."

I didn't know Jill, or Luke, but I was beginning to wonder if Doris's claim that Louise Haven was a matchmaking genius was a bit overblown.

"Well, thank you anyway for the attempt, Louise, but I'm going to be on a dating hiatus for the foreseeable future."

Louise gasped again. "Why would you do a silly thing like that?"

My eyes flicked to Doris. I didn't want to broadcast my mirror curse problem to everyone in town. She gave me a subtle nod. She understood.

"I'm still getting settled and there's so much to do here. I have a list of new recipes to try. Speaking of." I grabbed a spatula, slid it beneath a snickerdoodle, and set it on a napkin, then handed it to Louise. "Try this."

While Louise took a bite, I gave one to Doris.

The two women ate with expressions of deep concentration. Doris took another careful bite, as if still considering if she should like it or not, while Louise ate the whole thing.

"Delicious," Louise said around her mouthful of cookie. She wiped the crumbs from the corners of her mouth and swallowed. "Absolute heaven."

I beamed. "Yeah? They're good?"

My gaze moved to Doris. She knew the dirty little almond flour secret. Would that influence her opinion?

"She's right. Soft and chewy in the middle, crisp on the outside. You'd never know they aren't real."

"To be fair, they are real, they just have different ingredients."

"Well, that's it," Louise said. "I'm never making snicker-doodles again. I've been outdone."

I laughed. "Do you want to bring some home with you? These were just a test batch."

"Don't mind if I do."

I went to the front to grab a to-go box while she chatted with Doris and noticed a teenage boy in a blue hoodie loitering on the sidewalk just outside. That was odd. Wasn't it a school day?

He didn't make a move to come in, so I took the box back to the kitchen and wrapped up some of the snickerdoodles for Louise. She took it and said goodbye, muttering about not giving any to Garrett as she left, this time out the back door.

"I suppose I should go home and put my feet up," Doris said.

"Is your hip acting up again?"

"My hip, my knee, my back. You name it."

"Go home and get some rest. I've got things covered and Beth will be here soon."

"All right, honey." She gave me a hug and gathered up her handbag. "Call me if you need anything."

"I will. See you later." The front door opened, so I called over my shoulder, "I'll be right with you."

I walked Doris to the back door and wiped the cookie crumbs off my hands before going to greet my customer.

The door was just closing as I came into the front, and I caught sight of what looked like the kid in the blue hoodie dashing up the sidewalk. I blinked once and he was out of sight.

What had that been about?

Then I saw it.

The display nearest the door, which had moments earlier been filled with bagged sugar cookies and other sweets, was empty.

I'd just been robbed.

CHAPTER 4

Garrett

THE SCENT of something sweet caught my attention. It was nearly lunchtime and I'd skipped breakfast, so no wonder my stomach growled at the smell. I glanced up from the desk I used when I was in the office to see Deputy Spangler walking by with a pink box from Angel Cakes bakery. Whatever was inside, it smelled delicious.

My phone buzzed with a text, vibrating against the surface of my desk. I ignored it. Again. I didn't want to know why I was getting so many texts in the middle of the day. I wanted to get this report finished. Paperwork wasn't my favorite thing, but in this job, it was never ending. We had to document everything.

Which also meant I was going to ignore the treats in that pink box.

The sheriff's office could be abuzz with frenetic activity, a ghost town, or anything in between. It just depended on the day, and who was on duty. Mornings were busy, with deputies on day shift checking in for roll call before heading out on patrol. Mid-day was usually quieter—and a good time to get admin work done when I wasn't on a patrol shift—but there were still people coming and going, uniformed and civilian alike.

A man in a suit jacket, no tie, walked past with a large cookie on a napkin. Phillip Lancaster, one of the attorneys in the county prosecuting attorney's office, tipped his chin and veered my direction. He and his fellow prosecutors worked closely with our agency. As my field training officer had told me, we catch `em, they put `em away. It wasn't unusual to see him in the office, usually meeting with one of us about cases he was prosecuting.

"Got anything new for me?" he asked, pausing next to my desk.

That cookie smelled damn good. I clearly needed to get some lunch. I wasn't usually so distracted by food.

"Yeah, actually. Trent Jones. Frequent flier. Caught up with him at the scene of a stolen vehicle, likely with contraband inside. He ran and resisted."

"Name sounds familiar."

"I'm finishing up the arrest report."

"Sounds good. I'll be out of town for a few days, maybe out of cell range. But it's just a quick trip."

"Hunting?"

He smiled. "Fishing this time."

"Have a good one."

"I will. Thanks, Haven."

For a lawyer, Phillip wasn't a bad guy. I'd worked with him on quite a few cases over the years. Marie, one of our admin assistants, eyed him appreciatively as he walked out. Ever since he'd gotten divorced a while back, the women in the agency had taken extra notice of him.

I didn't worry about that. Wasn't my circus.

My phone buzzed again, demanding my attention. Reluctantly, I picked it up and swiped to see my messages.

Mom: *Give me a call when you get a chance. Not an emergency. But did you stand up Doris Tilburn's niece?*

Annika: *Not trying to pry, but what's the deal with blowing off a date? I heard she's nice.*

Marigold: *Sorry to bug you, but I just want to make sure everything is okay. There's some gossip going around, and of course I don't believe it, but I also want to know if you're all right.*

Zachary: *Dude, why would you blow off a date Aunt Louise set up? That was dumb.*

Luke: *Heard you blew off a date Aunt Louise set up. Probably a good call. What happened?*

Aunt Louise: *You better explain yourself, mister.*

I shook my head. I'd wonder how they all knew, but this was Tilikum. You couldn't sneeze without someone across town showing up to bring you tissues.

To be fair, I hadn't blown her off or stood her up. I'd texted her to let her know I couldn't make it. And it wasn't my fault crime didn't stop when my shift ended. Tell that to the bad guys.

Hey, could you stop the crime you're about to commit? I have a date.

Yeah, no.

I'd have to answer everyone at some point, but for now, I wanted lunch.

Usually I either packed a lunch or stopped at one of the restaurants downtown. But since we had leftovers at home, and Owen and I lived less than ten minutes from the sheriff's office, I decided to run home and grab something. That was a benefit of small-town living, unlike the rampant gossip and nosy family members.

I finished the last part of my report and hit save.

"What's up, slacker?" Kade Sheehan, one of my fellow deputies, paused next to the desk. Like me, he was in uniform —an army-green shirt and tan pants with his badge on the left side of his chest.

"Paperwork. What are you doing here? I thought you went home already."

"Overtime." He shrugged. "Got a call about ten minutes before my shift ended. Figured it wouldn't take long. I was wrong about that."

"I know what that's like. I missed a date last night."

"Oh, poor baby." The sarcasm in his voice was unmistakable. "Had to work past dinner on a day shift."

My brow furrowed. I wasn't sure where the snark was coming from. "Overtime on graveyard sucks, man. You should go home and get some rest."

"Yeah, not everyone gets the luxury of a desk job." He turned and walked off.

I watched him go, not quite sure what to make of him. He and I had started our careers at the same time, and, for a while, we'd been good friends. Years ago, I'd set him up with my sister Annika, but they hadn't hit it off. She'd gone on to marry Levi Bailey, and Kade was married to a woman named Erin. There hadn't been any hard feelings and he and I had stayed friends.

But lately, something was off. It was subtle, and if I hadn't been in law enforcement for as long as I had, I probably wouldn't have noticed. Kade had an edge to his voice, and he often seemed irritated—even angry.

Although maybe he was just cranky because he'd been on graveyard a lot lately. That could put anyone in a crappy mood.

I got up and left, nodding to a few people as I walked out. The early May weather was clear and warm. Nice time of year in the mountains. The snow had melted, the ensuing mud mostly dried, and the heat of summer hadn't set in yet. Maybe I'd take Owen hiking this weekend. It had been a while since we'd done something fun together.

Since I wasn't on patrol, I got in my personal car—a dark gray SUV I'd had for a few years—and headed home.

My house was on a quiet street, about a mile from my sister and brother-in-law, Annika and Levi, and my newly married brother Zachary and his wife, Marigold. Owen and I had lived there for several years and sometimes I wondered why I'd bought a house that was so big. It was a newer two-story, with four bedrooms and two-and-a-half baths, plus a three-car garage. We didn't need that much space, but I'd gotten a good deal and it was a nice place to live.

I pulled into the driveway and parked, the sight of Owen's bike leaning against the garage door making me furrow my brow. Hadn't he ridden to school today? And if he'd walked, why was his bike outside?

I checked my phone, but the doorbell cam hadn't registered anything. If Owen was home, he must have gone around to the back.

But he couldn't have been home. He was supposed to be in school.

Maybe it was my instincts taking over, but I quietly stepped out of my car, as I would if approaching a crime in progress. I made my way to the front door—nothing out of the ordinary. Just the welcome sign my sister had given me as a housewarming gift when we'd moved in.

I unlocked the door and opened it—slowly. Stepped inside and shut it behind me without making a sound.

The house seemed empty. No noise.

I glanced toward the back of the house. From where I was standing, I could see the door to the backyard. Owen's shoes were there, as if he'd kicked them off and left them where they lay.

Busted.

I crept forward from the entry toward the great room at the back of the house.

Owen sat on the couch, dressed in a blue hoodie and jeans, absently chewing something. He had a mug of hot chocolate on the coffee table, and it bothered me both that he wasn't using a coaster—he always left drips—and that I'd come to a place in my life where I worried about things like using a coaster.

He'd always looked more like me than his mom. Same brown hair and blue eyes. Same nose and sharp jaw. As much as he'd grown in the last couple of years, all he needed was some more muscle and a bit of facial hair and he'd be my mini-me.

His phone was turned horizontally, and the way his eyes were glued to it probably meant he was playing that racing game he was so obsessed with.

I walked around to the front of the couch. He didn't look up. Crossing my arms, I cleared my throat. Loudly.

His eyes met mine, widening in shock, and he spit crumbs all over the place.

"Why aren't you in school?"

He wiped his mouth with his sleeve and his eyes were wide. "Uh…"

I didn't say anything else. Just raised my eyebrows and waited for him to talk. Sometimes silence was plenty intimidating.

It dawned on me that I was thinking in terms of interrogation techniques with my son. Was that a good or a bad thing?

He drew his eyebrows together. "What are you doing here?"

"I'm asking the questions. Why aren't you in school?"

His mouth twisted and his eyes narrowed. His angry face wasn't nearly as cute as it had been when he was two.

When he finally answered, his tone was dripping with defiance. "I just felt like coming home, okay?"

"No. That's not okay. Get your stuff. I'm taking you back."

Rolling his eyes, he groaned. "I don't wanna go back."

I laughed, which was clearly the wrong move. It just pissed him off more. But what the hell was he thinking? I was going to just let him ditch school?

He didn't get up. Just glared at me.

I was about to lay down the law—this kid was not going to defy me—when a voice in the back of my head told me to slow down.

The voice that sounded suspiciously like my mom.

What was going on that he was so determined to stay away from school? Was I missing something?

I took a deep breath and softened my voice. "What's really going on?"

"Nothing."

"Seriously, Owen." I stepped closer to the couch. "Did something happen at school? You can tell me stuff, man. I can't help you if you don't tell me what's wrong."

His eyes widened again, like I was doing something alarming. What was going on with him? I was just walking toward him, not even that fast. He'd never acted afraid of me before. Why was he—

Then I saw it. His backpack was on the floor next to the couch, the compartment wide open. It was full of plastic bags, some of them open.

Cookies from Angel Cakes Bakery.

"Where'd you get those?" My voice was back to stern.

"I had money."

He was lying. Right to my face. Damn it.

"Owen, I know you're lying."

He crossed his arms. "I'm not lying. I bought them."

Great. Not only had he ditched school, he'd stolen something. It was the worst cliché. The deputy's kid decides to rebel and becomes a criminal.

My first instinct was to blow up at him. But I didn't. Somehow, I stayed calm.

"You don't have any money. You spent the last of it two weeks ago at the Quick Stop. I remember because you didn't have enough for the slushie and the giant bag of chips you wanted, so I spotted you two dollars. You're fourteen and you don't have a job, so unless you have another source of cash I need to know about, you wouldn't have had enough for all that." I gestured to the sugary contraband in his backpack.

"Fine. I stole them. What are you going to do? Arrest me?"

I thought about it. I really did. I wouldn't actually arrest him for stealing cookies. But toss him in the back of my car and take him to the station? Make him sit in an interrogation room for a while? Scare the shit out of him so he wouldn't dream of pulling a stunt like that again?

Seemed legit.

For a second, I felt the weight of being a single parent like a concrete block on my chest. A good mom could have helped in this moment. Soothed my temper, provided some balance. Instead, I had to play both roles. Which meant I had to stop, think, and consider the situation from more than one angle.

Was shock and awe the way to go? Scare the kid straight? He'd never done anything like this before. His grades were good, he never got in trouble at school, most of the time he was polite and respectful. He was great with all of his cousins. Overall, a good kid.

This was an aberration. Not that I was naïve enough to think now that he'd been caught once he'd never do it again, or that it might not be the start of a new pattern of behavior. But I could bring down the hammer, or I could get creative.

An idea occurred to me. I'd save the hammer for next time, if it became necessary.

"Grab your stuff."

A spasm of fear crossed his features. "Where are we going? Can you actually arrest your own son? They won't let you do that, will they?"

I let out a breath. "I'm not arresting you. This time. Put the rest of those cookies in your backpack and get your shoes."

"Where are we going?"

"Angel Cakes Bakery. You, my friend, are going to apologize."

CHAPTER 5
Garrett

OWEN SLUMPED in the passenger seat with his arms crossed. He hadn't looked me in the eyes once since getting off the couch and grabbing his backpack. He could be mad at me all he wanted. I wasn't letting him get away with this.

Silence seemed appropriate on the drive to the bakery. He knew he was in trouble. I'd let him stew in it for a while.

But damn it, why had he done that? What had been going through his fourteen-year-old mind when he'd decided to skip school and rob a bakery? There was no shortage of snack food at home. I tried to keep us healthy, but I wasn't a tyrant about it. If he was going to ditch school, why not just go home and raid the pantry? Why add theft to the mix?

I didn't want to make it about me, but what would happen if people got word that Deputy Haven's kid was a shoplifter?

We pulled up to the bakery and parked outside. The building was painted pink and white, with lines that evoked a fancy dessert. Black and white striped awnings shielded the windows and door from the worst of the mountain weather, and a sign in the shape of a cupcake said open.

I glanced at Owen. He hunkered down in the seat, as if he'd rather the ground open up and swallow him whole than go inside and apologize to Doris Tilburn.

"Here's the deal, pal," I said, deciding to give him at least the illusion that he had a choice in the matter. "You can go inside, apologize to Doris, and we'll figure out how to pay her back. Or I can take you in and hand you over to one of the other deputies."

He seemed to consider that for a second. When he answered, I could hear the hint of worry in his voice. "Fine. I'll go say sorry."

We got out and I motioned for Owen to go in ahead of me. He shuffled to the door, carrying his backpack, his shoulders hunched in defeat. I followed him inside and took off my aviators.

The scent of sugar, bread, and vanilla washed over me. Angel Cakes always smelled good enough to give me a head rush.

"Be right there!" a woman's voice called from the back.

Didn't sound like Doris. Maybe the woman who worked the front counter was there. Beth? Her name might have been Beth, but I didn't remember for sure.

I put a light hand on Owen's shoulder and nudged him farther inside. "We don't need to hang out by the door. It's not like you're going to make a run for it."

He looked back at me, eyes narrowed in a glare.

"Don't test me. I can still catch you."

"I'm not gonna run."

I didn't actually think he would, but I kept myself between him and the door anyway.

Habit.

My phone buzzed in my pocket, so I pulled it out to check. Aunt Louise again. I'd have to call her after I took care of this, or I'd never hear the end of it.

"Hi, can I help you?"

I looked up from my phone and froze.

It was like my brain completely turned off. All I could do was stare.

She was on the taller side with long blond hair tied in a low ponytail, a pink and blue floral headband keeping any loose strands off her face. She wore an Angel Cakes Bakery apron over her T-shirt and her eyes were a mesmerizing green. But it was her smile that almost knocked me over.

Big, bright, beautiful.

She was gorgeous.

I blinked. What was I doing there? Why was I standing in a swirl of sugar-scented air while this incredible woman smiled at me?

"Hi?" she said, her smile fading. "Do you guys need something?"

Owen hiked his backpack up his shoulder and looked at me like I was the most uncool, annoying person he'd ever seen in his life.

"Um…" I cleared my throat, hoping to restart my brain. It didn't work very well. "My uh, son…"

"Owen," he said when I didn't finish.

"Right, my son Owen." I paused again while she watched me, her big green eyes full of expectation. "He has something to say to you. Or to Doris, if she's here."

"No, I'm afraid she's not. My aunt is retiring and I'm taking over. I'm Harper."

Harper? *This* was Harper? The woman Aunt Louise had set me up with?

I'd bailed on a date with *her*?

Shit. I'd stood her up and my son had shoplifted from her. We were not going to be her favorite people.

Owen dropped his backpack between his feet and pulled out the bags of cookies he'd taken. He took them to the counter and set them in front of her, then hesitated for a second before speaking.

The words tumbled out of his mouth like he was desperate to get it over with. "I took stuff and I'm really sorry please don't let him arrest me."

Harper's eyes moved from Owen, to me, then back again. I glanced down, remembering I was in uniform. Yep, just your friendly neighborhood sheriff's deputy with his delinquent kid.

"Did he say he needed to arrest you?" Her voice was gentle with the slightest hint of amusement.

"He said he might."

She picked through the plastic bags, as if taking inventory. "Is this everything?"

He shook his head. "No."

"You ate some already."

"Yeah."

She tapped her lips. "Hmm. What should we do about this?" Her gaze moved to me again. "What do you think, Deputy…?"

Oh, shit. Here we go. "Haven. Garrett Haven."

Her eyes lit up in recognition. "Garrett Haven? As in Louise Haven's nephew?"

Owen looked back at me. "Dad, do you know her?"

"We haven't had the chance to actually meet," she said.

"Yeah, that's me," I said. "And I'm sorry about that."

"Oh, it's okay." She waved her hand, like it didn't matter. "It was for the best." She turned back to Owen. "Anyway, some of these are missing—in your stomach, of course—and others are broken or smashed. While I do appreciate, and accept, your apology, I can't sell these now."

Wait, for the best? Why? Had she met someone else while waiting for me?

I bet it was one of my brothers. Was it Luke? Theo? I'd have their asses.

"I don't have money to pay for them," Owen said.

"Hmm." She tapped her lips again. "I have an idea. Dad, can I see you back here for a minute?"

She was talking to me. I cleared my throat again, trying to rid myself of the anger at my brothers that they probably didn't deserve. I didn't know if either of them had even met Harper.

"Stay here." I leveled Owen with a stern dad-stare.

He nodded.

Harper's lips twitched in the hint of a smile and she motioned for me to come around the counter. I followed her into the kitchen and my heart beat a little harder as she stepped closer to me. She cast a quick glance toward the front of the store, then took another step.

Right onto my foot.

"Sugar cookies," she muttered, as if it was a curse word. "Sorry. I was just thinking, I don't want to step on your toes because you're the dad, and then I literally stepped on your toe."

I didn't feel a thing, except a mild pang of disappointment that she'd moved back. "It's fine. Didn't hurt."

"Good. Anyway, it seems like it would be a good idea for Owen to pay the bakery back somehow. And I don't mean you, I mean him. But, as he said, no money."

"What do you have in mind?"

"What if he works off the cost of everything he took? He could come in on Saturday. Do dishes, sweep the floors, that kind of thing."

"That's brilliant."

Her smile almost knocked me over again. "Yeah?"

Looking right into her eyes—and at that smile—my brain stopped working again. So I just nodded.

"Okay, great."

"I'm sorry about all this. He's usually a good kid. He's never done anything like this before."

"Yeah, he doesn't look like a hardened criminal. Yet." She winked.

She was killing me.

"I'll make sure he's here on Saturday."

"It's a plan."

We were done. I needed to go back to Owen. Take him to school or home or wherever I was going to take him so I could get back to work. But I couldn't seem to tear my eyes away from Harper.

"So, okay then." Her eyes flicked toward the front of the store. "You probably need to take him home or something. You know, before he goes on another crime spree."

"Right, yeah." I blinked, feeling like an idiot. "Sorry."

She just smiled.

I kept hesitating. Should I say something about our date? Let it go? She'd said it had been for the best. Why? Now that she saw me in person, she wasn't interested?

Ouch.

"And I'm sorry about last night. Work got in the way."

"It's fine. Like I said, for the best. I'm not really in a place where dating makes sense for me right now."

That eased the tension in my shoulders a little. At least she hadn't met someone else.

Or she was lying.

She didn't seem like she was lying.

I needed to go. I'd blown past awkward and was barreling straight toward mortifying.

"Thanks again."

I went back to the front of the store where Owen waited right where I'd left him. He cast a longing glance at the cookies on the counter and shouldered his backpack.

"Ready?" I asked.

"Yeah."

"Bye Owen," Harper called as we left. "I'll see you Saturday."

The door shut behind us and the fresh spring air replaced the decadent smells of the bakery.

"What did she mean, she'll see me Saturday?" he asked as we walked to my car.

"You stole from her. She can't recoup the cost of what you took and you don't have money to pay her back. So you're going to work it off."

"What?"

"You heard me. You're going to go to the bakery this weekend to help Harper until you've worked off your debt."

He sighed, his eyes downcast. "Okay."

"And no bike until I feel I can trust you again. I'll drive you to school and you'll go to Grandma and Grandpa's in the afternoon until I'm off work."

"I'm grounded from my bike?"

"Hey man, you're the one who broke trust. You have to earn it back. Maybe next time you're tempted to steal something, you'll think twice."

He nodded and opened the passenger door.

I got in and checked my messages. No new texts, and nothing from work either. That was a small miracle.

"What was wrong with you in there?" Owen asked.

"Nothing. What are you talking about?"

"You forgot my name."

"No, I didn't."

"Yes, you did."

I slipped on my aviators and turned on the ignition. "It was just a momentary blip."

"A blip? What's a blip? Is that like a senior moment?"

"A senior moment? I'm not even forty."

"I know, you're like super old."

I rolled my eyes. Nothing like a teenager to keep you humble. "Yeah, I'm old and it was a senior moment."

"Thought so."

Maybe it was better that Owen assumed age was getting

the best of his dad. Because the truth? That a woman I'd never met had just about dropped me to the floor with her smile? I did not need him to know that.

Because I certainly had no idea what I was going to do about it.

CHAPTER 6

Harper

MY FEET WERE KILLING ME.

There wasn't anything unusual about that—just the life of a baker. My day started at four in the morning and most evenings I stayed until after we closed. But it had been extra busy and Beth had gone home sick. I was so done.

I was almost finished cleaning up the kitchen, getting it ready for Horatio, who'd be in for his daily bread baking well before dawn. I'd be back early as well—tomorrow's desserts weren't going to bake themselves—but Horatio seemed to like doing his thing in the middle of the night.

Kind of wondered if he was a vampire or something. He was awfully pasty. But maybe that was because he worked at night and probably slept during the daylight hours.

Still. Vampire?

I wiped down the island and checked the time. Two minutes. I never closed even a minute early. Maybe I had a touch of OCD, but even on a day when I was so ready to go home, I had to leave the cupcake sign turned toward open until exactly five o'clock.

The front door opened and my heart sank a little. A customer right at closing.

I sighed. It was my fault. I could have locked the door a hundred and twenty seconds early, but did I? No, I did not.

"Hi." I did my best to be cheerful as I came out from the kitchen. "Can I help you?"

The man was probably in his late thirties, maybe forty, with a slightly receding hairline and a scraggly beard in need of a trim. Big, block letters on his T-shirt proclaimed, *True Crime All the Time.*

"Yeah." He eyed the pastry case, and when his gaze lifted to meet mine, the corners of his mouth turned up in a grin. "Oh. Hi."

The intensity in his expression was disconcerting, like he was mentally undressing me. I stepped away from the counter to put more distance between us.

"Is there something I can get for you?"

He didn't look at the pastry case. Instead, his eyes flicked down to my chest.

Lovely.

"Uh..." He ran a hand through his unkempt hair. "Did you bake all these?"

"Yes, I did."

"They all look so good, I don't know what to pick."

"Take your time."

"Did you know that in the nineteen seventies, a guy killed his parents and then led police on a chase that lasted four days before they finally caught him?"

His question was so out of the blue, it tripped me up. "Um, what?"

"They found him right here in Tilikum."

"No, I didn't know that." I pointed to his shirt. "True crime fan?"

He grinned. "Yeah. I like to do a lot of my own research."

"Oh. Interesting."

I didn't know if this guy was just a little bit awkward or if I had a reason for hoping he left soon. I didn't want to be judgy, but there was something about him that was making me uncomfortable.

Oh well. Wouldn't have been the first time. It was a hazard of dealing with the public. I'd just keep it professional and maybe clear my throat if he started staring at my chest again. Sometimes that worked.

"So, what can I get you?"

His eyes went straight to my chest. I cleared my throat, but he didn't seem to notice.

"Would you like a suggestion?" I asked, working hard to keep my tone friendly.

"Sure."

"The sugar cookies have been popular lately. Or the double chocolate chunk if you prefer chocolate."

"Chocolate," he said with a nod. "Are you new in town? I don't remember seeing you."

"Fairly new, yeah." I used a pair of tongs to get his cookie out of the case and put it in a white bag.

"Tilikum is a nice place, even if it has a lot of secrets."

"I suppose most places do." I rang him up and took his payment.

"Yeah, you'd be surprised. There was a woman out in Pinecrest who kept marrying different men and then killing them. Made them all look like accidents."

"Wow, that's terrible." I had a feeling this guy needed to find another hobby. His true crime fascination was a little much. "Can I get you anything else?"

"No."

I hesitated, waiting for him to go. He had his cookie. He'd paid for it. But he just stood there. His eyes roved over me again. He was really starting to make my skin crawl.

"Okay, then have a nice evening."

"You too. I'm Matt Rudolph."

"Harper. Nice to meet you."

"Nice to meet you too. I'm glad you moved to Tilikum. The old baker wasn't very pretty."

What was with this guy? "Well, she's my aunt, so…"

"You don't look like her."

I shrugged. "Maybe not."

He grinned again. "See you again soon, Harper."

"Bye."

I let out a breath as he finally left, then hurried over to lock the door and turn the cupcake sign to closed.

I couldn't put my finger on why that interaction had bothered me the way it did. Garrett Haven had stared at me when he'd been in with his son. That encounter had been arguably more awkward—it had seemed like he'd forgotten how to use words—but it had been cute, not weird.

Maybe I didn't need a solid reason. My intuition had been telling me something. What, I didn't really know, other than he'd made me uncomfortable. But I'd keep an eye out when I went to my car, just in case. You never knew these days. Even in a small town like Tilikum, there could still be a creeper deluxe.

Or worse. Matt seemed to know all about that.

I packed up the few desserts that were left to take to the food bank and made sure everything else was cleaned up. Tired as I was, I didn't mind the time it took. Matt was probably harmless, just a guy who let his eyes linger on my boobs too long, but hopefully this way he'd be less likely to stick around so he could "accidentally" run into me when I left for the day.

When everything was clean and tidy, I went out the back door and locked it. I didn't see anyone as I walked to my car. Just a few squirrels on the roof of the building next door and another in a wine barrel planter nearby.

I still locked the car doors as soon as I got in.

So far, my bad luck hadn't gotten me into serious trouble —no major car accidents or muggings or anything horrible like that—but I didn't want to tempt fate. And who knew, as the seven years drew to an end, maybe the mirror curse was gearing up to go out with a bang.

That was a disconcerting thought.

Then again, other than be reasonably careful, there wasn't much I could do about it. I turned on my car and flashed the lights once before putting it in reverse. I'd call that a habit, but it was probably more like a ritual. I did it every time I got in my car.

The drive home was uneventful, aside from a squirrel who seemed to value the candy bar it was carrying more than its life. It darted in front of me and I had to slam on the brakes to avoid hitting it. Without even glancing my direction, it bounded across the road, carrying the too-big-for-it loot.

Tilikum squirrels were interesting creatures.

I stopped at the food bank to drop off the leftover desserts and bread, then headed home. My house was less than ten minutes from downtown, in a little residential neighborhood with winding streets and lots of trees. It was cute, a two-story with a small yard and a two-car garage. That was going to come in handy in the winter. I wouldn't have to scrape ice off my windshield at four in the morning.

Inside were three bedrooms and two bathrooms. Like most rentals, the colors were all neutral, mostly beige and white. But it was clean and well-kept. And best of all, it had a great kitchen, especially for being a smaller house.

It wasn't just the maple cabinets, quartz counters, and farmhouse sink that I loved. It was the space. Most of the downstairs was open, great-room style, which left room for a big kitchen island and lots of counter space. And there was plenty of storage for my admittedly huge collection of baking supplies.

Despite the fact that I baked for a living, I still enjoyed doing it at home. Some of my best recipes had come from late night baking sessions in my own kitchen. But after my long day, I wasn't in the mood for more baking. Or cooking of any kind.

I went inside, put my things down, and went upstairs to change. There was nothing like the freedom of taking off my bra at the end of the day. So nice. I put on a tank top and flannel pajama pants, redid my ponytail, and went down to the kitchen to see what I could scrounge up for dinner.

My choices weren't exactly thrilling. I had food, I was just in a mood where nothing I had sounded good. After standing in front of my open fridge for a few minutes, I closed the door, pulled a ramen bowl out of the freezer, and popped it into the microwave. Not exactly health food, but at least it had a few vegetables in it.

Even with the hum of the microwave, my house seemed oddly quiet. I'd been living alone for years, but somehow it was taking a long time to get used to the silence of the small town.

It made me wonder what Garrett Haven was doing.

I'd been trying not to think about him, but alone in my house, in the quiet of the early evening, he muscled his way into my mind.

He was, well, big, for one. I was five-eight, so not exactly short, and he'd towered over me. And those arms. Did the sheriff's department have to order him custom uniform shirts? There was no way those were standard.

Add blue eyes, neatly trimmed stubble, a broad chest, and tree trunk thighs, and he was a dream in uniform.

Of course the guy who canceled on me would be freaking gorgeous. That was my luck.

The microwave beeped, so I grabbed my ramen and set it on the counter. He'd seemed like a nice enough guy, too. And I was impressed by the way he'd handled the situation with his son, especially considering he was in law enforcement.

He'd been firm with him, but calm. And even though Owen had begged me not to let his dad arrest him, there'd been no fear in his demeanor. He wasn't scared of his big, brawny, uniformed dad. Owen had been a bit sullen—no surprise, considering he'd been caught—but not afraid.

I stirred my ramen and took it to the couch. What was I doing? I was well on my way to letting the sight of Garrett Haven in that uniform live rent free in my head, and that was such a terrible idea. He'd stood me up once, which was not a mark in his favor.

And the mirror thing was a problem. A very real problem, despite what my mother and sister would have said about it. Aunt Doris had confirmed it. The bad luck would find me, every single time.

So I ate my ramen. Alone. And tried not to think about how much I would have liked to have someone to eat cheap, frozen food with.

Loneliness was a thing. And because of my bad luck, I was stuck with it.

CHAPTER 7

Garrett

WITH OWEN GROUNDED, my mom or one of my brothers had been picking him up from school and taking him to my parents' place. I was pretty sure I'd be relenting on the grounding sooner rather than later. At the very least, I wanted to give him a chance to earn back trust. If he ditched school again—especially to shoplift—he wouldn't be using anything with wheels until he was a legal adult.

It wasn't exactly a punishment for him to spend his afternoons with his grandparents. That had been the norm for a lot of his childhood, especially after my ex and I had split up. I felt guilty about that, but also grateful to my parents for stepping in and helping me out so often.

I did hope my dad had been making him do chores while he was there, though.

The past several days had been typical. I worked a lot. Had to put in some overtime, but that wasn't the end of the world. I'd been able to break away for Owen's final parent-teacher conference of the year. His recent poor judgment aside, he was doing fine in school, which was a relief. The shoplifting incident didn't seem to represent a downward spiral in behavior.

I hadn't been lying to Harper. He really was a good kid.

Despite plenty to occupy my mind—work, single father-hood, my son's recent bad choices—none of those things were in my head as I drove out to my parents' place to pick up Owen. All I could think about was Harper Tilburn.

That smile. Those eyes. I didn't know what was wrong with me. Her face was burned into my memory, like the after-image of the sun. I'd stared at her too long—and too awkwardly. I couldn't get her out of my head.

I'd never had that happen before. Sure, I'd crushed on girls when I was younger. Hell, when I was barely older than Owen, I'd been convinced I was in love with a girl at school. I'd cut her picture out of a yearbook and stuck it in the back of my binder. Until one day I saw her kissing Theo under the bleachers by the football field.

It hadn't been Theo's fault. He had no idea. And she prob-ably wasn't the only girl he'd kissed under those bleachers. I'd tossed her picture in the garbage and never looked back.

Even then, when I was young and basically an idiot, I'd never been so consumed by a woman. Especially a woman I'd only met once, and for all of five minutes.

I took the turn up my parents' driveway, determined to think about anything but Harper. I'd missed a date with her. So, what? She'd said it herself, it was for the best. She wasn't in a place to start dating anyone. And neither was I. Dating was not on my agenda, even if she was the most mesmerizing woman I'd ever laid eyes on.

Did she smell as good as her bakery? Were her lips as soft as they looked?

I needed to stop.

My parents lived up a long, gravel driveway. Their hand-built log home had views of Tilikum through the pine trees and I had countless memories of long days spent roaming the woods around their property.

I was one of seven kids—six boys and a girl—and we'd

grown up in a kind of semi-controlled chaos. Small-town living had probably helped. We'd been a little bit feral, but there were always neighbors and extended family members around to help keep us corralled.

There were worse ways to grow up.

I parked behind my brother Theo's truck. Next to it was a sixties-era black Chevelle. I didn't recognize the car, but it was probably Luke's. He restored classic cars for a living and tended to swap them out pretty regularly. It wasn't unusual to find one or two of my brothers there at any given time. Mom's cooking tended to attract us.

I went in without knocking and followed the sound of voices and laughter to the dining room.

My dad sat in his usual spot at the head of the table, dressed in a green flannel. His brown hair was streaked with gray, as was his thick beard. He had a solid presence, with his wide shoulders and well-muscled arms.

Whereas Paul Haven was all hard edges, my mom, Marlene, was soft—kind of like the blankets she was always knitting. She had a warm smile and kind eyes behind her blue-rimmed glasses. My sister-in-law Marigold had recently cut her hair, giving her a chin-length bob.

Rounding out the table were Owen, dressed in a blue hoodie despite the warm weather, Luke, and Theo.

Luke and I looked alike. Although his hair was a lighter brown, we had the same blue eyes and square jaw. The Bailey Customs T-shirt he wore was jarring, although the feud with the Baileys had ended years ago.

It did make me wonder if he'd lost a bet with Evan Bailey and that was the price he had to pay.

Theo wore a Tilikum High School hoodie. His hair was unkempt, like he'd been wearing a hat and Mom had made him take it off before he sat down to eat. He had broad shoulders and an athletic build. Professional football had been his dream, until an injury had sent him home to an early retirement. He'd channeled his knowledge and experience into becoming the football coach at Tilikum High School, and he was damn good at it.

"Good timing," Mom said. "Food's still warm if you want to make yourself a plate."

Owen's eyes pleaded with me not to make him go home yet. That probably meant there was dessert.

"Sounds good. Thanks, Mom."

The kitchen was homey and familiar, with slightly faded cabinets and dishes cluttering the counters. I got a plate, dished up a healthy serving of chicken and vegetable stir fry, and took it to the dining table. There was a spot next to Owen, so I sat.

"Get your homework done?" I asked.

"Yeah, Grandma made me finish before dinner."

I tipped my chin to her, and she smiled back.

"Thanks for picking him up from school," I said.

"You're welcome," she said. "Although tomorrow might be a problem."

"Are we talking after school?" Theo asked. "If you want to walk over to the high school, I can take you home. Is your bike in the shop or something?"

Owen slumped in his seat. "No. I'm grounded."

"Bummer," Theo said. "What'd you do?"

I watched my son, wondering if he'd confess in front of his uncles. It was clear from Theo's nonchalant tone that he expected Owen to admit to something minor, like a bad grade on a test.

He took a deep breath. "I cut class and stole stuff."

"Whoa," Theo said. "What'd you steal?"

"Cookies, mostly."

My parents already knew the story, of course, but my brothers looked at me, eyes wide with surprise.

"Little dude, that's not good," Theo said. "Was it from the Quick Stop?"

"No, Angel Cakes," Owen admitted.

"I mean, at least he went for the good stuff," Luke said.

Dad snorted.

I shot them both a glare. "That's not helping."

Luke put his hands up. "Sorry."

"I'm taking him to school in the mornings and he needs to come here in the afternoons for the foreseeable future," I said.

"Sure, I can drive him here," Theo offered.

"How long is the foreseeable future?" Owen asked.

"I don't know."

His brow furrowed. "Washington is a determinate sentencing state. That means punishments have a set length."

Dad's mouth twitched in the hint of a grin. So did Theo's. Luke coughed in an attempt to conceal his chuckle.

I glanced at Owen and raised my eyebrows. Smart kid. "It ends when I *determine* I can trust you again. How's that for a determinate sentence?"

"That's not what it means." Owen's tone took on a note of defiance. "It means you know the length of your sentence. It's not arbitrary."

"And if I'd arrested you and subjected you to state law, that would be applicable. But I didn't, so it's not."

"Dang it."

"Ever thought about going to law school?" Theo asked. "You'd make a good lawyer."

He shrugged.

"We can talk about this more at home."

"What about Saturday?" Mom asked. "Does he need a ride?"

"What's going on Saturday?" Theo asked.

"I have to go work at the bakery," Owen said. "Pay off my debt to society."

"I don't know about your debt to society," I said. "But your debt to Harper, yeah."

"Wait, who's Harper?" Luke asked.

Note to self: Luke doesn't know her, so he isn't the reason she said our missed date was for the best. My eyes moved to Theo. No recognition. He hadn't met her either.

Good to know.

"She's the lady Dad likes," Owen said.

Luke and Theo—who I have to point out are not biologically related to each other—somehow donned identical smart-ass grins.

"Ooooh," Theo said, as if we were all eighth graders. "Garrett likes a girl?"

"Is she cute?" Luke asked.

"I don't—"

Owen cut off what would have been a lame attempt at denial. Or at least deflection. "She's really pretty. Even prettier than Ms. Fallbrook. And basically every guy at Tilikum Middle School has a crush on Ms. Fallbrook."

That was kind of alarming. "Do *you* have a crush on Ms. Fallbrook?"

He shrugged. "I'm a guy, aren't I?"

Luke and Theo both laughed.

"She's an adult." I shot yet another glare at my brothers.

Owen rolled his eyes. "So?"

"Can we go back to the lady Garrett likes?" Luke asked.

"Luke, don't cause trouble," Mom warned.

"I'm not." He laughed. He was so causing trouble. On purpose. "I'm just curious what's going on in my brother's life."

Theo leaned forward and rested his chin on his fists. "Yes, Garrett. Tell us what's going on in your life."

"He was supposed to go out with Harper, but something came up and he wasn't able to make it," Mom said.

I looked over at her. "Now who's causing trouble?"

"I'm just providing context."

"You went out with the bakery lady?" Owen asked. "When?"

"I didn't go out with her."

"Right. He was going to," Mom corrected. "Owen, how do you feel about your dad dating? Has anyone talked to you about that yet?"

I tried, and probably failed, to keep the exasperation out of my voice. "I'm not dating anyone."

Owen shrugged. "Kinda weird that he doesn't. I'm fine with it as long as she's nice. And the bakery lady seemed really nice."

"And prettier than Ms. Fallbrook," Theo added.

I glanced at my dad, hoping he'd change the subject or something. But he just shrugged, as if to say, you're on your own this time.

"Look, I'm not dating Harper. I'm not interested in dating anyone."

"Why?" Luke asked.

"I don't have time. I have enough going on in my life as it is. And Owen and I are fine on our own."

"Yeah, but you totally like her," Owen said.

My kid could see right through me. "I don't even know her."

"You forgot my name."

"I told you, it was a blip."

Owen turned to his uncles. "He forgot my name when we were talking to her. Then he tried to blame it on a senior moment."

"What? No I didn't. *You* said it was a senior moment."

"If you're having senior moments, I might as well hang up my tool belt," Dad said.

"As soon as he saw her, he made this face." Owen tilted his head, widened his eyes, and stuck his tongue partially out. "Like, uh, you're so pretty, now I don't know my own kid's name."

My brothers were practically choking, trying to hold back their laughter.

I kept my expression neutral and my voice even. "You're so grounded."

"I'm already grounded."

"You're grounded longer."

"How long?"

"Until I say you're done."

"That's not fair. I need a sentence length."

"Five years."

His mouth dropped open. "You can't ground me until I'm nineteen."

"Fine. Four years. You're grounded until you're an adult."

"Da-ad."

"He can still play football for me next year, though, right?" Theo asked.

I locked eyes with Owen and watched as his filled with fear. The kid was dying to play for Theo when he got to high school next year. "As long as his crime spree is over."

"Was it really a spree?" Theo asked. "I'm thinking it was a one-time thing. He was like, crime curious."

"We've all been there, right?" Luke asked.

I was about to say I'd never stolen anything, but that wouldn't have been true.

And I didn't need Owen hearing that story.

"When did you steal something?" Dad asked Luke, his voice dangerously low.

"Never," Luke said quickly. "I'm just saying, we all make mistakes when we're young."

Dad eyed him with skepticism. It made me wonder if Dad knew about Luke's racing days. And whether he'd stopped, as he claimed.

"How about some berry crumble." Mom stood without waiting for a reply. "Owen, can you help clear the table, please?"

He nodded and got up from his seat. My brothers passed

their plates to him, and I finished my dinner while they got dessert.

Mom kept eyeing me with either curiosity or suspicion. I had a feeling she'd be on the phone to Aunt Louise as soon as I left. Conspiring over my love life—or lack thereof.

Owen and I hung out for a bit longer, then headed home. It was a school night, so I didn't want him up late. He settled on the couch with a video game while I got out my laptop and logged into our system to check on a few things.

The stolen car I'd recovered had been processed. I scanned the evidence list. Everything looked right. The bracelet I'd found in the dirt had been deemed non-relevant. No surprise there. It had probably been on the ground for years.

But something about it was tickling my instincts. My dad had always taught me to trust my gut. I had no idea what I'd find about a bracelet with *be kind... of a bitch sometimes* engraved on it, but the gut feeling was strong enough I decided to run a search through our database. Fortunately, most of our old case files had been digitized over the years. It would only take a minute.

To my surprise, I got a hit.

A silver bracelet with that engraving came up on the description of a missing person from about a decade ago. It was one of the things she'd been wearing when she was last seen.

But she wasn't just any missing person. She'd gone on to become one of the most notorious cold case murders in recent Tilikum history. Everyone knew the Jasmine Joyner case.

I'd been a young deputy, working graveyard. I hadn't been involved in the case at all. Too junior for something as important as a high-publicity homicide. But I remembered it well. It had been the talk of the town for months.

And then... nothing. It had gone unsolved.

Had I found something relevant to the case? I couldn't prove the bracelet had been Jasmine's, but it matched the description her family had given of what she'd been wearing when she disappeared. That was probably enough to get my superiors to let me dig a little deeper. See if this led to anything new.

Maybe Jasmine's case would heat up again—and I could catch the person who'd killed her.

CHAPTER 8

Harper

SATURDAYS WERE CRAZY.

Looking back, maybe I should have asked Garrett to have Owen come after school, rather than on our busiest day of the week. Having a teenage boy underfoot in the kitchen was proving to be a little chaotic.

It wasn't his fault. He was a nice kid, and, so far, he'd done everything I'd asked. Swept up spilled sugar, taken the trash out to the dumpster, folded to-go boxes, brought out batches of cookies to refill the case.

I peeked out front. Beth had a line that practically went out the door.

"I need to help get through those customers." I took my gloves off and glanced at the two timers I had going. "When those go off, can you come get me? The peanut butter cookies need to come out of the oven."

"Got it," Owen said with a solemn nod.

I grinned at him. He looked so much like his dad, just younger and without facial hair. Same blue eyes, light brown hair, and a jaw that was on its way to being chiseled. The kid was going to be a heartbreaker someday.

Not that I thought Garrett Haven was attractive or anything.

That was a huge lie. He was stupidly attractive.

I tightened my ponytail and went out front. Beth mouthed *thank you* as she boxed up someone's order. She was in her forties, with short brown hair and an impressive collection of earrings shaped like baked goods. Today's were donuts.

Cookies were flying out of the case and we'd run out of cupcakes well before closing. I wasn't going to have time to make more. I had four more custom cakes to finish and those had to take priority.

Beth and I made progress on the line. Fortunately, everyone was patient. One customer was there to pick up a birthday cake, so I went to the kitchen to get it out of the fridge.

"Can I help with that?" Owen asked.

Such a little gentleman. I slid the cake onto the island counter. "Sure. Can you get me one of the medium boxes?"

He retrieved the still-flat box and I put the cake on it, showing him how to fold up the sides then close the top.

"You want to carry it out for me?"

"Yeah, I got it."

He carefully picked up the box and followed me out front. I showed the customer the cake to make sure it was exactly what they wanted, then handed it over.

"Have a great day," I said.

Next in line was a nice-looking guy, probably about my age or maybe a few years older. He looked familiar, but I couldn't remember where I'd seen him before. He flashed a friendly smile, then seemed to notice Owen.

"Hey, pal. What are you doing here?"

"Hi, Uncle Z." Owen glanced at me, his eyes pleading, as if to say, please don't make me tell him.

"He's my helper today," I said. "Just, um, learning about working in a bakery."

"Sweet. I'm Zachary Haven, one of Owen's uncles."

"Oh yeah?" I glanced at Owen. "You have a lot of uncles?"

He sighed. "So many uncles."

"Well, it's nice to meet you, Owen's uncle Zachary. What can we get for you?"

"Good question." He eyed the pastry case. "O, what do you think Auntie Marigold would like?"

Owen tilted his head and pointed. "What are these?"

"Coconut macaroons."

"No." He pointed to the next row. "What about these?"

"Lemon lavender cookies."

"That sounds like Auntie Mari."

Zachary grinned. "Yeah, it does. Good call. I'll take two. No, make it four."

"Can I do it?" Owen asked.

"Absolutely." I handed him a set of tongs. "Since he wants four, we'll box them up."

Owen gently pulled four lemon lavender cookies out of the case and set them in a pink to-go box. I rang up the order while he folded the top down and added a little Angel Cakes sticker to hold it shut.

"There you go, sir." He handed the box to his uncle. "Have a nice day."

"Thank you." Zachary tipped his chin to him, then smiled at me before taking his box and leaving.

Owen froze, his eyes wide, and sniffed the air. "Harper."

"What's wrong?"

"The cookies. I wasn't listening for the timer."

Oh, no. Was that smoke?

Gasping, I ran to the kitchen.

Right as the fire alarm went off.

"Sugar cookies," I mumbled to no one in particular as I scrambled to turn off the oven. "It's not even that smoky back here."

The mirror curse was rearing its ugly head again.

"Should I open the back door?" Owen asked over the sound of the blaring alarm.

"Yes, please!" I shoved on a pair of oven mitts and opened the oven. A cloud of smoke rolled out and billowed toward the ceiling. To the surprise of no one, the cookies were ruined. Not as black as you'd think, given the way the smoke alarm was being such a drama queen, but not fit for sale.

"The fire department's here," Beth called back.

I put a tray of ruined cookies on the island. "Are you kidding? How did they get here so fast? Is that thing monitored?"

"Mr. Bakerfield called."

A man's voice came from the front of the store. "You're welcome!"

I groaned and took out another tray. Great. Now I had dozens of garbage cookies I couldn't sell, and the fire department was going to evacuate the bakery.

Beth disappeared into the front of the store, and a moment later I heard voices directing people outside.

The stupid fire alarm didn't stop.

"We get it, we get it." I grabbed a clean baking sheet and waved it in the air in front of the fire alarm. "There's no fire. You can shut up now."

Owen opened and shut the back door, trying to fan out some of the smoke. Finally, it stopped.

"Hey, Owen. What are you doing here?" A firefighter dressed in full uniform—the yellow pants and everything—came into the kitchen.

"Oh, hey, Uncle Levi."

"Wow, you really do have a lot of uncles."

"Told you."

A carbon copy of the first firefighter appeared in the back door. If it weren't for the slightly different haircuts, I would have thought I was seeing double.

"What's going on, bro-wen," the second firefighter said.

"Another uncle?" I asked.

"Sort of?" Owen said, like he wasn't sure how, or whether, they were related. "Logan's my cousins' uncle, and my uncle's brother, so..."

I didn't try to parse that out. I had bigger problems. "I'm so sorry someone called you guys. It was just burnt cookies."

Logan walked over to the island and glanced down at the overly browned peanut butter cookies. "Yeah, I see that. Are you sure my wife isn't here somewhere? She tends to burn cookies too."

I sighed. "We were just busy and I didn't hear the timers."

"It's my fault." Owen's voice was glum. "I was supposed to pay attention to the timers but Uncle Z came in and I forgot."

"No, it's okay," I said. "Sometimes things like this happen when we're busy."

Levi jerked his thumb over his shoulder toward the front of the store. "I'll let everyone know it's safe to come back in."

"Sounds good, brodentical." Logan picked up a cookie and took a bite. "A little crispy, but these aren't bad."

"You can take some with you, if you want. I can't do anything with them."

"Yeah, some of these are salvageable. My boys will eat them."

"That's a silver lining, I guess." I grabbed a box for him. "That was quite the response time. I think the alarm had been going off for all of thirty seconds when you walked in the door."

"We were driving right by," Logan said. "Must be your lucky day."

I laughed weakly. "Yeah. Lucky."

He picked through the still-hot cookies, holding them with the tips of his fingers, and put half a dozen or so in a box. "Thanks for these. And I'm glad your bakery isn't on fire."

"Me too."

"See ya, Owen."

"Bye, Logan."

He left out the back door and shut it behind him.

"Well, that was an adventure." I pulled out my hair tie and redid my low ponytail. "Looks like I have more cookies to bake. And four cakes to decorate."

"What do you want me to do?"

"Let's go help Beth do damage control with the people who were in line. We'll give them a free cookie. Then we'll get baking."

Owen followed me to the front where the line was re-forming as people came back inside. The evacuation hadn't lasted long, but I knew how quickly customers' patience could wear thin. I put on my best smile and had Owen pass out free cookies from what we had left in the case to the people who were waiting. That seemed to help.

I also made a mental note to drop off treats at the fire station.

Once we got through the line, the pastry case was pretty decimated. I decided to abandon peanut butter cookies for the day—didn't want to test my bad luck on those again—and focus on our best sellers. Chocolate chip and sugar cookies.

Owen and I got to work in the kitchen. I had him fetch ingredients—he was amazed by the size of the sacks of flour and sugar—and made sure to sprinkle a pinch of flour on the counter before I got started.

"What did you do that for?" he asked.

"It's something I picked up from my aunt. I always sprinkle a little flour before I start a new batch of anything. For good luck. And trust me, I need it."

"Did you forget before you started the peanut butter cookies?"

I paused, trying to remember. "That's a good question. But I don't think so."

"Didn't work very well, did it?"

I turned on the large stand mixer. "I guess a pinch of flour isn't enough to counteract my bad luck. I have a lot of that."

"It was kind of weird that the fire department was right outside. If there'd been a real fire, that would have been lucky. But there wasn't, so it was sort of the opposite."

"Yes," I said vehemently. I liked this kid. "That's exactly it. First, we missed the timers. Then, the smoke alarm went off when there wasn't even that much smoke. Then, the fire department was right outside, so it turned into a whole thing when it was nothing more than some burnt cookies."

"Definitely sus."

Nodding, I poured the chocolate chips into the mixer and let them incorporate into the dough. When they were mixed in, I turned it off and dumped the dough onto the island work surface.

"Do you want to do this?" I grabbed a cookie scoop and held it up.

"Sure. What do I do?"

"Use this to make them uniform." I scooped a glob of dough to show him how. "Then just put it on the tray. Leave room between them, since they spread. Like this." I put another next to the first one.

"Okay. I can do that."

He started scooping cookies while I got a batch of sugar cookie dough going. When the trays of chocolate chip went into the oven, I set the two timers, plus the timer on my phone, just to be extra careful.

Then I turned my attention to finishing up the last of the cakes for the day.

I chatted with Owen as I piped frosting, showing him how I used the different tips to make particular shapes. Since he seemed interested, I gave him some to try on a few day-old sugar cookies. He wasn't half bad.

The afternoon flew by. Before I knew it, we'd finished the cookies and added them to the case—to the delight of the waiting customers—and put the last touches on the custom cakes. I was about to start cleaning up the cake mess when Garrett Haven appeared, startling me.

I gasped and my icing spatula clattered to the floor. He was almost as wide as the doorway, and that uniform made him look so intimidating.

Then again, he was probably intimidating in regular clothes.

"Sorry." His deep voice sent a tingle down my spine.

"That's okay." I tried to ignore the way my heart sped up. "I just didn't see you there."

His eyes didn't leave mine, holding me captive for a moment. They were a stormy blue-gray. So intense. Like he carried the weight of the world on those broad shoulders.

"Dad?" Owen asked. "You're doing it again."

Looking away, Garrett cleared his throat. "You ready?"

"Yeah, I guess so."

"Wait!" They both looked at me like I had a wooden spoon growing out of my head. "You need some cookies to take home."

I brushed past Garrett and grabbed a to-go box.

"That's okay," Garrett said. "You don't have to do that."

"I know, but I want to. Besides, he helped make these."

I put half a dozen chocolate chip cookies in the box and turned around to hand it to Garrett.

He watched me like I didn't make sense, a furrow in his brow that was so unintentionally sexy.

Didn't matter. I wasn't dating anyone. Least of all Garrett Haven.

I held the box out. "They're still a little warm."

He hesitated for a second, then took it. "Thanks."

A girl could really get lost in those turbulent eyes.

"Owen was great, by the way. It was fun having him. Things got a little crazy earlier, but don't worry, there wasn't a fire. The fire department happened to be close when the alarm went off and we ruined the cookies, but that wasn't Owen's fault or anything." I was making next to zero sense, but I couldn't seem to stop talking. "Anyway, he was a big help and he'd make a pretty good cake decorator if he practiced."

The corners of Garrett's mouth lifted in a subtle smile and my knees almost buckled. It changed his entire face, warming his expression. I had a feeling that grin didn't come easy, and seeing a hint of it made me want to do anything to get him to smile at me again.

I laughed, almost cringing at how awkward it sounded. "Well, have a nice afternoon."

"K, Dad," Owen said. "I served my time. We can go now."

He glanced at his son as if he'd forgotten he was there. "Right. Yeah." He held up the cookies. "Thanks again."

I watched them leave, still a little awestruck by Garrett's smile.

"Uh-oh," Beth said as the door shut behind them.

I jumped. I'd totally forgotten she was there. "What?"

"Nothing." Her voice was full of mock innocence.

A customer came in before I could press her. I let her handle it and went back to the kitchen to start cleaning up.

A teenage helper. Burnt cookies. A fire alarm. First responders evacuating the bakery. It had been a big day. But were any of those things on my mind as I washed dishes and put things away?

Nope. All I could think about was Garrett Haven's smile.

CHAPTER 9

Garrett

"DAD, you have to try one of these," Owen said around a mouthful of chocolate chip cookie. "They're so good."

I eyed the box of cookies on the kitchen counter like they might bite. They certainly looked good. Perfect, even. Uniformly round and all the same size. Lightly browned edges and dotted with gooey chocolate chips.

What was I afraid of? That if I ate one of Harper's cookies, it would cast a spell on me and I'd become hopelessly obsessed with her?

Yes. That's exactly what I was afraid of.

I was already halfway there.

But the cookies did smell good. And if I didn't eat one, Owen was going to inhale them all.

I picked up a cookie and the scent made my mouth water. I took a slow bite. Slightly crispy edges, chewy and warm in the middle. My eyes closed and I groaned.

"Oh my god."

"Told you."

"Don't eat them all." I batted Owen's hand away as he tried to take another one. "You get half."

"I helped make them. I should get four."

"You were there because you shoplifted. You should have to watch me eat them all."

"Fine. Half is fair. I'll save my last one for later." He walked out of the kitchen and disappeared upstairs.

I took another bite. They were so buttery, with just the right amount of chocolate. I could have eaten a dozen of them.

But that didn't mean I was going to obsess about Harper. Any more than I already was, at least.

She'd turned me into an idiot again when I'd picked up Owen. I wasn't like my brothers Luke and Zachary, or even Theo. They always seemed to know what to say to women. I wasn't like Josiah, either, who communicated mostly in lumberjack grunts, like our dad. But that star struck, tongue tied thing I did every time I saw Harper? That wasn't me, either.

What was it about her?

I didn't know. But I grabbed another cookie. They were too much for any man to resist.

———

The scent of cookies wafted past the desk. I glanced up to see Kate, one of our deputies, walk by with a pink Angel Cakes box. I started to get up, like a cartoon character following his nose, but managed to stop myself.

I had to go out on a half-day patrol shift soon, which was good. The scent of whatever Kate had brought from the bakery lingered in the air. But the cookies weren't the problem.

It was Harper. She was the real temptation.

So far, I'd resisted the urge to stop by Angel Cakes—or even just circle it a few times. I kept telling myself I didn't want a relationship. I didn't want to date. I didn't have time and it wasn't worth the risk.

And all of those things were true. The thought of navigating a new relationship, trying to integrate another person into my life—and Owen's—was too daunting.

Yet, I couldn't stop thinking about those green eyes. That dazzling smile. The way all that long blond hair would look fanned out over my pillow.

"Haven." Kade's voice broke me out of my stupor.

"Hey, Sheehan."

He took a bite of a large cookie. "Just a heads up. Trent Jones is back on the streets. He made bail."

"Shit," I muttered under my breath.

"Yeah, he's a fun one. So I hear Sarge let you take the Joyner case."

My brow furrowed. "I talked to him this morning. How do you know about it already?"

He shrugged. "Word gets around. You really have time to dig into a cold case?"

"In between everything else, I guess. I just want to see if there's something we missed back then. You didn't work the case at all, did you?"

"Nah. I was too green, just like you."

"Didn't think so."

"You're a brave man, Haven."

I glanced up at him. "Why?"

"That case is basically cursed. I wouldn't touch it with a ten-foot pole."

"Cursed? I didn't think you were the superstitious type."

"I am when it comes to unsolvable cold cases that are going to make the town gossip line go nuts. I wouldn't want to be the object of that kind of scrutiny."

"The case is over a decade old. I'm sure the gossip line won't pick it up."

"Don't be so sure. I bet half the town knows already."

"We're already getting calls," Brenna said as she walked by. She was my favorite dispatcher when I was on patrol.

"Calls about the Joyner case?" I asked.

"Yep. Did we catch the killer? Is the killer still out there? Are the trails safe? You'd think it just happened."

"How the hell does anyone know I'm looking into it? I just started reviewing the case files."

Brenna shrugged and glanced at Kade, who shrugged back.

It wasn't confidential or anything. But it annoyed me that it was already town gossip. Freaking Tilikum.

"Did you try one of these?" Kade held up the remnant of his cookie. "They're amazing."

I shook my head. It didn't make rational sense, but I was worried that if I ate one of Harper's cookies, I'd black out and wind up at Angel Cakes Bakery, staring at her like a kid ogling cotton candy at the summer Mountain Man Festival.

"Your loss." He walked away.

At least he'd left the sarcasm at home.

Ignoring the temptation of baked goods—and Harper Tilburn—I went back to reviewing the Joyner case. There was so much information to sift through. Interviews with family and friends, the hundreds of tips that had come in, the medical examiner's findings, the evidence—or lack thereof— at the scene.

The murderer had been meticulous. He hadn't left a shred of DNA. She hadn't been sexually assaulted, which was inter- esting in and of itself. Murders of women were often sexually motivated, but this one didn't seem to have been. And there hadn't been so much as a hair or spot of blood on her body that wasn't hers.

She had a minor head injury, ligature marks on her wrists that indicated restraint, and the cause of death was stran- gulation.

The working theory had been crime of opportunity. She'd been on a hiking trail where the perpetrator had assaulted and killed her. No one had come up with a motive, and a lot of people in town had decided it had been a vagrant. Some random criminal passing through had attacked the poor young woman and left, never to be seen again.

But had they missed something?

The location where I'd discovered the bracelet wasn't where Jasmine's body had been found. If it was her bracelet, how did it get there? Had she lost it before she went missing? How reliable was the description of what she'd been wearing when she disappeared?

There was one way to find out.

Her older sister, Jocelyn, had been the last person to see her alive. I found the interviews they'd conducted, both before her body had been found, and the follow up later. Sure enough, Jocelyn had listed the bracelet among the things she'd been wearing. They had a matching set and never took them off.

I kept reading through the interviews with Jocelyn. She'd been concerned that Jasmine's ex-boyfriend might be involved. Not long before she was murdered, Jasmine had left what her sister described as a toxic relationship. I searched through the case notes and found the interview with the ex. He'd been on a fishing boat in Alaska when Jasmine had been killed—his alibi corroborated by numerous witnesses.

He'd been taken off the person of interest list, but as I kept reading through Jocelyn's interview, something stood out. She said in the weeks prior to Jasmine's initial disappearance, she'd received two packages from an unknown sender.

I kept reading, but the contents of the packages weren't listed. I didn't see another mention of them anywhere.

Hadn't anyone looked into that? It seemed impossible that they hadn't, unless it had been confirmed that the packages weren't related. But why wasn't there something in the file to indicate that?

I wondered if Jocelyn Joyner still lived in Tilikum. I

wanted to talk to her—find out what the packages had been about. If I was lucky, maybe she still had them.

Probably not after a decade, but you never knew what people would hang onto.

Sergeant Denny, my direct supervisor, walked by and glanced at me, eyebrows raised. I had to head out on patrol to cover for another deputy who was on paternity leave. It was hard to tear myself away from the Joyner case, but I didn't have much choice. Sometimes that was life in law enforcement—you did what you were told.

I stood. "Heading out, Sarge."

"Be safe out there."

"Will do."

I went out to my patrol car and performed the requisite inspection, checking for dings or dents. I opened up the back seat and looked around, making sure there wasn't any contraband left behind. The routine was part of protocol.

Then I got in and checked with dispatch to let them know I was available for assignment. "Squad seven, 10-8."

"10-4, squad seven. Squad nine is responding to family trouble at 306 West Cherry Street. Stay in the area in case they need assistance."

"10-4. Thanks, Bren."

I headed out and drove around town, keeping my eyes open and listening to the radio chatter. Deputy Spangler was squad nine and he handled the family trouble call without needing anything from me. Family trouble usually meant a disagreement between family members that wasn't domestic violence. It wasn't a surprise Spangler was able to de-escalate whatever had been going on. He was good at it.

I drove past Lumberjack Park, where it looked like the Squirrel Protection Squad were having a meeting. A few of the members turned and waved as I passed. I lifted a hand to wave back. Law enforcement had an amicable relationship with the grassroots group. They'd ostensibly formed to help protect the local squirrel population in a time of crisis, but everyone knew they were really Tilikum's civilian security force.

They'd watched out for my sister-in-law, Audrey. And helped with the search when Marigold had gone missing. As long as they didn't get in the way of an investigation, I was happy to let them do their thing.

I came to the turn that would take me to Angel Cakes and I swear, the steering wheel moved on its own. I jerked it back so I'd go straight instead of turning. My Harper obsession was getting out of hand. I could have caused an accident.

Granted, no one else was on the road. But still. I needed to get her out of my head.

I circled the block and stopped at a four-way. Another car went through and the driver caught my eye as she passed.

Oh, shit. It was her.

Harper.

Without thinking, I pulled out behind her. What was I doing? She was probably on her way home. Was I going to follow her? What was that supposed to accomplish?

We came to another four-way intersection. She turned right.

So did I.

She also didn't use a turn signal, but there was no way I was pulling her over. Next time she turned, I'd go the opposite direction. I couldn't keep following her. I slowed down, putting more distance between us.

But when she turned left, what did I do? Yeah. Turned left.

She used her turn signal that time.

Turn around, Garrett. Do it. Turn around and stop following her.

Did I?

No. No, I did not.

She turned right and once again, didn't use her turn signal. It was probably burned out on that side. Before I could contemplate what I was doing—or talk sense into myself—I flipped on my lights.

She slowed and pulled to a stop. I parked a short distance behind her.

What the hell was I doing?

I keyed my mic. "Squad seven."

"Go ahead, squad seven."

"Put me out with a traffic stop at 5806 West Cedar. White Toyota RAV4, one female occupant. Reason for stop is failure to use a turn signal."

Brenna hesitated. "10-4, squad seven."

"I'm just going to let her know. It's probably out."

"Uh-huh. 10-4."

I rolled my eyes. Brenna knew me. She knew I didn't usually pull people over for little things.

And what was I supposed to do now? Walk up to Harper's car and ask her out?

Actually…

I got out of my car. I wasn't going to do it. I was absolutely not going to ask her out. I didn't want to start a relationship. I didn't have time.

Except I couldn't stop thinking about her. It was driving me crazy.

She was driving me crazy.

I approached her car and she lowered her window.

"Um, hi officer. Is there a problem?"

I took off my sunglasses. "Hi, Harper."

Her eyes widened in recognition. "Oh! Garrett. Wait. Why did you pull me over? Was I speeding? I'm sure I wasn't speeding. What did I do?"

Her rambling was so cute, I couldn't help but crack a smile. "Nothing. It's just…" There my brain went again, forgetting how to use words. "Your turn signal. It might be out. You didn't use it. Twice. Just the right one."

That was probably the least eloquent I'd ever been in my

entire life, but at least I'd gotten to the facts.

"My turn signal? That's weird. Can you check it for me?"

"Sure, yeah." Exactly what I should have suggested. My brain really needed to catch up and start working. "Go ahead with the left one."

She turned it on. I stepped back to make sure the lights were blinking. They were.

"That one works. Now the right."

She pushed the lever down.

I walked around the car to check, then back to the driver's side. "Passenger side rear is out. Front works."

"Well that sucks."

"Is there an indicator light on your dash or anything? A lot of cars alert you when a light is out."

She glanced at her dashboard. "There might be but if there is, it didn't work. That would be my luck. Do you know where to get a replacement light?"

The hint of worry in her voice tugged at something in my chest. A busted light wasn't my problem, and it wasn't even a big deal. But I had to fix this for her.

"I can grab one and help install it if you want."

She gazed up at me and her big green eyes locked me in place. A car could have flown by at ninety miles an hour and I'd have been hard pressed to notice.

"Um." She shook her head a little, as if to clear it. "That's okay. I'm sure I can figure it out. There's an auto parts store in town, right? I think I've seen it. I don't know why I asked that question. I'll be fine."

I cracked a smile. She was sexy when she was flustered. "I really don't mind."

"I'm sure you're busy with, you know, police stuff. Or, sheriff stuff or whatever you are."

My smile grew. I put a hand on the top of her car and leaned down. "Sheriff's deputy. How about this? We have dinner and I fix your turn signal."

Oh shit. I'd just asked her out.

"Like, right now?"

"I'm on duty until six and then I have to pick up Owen from my parents' place." Despite the slight panic rising in my chest, I'd already said it. No going back now. "So how about tomorrow? Are you free?"

Her eyebrows drew together. "I don't know if dating is a good idea for me right now."

She'd just given me an out. I could have accepted her polite refusal, let her go about her business, and moved on.

Except, I couldn't. I couldn't do it.

"It's just dinner. No pressure. And I promise I won't miss this one."

Her expression softened. "You promise?"

"Yes. Even if I'm chasing a bad guy. It'll be his lucky day."

She looked forward, rubbing her lips together, and gripped the steering wheel. It took her two, maybe three seconds, but the wait just about killed me.

"Okay, Garrett Haven. Dinner. And you fix my blinker."

"Deal."

"You're not going to give me a ticket, are you?"

That almost made me laugh. "I'll be lenient this time."

Her lips turned up. "Thanks, deputy. Am I free to go?"

That smile was going to be the death of me. "Yes, ma'am. Be safe out there."

"You too."

She raised her window as I stepped back, her smile disappearing behind the glare of the sun on the glass.

I walked back to my car, half in a daze. Had I really just pulled her over, then asked her out?

And she'd said yes?

Practical, sensible Garrett Haven would never have done that.

I got in my car with a slight grin on my face, kind of glad that guy had gone missing for a minute.

CHAPTER 10

Harper

WAS this date a good idea or a bad idea? I was so torn.

All day, I'd waited for something bad luckish to happen. Nothing. No failed timers, no burnt cookies, no smoke alarms or evacuations.

In fact, it almost seemed as if my day had been filled with good luck.

Every batch of cookies had turned out perfect and my cupcakes looked magical. After the morning rush, things had slowed down just in time for me to take an actual lunch break. My blinker randomly started working again, and when I came back to work after grabbing some food, my spot in the parking lot was still open.

Bad luck had to be lurking, just waiting to strike.

Which meant this date was probably going to be a disaster. Or he was going to get a huge promotion in another country tomorrow and I'd never see him again.

There was a knock at my door and I glanced at the clock on the microwave. He was right on time, to the minute.

Wow. Okay. So, not blowing me off, missing our date due to work, or anything in between. That was a good start at least.

With a deep breath, I smoothed out my black dress and fluffed my hair, then answered the door.

Garrett Haven stood on my doorstep, looking like a dream in a dark gray coat over a button-down shirt with the collar undone and a pair of extremely well-fitting gray slacks.

I don't know why it surprised me so much to see him out of uniform. Of course he'd be dressed in regular clothes.

And of course he'd look that good.

Wow. Again.

He gave me that smile of his and I hadn't even said anything. The words *I'm so lucky* ran through my head.

Wait. No. I wasn't lucky. Like, ever.

"Hi." His voice was pleasantly deep. "You look beautiful."

My cheeks warmed and I felt a pleasant fluttering in my stomach. "Thank you. So do you. I mean, you look nice."

"Thank you. If you unlock your car, I can get that blinker replaced for you."

"You know what's weird? It works now."

"Really?"

"Yeah. I checked it a couple of times to make sure I wasn't imagining it. But it works fine. I don't know what was going on yesterday."

"All right. Are you ready, then?"

I nodded, grabbed my purse, and put on a jacket since it was raining. He led me to his car—not his patrol car, of course, it was a dark SUV—with a light touch on the small of my back, making the butterflies in my stomach take flight.

We got in and I let out a small breath. Feeling this jittery, I was bound to be the cause of my own bad luck. Self-fulfilling prophecies and all. I didn't want to trip over my feet or blurt out something embarrassing, not because of the mirror curse, but because I let myself get too flustered.

I glanced at Garrett as he drove. At his strong stubbly jaw and broad shoulders.

Flustered it was. I couldn't help it. He was such a heady

combination of handsome, intimidating, and drop dead sexy. The kind of man who made you contemplate breaking the law just so he could arrest you.

Excuse me, deputy? I think you need to handcuff me…

"How was your day?"

I startled at his voice and blinked away the fantasy. "My day? It was… fine. Busy, but that's just my life. How about yours?"

"It was all right. Long."

"I hope you didn't have to let any bad guys get away to pick me up on time."

He cracked a smile. "Not this time."

We made a little more small talk on the way to the restaurant. It wasn't far, on a side street downtown near the bakery. I glanced at the parking lot up ahead. It looked packed. There wasn't any parking on the street, either. I wondered how long we'd have to circle before we found a spot, or how far we'd have to walk.

And how wet we were going to get. Bad luck about to strike?

As if the rain knew we were about to get stuck in it, it came down harder. Garrett turned up the windshield wipers and slowed as we approached the restaurant.

"I might have to circle—" He stopped as reverse lights lit up in front of us. "Never mind. They're leaving."

The spot was right in front of the restaurant. That was… I wasn't going to say lucky. Convenient. It was convenient, especially with the rain.

Garrett parked, then told me to wait and ran around to my side to open my door. He used his jacket to shield me from the rain as we ran to the entrance.

We went inside and he draped his coat over his arm. The restaurant was cozy, with a low hum of conversation filling the air.

I smoothed down my hair, although it hadn't gotten wet. "Thank you."

He smiled.

So many butterflies.

Although the restaurant looked full, there was a table available and we were seated right away. The ambiance was charming and romantic, with white tablecloths and flickering candles. We perused our menus for a few minutes and I waited for the jittery feeling to let up.

It didn't.

Was I nervous because this was a first date? Or because I was convinced something was going to go wrong?

Maybe a bit of both.

The server came to our table and we ordered wine and dinner. I almost knocked over my water glass handing the server my menu, but Garrett grabbed it before it could splash all over me. I thanked him with a laugh.

When it happened again—that time just trying to pick up my wine glass after the server had poured—I rolled my eyes and shook my head.

"Sorry. I don't know why I'm so clumsy all of a sudden."

His smile was soft and so genuine. "It's fine. No harm done. So how did you become a baker? Did you go to culinary school?"

"I did, but I mostly learned from my aunt Doris. When I was a kid, my sister and I used to come stay with her sometimes. Aunt Doris and I would spend most of our time baking."

"She did the world a service. The cookies you sent home with us the other day were probably the best thing I've ever eaten in my life."

I smiled, and a warm, giddy feeling spread through me. "Thank you. Owen was a big help."

He raised his eyebrows. "Really?"

"Absolutely. He did everything I asked without a single

complaint. I think he might have even enjoyed himself when I let him scoop the cookie dough."

"It would be nice if he could bring some of that good attitude home when it's time to do the dishes." There was humor in his voice and the corners of his lips lifted in a grin. "He is a great kid, though."

"He is. You've done a great job."

A flicker of surprise crossed his face. "Thank you."

My curiosity about Owen's mom was growing, but it felt awkward to bring it up. Aunt Doris had said Garrett was divorced. But was she still around? Did they share custody? If Garrett and I actually started dating, would it be complicated?

I'd thought about that before, when Doris had set us up the first time. But knowing Owen made it all the more real.

But this was just one dinner. I didn't need to dig into his past if this wasn't going anywhere.

The server brought our dinners and we started eating.

"How did you get into law enforcement?"

"It's what I wanted to do since I was a kid. I was always the good guy when my brothers and I played. Always the cop, catching the bad guys."

"How many brothers do you have? Owen said he has a lot of uncles."

"Five brothers and one sister."

My eyes widened. "There are seven kids in your family?"

"We were three and three at first. My dad had me and two of my brothers, Josiah and Luke, with his first wife. And my mom had three boys, Reese, Theo, and Zachary. Then they got together and had our sister, Annika."

"Kind of like the Brady Bunch, except… different."

"Yeah. We were all close in age too. It must have been chaos. I don't know how they did it."

"That's amazing."

He chuckled softly. "I mostly remember it being loud."

"With six little boys, I can imagine. What did you all think of your sister?"

"We loved her. We tended to torture each other, but we protected her like it was our job."

"That's so sweet. Are you all close now?"

"Yeah, I guess you could say we are. Most of us, at least. Zachary and I used to get into it a lot, but we went through some stuff together and it changed things. And now that he's married, I probably won't have to arrest him again, so that helps."

My mouth dropped open. "You've arrested your brother?"

"Yeah. A couple times."

"For what?"

"Disorderly conduct. He used to have a tendency to start trouble, especially when alcohol was involved. He was never booked or had charges brought up or anything, but I had to haul him in a couple times to break things up. Didn't make him like me all that much."

"But you get along better now?"

"Yeah." His lips turned up in a subtle grin. "I was the best man at his wedding."

"Wow. I love that. What about your other brothers?"

"They're good guys. Josiah got married in January. He's not exactly a people person, but his wife Audrey is great. Theo coaches football at the high school. He played professionally for a while but he got injured."

"He's not married?"

"Nope. Neither is Luke. He owns a custom auto shop. Rebuilds classic cars and that sort of thing. My sister, Annika, is married, and has been for a while now."

"Oh, to the firefighter?"

"Yeah, how did you know?"

"He was one of the responders when the fire alarm went off at the bakery. Owen said he was his uncle."

"Levi Bailey. He's a great guy."

"Does he have a twin or was I hallucinating?"

"Yep, identical. That's Logan."

"Okay, things are making more sense. So there's you, Zachary, Josiah." I started counting off brothers on my fingers. "Theo, Luke, and who was the other one?"

"Reese."

"What does he do?"

"Honestly, I have no idea. He left town a long time ago and never came back."

I could hear the hurt in his voice. It was subtle, as if he were trying to hide it, but it was definitely there.

"What happened?"

"I don't know. I've always assumed he had a falling out with Dad, but I don't know what actually went down. Or why he's stayed away so long."

"That's sad. I bet your parents miss him."

"Mom does for sure. I think he's contacted her a few times over the years, just to let her know he's still alive. But he could be anywhere. What about you? Just the one sister?"

I nodded. "Her name's Holly. Obviously my mom had a thing for H names."

"What about your dad?"

"I don't really know him. I don't want to say my mom dated him just long enough for him to get her pregnant because she wanted a baby. But I think that's what she did."

"Really?"

"Yeah. I try not to be judgy about it, but I'm pretty sure that's what she did with my sister's dad too. Of course, she doesn't describe it that way, exactly, but Holly and I both have the same theory. My mom is… interesting. She's super independent. I think it was hard for her to share her space with her own kids, so the idea of letting another adult in her life permanently was sort of unthinkable."

"But she had you two on purpose?"

"Yeah. She wanted kids, so she found a way to make it

happen. And she was a good mom, in her own way. I love her, but we're not very close. I'm so different from her, and my sister. Neither of them really get me. There's no animosity or anything, our relationship is friendly. But it's just that. Friendly. That's probably why I'm close to my aunt. We both love baking and we're, I don't know, weird in the same ways."

He grinned a little. "How are you weird?"

A tingle of nervousness swept through me and I let out a breath. Vulnerability is hard. "Okay, so I'm a little bit superstitious. And by a little bit, I mean a lot."

He kept smiling at me. "What are you superstitious about? Like walking under ladders and stuff?"

"Oh, I'd never walk under a ladder."

"Black cats?"

"No, black cats aren't a problem. I don't know why, it makes sense in my head. But if I spill salt, I always toss a bit over my shoulder. Whenever I start baking anything, I have to take a pinch of flour and toss it on my work surface. And I knock on wood whenever necessary."

"Is that it?"

I wondered if I should tell him about the mirror curse. If he didn't believe me, he might think I was a little bit crazy. And if he did believe me, he might not want to risk it rubbing off on him.

"There's probably more, but that's what I can remember off the top of my head."

"That doesn't seem too weird."

I smiled. "Thanks. That's good to hear."

We spent the rest of dinner chatting about all sorts of things. He told me stories about growing up in Tilikum, especially pranks he and his brothers played on the Bailey brothers in the days of the feud. I shared some of my ideas for new cookie flavors, and about the time I'd worked for a chef who'd barked orders like a military commander. We laughed a lot and it was just so… easy.

As the evening went on, it felt less and less like a first date with someone I barely knew. Somehow, he felt like someone I'd known for a long time. Like something in him was deeply familiar in a way I couldn't explain.

I didn't want our evening to end, but it was getting late—for me, at least. Such is life when you start work at four in the morning.

When I barely hid a yawn, he asked if I was ready to go. I wasn't—I was really enjoying myself—but I didn't want to nod off and bump my head on the table. Or make him think I was bored.

The rain had stopped by the time we left the restaurant, so he didn't shield me with his jacket. But he did open the door and offer his hand to help me in. It was such a sweet gesture, and when I caught a glimpse of his subtle smile, I almost melted into a puddle.

Why thank you, Deputy Dreamy. Now, about that crime I committed earlier. Are you going to cuff me?

I rested my hands on my thighs on the drive back to my place, hoping he'd reach over and hold my hand. Silly? Maybe. But I was craving contact with him, wishing he'd initiate even a light touch. His presence left me feeling warm and content—and wanting more.

When we got to my house, he walked me to my door, and it occurred to me that nothing bad had happened all night. Sure, it had rained, but that wasn't bad luck, just weather. I'd almost spilled on myself—twice—but hadn't. No dropped forks or food in my teeth or tripping on the way out.

Maybe dating Garrett Haven wasn't such a bad idea after all.

Or maybe I just hoped it wasn't.

Because looking up into his blue-gray eyes, I realized

something. I really, really liked this guy. And I didn't want my bad luck to ruin it.

Okay, luck, I thought, silently projecting out into the universe. *If you're going to mess this up, go ahead and do it now. Show me he doesn't like me and I can move on, before I get too attached.*

"Look, I need to be really honest with you." His gaze was intense, and my heart sped up.

Oh, no. Here we go. "Okay. Honest is good."

"I don't know if I can make a relationship work."

My heart sank. *Okay, luck, you win.*

"But," he said vehemently, and hope surged like a wave. "I don't know what it is about you. I keep telling myself I don't have room for this, I don't have time. And it's like something in me just won't listen. I can't get you out of my head. And the truth is, I don't want to."

I could feel my pulse in my neck, beating hard. He shifted closer, ever so slightly, and my breath caught.

His eyes didn't leave mine. "Can I see you again?"

Words, Harper. Say something. "Yes. I'd love that."

The way his mouth turned up in a smile sent tingles down my spine. He moved in and I tilted my chin up, ready for his kiss.

His phone rang and he paused, his lips just inches from mine.

"Sorry." He straightened and pulled out his phone. "Just in case it's Owen."

"That's okay." My voice was breathy and my head slightly dizzy.

He answered. "Hey, bud. Is everything all right?"

It was Owen. Totally understandable. I loved that he kept his phone on to make sure his son could reach him.

"Yeah, that's fine. Thanks for asking first. I'll be on my way in a minute." He ended the call and pocketed his phone. "Sorry about that."

"Don't apologize. Tell Owen I said hi."

His smile was back. "I will. So, I'll call you?"

Or maybe come inside?

No, don't say that, Harper. Too soon.

My body protested, my lady parts trying to usurp control from my rational brain. Our night had gone so well. And I wasn't just *interested* in him, I was *insanely attracted* to him. I'd never been one to jump into bed with a man, but for Garrett Haven, I would have made an exception.

However, my bad luck was still lurking. I needed to be careful.

"That would be great," I said. "As long as you mean it."

"I'm a man of my word. I'll call you."

Swoon city.

"I had a great time tonight. Thank you."

"I did too." He took a deep breath, and I hoped he'd move in to kiss me again, but it seemed as if the moment had passed. "Goodnight, Harper."

"Goodnight, Garrett."

I went inside and paused, listening to the sound of his car leaving. That had been the best first date I'd ever had.

But I sighed, knowing what that probably meant. He'd call, sure. To tell me he'd just been offered a job with the FBI and had to move to Washington, D.C. or something.

Or maybe not. He seemed to have sidestepped—or averted—my bad luck all night. Maybe the mirror curse had just met its match.

CHAPTER 11

Harper

THE TIMER DINGED and I rushed to the oven to take out the cake. Thanks to my alarm, that was definitely set to *on* and somehow did not wake me up, I'd started my day behind. Coincidence? Bad luck? I didn't have time to contemplate. None of the day's treats were going to bake themselves.

It was already mid-afternoon, and although it had been a hectic day, I was handling it. Plus, I was in a great mood, still riding the currents of post-first-date giddiness.

I can't get you out of my head.

His words, delivered in that deliciously masculine voice, echoed in my mind. The feeling was mutual. I couldn't get him out of my head either.

Letting out a little sigh, I set the cake on the island to cool. One date with Garrett Haven and I was a big gooey mess of feelings.

And temptations.

I leaned against the island. What would that stubbly jaw feel like against my face? Or… lower? For a moment, I got lost in a daydream, imagining Garrett's big hands hauling me against him. The way his thick arms would feel wrapped around me, his strong body—

"Hey, Harper?" Beth asked.

I jolted back to reality and felt my cheeks instantly flush. Beth wasn't alone.

Owen stood with her in the doorway between the front of the bakery and the kitchen.

"Hey, Owen!" My voice had far too much enthusiasm. I was just hoping he couldn't tell I'd been about to imagine myself getting naked with his dad. "What's up?"

"Go ahead." Beth nudged him into the kitchen.

He wore a gray hoodie and had his hands shoved in the front pockets of his jeans. "Um… I was just wondering…"

I tilted my head and waited, but he didn't continue. "Wondering about what?"

Oh no. Was he upset I'd gone out with his dad? Had he come to ask me to stop dating him?

He kept his eyes lowered. "Do you need help with anything today?"

For a second, I almost lost my mind and ran over to hug him. He was just so dang sweet, with his mild embarrassment and slightly forlorn expression.

"Do I ever. I woke up late this morning, and I've been behind all day. So if you're offering, I ain't saying no."

His gaze lifted and his mouth turned up in the hint of a smile.

Just like his dad.

"I'm offering."

"You're basically my hero today." I pointed to a row of hooks with extra aprons. "Grab an apron, wash your hands, and let's bake."

With a big grin, he pulled off his hoodie, donned an apron, and went to the sink to wash his hands.

I didn't know where this was coming from—whether he'd enjoyed himself the other day and wanted to learn more about baking, or if there was some other motive—but I wasn't about to turn down his offer. Was he bored? Lonely? It was hard to tell. I didn't have a lot of experience—or, any experience—with teenage boys, and I wasn't sure how to read him.

But I was grateful for the help. Plus, I really liked him. And not even because I was lusting after his dad.

We got to work on a batch of cherry chocolate chunk cookies. He got the flour and sugar without me having to ask and I walked him through the recipe.

"So, did you come here after school?" I asked. "How was that?"

"Yeah, I had school. It was okay."

"Does your dad know you're here?"

"Yeah, I texted him. I was grounded, but he let me off early for good behavior." He glanced up at me. "By the way, I know you guys went on a date last night."

"Oh, good, I'm glad you know. Now I don't have to worry about whether I'm allowed to mention it. I don't really know how this works." I paused, a twinge of nervousness in my stomach. "Are you okay with it?"

"Sure, it's fine." His tone was matter-of-fact. "I knew he liked you, even when he denied it."

That made me laugh. "He denied it?"

"Yeah. He hasn't dated anyone since my mom, so I guess it's kind of hard for him."

The twinge of nervousness grew. He'd mentioned his mom. Could I ask? "Would it be awkward if I asked about your mom?"

"No." Still matter-of-fact. "What do you want to know?"

"Did they get divorced a long time ago?"

He paused. "Six years ago? Something like that."

"Was that hard for you?"

His shrug spoke volumes. I could practically see him trying to push down his feelings. "She was already gone a lot, so it didn't change things too much."

"So, she's gone a lot now?"

"I don't see her."

That hit me like a punch in the stomach. He didn't see his mom? Like, ever?

"Not at all? Did she move away?"

"I don't think she lives in Tilikum anymore. But no, I just don't see her."

The urge to hug him was so strong. "Owen, I'm so sorry. That really sucks."

"I guess. We weren't close anyway."

"I feel that. I'm not close with my mom either."

He looked up, his expression full of interest. "Really?"

"I don't want to say my relationship with my mom is like yours, considering I do actually see her. But only a couple of times a year at most. We talk a little bit, but not much. There's just this weird gap between us. I can't really explain it."

"That sucks too, doesn't it?"

I nodded. "It does sometimes. I think, as humans, we all have a basic need to be understood. To be seen. It's hard when one of the people who ought to really see you, just... doesn't."

"Yeah." His brow furrowed. "It is annoying that my mom just bailed on us."

I had a feeling it was a lot more than annoying. The hurt he was trying to hide was plain in the set of his shoulders, the stormy look on his face.

Maybe I could read him a little bit.

"Yeah, that's rough." I wasn't sure what else to say. *Your mom sounds awful, what did your dad ever see in her?* No, that was a terrible question. "She doesn't know what she's missing."

He met my eyes again and a smile tugged the corners of his mouth. "You're just saying that because you like my dad."

"I'm saying it because it's true. But you're right, I do like your dad. Is it weird if I say that to you?"

"It's okay if it's weird. Is the dough ready?"

"It is. You want to start scooping?"

He held up the cookie scoop. "On it."

I let him dump the cookie dough onto the work surface and got out a few baking sheets. He remembered how to do it, so I left him to it while I washed out the mixer so I could get started on the next thing.

Beth poked her head into the kitchen. "How are we doing on cookies?"

"They're going into the oven in just a minute. How's the case looking?"

"Pretty bare, but it's not busy. We're fine, I just wanted to check."

"Sounds good. Thanks, Beth."

Once Owen finished scooping cookies, he and I put the trays in the oven. We shared an amused look as I set two timers—no fire-cookie fiasco today—and I went looking for the coconut flakes. I wanted to whip up a batch of pistachio coconut drop cookies for the evening rush.

"I know I ordered more," I said, more to myself than to Owen as I kept searching through the shelves and cupboards. "Where are—oh no."

"What's wrong?"

"I'm out of coconut flakes. I'm sure I ordered more, but it probably got lost."

"That sucks."

"It's okay, this stuff happens to me all the time." I sank down on one of the tall stools. "I'm sort of cursed."

"What do you mean?"

I sighed. "You want the truth?"

He nodded and pulled up another stool.

"I broke a mirror. And it wasn't just any mirror. It was my grandmother's full-length antique mirror in this fancy, gilded frame. When I was little, I used to love to stand in front of it and twirl. I guess she remembered that because she left it to me. Literally the first day I had it in my possession, I broke it."

His eyebrows drew together. "But why does that make you cursed? You don't really think your grandma would curse you from the afterlife or something, do you? Over a mirror?"

"No, I don't think she did it. It's not her fault, it's just… the physics of luck, you might say. I broke a mirror. That's seven years bad luck. Although to be honest, I do think it's worse because it was a special mirror."

He eyed me like he was suddenly not so sure that hanging out in my bakery was such a great idea.

"I know, I know, it sounds crazy. It's okay if you don't believe me. Most people don't. I think my aunt is the only one who understands. My mom and sister certainly don't. They think I use it as an excuse so I don't have to take responsibility for my problems."

"Grown-ups love to say stuff like that."

I laughed. "Very true. I deny it, though. I know bad luck isn't to blame for everything. Not even my biggest life problems. It's mostly a lot of little stuff that's inconvenient. Although it tends to build up after a while."

"How much longer do you have?"

"Until the curse ends? Around six months now."

"That's not bad. It's almost over."

"Let's hope so."

Beth came back into the kitchen. "The lobby is clear for now. Do you mind if I take a quick break? I have an errand to run."

"Of course. We've got this." I winked at Owen.

I grabbed one of the cookie timers and brought it up front. Owen came with me, and I was about to ask him what he liked to do when he wasn't hanging out at Angel Cakes, when a customer came in.

My heart sank a little. It was… what was his name? Matt. He looked unkempt with a hole in his shirt and worn jeans.

The smile that lit up his face was too suggestive to be described as friendly.

"Hi. Harper, right?"

I nodded. "Can I help you?"

He didn't look in the case. Just came up to the counter, his eyes locked on me. "How have you been?"

"Fine, thanks. Is there something I can get for you?"

"Oh, yeah." He started perusing the pastry case. "Man, everything looks good."

Owen turned so his back was to the customer and gave me a look.

I tried not to giggle.

"What do you suggest?" Matt asked.

"We have butterscotch chip today. Those are very popular."

"You made them?"

Why did he always ask that? "Yes."

"Okay. I'll take one of those."

"I got it." Owen jumped in front of me and put a butterscotch chip cookie into a bag.

"I was listening to a podcast last night," Matt said. "It reminded me of you."

I didn't like where that was going. "Oh?"

"The victim worked in a bakery." His eyes were intense. "Just like you do."

"Um…"

"And her killer was a customer who was obsessed with her."

"That's incredibly disturbing."

He grinned. "I know, right?"

Owen cleared his throat and held out the bagged cookie. "Here you go."

"Thanks." Matt took it, paid with cash, and I handed him his change.

"Thanks for coming in."

"Nice to see you again. Are you open every day?"

"We're closed on Mondays."

"Got it." He took a slow step back. "Maybe I'll see you around."

Note to self: stay home on Mondays. "Enjoy your cookie."

Finally, he turned and left. The door shut behind him and I let out a breath.

"Bruh, he was sus."

I turned to Owen, pressing my lips together so I wouldn't smile like a dork. He'd just called me bruh. That meant he liked me, right? I was in. It was all I could do not to squeal.

"So sus," I managed, and almost sounded like I used that word regularly. "It wasn't just me?"

"No, he definitely lives in his mom's basement."

I burst out laughing. "Oh my gosh. Poor guy. His true crime fascination is disturbing. Do you know who he is?"

He shrugged. "I've seen him around."

The timer went off with a ding. "Hey, look at us, not burning the cookies."

"Do you get to eat the stuff you bake?"

"Is that code for can I have a cookie?"

His sheepish grin was adorable. "Maybe?"

"Someone needs to taste test them," I said, my voice solemn. "Come on, let's get them out of the oven. We can start on a cake while they cool. And yes, *we* get to eat the stuff we bake."

We went into the kitchen and took out a perfect batch of cherry chocolate chunk cookies. A few more customers came in while we waited for them to cool, then we dove into our taste test. They were rich and chewy with a light crispness at the edges, and the cherry and chocolate flavors complemented each other nicely.

Owen wiped his mouth and checked his phone. "I should probably go. Homework."

"Okay. I'm glad you stopped by."

He took off his apron and hung it on a hook, then donned his hoodie. His expression had gone sheepish again, like he wasn't sure what to say. He finally settled on, "Well, bye."

"Thanks for your help today."

"You're welcome."

He shoved his hands in the front pocket and started shuffling toward the front.

"Hey, Owen?"

"Yeah?" He turned and the hope in his eyes melted my heart.

"You can come anytime. Even if you don't want to help and you just want cookies. I'll always have some for you."

The corners of his mouth lifted and once again I was struck with how much he looked like his dad. "Thanks."

"Anytime. I'll see you later."

He nodded and left out the front.

With a sigh, I sank onto a stool. It was probably silly, but I couldn't stop smiling.

He'd called me bruh.

CHAPTER 12

Garrett

MY FEET HIT the pavement in a steady rhythm and sweat dripped down my temples. It was a nice day for a long run. Clear sky, but not hot. A gentle breeze coming down from the mountain peaks.

It was a much-needed day off. Juggling patrol shifts with investigative work and all the requisite paperwork was a lot. The day before, I'd responded to a call that had turned into a mess. A neighbor had reported a loud argument that had turned out to be a mother and her adult son. She was trying to kick him out of her house and he was refusing to leave. I'd done what I could, but he didn't have any warrants and, despite the mom insisting I take him to jail, I had no cause to arrest him. Although I'd basically taken his side, he hadn't been happy with me either. Fortunately, I'd de-escalated the situation, but it didn't seem like I'd helped them resolve anything.

And the Joyner case was never far from my mind. Something about it ate at me, my instincts prickling like there was a lead just out of reach that I couldn't quite see.

I checked my watch and picked up the pace, deciding to push it for the next half mile or so. Mayor Bill Surrey drove by and lifted his hand in a wave as he passed. I waved back. My legs started to burn and my breath came faster as I took a right at the corner, then stopped in my tracks.

Harper's street. I was about to run right by her house.

I stood there, hands on my hips, breathing hard. I hadn't planned on passing her house, but my subconscious must have been working overtime to get me there.

Her car was in her driveway. I could see it, just up the street from where I was standing.

I was planted to the spot, my eyes locked on her house. It must have been her day off. And there I was, several miles from home, and I couldn't seem to make myself turn around.

What was it about her? We'd gone out once. Just one date. I hadn't even kissed her. I still had all the regrets about that. I should have. I'd been thinking about it ever since.

I wanted to know what she tasted like.

Somehow, this woman had gotten deep under my skin. The fact that my son liked her only made it worse. I couldn't hide behind the single dad thing as an excuse.

I wanted to be cautious. To hold back and take things slow.

But I also wanted to fuck her brains out.

That wasn't like me. I was the responsible one. The guy who did things by the book. Zachary made fun of me for it, but it wasn't a bad thing. It made me a good father, especially under less than ideal circumstances. It made me good at my job.

I couldn't just show up at her house.

Could I?

No.

I was standing on a residential street corner, sweating all over my T-shirt and shorts, not moving. Someone was probably going to report me for suspicious behavior.

That got me walking again. But instead of turning back the way I came, I was heading toward her house, as if an invisible line had hooked me right in the chest and kept pulling me closer.

I was not normally a spontaneous guy, but she was right there.

And she was irresistible.

I jogged up to her door and knocked. That was when I realized I might not smell the best, considering I'd just run several miles.

Too late. She opened the door, greeting me in a black tank top and knee-length skirt, her hair loose around her shoulders. The smile that lit up her face just about knocked me on my ass.

"Hi there. This is a nice surprise." Her green eyes sparkled without a hint of suspicion. She looked genuinely excited.

By me.

"Sorry to just show up. I was out for a run and wound up on your street. Thought I'd stop by."

"I can see that." She gestured to my workout clothes. "Day off?"

"Yeah. You?"

She nodded. "We're closed one day a week so I can pretend I'm a normal human."

"Feeling like a normal human once in a while is good."

"It really is."

My eyes drifted to her mouth. I wanted to taste those soft, pink lips. I'd missed my chance the other night. I wasn't making that mistake again. "I know I already said I had a good time the other night. But I'm not exactly happy with how it ended."

"No?"

Shifting closer, I reached out to slip a hand around her waist. "No."

She didn't resist as I drew her near. There a gap between her tank top and skirt, right in the middle of her back, and my heart sped up as I felt the heat of skin against my fingertips.

Her lips parted and she drew in a quick breath.

I pulled her tight against me and inhaled her vanilla scent. With one hand splayed across her back, I tilted her chin up with the other.

"I wanted to do this."

Dipping my mouth to hers, I took her lips in a kiss.

I'd meant for it to be a do-over goodnight kiss. Just a taste.

I didn't stop at a taste.

Parting her lips with my tongue, I delved into her mouth, suddenly ravenous for more. She threw her arms around my neck and pressed herself against me while my hands slid down to cup her ass.

She tasted minty and sweet. I couldn't get enough. I kissed her deeply, enjoying the velvety smoothness of her tongue, the wetness of her mouth. The fact that we were making out on her doorstep in broad daylight didn't even register.

I just wanted more.

She pulled back slightly and our lips parted. "Come inside."

Every molecule in my body ached for this. "You sure?"

"Yes." Her voice was breathy and she fisted my shirt, pulling me in. "Now."

Fuck, yes.

I kicked the door shut behind me and pounced like a predator, hauling her against me. Our kisses were frantic—we were hot and desperate for each other. I backed her into a wall, instinct taking over. The feel of her body set me on fire. She moved her hips, rubbing against me, and I growled into her mouth.

Clothes. Too many clothes.

Pulling away, I met her eyes and she nodded. She hiked up her skirt and slid her panties down her legs while I yanked my shorts down.

I hesitated. "I don't have anything with me."

She grabbed my shirt and pulled me close. "I have it covered."

With a low growl, I picked her up and pressed her against the wall. Her legs wrapped around my waist and before I knew what was happening, I was deep inside her.

My eyes rolled back and I groaned as we started to move. Up against the wall wasn't the easiest maneuver, but with the adrenaline coursing through my veins, it was effortless.

Our bodies fit together like we'd been made for this. She held on, fingers digging into my back, moaning with each thrust of my hips. It was sweaty and rough and hard. And so fucking good.

Her breathy string of yeses in my ear intensified, spurring me on. I picked up the pace, my breath ragged. It was too much. She was too much. I'd never been so consumed, so obsessed. With her taste on my tongue and her body wrapped around me, I let go, losing control.

I felt her climax begin and I unleashed.

Growling into her neck, I let the waves of pleasure rip through me. She held on, her body pulsing, her moans raw and uninhibited.

As I felt her grip on me loosen, I gently set her down and placed my palm against the wall, leaning on it to catch my breath.

"Oh wow," she said, a lazy smile lifting her swollen lips. "What did you just do to me?"

One corner of my mouth tugged upward. "I didn't plan that."

She brushed her hair out of her face and rested her head against the wall. "Either way, I'm glad you stopped by."

I leaned in and kissed her, softly this time. She smiled against my mouth and warmth spread through my chest. I didn't know what it was about that smile, but it got me every time.

"Would you like to come all the way inside? Maybe have coffee or something?"

"Maybe we should have done that first."

"No, this was great." She tilted her chin up and kissed me. When she pulled away, her expression shifted, eyes widening in alarm.

It sent me into instant protector mode. "What? Is everything okay?"

"I have cookies in the oven." A timer started to beep and her shoulders relaxed. "Never mind. They're fine. I thought maybe I missed the timer."

I tugged my shorts back up. "Want me to get those out for you?"

She looked down at herself. "Would you? I should clean up."

"I've got it. Do what you gotta do."

She scooped her panties off the floor and headed up the stairs as I went into her kitchen. The timer had stopped beeping—must have been automatic—so I put on the oven mitts she'd left sitting on the island and took out a sheet of cookies.

The warm, sweet scent filled the room. I wanted to grab one and bite into it, but of course they were too hot to eat.

My head was starting to come back to reality. But it wasn't regret that filled me. I wanted her to come down so I could touch her again. Get another taste of her mouth.

She appeared in her tank top and skirt with her long hair loose around her shoulders and a flush in her cheeks.

I liked that I'd done that to her.

"Hi," she said.

I approached and slipped my hands around her waist. Leaning in, I brushed a soft kiss against her lips. "Hi."

She wound her arms around my neck. "That was, um…"

"So good," I growled.

"That's an understatement. Thanks for getting the cookies."

"Is this what you do on your day off?"

She shrugged. "Sometimes. I like to experiment and I don't always have time, especially when the bakery is busy."

"They smell incredible." I leaned in to her neck and inhaled. "Almost as good as you."

She giggled. "You smell good too."

I leaned back and raised an eyebrow. "I'm sure I don't."

"No, you really do." She dropped her hands and took a quick breath. "Okay, before I lose my mind and start taking my clothes off again, do you want some coffee?"

Taking our clothes off sounded great, actually, but I didn't push. "Sure. But only if I get one of those cookies."

"I'm warning you, they're experimental. I have no idea if they're good."

"I'll take my chances."

She started the coffee maker and slid all the cookies onto a wire rack. They were dark and chocolatey looking with little flecks on the top.

"What are they?" I asked.

"Grain-free chocolate coconut cookies. They're made with almond flour and sweetened with maple syrup, so they're a little different than my usual."

I picked one up with the tips of my fingers. It wasn't too hot. I took a bite and groaned. It was unreal. Crisp edges with a rich, fudgey middle, and the flakes of coconut added the perfect contrasting texture.

"These are amazing."

"Yeah? I hoped they'd be good." She picked up a cookie, took a bite, and chewed slowly. "Oh yeah. That's not bad."

"Not bad?" I resisted the urge to shove the rest in my mouth and start devouring another one. "They're incredible."

She put the rest of her cookie down. "Thank you. I'm glad you were here to taste test."

I set the rest of mine on the counter. Suddenly I wasn't nearly as interested in chocolate coconut cookies as I was in the irresistible woman in front of me.

What was it about her that made me so insatiable?

I didn't stop to ponder. Instead, I pulled her close and kissed her, tasting the chocolate on her tongue.

Clothes came off, and as we stumbled to the couch, our kisses intense and frantic, I couldn't help but think I had to be the luckiest guy on the planet.

CHAPTER 13

Harper

IT HAD BEEN a quieter than usual day at the bakery, but I didn't mind. The slower pace had given me a chance to get ahead on special orders. Although it was only May, wedding season was already in full swing. Aunt Doris had come in for a few hours to decorate wedding cakes, which had also helped ease the stress of deadlines. Plus, it was great to see her feeling up to it.

I finished boxing up the day's leftovers to take to the food bank and put them in a paper bag. There wasn't a lot, so I took some bread off the shelf that could have sold the next day and added it to the top. I grabbed my things, switched off the lights, and with a contented sigh, let myself out the back door.

Although I was tired from the long day, I wasn't going straight home. I had a hair appointment at a local salon, Timeless Beauty. One thing my mother had given me was thick hair. I kept it long—less maintenance, and I could pull it back or wear it up to keep it out of the way—but the ends were looking pretty sad. I was overdue for a trim and looking forward to a little pampering.

The salon was walking distance from the bakery, but I

wanted to leave the food bank donation in my car, so I went to the parking lot behind the building. I dropped it off, leaving it in the back seat, locked the doors, and headed through the alley to the sidewalk.

He'd never been far from my thoughts, but with the busyness of work over, Garrett Haven rushed into my mind like a tidal wave.

I'd been surprised to see him when he'd come to my house. But nothing could have surprised me more than what had happened next.

That kiss. Those hands. His lips had been a little salty, his body hard and warm. As soon as his mouth had hit mine, I'd wanted him. All of him.

And the way he'd backed me up against a wall, like he was desperate for me? My panties had come off in a hot second and I had zero regrets about that.

Honestly, I'd always thought the sex up against the wall thing was a myth. No one could actually do that, right?

Garrett Haven could.

And he hadn't just managed it. He'd blown my mind.

The memory made my cheeks warm and my stomach tingle as I walked. I still felt a hint of giddiness, the warmth and contentment lingering. How had I gotten so—

Nope. I wasn't going to say lucky.

Regardless, I'd been in a great mood ever since. The only downside was how much I wanted to see him again. Not even just for the up-against-the-wall passion, although I'd happily do that again. I missed him.

That part was mildly disconcerting. I didn't want to get too attached too quickly. Something always seemed to go wrong. I hated feeling like I was always waiting for the other shoe to drop. But it always did, so…

At least he hadn't gotten a sudden job offer in another country, or the promotion of his dreams that also meant he had to break up with me.

A squirrel with something stuffed in its cheeks darted in front of me and raced up the drainpipe. I blinked and glanced around. The salon was behind me. Lost in daydreams of Garrett, I'd walked right by.

"Thanks, little buddy," I said as the squirrel disappeared onto the roof.

I turned around and went back to Timeless Beauty. A little bell above the door tinkled when I went in and a woman with long, dark hair smiled from behind the front counter.

"You must be Harper?" Her voice was friendly and professional.

"Yes, I have an appointment with Marigold."

"I've got you all checked in. She'll be right out."

"Thanks."

The salon was elegant, with a velvet chaise, ornately framed mirrors, and vintage artwork on the walls. Two women came out from a back room. One wore a navy dress and wedge sandals and her long brown hair hung in loose waves around her shoulders. The other, with blond hair and a pretty floral top, looked younger. Maybe twenty at the most.

"Night, Brielle," the first woman said. "Thanks for your help today."

"You're welcome. See you tomorrow." Brielle gave her a hug, then left.

The brunette had an infectious smile. "Hi, Harper. I'm Marigold. It's so nice to finally meet you."

I shook her outstretched hand. "Nice to meet you, too."

"Come on back and we can talk about your hair."

She gestured to a chair and I took a seat, then pulled out my low ponytail.

"The ends are so dry. I like the length overall, but it needs a trim."

She ran her fingers through my hair, then held a section between two fingers and inspected the ends. "If you're comfortable with it, I can take off about two inches and make you feel like a new woman."

"That sounds great."

She took me to the washing station and I relaxed while she washed and conditioned my hair. The scalp massage she gave me was worth whatever the haircut was going to cost. When she finished, she wrapped my hair in a towel and took me back to her station.

She got started combing out my hair. "I don't know if you remember, but you did my wedding cake."

My eyes widened in recognition. "I do remember. That was the day I first got into town."

"We thought we might be without a cake until you arrived. And it was delicious, by the way."

"Thank you so much. I'm glad I was able to get it to your reception on time. Sorry about that."

"Oh goodness, no need to apologize." She set the comb down, picked up her scissors, and started cutting. "How's your aunt doing? I heard she's had some health problems."

"She's doing quite a bit better now that she's not working such long days."

"I'm so glad to hear that."

"Congratulations on your wedding, by the way." I paused, putting the pieces together. "Wait, you're married to a Haven, aren't you?"

Her smile lit up her whole face. "Zachary."

I almost blurted out, *what a coincidence, I just slept with his brother!* Fortunately, I stopped myself. "He's Garrett's brother?"

"He is," she said, her tone lifting, as if to say, go on.

"I kind of went out with him the other night."

She gasped, her eyes widening. "You're kidding!"

"No. Why?"

"Sorry, I'm just surprised. Last I heard, he stood you up

and then stubbornly insisted he's not interested in dating. This is a lovely turn of events."

"Thanks. We had a good time, so, um, hopefully…"

She raised her eyebrows, the corners of her mouth lifting.

"You know how it is when things are new, right? I haven't lived in Tilikum very long, and I've had a string of bad luck in relationships. Actually I've had a string of bad luck in general, so it's a little scary to get hopeful about something like this."

"I completely understand."

"And I'm not usually one to let temptation take over, but he stopped by yesterday, kind of randomly, and let's just say things got a lot hotter than I expected. I'm talking, up against the wall hot. Marigold, I didn't even know that move was real. It was incredible. I'm talking the best orgasm I've ever had." I stopped, my eyes widening. "Why am I telling you all this? I'm so sorry, we just met, this is so inappropriate, I need to stop talking and I can't seem to."

She put down her scissors and squeezed the sides of my shoulders. "Don't be sorry. This happens all the time. I promise, it's all safe with me. What's said in the sacred chair of hair, stays in the sacred chair of hair."

"You're just very nice and so pretty, it makes me want to trust you."

"You can trust me." She squeezed my arms again, then went back to my hair. "You can trust Garrett, too, by the way. He's a really good guy. And I'm not just saying that because he's my brother-in-law. He helped save my life once."

"Really?"

She nodded. "He did. His loyalty is unmatched. Plus, he's a great dad and a well-respected deputy."

"That's the thing, it's all too perfect. Things like this don't work out for me. The other shoe always drops."

"It sounds like Garrett is exactly what you need. Besides,

sometimes the best thing comes along when we least expect it."

"Is that what happened with you and Zachary?"

"You could say that." She fluffed out my hair. "Let's get you dry, then I'll finish up."

She blow dried my hair and I loved how she made it so shiny. It already looked so much healthier. And despite the fact that I'd unintentionally told her too much—best orgasm I'd ever had?—it had felt good to tell someone.

Starting over in a new place was hard.

Before I paid, she gave me her number and suggested we get together sometime. I loved that idea and hoped she meant it. Starting a new relationship was great, but the way I'd babbled to her reminded me I probably needed to try a little harder to make some friends.

I left, feeling pretty, and not quite skipped down the sidewalk back to my car. I got to the parking lot behind the bakery and paused. Something red and shiny caught my eye. It was a gift bag, hanging from the driver's side mirror of my car.

My first thought was Garrett. Had he left me a surprise gift?

The bag was glossy, a dark red background with lighter red hearts that caught the sunlight. It looked like the sort of thing you saw in stores around Valentine's Day. And it seemed a tiny bit odd. Maybe a touch too on the nose for a guy like Garrett Haven.

Then again, despite the fact that I'd happily let him take me up against a wall, and again on my couch, I didn't really know him all that well. Not yet. Maybe gift giving was one of his love languages.

I untied the string holding the bag to the mirror. There wasn't any tissue paper or other filler, and I pulled out a brown teddy bear with a bright red ribbon around its neck.

Huh.

I checked the bag for a note, but didn't find anything. There wasn't anything attached to the bear, not even a little scribble on the tag. And no sign of a note or card on the ground, either.

The bear was kind of cute, if you liked that sort of thing. I didn't want to be ungrateful. If Garrett had thought I'd enjoy a stuffed animal, I absolutely appreciated it. But it looked a bit worn, as if it wasn't brand new. With a tickle of apprehension in my stomach, I brought the bear to my nose and sniffed. It had a hint of mustiness to it. Definitely wasn't new.

I glanced around again, wondering if the gift giver was watching me. It couldn't have been Garrett. Could it?

If it had been, I was going to start questioning some very big choices I'd recently made. Particularly the one involving a wall and a lack of underwear.

I dropped the bear back in the gift bag, got in my car, and locked the doors. It felt weird to stand in the open air with that thing. But I had to know. I dug my phone out of my purse and called Garrett.

"Hey, Harper."

"Hi. You're probably working and I'm so sorry to bug you. But… did you leave a gift on my car?"

"No. What is it?"

"A teddy bear."

He hesitated, as if he were as confused as I was. "There was a teddy bear on your car?"

"It was in a gift bag hanging from the side mirror. Whoever it was, they didn't leave a note. I wonder if it was a mistake and they put it on the wrong car."

"Okay, walk me through it. Did you discover the bag just now?"

"Yes."

"What were you doing before that? Did you just leave the bakery?"

"No, I went to the salon and got a haircut."

"Got it. Did you drive to the salon or was your car outside the bakery the whole time?"

"It was outside the bakery. I walked to the salon."

"When you left the bakery, did you notice anything on your car at that point? Did you look?"

He was totally using his cop voice. It was such a turn-on.

"There wasn't anything there. I'm sure of it. I brought the day's leftovers to the car before I went to my appointment and didn't see anything."

"So whoever left it on your car must have put it there after you left for your salon appointment. What time was that?"

"Um, I guess I left the bakery at about five-thirty. My appointment was at five forty-five."

"Okay, I want you to check the bear. Are there any zippers, buttons, or other openings?"

I turned it over and around, inspecting all the seams. "No."

"What about the neck?"

"Nothing there, either. It has a bow, but it's just a ribbon and there's nothing underneath."

"Squeeze it. Anything hard inside?"

"Are you thinking it has a camera in it or something?"

"Yes."

I started squeezing it all over, including the stubby arms and legs. I hadn't even thought about a hidden camera. But why would someone give me a bear with an old school nanny cam in it? It wasn't like I had a bakery rival who wanted to steal my recipes or something.

"It's soft all over. I don't feel anything. Just stuffing."

"Got it."

The seriousness in his voice made me smile. "Are you writing all this down like you're investigating a crime?"

"I'm documenting, yes."

"So professional."

"I'm just trying to put the pieces together to see if we can figure out who did this."

"I know. I'm just saying, you must be very good at your job." My tone was light and flirtatious. "You're certainly good at other things."

The way he cleared his throat was so cute. Had I flustered him a little? "You bring out the best in me."

I leaned back against the headrest, my cheeks warming as heat burst between my legs.

"But listen," he continued, "I'm concerned about this. Are you home?"

"Not yet. I'm still in the parking lot."

"Lock your doors."

"I already did."

"Good. Head home but watch for any sign that you're being followed. If you see anyone, don't go home. Come here to the sheriff's office."

My back tightened. The situation, and his response, was making me increasingly nervous. It had to be a mistake, right? Someone left it on the wrong car. I barely knew anyone in Tilikum. Who would leave a weird teddy bear in a shiny heart bag?

"Okay, I'm going home now. I'll call you if anything else weird happens."

"Do that. It might be nothing, but let's not take any chances."

I could tell by his tone that he didn't think it was nothing. Of course, that was his job, to find the something—the who and the why in every situation.

"No chances. Doors are locked. I'll watch behind me and go to the sheriff's office if there's anything sus. I mean, suspicious."

He chuckled softly. Wow, I loved making him do that.

"Talk to you later," he said.

"Yeah. Bye."

I ended the call and left. Instead of going straight home, I took a round-about route. There weren't any cars behind me until I was already a mile or so from downtown. It was a guy in an old truck and he didn't stay behind me for long—just a few blocks—before turning left. I clearly wasn't being followed, not even at a distance.

Once I was safely home, I parked and gave the gift bag the side eye. On a whim, I held the bear up and took a picture, then texted it to Owen.

Me: *Look what someone left on my car. Tell me that's not weird.*

Owen: *Who left it?*

Me: *I don't know. No note.*

Owen: *Sus*

Me: *That's what I said!*

Owen: *Did you tell my dad?*

Me: *Yeah. He thinks it's sus too.*

Owen: *He'd know.*

Me: *It's so creepy. Not even brand new. Like someone had this in a closet somewhere.*

Owen: *Looks like a bad prank. I'd blame my uncles, but they're better than that. That's just sad.*

Me: *If it's a prank, I don't get it.*

Owen: *What are you going to do with it?*

Me: *I don't know. Probably show it to your dad for evidence or something.*

Owen: *Sounds about right. Be careful, K?*

Me: *I will. Don't worry.*

Owen: *Don't bring it in the house. I'm not saying it will come to life at night, but…*

Me: *With my luck, I'm not taking any chances. It lives outside.*

Owen: *Good plan. Garage, maybe, so the squirrels don't steal it.*

Me: *Tilikum squirrels on the loose with a creepy bear? Sounds like a horror movie.*

Owen: *Exactly.*

Laughing, I put the bear back in the gift bag. Owen cracked me up.

Of course, there was no way I was bringing that thing inside. I didn't really believe inanimate objects could come to life at night. But still, why tempt fate? Especially when I was still under the dark cloud of the bad luck curse. If anyone was at risk of being murdered by a creepy teddy bear, it would be me.

I got out and deposited the gift bag in the corner of the garage. I stepped back, eying it for a second, then found a moving box I hadn't recycled yet and put it over the top. If it did come to life after dark, I didn't know if a cardboard box would stop it. But the barrier, however flimsy, made me feel a little better.

So did the text from Garrett that came through a moment later.

Garrett: *Did you make it home okay?*

Me: *Yep. Nothing unusual. I'm leaving the creepy bear in the garage though.*

Garrett: *Good. I'll take a look at it when I can. I'll also see if any of the businesses have a camera on that parking lot. See if I can pull footage.*

Me: *It's okay, you don't have to go to all that trouble.*

Garrett: *Yes, I do.*

That made me smile. His concern was comforting.

Me: *I don't think Aunt Doris ever put up cameras, but maybe one of the neighboring buildings did.*

Garrett: *Let's hope so.*

I didn't want to stop talking to him, even just over text, but I wasn't sure what else to say. I went inside and made sure to lock the deadbolt on the door from the house to the garage. Not because I thought a murderous bear would come rampaging inside. But because it was weird that someone had left it on my car. And while no one had followed me home, this was a small town. It wouldn't be hard for anyone to find out where I lived.

The whole thing was just strange.

But I felt a lot better knowing I had Garrett Haven looking out for me.

CHAPTER 14

Garrett

THE NOISE LEVEL AT MY PARENTS' place reminded me of my childhood.

There weren't quite as many kids running around, but our family had certainly grown. Annika and Levi had brought their four kids to visit Grandma and Grandpa. Mom had called to ask if Owen wanted to join them. He was older than his cousins, but he still had fun with them, so we'd come up for the afternoon.

Somehow it had turned into an all Havens on deck situation. Zachary and Marigold were there, as were Luke and Theo. About ten minutes after we'd pulled up, Josiah and Audrey had arrived, adding to the chaos with their two dogs, Max and Maggie.

The yard had turned into a free-for-all, and it wasn't just the kids. Zachary chased our nieces, Emma and Juliet, around the swing set while they shrieked with glee. Theo had started a four-and-a-half man football game with Luke, Owen, and our nephews Thomas and Will. Half because Will was only three, although what he lacked in size, he made up for in determination. The dogs happily ran around, zig-zagging through people's legs.

Mom watched it all from off to the side. She stood in the grass, dressed in a light blue shirt and khaki shorts, her hair pulled back. I wondered if she was thinking about the days when she'd had seven little kids playing in that very spot.

Although, my brothers and I had been crazier.

Dad brought her a glass of lemonade and leaned in to give her a kiss on the cheek. I'd thought about it before, but as I watched them, it brought to mind something Dad and I had in common—a rough divorce. Not in the sense that there'd been a lot of fighting involved. My biological mother had essentially done what my ex did years later—just up and left.

But Dad hadn't let it make him bitter. When he'd met Mom, his hurt hadn't kept him from loving someone again. And our family was infinitely better for it.

It made me think of Harper and what it would be like if she were there, at my side. Which was crazier than two people with six little kids between them starting a new family together. Whatever was happening between us, it was still early. I shouldn't have been missing her like I was, or thinking things like the L-word.

I needed to be cautious. I'd already gone from *I'm not dating anyone* to pursuing a woman pretty aggressively. And I'd thrown caution completely out the window once already.

That kind of spontaneity wasn't like me.

My sister-in-law, Marigold, wandered over to stand next to me. She pressed her lips together, like she was trying to hide a smile.

"Why are you looking at me like that?"

Her smile widened. "I met Harper the other day. She came into the salon. I really like her."

Just hearing her name tugged one corner of my mouth upward. "Yeah, she's um…" *Completely irresistible… The sexiest woman I've ever met…* "She's great."

She lowered her voice. "I won't make a big deal out of it,

since you don't seem to be sharing anything right now. But she sure seems to like you a lot."

Suddenly I was like a kid on the playground, dying to know what my secret crush had said about me. "What did she tell you?"

"I can't share specifics. Hair stylist confidentiality and all that."

I furrowed my brow.

"Trust me, it's a thing. Anyway, it wasn't so much what she said as how she said it. Her whole face lit up when she talked about you. It was really sweet."

On the outside, I tried to keep my cool, but on the inside, a potent combination of warmth and elation spread through me.

"Things are good so far."

Good so far? Way to sound apathetic.

But damn it, I had all these feelings and I didn't know what to do with them. Especially because Owen kept looking at me like he knew I was hiding something.

Maybe he did know I was hiding something.

Obviously not that I'd gone out with Harper. I didn't need to keep that from my son. We were going out again, and he knew that too. But my unexpected visit to her house? He didn't need to know about that.

Marigold touched my arm. "I think it's great."

"Thanks, Mari."

My family didn't need to know either. Not yet. They'd make a thing out of it and I didn't know if this was a thing yet or not.

Fucking her up against a wall did kind of take things to the next level, though.

"Hey, Dad?"

I blinked back to reality at the sound of Owen's voice. "Yeah?"

"Can I go get the cookies I brought?"

"Cookies?" Luke turned and the football nailed him in the side of the face. "Hey!"

"Who has cookies?" Zachary asked.

"Cookies! Cookies! Cookies!" my nieces started chanting. Will joined his sisters. "Cookies! Cookies! Cookies!"

"I think that's a unanimous yes," Mom said. "Need help?"

"No, I can get them," Owen said. "I'll be right back."

Owen went through the house to get the box he'd brought home from Angel Cakes. He hadn't let me look and the smell had tormented me all the way there.

Mom moved closer to me and tucked her hand in the crook of my elbow. "Owen isn't wearing his hood."

"What?"

"His hood. For the past, I don't know, six months to a year, every time I saw him, he had his hood up. Like he was trying to hide. He's not even wearing one today."

I thought about it for a second. She was right. He had started wearing a hoodie almost every day, no matter the weather, and often kept the hood up. I probably saw him with it down more than she did, since he didn't always wear it at home. But today he was in a T-shirt, no hood to be seen.

I'd figured the hoodie was just a middle school thing. But was it more? Had I missed something?

"You think he was hiding? From what?"

"I'm not sure. But I suspect he has a lot more going on in his head, and heart, than he lets anyone see."

Before I could ask her more about what she meant, Owen appeared with the pink Angel Cakes box and his cousins went nuts.

Let's be honest, my brothers did too.

"Watch those grabby hands," Mom said. "Just one cookie each."

Mom and Dad helped Owen pass out chocolate chip cookies to everyone. I took one with an odd sense of excitement. It was just a cookie, I didn't know why it made my pulse speed up.

Except it wasn't. It was one of Harper's cookies.

The little kids took theirs and ran back toward the swing set. Several of the adults followed, including Annika and Levi.

Theo groaned. "This is so good."

"Angel Cakes makes the best cookies," Luke said.

"Did you help with these?" Mom asked Owen.

He grinned. "Yeah. I pretty much made them. Harper told me what to do, but she let me do most of it."

"Hang on," Theo said. "Harper, as in the lady your dad likes?"

"Bro, is your son creeping in on your girl?" Luke asked.

"No, Uncle Luke." Owen rolled his eyes. "Dad's dating her. I was just helping at the bakery."

"Hang on again," Theo said. "Since when is your dad dating?"

Owen shrugged as he took a bite of cookie. "Since he took Harper on a date. They're going out again tonight."

All eyes swung to me.

"Why are you all looking at me like that?"

"I can't imagine, Mr. I'm-not-dating-anyone," Theo said around a mouthful.

Luke grinned at me. "Yeah, you were pretty adamant about the whole not dating thing."

"Can you say, denial?" Theo snickered.

"You guys." Marigold shook her head. "Don't give him such a hard time."

"Have you met us?" Luke asked.

I crossed my arms. "We're seeing whether or not we're compatible. There's nothing wrong with me modeling a healthy dating relationship for my son."

Zachary groaned. "Way to make it boring. Just admit you're into her and you hope you'll get in her—" He glanced around at the kids. "That she'll be down for some grown-up playtime."

Marigold laughed. "Good save, honey."

He grinned and winked at her.

"The little kids aren't listening, Uncle Z," Owen said. "And I know what that means."

"Can we change the subject, please?" I asked.

"Dad, it's fine. I know people have sex. This isn't news."

My dad took another cookie out of the box. "Who's having sex and why does Owen know about it?"

I cleared my throat, hoping Dad would get the hint and let this one go.

"No, Grandpa, I just mean in general. I'm fourteen, I've had the talk."

Dad gazed into the distance, a faraway look in his eyes. "I had to give the talk. To six boys." He shuddered.

Mom put a hand on his shoulder. "It wasn't that bad."

"Josiah and Reese took it well. Just nodded so I knew they heard me, left it at that. Garrett and Luke were a bit shocked, but they got over it. But Zachary and Theo?" He shuddered again. "Zachary had questions. Lots and lots of questions."

"That tracks," Zachary said.

"What about Theo?" Mom asked.

"I'll never forget the look on his face. You'd have thought I murdered someone in front of him. He said, 'Dad, why did you tell me that?'"

Zachary and Luke burst out laughing.

"I did not," Theo said.

"You did," Dad said. "I thought you were going to cry."

Theo took another cookie. "That's so not true."

Owen walked over and patted Theo's shoulder. "It's okay, Uncle Theo. I had a hard time with it, too."

"You did?" I asked. "Since when?"

"It was fine, Dad. You were just… sort of robotic about it."

"I told you the facts."

"It was a lot of biology. And it's weird hearing your dad say the word vagina so many times." Owen shuddered just like his grandpa.

"I have a vagina!" Juliet said happily.

Apparently none of us had noticed her make her way back to the picnic table. She stood there, wearing a purple dress and matching bows in her hair, with an enthusiastic smile on her face. My brothers and I all exchanged similar, I-have-no-idea-what-to-say-to-that looks.

"Yes, you do, sweetheart," Marigold said, her tone matter-of-fact.

"Juliet!" her twin sister Emma said. "Don't say that!"

"Don't say what? Vagina? You have one too. But Thomas and Will have penises."

Emma gasped. "You can't say that either."

Juliet appeared to ignore her sister. "Penises are on the outside. Vaginas are on the inside."

"We keep penises inside our pants!" Will exclaimed happily from the swing. "Except to go pee pee."

His dad, Levi, just nodded. "Yes, son, we do."

"I have a penis and nuts!" Will said.

Levi and Annika both shot Zachary a glare. Apparently he was responsible for teaching Will the term *nuts*.

"The proper word is testicles, buddy," Annika said.

"Test-wickles?" Will asked.

"Close enough," she said. "But let's stop talking about all our body parts, okay?"

"I keep my test-wickles in my pants too."

"Yes, you do. That's appropriate."

I shook my head. I didn't remember Owen shouting about his boy parts when he was little. But my nephew Will had a big personality. He reminded me of a cross between Zachary and Levi's brother, Gavin Bailey. Kind of a scary combination.

Owen caught my eye and shrugged, as if to say sorry, I didn't mean to start something.

I shrugged back. Not your fault, and not a big deal.

"So, Owen," Theo said. "Committed any crimes lately?"

Owen elbowed him in the ribs.

"Ow." Theo rubbed his side. "I probably deserved that."

Thankfully, the shoplifting incident didn't seem to have been the start of a pattern of behavior. I didn't know if I could take credit for handling it well, or if he'd decided getting in trouble wasn't worth it. Maybe a bit of both. But I was grateful I didn't have the added complication of a kid turning to crime.

And later, I had a date with Harper. I felt a tug in my chest, a longing to be with her again.

Whatever was happening between us, it was a lot more than my clinical description. It wasn't an attempt to model a healthy dating relationship or explore our compatibility. It was deeper than that. Much deeper.

And I was glad rational, responsible Garrett had hung up his gear for a little while.

CHAPTER 15

Harper

MY HEAD RESTED against Garrett's bare chest and my arm draped across his toned midsection. He traced idle circles on my shoulder as we laid in bed together. We originally had plans to go to dinner, but there was something about him I couldn't resist. Apparently he felt the same way.

At least we'd made it to the bed that time.

I didn't think either of us had meant to tear each other's clothes off as soon as he'd arrived to pick me up, but you wouldn't hear me complaining. I was relaxed and happy, my body content.

He kissed the top of my head, and the strangest thing happened. A lump formed in my throat and tears gathered in the corners of my eyes. I tried to swallow the rush of emotion. I didn't want to freak him out. But the gesture was so gentle. So sweet. Intimate on a deep level.

It was overwhelming.

While a part of me wanted to sink into this newfound intimacy, bask in it until morning, another part of me wanted to untangle myself from him. Maybe even call it a night. It felt as if we were rushing headlong into a fog and we couldn't see where the path led. Was there a cliff out there? Were we going to fall off and hit the bottom?

Because there was always a cliff. And I always fell.

His arm flexed, pressing me tighter against him. I closed my eyes and breathed him in, let the strength of his embrace surround me. Whatever was happening between us was so new. Couldn't I just enjoy it for what it was, without worrying about whether it was doomed to crash and burn?

Probably not entirely, but for the moment, I'd at least try.

Garrett kissed my head again, then broke the comfortable silence. "I saw my family today."

"Is that why Owen wanted the cookies?"

"Yeah, everybody loved them."

I smiled. "I can't take credit. He did all the work."

He paused, as if considering what to say next. A flutter of nervousness swept through me.

"So, it kind of came up that we're…"

My eyes widened and I lifted my head to look at him. "That we're?"

"Dating."

I let out a relieved breath. "I thought you were going to say something else. I know Owen is fourteen, not four, but I don't think he needs to know about… you know," I looked up and down at our bodies tangled in the sheets, "this."

"No, that's not what I meant. Just that my family knows we're seeing each other."

The corner of my mouth lifted and I glanced pointedly down his body again. "Yeah, I'm seeing a lot of you lately."

His subtle smile was so satisfying. I loved making him do that.

"Sorry, I'm teasing. I take it that was a big deal? To tell them?"

"I guess it was. I haven't dated anyone since my divorce. In fact, I was pretty determined not to."

"Is it okay if I ask about that?"

"Of course. You can ask me anything."

"Owen said he doesn't see her anymore. Did she just... leave?"

"It was more gradual than that. When we first split up, she made an effort to see him. Not as often as I would have if our roles had been reversed, but some. It didn't take long for those visits to become fewer and farther between until eventually they stopped."

"I just don't understand that."

"I don't either." He took a deep breath, his chest expanding against me. "That was why I stayed married to her as long as I did. I thought I could hold our family together for Owen's sake. Because deep down, I knew if we split up, she'd drift away. He'd lose his mom, just like I did."

My chest tightened with sympathy. "Your mom left you too?"

"Yeah. I don't remember it, really. I was very young; a lot younger than Owen when his mom left. And I was lucky. My dad married Marlene, and she's my mom. Doesn't matter if we're related by blood or not. She's my mother."

"Sounds like she's pretty great."

"She is. Having my own son, especially with what we've been through, really made me see her through new eyes. Even though she already had three boys, she loved us like we were hers. There was never any difference."

"Do you ever hear from your biological mother?"

"No."

The hurt in his voice was clear. And I understood it. My family situation was different, but I knew what it was like to feel abandoned by a parent. My father knew I existed, but my mom had planned it so he wouldn't be a part of my life. For all I knew, he didn't want to anyway.

When I buried my face in his chest and held him, he wrapped his arms around me and leaned his cheek against the top of my head. A rush of emotion poured through me. I wanted to soothe all his hurts. Hold him and kiss him and lo—

I couldn't say it. I couldn't even think it.

The intense intimacy of the moment finally got to me. I needed to get up. Put some space between us and maybe bake something. Escape into my go-to form of stress relief.

Turning to baking when things got heavy was probably why I thrived as a professional baker, even though it was fast paced and demanding. And things were definitely getting heavy.

I pulled away but smoothed my expression. "Are you hungry? I'm hungry."

His mouth lifted in a grin. "I could eat."

"How about we stay in? I'll cook."

"Are you sure?"

"Absolutely. I'm in the mood for it."

His smile grew. "Great."

I was about to get up when he reached out and wrapped a hand around the back of my neck, gently pulling me in for a kiss. His mouth felt so good against mine—soft, warm, delicious.

And more than a little bit dangerous.

I needed to clear my head. He was getting under my skin, and as much as I loved it—craved his closeness—it was starting to freak me out.

Kitchen. That was what I needed.

I got up and, since we were staying in, put on a tank top and a pair of jeans instead of the dressier date attire he'd taken off me. I pulled my hair back into a ponytail and left him to get dressed while I headed for the kitchen.

Just standing in the space soothed my too-fast heartbeat. I looked through the fridge, mentally assessing what I could whip up on the fly. I wasn't going to feed him cookies for dinner, but my kitchen talents didn't stop at baked goods.

And I enjoyed a challenge. Throw me in a kitchen with five ingredients and an oven, and I'd make your taste buds sing.

Fortunately, I had more than five ingredients.

I'd been experimenting with a recipe for cherry hand pies on my last day off and had made extra pie dough. A baker never knew when she'd need to whip up a flaky crust. And since I already had the dough in the refrigerator, I decided on a quiche.

Garrett came out, dressed in a short-sleeved shirt and jeans, while I was rolling out the dough for the crust on the island.

"You know Owen's come to the bakery after school a few times, right?" I asked.

"Yeah. He told me."

"He's such a great kid. It's hard to believe the first time I met him, he'd shoplifted from me. I guess even good kids make mistakes."

"I sure did."

I smiled. "It's hard to imagine you doing something like shoplifting, though. Weren't you always the cop chasing the bad guys?"

He glanced away. "Usually. Although, when we pulled pranks on the Baileys, we pushed the boundaries of the law a lot. And then there was this one time…"

I waited a moment for him to continue, but he didn't. I gave him a quizzical look. "You can't leave me hanging like that. I really need to hear this story."

"We all knew how to pick locks. Us, the Baileys, it was just part of the feud. But one summer, Reese and I were being particularly idiotic and decided to see if we could break into the Sugar Shack."

"The candy store?"

"That's the one. We did it a few times. Took just enough stuff so if we got caught it would look legit, like we could have bought it. I felt so guilty, I broke in again and left some cash on the counter by the till."

I couldn't help but laugh. "That's too adorable. What about Reese? He didn't feel guilty?"

"Not that I know of. He kept trying to goad me into going back, but I wouldn't do it."

"I take it Owen doesn't know that story?"

"No. He can hear about it when he's older. I want him to keep thinking his dad is above suspicion for a while longer."

"That's fair. Did he ever tell you why he did it? Whether he maybe did it for attention? I'm not implying you don't give him enough of it. I think you're a great dad. I really mean that." I paused. "But I think we both know what it's like to be a kid with some big hurts."

He nodded slowly. "Maybe I've been assuming he's fine when he isn't. It's tough because he's a Haven. We're good at holding things in. He's seemed a little different lately, though. Happier."

That made me smile. "Yeah? That's good to hear."

"I think you might have something to do with that."

I kept my eyes on the dough, but my heart soared. "I don't know about that. I've been making him work."

"Apparently he doesn't mind, if he keeps coming back."

"He called me bruh." I lifted my gaze to meet his.

"Wow."

"I know! That means he likes me, right? I'm cool?"

"Definitely means you're cool."

I smiled. "I texted him a picture of the creepy bear. He said it was sus."

"He's not wrong. That reminds me, can I see it?"

"It's in the garage." I nodded toward it. "I put an empty moving box over it."

His brow furrowed.

"Don't judge. Your son put the idea in my head that it might come to life at night and go on a murderous rampage."

"Sounds like Owen."

I finished the quiche filling while Garrett went out to the garage to inspect the bear. He came back in a moment later, carrying the gift bag with one finger, as if he didn't want to touch it.

"Worried about getting your fingerprints on it?" I was half-joking, but maybe that was a concern.

"Sort of. Also, habit." He set it down on the counter. "Do you have gloves?"

"I do, actually. There's a box of disposable ones in that cupboard." I pointed to where he could find them.

"Thanks."

"So what are you going to do? Dust it for prints or something?"

He pulled a pair of gloves out of the box. "Probably not, although I'm tempted. But there's no crime involved and our forensics lab is already overworked."

"That's fair."

His brow furrowed as he lifted the bear out of the bag. I watched while he thoroughly inspected it. He went over the seams and pressed every bit of it, looking for evidence of something hidden inside.

"I think it's just a bear." He brought it closer to his nose and sniffed. "An old bear."

"That's why it's so creepy. It's weird enough that someone left it without a note. But who digs an old stuffed animal out of their basement or whatever, puts it in a gift bag, and leaves it on someone's car?"

"That's a great question."

"I keep hoping it was a mistake and meant for someone else. Although I feel bad for thinking that. Then someone else was supposed to get the creepy bear."

He tilted his head. "Maybe it was meant for someone else but there's a reason that someone would want an old bear. Some nostalgia behind it."

"Oh, good point." My voice brightened. "Maybe it's a cherished childhood memento. I wonder how I could figure out who it was meant for. I'll ask Aunt Doris. She might have some ideas. Oh! Or maybe someone will report it missing."

"A missing stuffed animal?"

"I mean, they might think it was stolen or something. Who knows, you might hear about it."

"It wouldn't be the weirdest call we've ever had."

I put the quiche in the oven and set the first timer. "What is the weirdest call you've ever had?"

He paused for a moment. "We get squirrel calls a lot. When Sheriff Cordero was new, we got a call about a squirrel stealing someone's wallet. He got on the radio to chew out the deputy for responding to an obviously bogus call. We had to explain to him that the squirrels around here actually do steal things. The wallet was recovered."

I laughed. "A wallet?"

"Wallet, keys, picnic lunches. Once I responded to a call at this older gentleman's home. He had a garden in his backyard and he swore up and down that his neighbor was stealing his peppers. Turned out it was a squirrel."

"How did you figure it out?"

"Set up surveillance."

"You set up surveillance to catch a squirrel stealing garden peppers?"

"It was just one of those doorbell cameras. Right after dawn, a little squirrel sat there, helping himself to the guy's peppers."

"Were they spicy?"

"That was why the guy was so convinced it had to be his neighbor. Squirrels don't usually eat anything spicy. Apparently that one was the exception."

"Hopefully he made up with his neighbor."

"I think he did."

"Keeping Tilikum safe, even from the squirrels."

"Just doing my job."

Fortunately, bad luck didn't strike. The quiche came out perfectly, I didn't drop anything, and my mom didn't call unexpectedly in the middle of dinner—all things my bad luck could have done to mar our evening.

The surprising thing was, it was all so easy. The conversation, the connection. Garrett loved my cooking, and we ate and talked until I was having a hard time staying awake. I apologized but he didn't mind.

I found myself wishing he didn't have to leave. That, instead of a long goodnight with tempting kisses, we were heading to the bedroom together.

Too soon, right? Way too soon to be thinking like that.

But sugar cookies, he was everything. And my heart wanted more.

CHAPTER 16

Garrett

I'D HIT on a stroke of luck and found the sister of my cold case victim. Jocelyn Joyner, who'd gotten married and now went by Jocelyn Smith, still lived in the area, in a small neighborhood on the south edge of town. We didn't have a current phone number, so I was hoping my luck would hold and she'd be willing to talk to me if I just showed up at her front door.

Instead of my uniform, I'd worn plain clothes—a button-down shirt and slacks. I had my badge and ID with me, but people were often more willing to talk to a guy in regular clothes than a deputy in uniform. I wanted to make her comfortable, especially since I was there to talk about a difficult topic.

Her house was nice, a big two-story with a well-maintained yard. No cars out front, but they might have been in the garage. I parked on the street, went up to the front door, and knocked.

A woman with long dark hair pulled back at the nape of her neck answered the door. She wore a blouse and slacks, like maybe she'd recently come home from work. "Can I help you?"

"Afternoon. Sorry to intrude, but are you Jocelyn Smith?"

"Yes."

"I'm Deputy Garrett Haven with the Tilikum County sheriff's office. I'm wondering if I could ask you some questions about your sister, Jasmine."

"What about her?"

"I'm looking into her case."

"Did you find something? Oh my god, you have to tell me."

"Possibly, but nothing conclusive. Would you be willing to talk to me?"

"Yes, yes." She stepped aside and ushered me in. "Please come in."

I nodded to her. "Thank you."

She led me past a row of hooks with backpacks and shoes shoved underneath.

"Kids?" I asked.

"I have three. They're at the store with their dad. I hate to think what kind of junk food they're going to bring home. He's a softie when it comes to that stuff."

"Sounds like fun."

I followed her into the dining room where she offered me a spot at the table. A painting of a mountain meadow hung on the wall.

"Can I get you something to drink?" she asked.

"No, I'm fine. Thank you."

We both took a seat at the table. She clasped her hands together and fidgeted in her seat.

"First of all, I'm sorry for your loss."

"Thank you. But what's going on? Did you find something in her case?"

"Possibly. I found a bracelet in the woods matching the one you reported she was wearing when she disappeared."

Her mouth opened slightly and she held up her wrist.

Sure enough, she wore a silver bracelet. "We thought they were so funny back then, we each bought one."

"You're certain she was wearing it that day?"

"Positive. She never took it off. They're a little tricky to get on if you don't have someone to help fasten the clasp."

"Do you keep yours on all the time?"

"I take it off to shower and when I go to bed. But my husband helps me put it on every morning. It makes me feel like I still have a little piece of her with me."

"I can't prove the bracelet was hers, but it matches the description you gave, down to the engraving. And it shows the wear expected with exposure to the elements. If nothing else, it prompted me to take a look at your sister's case."

"Well thank goodness for that. It's about time someone did."

"I understand. We all want answers. When you initially reported your sister missing, you told investigators you were concerned that a man named Tanner Leeman might be involved."

"Yes, Tanner was her ex-boyfriend. She'd broken up with him a few months before she disappeared. He wasn't happy about that. But the police were sure he didn't kill her."

"Because he was on a fishing boat in Alaska."

She nodded. "I thought it had to be him. Jasmine didn't have any enemies. Everyone loved her. But even I had to admit it wasn't possible for Tanner to be in two places at once."

"The report also said in the weeks leading up to her disappearance and murder, she received packages from an unknown sender. Do you remember that?"

"Oh, yes. It was terrible."

"Why? What was in them?"

She took a deep breath and looked away, as if recalling the incidents. "The first one had a pair of her underwear."

"How did she know they were hers?"

"Same brand, same size, same color. They were her favorites, and not something you could get locally. She ordered them online."

"Was any of her underwear missing?"

"To be honest, it was hard to tell. It could have been a different pair. But who would have known what kind of underwear she wore, other than Tanner?"

"So she believed Tanner had sent them to her."

She nodded. "She was afraid he'd been in her house. That he'd done it to show her he could still get to her."

"Did she report the incident to the sheriff's department?"

"No. I told her to, but she wouldn't listen. She said they wouldn't do anything, so why bother."

"Did Tanner have a key or other access to her home?"

"He shouldn't have. She changed the locks when they broke up. Not that it stopped him."

"Was she aware that someone had been in her house? Were there any other signs of a break in?"

"Not that I know of."

"You said she received packages, as in more than one. Do you recall how many there were?"

"There were two."

"What was in the second one?"

Her eyebrows drew together. "Flowers."

"Fresh flowers, or dried?"

"Fresh. A bouquet. She thought Tanner was trying to apologize, but there wasn't a note."

"What kind of flowers were they?"

"They were all white, with lilies."

"Do you know where they came from? Was it a local florist?"

"I don't know. I remember the box they came in was like the first—blank. No logo or stickers or anything."

"Was there postage on the packages? Had they actually been shipped?"

She paused, as if considering. "You know, I don't remember. It seems like there was, but I don't actually know for sure."

Damn.

"In the case notes, it indicates that you told law enforcement about the packages. But it doesn't look like they took them into evidence or treated them as part of the case. What did they tell you about them?"

"They said it was probably Tanner. Seemed like something an angry ex would do. Without any evidence that he'd broken in, there wasn't much they could do about it. And I think once they realized he couldn't have killed her, whether or not he sent her a pair of her own underwear or flowers was irrelevant."

"Do you know if he ever admitted to sending either package?"

"I don't know. I'm not sure if they ever asked him."

"The case notes indicate he was cleared as a suspect because he was in Alaska at the time of her disappearance. Was there any indication that the packages came from Alaska?"

"No, but he'd only just left, I think the day before she disappeared. He could have done it before."

"Do you remember when the flowers arrived, relative to when she disappeared?

"A day or two before, I think."

I kept my expression carefully neutral, but inside I was seething. It was possible those packages had come from her ex-boyfriend. But what if they hadn't? How could the investigators have been sure? Those items should have been taken in as evidence. How could someone have dropped the ball so badly?

"You don't happen to have those packages or any of the things they contained, do you?"

"No, I don't. It seemed sort of morbid to keep them."

"Of course."

"Why are you so interested in them? I thought they didn't have anything to do with her murder."

"I'm just looking at her case with fresh eyes. Were there any other strange incidents you can recall around the time of her initial disappearance? Any indication she was being watched or followed?"

"She did seem preoccupied. Like she was nervous. I remember because she wasn't usually like that. She was such a happy person. It was like there was a cloud following her around. But she didn't tell me why, so I don't know what was making her feel that way."

I hesitated before asking, but I had to know. "She didn't happen to get anything on her car? A gift bag, maybe with a stuffed animal in it?"

She shook her head. "No, nothing like that. At least not that I know of."

That was a relief. "Okay. Thank you for your time and I apologize for poking at a painful wound."

"Don't be sorry. I'll help in any way I can if it will get my sister's killer behind bars."

"Of course. I'm doing my best."

"Thank you, deputy?"

"Haven. Garrett Haven."

We got up and she walked me to the door. I gave her my card and asked her to call me if she remembered anything else that might help.

I left and went back to the station. Someone had brought in goodies, but they were just donuts from the Quick Stop. Easy to ignore. And I had bigger things on my mind.

Jasmine's murder had been considered a crime of opportunity. She'd been taken off a hiking trail, a simple wrong place, wrong time situation.

But was that it?

The location of her bracelet still bothered me. It was too

far from where her body was found, and not on a hiking trail. How had it gotten there?

And the packages. I wasn't convinced they'd been sent by her ex. I'd have to see if I could track him down and ask him myself. If he admitted to doing it, fine, I could move on and find another lead to follow.

But this trail was beckoning to me, tickling my instincts. A package with her underwear in it meant someone had broken into her house. That wasn't a crime of opportunity, that indicated research and planning. And it had been meant to send Jasmine a message.

Someone had been watching her. She hadn't been a random victim. She'd been a target.

I went to my desk and sat down, intending to dive back into Jasmine's case files, but Sergeant Denny appeared as if from nowhere. He crossed his arms, and by the groove between his eyes, I could tell he wasn't happy. "Prosecuting attorney's office dropped the Jones case."

"What?"

"Botched reports, missing evidence. The whole thing's a mess. I know you're a rookie investigator, but you should know better."

I had no idea what he was talking about. I'd followed protocol to the letter. I always did. "That doesn't make sense. What's missing? Who else had access?"

His gaze darkened into a glare.

"I'm not implying someone tampered on purpose, I—"

"Look, mistakes happen," he said, cutting me off. "But don't get too deep into that cold case. I know you want to be the guy who catches a killer, but that doesn't mean you can get sloppy on smaller cases."

I wanted to argue that I hadn't gotten sloppy, but I knew it was better to keep my mouth shut. Especially if he was just going to blow off steam at me, not write me up. So I nodded once.

He nodded in return and walked away.

I let out a frustrated breath. It certainly wasn't the first time one of my superiors had given me a hard time about something. Sergeant Denny could be a hardass. It was just part of the job.

The hairs on the back of my neck stood on end, like I was being watched. I glanced up and saw Kade standing on the other side of the room, leaning against a pillar with a cup of coffee in his hand. His expression might have seemed neutral —just a guy taking a quick break before going out on assignment again. But even at a distance, I could see the tightening at the corners of his eyes, the slight hitch in his jaw.

He wouldn't have tampered with something to make me look bad, would he?

That seemed like a stretch. Just because he'd been in a bad mood a lot, didn't mean he had it in for me.

Pushing Kade out of my mind—he wasn't my problem—I got up and went outside. I wanted to clear my head, but I also had a call to make, and I didn't want an audience. Sarge had said the prosecutor's office had dropped the case. I had a pretty good relationship with Phillip Lancaster, one of the prosecuting attorneys. Maybe he could shed some light on what was going on.

"Lancaster," he answered.

"Hey, Phillip. Garrett Haven. Got a minute?"

"Sure thing."

"I just got word about the Trent Jones case being dropped. Seemed pretty open-and-shut. Any idea what happened?"

"Yeah, this is a tough one." He paused, and his voice was hesitant when he continued. "There were too many things in your report that weren't accounted for in the evidence room. Started to make it look like you were exaggerating or you'd mishandled things. And forensics found your prints on the car."

"Mine? I wore gloves the whole time. That's not possible."

"I don't know, that's above my pay grade. All I know is, a jury would rip the case to shreds. We both know Jones is a problem, and believe me, I want him off the streets as much as you do. But the missing evidence alone is a bad look. Sorry, man. I hate to be the bearer of bad news."

Fuck. Missing evidence? My prints on the car?

"Look, I have no idea how that happened."

"Don't sweat it too much. But if the guys on your end aren't keeping things buttoned up, there's only so much I can do."

"Right. Got it."

"Just… be careful. You have a good reputation. Don't want to lose that."

"No, I don't."

"While I have you, how are things going on the Joyner case? Making any progress?"

"Nothing substantial yet. I talked to the victim's sister. There's an angle they didn't pursue. I think the victim might have been targeted before she was taken. Someone might have even broken into her house."

"You're kidding."

"No. But don't worry, I'll be meticulous with everything. If I have any shot of finding this guy, I'm not going to let any stupid mistakes get in the way."

"Good. And thanks for following up. I'm always available if you have questions."

"Thanks, Phillip. Appreciate it."

I ended the call.

Part of me wanted to throw my phone. Anger simmered in my gut. Mistakes? I didn't make mistakes. Not like that. It wasn't just that this made me look bad—which it did—it also kept a criminal on the streets. And a frequent flier like Jones would most likely offend again.

I just hoped if he did, no one would get hurt.

My phone buzzed with a text and, despite my frustrations,

the corners of my mouth turned up in a smile at seeing Harper's name. My anger cooled.

She'd sent a picture of herself holding a cupcake with pink and yellow swirled frosting.

Harper: *Pink lemonade cupcakes. Aren't they cute?*

Me: *You're cute.*

Harper: *Want me to save one for you?*

Me: *How about you save some frosting. I can lick it off you.*

Harper: *How soon can you be at my place? Not really, I can't leave work. But now I'm all tingly in, you know, places.*

Me: *What places?*

Harper: *Secret places.*

Me: *Delicious places.*

Harper: *You're killing me right now.*

Me: *Not sorry.*

Harper: *Can't wait to see you again.*

Me: *Me too.*

The urge to type *love you* hit me like a punch to the jaw. Love you? It was too soon for that. Spontaneous Garrett might have taken over for a while, and I didn't regret that, but I still needed to be careful.

And I needed to stay focused. If I really had made mistakes, I couldn't let it happen again. My job was at stake.

CHAPTER 17

Harper

THE SCENT of vanilla sponge cake filled the bakery kitchen. It had been pouring rain all day, which probably accounted for the lack of customers. Fewer people out and about, fewer still stopping in for a treat.

It was nice to have a breather. With no more need for cookies and cupcakes, I had time to work on custom cake orders. And for a cup of tea.

I pulled a stool to the island and sat, giving my feet a rest.

My phone buzzed with a call, giving me a zing of anticipation. Was it Garrett?

I was probably a little too excited about that.

But it wasn't. It was my sister, Holly. That was odd. She didn't call very often.

"Hey, Holly. Is everything okay?"

"Yeah, fine. Do you have any idea what happened to Grandma's vintage cameo brooch?"

"Um, no. I don't think so."

"You didn't end up with it?"

"No."

"Are you sure?"

"I think I'd remember if she left me that brooch. It was beautiful."

Holly let out an irritated breath. "So you're sure you didn't lose it?"

I was trying not to get annoyed that she assumed if it was missing, it must have been my fault. "I'm positive. I never had it. Why?"

"I bought a new dress and the brooch would look perfect with it. I was hoping you had it."

"Did you ask Mom? If Grandma didn't leave it to you, she probably has it."

"No, I'll have to call her."

"Yeah." I hesitated. Holly's familiar voice stirred up an old longing. I'd always wished we were closer. The kind of sisters who shared secrets. "So, how have you been?"

"Good. Just busy."

"Work busy or socially busy? Or both?"

"Mostly work. Why?"

"I'm just wondering. Did Mom tell you I moved to Tilikum?"

"No. Why would you do that?"

"Aunt Doris was struggling with the bakery, so I came out to help."

"Just temporarily?"

"Probably not. She really needs to retire."

"What does that have to do with you?"

"I mean, I'm a baker, so…"

"Sure, but she should be able to find someone out there. She can't expect you to just drop everything and come bail her out."

"She didn't expect me to, I decided."

"But it's a tiny town in the middle of nowhere."

"And?"

"And it sounds like my nightmare."

"I guess that's one of the things that makes us different. I like it here." I hesitated again. "I'm kind of seeing someone."

"A small-town guy? Oh my god, please tell me you're kidding."

"What? Why?"

"Lovely. Now you're going to be stuck in that backwoods dump with a flannel-wearing hick who chops wood and wants to keep you barefoot and pregnant. And isolated, I might add. All I can remember about Tilikum is that there's zero decent shopping."

"Wow, way to stereotype."

"We both know I'm right. He probably grew up there and has never lived anywhere else."

"His family lives here, but I don't actually know where else he's lived. I don't have his entire life story."

"How much can there be to tell?"

"Probably a lot. Just because he grew up in a small town doesn't mean he's a hick. He's a sheriff's deputy, thank you very much."

"Okay."

I rolled my eyes at the skepticism in her voice. "He's a great guy. He's been divorced for a while and has a teenage son who's the coolest kid. He's been coming into the bakery to help after school and I'm pretty sure he likes me."

"Harper, you're killing me. He has a kid already?"

"What's wrong with that? I told you, he's a great kid."

"For now. Besides, why would you even consider saddling yourself with someone else's child?"

"He's a single dad. That means they're a package deal."

"Exactly. That should have been a hard no."

"Maybe for you it would be. But Garrett is amazing. I really like him, and I like his son."

"Okay, well, kiss your dreams goodbye."

"I'm sorry I mentioned it."

"Don't be like that, Harper. You need to learn to take criticism."

"I work in a bakery serving the public, I take criticism all the time. I just thought my sister would be happy for me."

She sighed. "I just think you sell yourself short. You could achieve so much more."

"Sorry I'm not fancy enough for you. And he's not a hick and he doesn't want me barefoot and pregnant."

"Oh my god, stop being so sensitive."

I was about to argue with her, insist I wasn't being sensitive, but I knew where that would lead. We'd talk in circles until she gave up, too exasperated to deal with me. "I hope you find the brooch."

"Listen, I know you don't think you have it, but just look around, okay? It wouldn't be the first time you lost something."

I closed my eyes. "Sure, Holly. I'll take a look when I get home."

"Thanks. Talk to you later."

She ended the call and I set my phone down. My shoulders slumped as I stared at my tea. That had been an awful conversation. But what had I expected? Holly—and our mother for that matter—was perpetually disappointed in me. I was the university dropout. Never mind that I'd gone to culinary school. To them, baking wasn't a real career. And every man I dated was lacking. Not that they'd ever met any of them, they just assumed.

They always expected me to fail.

My phone buzzed against the island. Great. With my luck, it was my mother.

I turned it over and it didn't even surprise me. It *was* my mother.

The mirror curse struck again. No one could convince me that was a coincidence.

Against my better judgment, I answered. "Hi, Mom."

Doris came in the back door and winced. I shrugged.

"Harper, what's this I hear about you dating some man out in Tilikum?"

"Did you just talk to Holly? I hung up with her like two minutes ago."

"Yes."

"Why did she call you? I'm going out with a guy. I don't think that's a family emergency."

"She called about your grandmother's brooch. The subject of your questionable life choices also came up."

"My questionable life choices? Mom, I've been out on a couple of dates. Why did this warrant a phone call?"

Doris shook her head slowly.

"I didn't say anything when you moved to Tilikum. I thought it would be temporary. But darling, is that really the best you can do? It's very… provincial."

"I'm sure you mean that in the worst way possible."

"What sort of life could you have there? I'm concerned."

"That I'm going to get stuck with a flannel-wearing hick who wants me barefoot and pregnant."

"Yes."

I rolled my eyes again. Much more of this and I was going to get an eye-roll headache.

It's totally a thing.

"He's a good man. And I like Tilikum. It's quiet here, and friendly."

"Well, don't say I didn't warn you."

She kept talking for another minute or so. Something about small towns and the sort of people who lived in them. I held the phone away from my ear while Doris laughed softly behind her hand.

"Mom, I'm at work, I need to go. Thanks for the advice."

"Anytime. You think this through, all right?"

"Yeah, I will. Bye."

I ended the call, and, with a groan, dropped my forehead to my arms.

"Sorry, I didn't mean to eavesdrop," Doris said.

"No, it's okay. If it had been private, I would have let you know."

She placed a gentle hand on my back. "I figured. Don't let her get to you."

I sat up. "I shouldn't have said anything to Holly."

"Is that what happened?"

"Yeah. Holly called and I made the mistake of telling her I'm dating someone. She immediately called Mom, like it's some sort of crisis."

She pulled up the other stool and sat. "Your mom always has her own ideas about things."

"What does she have against small towns? I didn't even know that was a thing with her."

"I don't know. She'd probably say they're uncivilized, but I think it has more to do with status. She's always been very concerned with how people perceive her, and her idea of success is very specific."

"I wish she didn't have to project all that on me. So what if I like living here and being a baker and dating Garrett Haven? There's nothing wrong with that."

"Of course there isn't."

"It's not like we're getting married. It's a new relationship. She could simply be happy for me."

"For what it's worth, I'm happy for you."

I placed my hand over hers. "Thanks, Aunt Doris. That's worth a lot."

"Hey, Harper?" Beth poked her head through the doorway. "Are you good to watch the front until closing?"

"That's right, dentist appointment." I squeezed Doris's hand, then stood. "Sorry, I wasn't paying attention to the time."

"No problem. I just need to get going."

"Go ahead. I've got this."

"Thanks. See you tomorrow."

"What can I help with?" Doris asked.

"There's a cake in the fridge that needs to be frosted. The order form is over there." I pointed to the small stack of orders. "Other than that, we're in good shape today."

I left Doris to work on the cake while I went up front. Outside, the rain had stopped and the sun had finally come out. The pastry case was looking pretty bare, but it wasn't long until closing.

The door opened and my stomach went queasy. Matt walked in with a creepy leer on his face. His hair was either wet or very greasy—maybe a bit of both—and his shirt had what appeared to be a mustard stain on the chest.

"Hi, Harper."

"Hello. What can I do for you?"

"How's it going?"

"I'm fine, thank you. Can I get you something?"

No matter how hard I tried to use my customer service demeanor, he never took the hint. He approached the counter, his eyes roving over me in a way that made me enormously uncomfortable.

"Just thought I'd stop by and say hi."

I wished I knew whether Matt was just a bit awkward, or actually dangerous. I honestly couldn't tell. I didn't want to be judgmental. Just because he was habitually unkempt didn't mean he was a bad person.

But he also looked like he might have a cage in his basement waiting for his next victim.

"Oh, well, hi. Sorry the selection is a little lacking, but that tends to happen at the end of the day." I stepped back, hoping I could excuse myself into the kitchen. "Let me know if you want something from the case."

"What's your favorite?"

"It would be hard to choose one."

"You're just such a good baker."

"Thank you. If you liked the butterscotch chip before, we still have some of those."

He grinned. "You remembered."

Oh no. "I did?"

"I did get a butterscotch chip last time. I knew you—"

Before he could finish, the door opened. It might as well have been a knight in shining armor, only it was a big man in aviators and a deputy uniform.

I couldn't help the enormous smile that stole over my face. Giddiness bubbled up inside me, chasing away the queasy sensation. I would have been happy to see Garrett anyway, but his timing was perfect.

Owen came in behind him, his hands stuffed in the pocket of his hoodie. He flicked his head to get his hair out of his eyes and smiled.

"Hi, you two."

Garrett took off his aviators and gave me a subtle grin. "Hi."

Just that little word, delivered in his deliciously deep voice, sent a tingle down my spine.

Owen's brow furrowed and his eyes moved to Matt, then back to me.

"Sorry," I said, turning back to Matt. I'd basically forgotten he was standing there. "Did you decide?"

He wasn't looking in the case, and he wasn't looking at me—my face or my boobs. His gaze was on Garrett. And he did not look happy. His round cheeks were splotchy red and his glare was unmistakable.

Garrett's expression didn't change. I could practically see him sizing up the situation—noting the variables, calculating the risks. He looked calm and completely in control.

Matt, not so much. He clenched his fists and his upper lip curled in a sneer.

"Go ahead and go to the kitchen." Garrett nudged Owen

but his eyes didn't leave Matt.

Owen widened his eyes at me, as if to say, *this should be interesting*, as he headed around the counter.

Garrett followed Owen to my side of the counter, but didn't go into the kitchen. He locked his gaze on me, his expression intense. I could feel Matt watching, but I couldn't take my eyes off the man moving toward me.

One corner of his mouth lifted slightly as he placed a knuckle beneath my chin to tilt my face up. He brushed a soft kiss against my lips, then shifted to stand right behind me, one hand on the small of my back.

Garrett's move wasn't lost on Matt. He'd just declared, in no uncertain terms, that I was his.

If Owen and Aunt Doris hadn't been in the kitchen, I would have dragged him back there and let him defile me in a hundred different ways.

Garrett leaned in and spoke low into my ear. "Sorry. I'll let you finish with your customer."

Matt looked like his head might pop. His face had gone from splotchy red to purple, and his eyes were bloodshot. He was way too angry for a regular bakery customer who'd just witnessed the baker get a tiny kiss.

And he was way too angry for a guy who was just a bit awkward and didn't seem to remember to wash his clothes.

Did he have a cage in his basement? And was he thinking about putting me in it?

I swallowed hard. "Did you want something?"

He tore his eyes from Garrett and turned his glare on me. Although his expression softened, the intense eye contact was unnerving.

"Butterscotch chip."

I did my best to smile as I got the butterscotch chip cookie out of the case and put it in a bag. His anger seemed to be starting to cool, his face returning to its normal color. He took the bag and paid with cash.

"Have a nice day." I handed him his change.

"Thanks, Harper." His voice still had a note of strain, and when he lifted his eyes, they narrowed at Garrett. But there was more annoyance than malice in his gaze as he turned and walked out the door.

I let out a long breath while Garrett gently rubbed my back. "Well that was awkward."

"Has he been in before?" he asked.

"A couple of times, yeah. He's always struck me as a little off."

"He did not like seeing me here." He slipped a hand around my waist and turned me toward him. "Are you okay?"

"Oh yeah, fine. It wouldn't be the first time I had a customer I wasn't thrilled to see return."

He glanced at the door. "Do you think he left you the bear?"

"I hadn't thought of that, but maybe?" I paused. "Kind of fits, doesn't it?"

"He didn't say anything about it?"

"No, but he was only here for a minute before you walked in."

Garrett nodded slowly, as if considering.

"Do you know anything about him?" I asked.

"Not really. I've seen him around town but he's never been in trouble. Not here, at least."

"So maybe he is just kind of weird."

"Bro's a creep." Owen appeared in the doorway. "Dad, you should arrest him."

Garrett let go of me and stepped back. "I can't arrest someone without cause."

"He probably has a fridge full of jarred human organs."

Garrett shook his head with a soft chuckle. "That's helpful, Owen, thank you."

"I'm just saying. Harper, he totally left you the murder bear, by the way."

"You think so?" I asked.

"Definitely. Fits the profile."

"What profile?" Garrett asked, a hint of amusement in his voice.

"You know what I mean. Weirdo obviously has a crush on Harper. Seems like the type who'd leave an old stuffed animal on her car."

I looked at Garrett and shrugged. "He's not wrong."

"Guy's got no rizz, though," Owen said.

Garrett met my eyes, his brow furrowed. I shrugged. Apparently we both needed a teenage slang lesson.

"Rizz?" Garrett asked, turning to Owen.

Owen rolled his eyes. "Rizz, like charisma. Means he can't get a girl."

"Oh." I nodded. That actually made some sense. "Matt definitely lacks rizz."

Owen shook his head and let out a soft laugh. "Bruh."

"What?" I asked.

"Nothing."

"If he does anything, and I mean anything, that makes you uncomfortable, call me," Garrett said. "Immediately."

"Okay. I will."

He brushed a wisp of hair off my face. His eyes flicked to Owen and he lowered his hand.

Oh my gosh, he was shy about touching me in front of his son. Why was that so cute?

"Dad, you're so weird." He turned and started back into the kitchen. "I'll go in here so you can kiss your girlfriend."

Girlfriend? My heart fluttered and I tried to keep myself from smiling too big.

But something tickled the back of my brain, a voice whispering doubts. Garrett Haven was too good to be true. And my bad luck was going to ruin it somehow.

CHAPTER 18

Harper

RUNNING errands in Tilikum was so easy. Everything was close and there was never any traffic.

Which was great, because I was dragging. I'd even slept in late, but for some reason, I was still tired.

The clouds had blown through and hints of summer were in the air. Flowers bloomed in wine barrel planters around downtown and the temperature was climbing. I remembered from my visits with Aunt Doris that summers were hot in the mountains. I made a mental note to have the air conditioning unit at the bakery serviced. With my luck, it would go out on a hundred-degree day at the height of wedding season and all my cakes would melt.

Not good.

I'd already stopped by the hardware store for a few odds and ends and put gas in my car. I still needed to hit the grocery store, but two tasks out of three sounded like a latte was in order.

Treat yourself, am I right?

I parked outside the Steaming Mug, Tilikum's adorable coffee shop. It was right up the street from the bakery, so I'd been in quite a few times when I needed an afternoon pick me up.

Of course, just about everything was right up—or down—the street from the bakery. I freaking loved this town.

The Steaming Mug had a charming ambiance, with an exposed brick wall behind the teal counter and a large chalkboard menu. There wasn't a line, but before I could place my order, a familiar voice called out to me.

"Harper, dear!" Dressed in a peach tracksuit with yellow and white stripes at the shoulders, Louise Haven waved me over to her table.

"Hi, Louise."

She was seated with a few silver-haired women. One moved over and offered me her chair next to Louise.

"Sit, sit." Louise patted the chair. "Tell me how you've been. Although I think I have a pretty good idea." She winked.

I lowered myself into the chair, not sure what the wink was about. "I'm doing well. How about you?"

"Fine, dear, fine. But what's new?" Her eyebrows lifted and she smiled expectantly, leaning forward as if I were about to drop a juicy tidbit of gossip.

I'm recklessly sleeping with your nephew.

Thankfully, that didn't fly out of my mouth.

"Let's see. Everything at the bakery is good. We've been so busy I need to hire another baker. At least someone part-time."

She nodded along, her eyebrows still lifted.

Apparently she wanted more. "Doris is doing well, but you probably know that already."

"I do. I had tea with her just the other day."

"That's great."

She leaned a little closer. "And?"

"And... I've been out with your nephew Garrett a few times."

"I knew it!" She turned to her friends. "Didn't I tell you? I was right about them all along."

They gave her appreciative nods.

"I don't mean to brag, but I have some skill as a matchmaker. When Doris told me you were moving to Tilikum, I said, Doris, we need to set her up with my nephew Garrett. They're perfect for each other."

"Did you really say that?" one of her friends asked.

She waved her off. "Something like that. I might have said Luke initially, but that was before I'd gotten a good look at you."

I laughed. "I guess you were right about Garrett."

"You're such a dear for letting that first date incident go. I'm sure it wasn't his fault."

"Oh, I know. He was chasing a bad guy. Literally."

She sighed. "That's our Garrett. He's a good man. An honorable man. Although hopefully not too honorable, if you know what I mean." She smirked at me.

My cheeks warmed. She had no idea. "He's been... very much a gentleman."

Even when he was slamming me up against a wall.

Sugar cookies, I needed to stop thinking about that. Especially when I was talking to his aunt.

"I'm sure he has. Always walked upright, that one. Even when he was little."

"He sure is handsome in that uniform," her friend added. "I see him out and about occasionally and he makes me want to steal something just so he'd have to arrest me."

Louise's friends all giggled. She lifted her eyes to the ceiling and shook her head.

"Ladies, he's my nephew." She leaned closer to me and lowered her voice. "Although they're quite right, he is a handsome man. And he's a Haven, which comes with its own set of perks."

I wasn't quite sure what to say to that. "Good to know."

She pointed downward a few times. "I mean in the manhood department, dear. I'm quite sure you won't be disappointed."

My eyes widened and my cheeks blazed. No, I was definitely not disappointed. But coming from his aunt?

"My goodness, Louise," her friend said.

"Don't be such a ninny." She waved her off again. "Women should talk about these things. It's important." She turned back to me. "I'm not saying I know something I shouldn't. I'm his auntie, after all. But the Haven men are uniquely gifted."

"Well, this has been lovely, and weirdly educational." I stood and jerked my thumb in the direction of the counter. "But I should get my coffee and go. I have more errands."

"Of course, dear, of course. Don't let me keep you." Louise wiggled her fingers at me. "Ta ta, Harper. Tell my handsome nephew I said hello. And he can thank me later for making sure the two of you got together."

I laughed. "Okay, Louise. I'll do that. Have a nice afternoon." I waved to her friends and went to the counter to order my latte.

It might have been my imagination, but it seemed like the two baristas working the front counter were talking about me while I waited for my coffee. They leaned in and spoke in quiet voices, casting quick glances at me over their shoulders. And I was pretty sure I heard the words Garrett Haven.

One thing I wasn't used to—having moved to Tilikum from a larger city—was the small-town gossip. Maybe the baristas weren't talking about me, but the two cashiers at the hardware store certainly had been. I'd heard them loud and clear—*she's the new girl in town and I hear she's dating Deputy Haven.*

It had happened at the Copper Kettle too, one of the diners in town. I'd stopped in to pick up a to-go order and noticed the whispers as I left. Something about the one to finally catch the eye of Deputy Haven.

I wasn't sure what to make of it. Was it because I was new in town? Or because people were surprised? Maybe they thought I wasn't pretty enough and didn't understand what the hot law enforcement officer saw in the baker.

Or maybe I was overthinking it and it was just the way things were in a small town. It seemed like pretty much everybody knew everybody, and they all knew your business. Even when it was none of theirs.

The barista gave me my coffee and I left, trying to shake off the feeling that she was analyzing my face and judging whether I was cute enough to be with the handsome Haven brother.

I opened the door and stepped out onto the sidewalk. Out of nowhere, a man appeared right where I was walking. I smacked into him, spilling hot coffee all down my front.

"Sugar cookies." I jumped back, holding my dripping cup away from myself.

"Watch it, lady." The man was scruffy with unkempt hair and a scraggly beard. His lip curled in a sneer.

"I'm sorry. I didn't see you there."

"If you get burned, it ain't my fault."

That was an odd response to an apology. "I didn't say it was. Did I spill on you?"

He looked down at his T-shirt. It had a wet splotch on the front. "Ruined my damn shirt."

"I'm so sorry. That was totally my fault."

"Damn straight it was. Don't go tattling on me to your cop boyfriend. The dick'll probably haul me in again. I didn't touch you. We clear?"

"I never said you did."

He pointed a finger at me and opened his mouth to say something else, but another male voice cut him off.

"Move on, Trent. No need to make a scene."

I glanced at the new arrival. He was a nice-looking guy, probably mid-thirties, with light brown hair and blue eyes. He wore a black T-shirt and jeans, and although his voice was calm, his posture was like a coiled spring.

"The fuck's your problem, Haven?" Trent asked. "Trying to start something?"

Haven? Was he one of Garrett's brothers?

"The only one trying to start something here is you. She spilled a little coffee and she apologized. Let's all go on with our day."

"Tell your brother to fuck off." He spat on the sidewalk and kept walking.

"Are you okay?" the other guy asked.

I looked down at my mess of a shirt. "Yeah, fine. Not the first time I've spilled coffee all over myself. Thanks, by the way."

"No problem. I'm Luke, Garrett's brother."

"Nice to meet you. I'm Harper."

"Good to meet you too."

"Who was that guy and why was he so angry? I mean, I wouldn't be happy if someone ran into me on the sidewalk and spilled coffee on my shirt. But wasn't that a little excessive?"

"Trent Jones. He's a local, and kind of a hothead. Likes to steal cars."

"Seriously?"

"Yeah, he has a reputation. Sometimes you hear wild stories about people in this town, but in his case, they're mostly true."

"Wow. I wonder if that's why he said Garrett would probably haul him in again. Do you think Garrett's arrested him before?"

"More than likely."

Trent had disappeared around a corner but my heart still felt jumpy.

"Don't worry about him. Guys like that are the exception in this town, not the rule. Most of us aren't rude car thieves."

"That's good to know. And your chivalry just now totally made up for his rudeness. You didn't have to stop and help me."

He shrugged, like it was no big deal. "I saw you run into him from across the street and I had a feeling he'd be a dick about it."

"Thank you."

"Do you want another coffee?" He put up a hand. "I'm not hitting on you or anything. I know you're dating my brother."

Holding up my cup, I sighed. "No. With my luck, I'd just run into someone else and have twice as much coffee on my clothes."

"Fair enough. It was good to meet you. I'm sure I'll see you around."

"Yeah, you too."

With a smile, he turned and walked back across the street.

I shook off the last bit of coffee still dripping from my hand and tossed my cup in a trash can. Thank you, mirror curse. I'd not only run into someone and dumped my much-anticipated latte all over myself, I'd run into a rude car thief. Luke walking by had been—dare I say it—lucky? But not enough to cancel out the bad luck.

Harper: zero. Broken mirror: about a million.

CHAPTER 19

Garrett

CRUISING DOWN THE WINDING HIGHWAY, I headed back toward town. I'd been out on patrol all morning, checking on some of the more remote areas of the county. Nothing much was happening. I'd noted an old truck with a taillight out and pulled him over just to let him know. Other than that, it had been a quiet morning.

I wore my aviators against the glare of the sun and my mind drifted as I drove. Town chatter about the Joyner case hadn't died down. New leads were coming in, which would have been great, if they'd been legit. But mostly they were just wasting our time.

Brenna's voice came over my radio. "Possible breaking and entering at 45 West Sunnybrook Lane."

"Squad seven," I replied.

"Go ahead squad seven."

"I'm not far from that location. I can go take a look."

"10-4, squad seven."

"Proceeding to 45 West Sunnybrook Lane."

I drove to the location and parked outside a small white house. On the porch, dressed in a pink housecoat, was a little old lady every first responder in Tilikum knew all too well. Mavis Doolittle.

I keyed my mic. "Squad seven."

"Go ahead, squad seven."

"Put me at 45 West Sunnybrook Lane, possible breaking and entering. But Brenna, this is Mavis Doolittle's house."

"That's correct."

Kade's voice cut in. "Better you than me."

I sighed. Mavis Doolittle was notorious for her questionable emergency calls. It had been a while since she'd called anything in, probably because the fire department had threatened to fine her.

"Maybe I need backup on this, Sheehan. How soon can you get over here?"

Kade chuckled. "I'm sure you can handle anything Mrs. Doolittle can dole out."

"I'll check it out. But, Brenna, this better not be a bogus call."

"She was insistent," Brenna said. "Said she came home from the salon and found evidence of a break in."

Maybe someone really had broken into her house. She was unreliable, but we couldn't blow her off.

Mavis was probably in her eighties, a tiny lady with a head full of tight, white curls. She patted her hair, then wrung her hands together.

"Deputy, I'm so glad you're here. It's terrible. Just terrible."

"Afternoon, ma'am. Can you tell me what happened?"

She leaned against the railing and took halting steps down the stairs. "I was at the salon. A woman has to maintain her appearance."

I waited while she stopped in front of me and patted her hair again.

"When I came home, I went inside and I knew something wasn't right."

"Was your door open or anything broken?"

"No, nothing like that."

"Okay. Then why do you think someone broke into your house?"

"He ate the cookies I left out on my kitchen table."

I hesitated. Not a bogus call, my ass. "Someone broke in and ate your cookies."

"Yes." She grabbed my arm, as if to tug me closer. Her eyes brightened and she squeezed a few times. "Oh my. They really did send me a nice, strong man, didn't they?"

I gently eased out of her grip. "I'll have you stay out here while I go inside and check things out. Make sure it's safe."

"Oh, it's not safe. He's still in there."

A ripple of tension swept through me. "Still in your house?"

"I think so."

Something wasn't adding up. She was awfully calm for an elderly woman with a suspect in her house.

A cookie-eating suspect?

"Wait here, please."

She touched my arm again. "Be careful."

"I will, ma'am." I keyed my mic to report in to dispatch. "Squad seven."

"Go ahead, squad seven."

"Mrs. Doolittle claims someone broke in and stole cookies. I'd chalk it up to typical Mavis, but she also says the suspect is still inside. I'm going in to take a look."

"Stole cookies?" Brenna asked.

"That's what she said."

The door was unlocked, so I eased it open and scanned the entryway. Nothing unusual, other than the cloying scent of something floral. It was so strong it almost made my eyes water.

"Tilikum Sheriff's department," I called out to identify myself to anyone who might be inside.

I didn't hear any movement. The living room off the entry was empty, just a couch with a plastic liner and an antique-looking coffee table. Senses on high alert, I made my way toward the kitchen.

In the center of her small kitchen table was a dessert massacre. Crumbs and pieces of broken cookies were every-where. It looked like what would happen if my three-year-old nephew, Will, had been left alone with a plate of cookies for more than a few minutes.

No wonder Mavis thought someone had broken into her house.

But who would do that? And why leave such a mess?

A rustling sound made me turn, my hand straying near my sidearm. "Mrs. Doolittle, is that you? I need you to wait outside."

No reply.

Taking slow steps, I moved in the direction of the sound. A piece of cookie crunched under my shoe. My brow furrowed as I glanced into the dining room. I didn't see anything, until—

A streak of gray fur flew through the air. Instinctively, I put my arms up to shield my face.

The squirrel landed on my shoulder, its claws pinching through my uniform. It scampered across my back and leaped onto the floor.

"Damn it."

I followed it into the kitchen, wondering how the hell I was going to get a squirrel out of Mavis Doolittle's house.

I keyed my mic again. "Squad seven."

"Go ahead, squad seven."

"Suspect is a squirrel. On the loose in the house."

"Now this makes sense," Brenna said. "Be careful. Those little things are shifty."

"Yeah, tell me about it."

I didn't see the squirrel in the kitchen, so I backtracked

toward the front door and checked the living room. Not there, either. Had it run upstairs?

And how had it gotten in, anyway?

A quick trip upstairs revealed the mode of entry. One of the windows in Mrs. Doolittle's bedroom was open. The tree outside had a few branches that reached toward the house, close enough that the squirrel could jump the distance and scamper inside.

Was it too much to hope the little guy had escaped the way it had come?

I couldn't leave until I was sure. I searched upstairs, closing doors behind me so it wouldn't run into one of the bedrooms if it was still inside. With no trace of it, I grabbed a towel out of the hall bath in case I needed to catch it, and went down to the main floor.

Maybe it was gone.

A chattering sound coming from the kitchen made me freeze in my tracks. Holding up the towel, I tried to be as quiet as possible as I moved toward the noise.

The little asshole sat on the table, right in the center of the cookie carnage, stuffing its face. Its fluffy tail twitched and it looked right at me, but didn't stop eating.

I kept the towel raised, ready to throw it on the squirrel, and slowly moved closer.

That's it, little thief. Keep shoving food in your face. Don't worry about what I'm doing.

As soon as I tossed the towel, it bolted, scattering crumbs everywhere. In one quick motion, I grabbed the towel and pivoted. The squirrel dashed across the kitchen, climbed onto the counter, and ran across the front of the sink. I threw the towel again, aiming ahead of it, but it jumped on top of the fridge and disappeared.

"I know you're up there." I picked up the towel again. "You're backed into a corner, my friend. Nowhere to go."

A streak of fur flew from the top of the refrigerator and

slid across the kitchen floor, back legs splayed. I dropped the towel onto it, but I was a second too late. Before I could wrap it up, it escaped out the other side.

I followed it into the living room, where it climbed the curtain and paused to look at me, beady black eyes full of... well, fear, most likely. But in the moment, it looked like rebellion.

I couldn't keep chasing this thing around the house. I needed a new plan.

You worked in law enforcement in Tilikum long enough, you learned a few things. This wasn't my first squirrel rodeo.

I left the squirrel hanging from the curtain and went back to the kitchen. A quick peek through Mrs. Doolittle's cupboards, and I found what I needed.

Peanut butter. I just hoped the squirrel wasn't too full of cookies for this to work.

I scooped out a big spoonful and stuck on some cookie pieces for good measure. Then I set it on the floor, crouched with the towel, and waited.

The scent lured it. Within moments, the squirrel came in, fluffy tail twitching. It stopped on its hind legs about a foot from the peanut butter and scrunched its nose. Despite having already decimated a plate of cookies, it went in.

I waited, my heart beating hard. The squirrel seemed to ignore me, intent on its snack. In my head, I heard the voice of William Wallace in the movie *Braveheart*.

Hold... Hold... Hold...

Now!

I scooped the squirrel into the towel and held the sides together, making a little sack. It thrashed around, trying to get out as I rushed to the back door.

"It's okay, I'm not going to hurt you."

I opened the door and hurried out into Mrs. Doolittle's backyard while the squirrel tried to tear its way out of the towel. As gently as I could, I set it on the grass and let go, jumping away in case it came out heading toward me.

The towel fell open and the squirrel darted out, but stopped a couple of feet away. It turned, black eyes wide, and stared at me, as if to say, what the fuck, man?

"Pretty sure you ate a week's worth of food in there. You'll be fine."

With that, it scampered away.

Blowing out a breath, I picked up the towel and took it inside.

I went to the front to let Mrs. Doolittle know she could come back in.

"Did you find him?" she asked as she followed me into the house.

"Were you aware it was a squirrel, Mrs. Doolittle?"

"Was it? Oh my goodness gracious, no wonder it left such a mess."

I eyed her with skepticism. She just beamed up at me, eyes crinkling at the corners.

"You should consider putting a screen in the bedroom window upstairs. I think that's how it got in."

Her mouth twitched in a grin. "The bedroom, you say? Perhaps you should show me."

"I borrowed a towel to catch the squirrel and used some of your peanut butter as a lure."

"Smart and handsome. Such a combination."

I ignored that. "Do you need help cleaning up?"

"No, no." She waved a hand. "I'll take care of it. Would you like to stay? I can fix you a snack. Maybe give you a nice foot rub. It's the least I can do."

"Thank you anyway, ma'am, but I need to get back to work."

"Are you sure? These hands don't look like much now, but I still know how to use them."

I didn't know if she was still talking about a foot rub, or something else. And I didn't want to find out.

"Have a good day, ma'am."

Without waiting for a reply, I left through the front door and went straight for my car.

I keyed my mic to check in. "Squad seven."

"Go ahead, squad seven."

"Squirrel was safely removed. I'm heading into the office."

"You get out in one piece?" Brenna asked, a hint of humor in her voice.

"She offered me a foot rub before I left."

She laughed. "At least that was all."

"We should send Kate if she calls again. She gets a female deputy enough times, she might go back to calling the fire department."

"Good idea."

I shook my head and pulled out of the driveway. At least it hadn't been a totally bogus call. There really had been an intruder in her house. And it certainly wasn't the first time I'd been on a squirrel call. Happened all the time in Tilikum.

The corners of my mouth lifted as I imagined the way Harper was going to laugh when I told her that story.

For once, instead of worrying about what it all meant, and whether we were moving too fast, I let thoughts of Harper run uninhibited through my mind. And I smiled even bigger.

CHAPTER 20

Garrett

DESPITE SPENDING SO much time at Mavis Doolittle's house trying to wrangle a squirrel, I was in a good mood as I parked my patrol car and went inside. Technically, I was off, but Owen was going to a pizza party at a friend's house, so I figured I'd get some more work done before I headed home.

The station was quiet. Most deputies were out on patrol or working shifts in the jail. I went to the kitchen to fill my water, then took a seat at my desk.

I'd just gotten started on some paperwork I needed to finish when Sheriff Jack came by.

"Can I see you in my office?" he asked.

"Sure."

Jack Cordero was a popular figure in Tilikum, and he was well-respected by the men who served under him, myself included. He'd spent a lot of his career with the Seattle PD and moved to Tilikum for a change of pace.

But as much as I liked, and respected, him personally, no deputy wanted to be called into his office.

I followed him back, the feeling reminiscent of being taken to the principal's office in school. Not that I'd had that experience very many times. Zachary had been the troublemaker of the family, not me.

Still, I was concerned.

"Have a seat." He gestured to the chair on the other side of his desk.

I lowered myself onto the edge of the seat, my spine straight. "Is something going on?"

"Yeah, there is. A few days ago, we had an anonymous misconduct complaint. About you."

My brow furrowed. "Me?"

"Obviously when someone won't identify themselves, it's more or less impossible to investigate or substantiate their complaint. I wouldn't have thought twice about it, except we had another one. This time it wasn't anonymous."

"Two complaints against me?"

"Actually, now there have been three. We had another one this morning."

I stared at him in shock. I'd never had a complaint filed against me. Not a legitimate one, at least. Trent Jones had tried after I'd arrested him the first time, but I'd done everything by the book. He'd just been pissed off that he'd gotten caught and had been throwing spaghetti at the wall, trying to find a way to get out of the charges.

"What are the complaints?"

"The anonymous one had to do with a traffic stop. The caller claimed you ordered him out of his car and frisked him without cause."

"There's no way that's legit."

"Like I said, I would have blown it off as nothing, considering the guy wouldn't give us his identity. Just insisted it was you who pulled him over and you mistreated him. But the second one gave us his name and contact info. He wants to file a formal complaint."

"About what?"

"He claims you harassed him. It was a family trouble call, neighbor reported loud arguing."

"Adult son living with his mother?"

Jack nodded.

"She was trying to kick him out and thought I should arrest him. I didn't harass him, I practically took his side."

"He said you threatened him."

Suddenly I really wished we had standard issue body cameras. We were one of a handful of sheriff's departments in the state that didn't. We'd applied for funding, but it hadn't come through yet. One of the perils of being a small agency.

"I had a conversation with the guy. I didn't threaten him."

"The latest one is a guy who also said you harassed and threatened him. At Angel Cakes Bakery, to be exact."

"You've got to be kidding me."

"His story is that he was innocently buying baked goods when you arrived and used your position and authority to intimidate him."

"He was making my girlfriend uncomfortable." The word girlfriend rolled off my tongue all too easily. "I probably glared at him, but I didn't harass him."

"Were you in uniform?"

"Yeah, but I didn't even have words with him."

Jack pressed his lips together and glanced away. "You've had an impeccable history. Until recently. I can chalk up the mistakes with Trent Jones's arrest to rookie mistakes. It's not your fault you're learning the ropes on your own. But then we start getting complaints, and not just one. That's either one hell of a coincidence, or it's the beginning of a pattern."

"There's no pattern. You said yourself, the anonymous claim can't be substantiated. It's irrelevant. I don't know why the freeloader would want to file a complaint against me, but I'm telling you, it's bullshit. And Matt might very well be the one doing the harassing."

"What's going on at home lately? How's Owen?"

I shifted backward in my chair, the abrupt change of subject rattling me a little. "He's fine. Why?"

"I know about the shoplifting."

"Come on, Jack. I'm his father. I handled it."

"I'm not saying you did anything wrong. I'm just wondering what's going on. Owen's never been in any kind of trouble, has he? Even at school?"

I shook my head. "He's a good kid, he just made a mistake."

"I know, sometimes they do that," he conceded. "And sometimes the reason behind it is worth digging into."

"What are you getting at?"

"That I see some things that give me cause for concern. I don't know if it's your new role or things are rocky at home. Maybe it's your new girlfriend. Or all of the above. But whatever is going on, I need you to address it."

"Look, I don't have issues at home. Owen's fine. And Harper certainly isn't a problem."

He paused and the gravity in his expression made me more than a little bit nervous. "What about the Pasco incident? You still struggling?"

"No." My voice was filled with honest conviction. I'd shot a man in the line of duty and I had zero regrets. It wasn't that I was flippant about what I'd done. I'd taken a man's life and that was no small thing. But he would have killed my brother Zachary, and Marigold.

In the aftermath, I'd been put on administrative leave while the agencies involved did their investigations—standard protocol. I'd met with a therapist a few times to process the incident, then been allowed to come back to work.

"The situation in Pasco was intense," I continued. "But I'd do it again if I had to."

"We all know you saved lives that day. But sometimes that stuff comes out when you don't expect it."

"Are you suggesting I'm suddenly going around threatening and intimidating people because I had to take the life of a human trafficker in order to save my brother? Or because I'm raising a teenager? Or maybe it's because I'm dating someone. Is that it?"

"Don't get defensive—"

"Of course I'm going to get defensive."

"Here's the bottom line. I don't want to put you on leave. I need you out there doing your job. But I do have to look into these claims. It's protocol. And the timing of everything is... troubling. So if there's something going on in your personal life that's bleeding into your work, deal with it."

"I'm telling you, there isn't anything. It's just normal life stuff."

He paused, his dark eyes scrutinizing me. "I'll take you at your word. For now. And maybe it is a coincidence. I'm not saying I don't trust you, just that I have to tread carefully. I'm not only responsible for the safety of the citizens in my jurisdiction, I'm responsible for maintaining their trust. We enjoy a good relationship with the people in this town. I don't want to compromise that."

"I hear you." Trust in law enforcement could be a fragile thing. I knew that as well as anyone. "Just don't put me on leave. I've got too much to do."

"I won't unless I have to."

"Fair enough." I stood. "Anything else?"

Jack shook his head. I could tell he wasn't happy about any of this, for my sake as well as his. He wanted to believe me, but he had to do his job.

I left his office and went back to my desk. The complaint filed by Matt was particularly troubling. I hadn't threatened him. Not even close. I'd barely interacted with him at all. Okay, so I'd kind of marked my territory. But one look at him and I'd been able to tell he was trying to hit on Harper. A guy could see that sort of thing. Of course I was going to put an end to that. Definitively. That wasn't a threat, whether I'd been in uniform or not.

Just a man protecting his woman.

But the whole situation was unsettling. No formal complaints in my entire career, and suddenly there were three? How was that possible? The threat to my job pissed me off. Not only was it my livelihood, it was my life.

The hair on the back of my neck stood up, but no one was around. Was I being paranoid? Or was something off?

I didn't know. But I had to stay sharp if I was going to find out.

CHAPTER 21

Harper

MY EYELIDS WERE STRANGELY heavy as I piped cream cheese frosting onto a batch of red velvet cupcakes. It seemed like I'd slept fine the night before, but maybe I'd tossed and turned more than I thought.

I put the piping bag down and sank onto a stool. For the last week or so, I'd been getting tired in the afternoon. I kept wondering if I was about to get sick. It felt like my battery was running low.

Maybe I needed some fresh air. I loved the fast pace of my job, but it also made it easy to forget the outside world existed. A little sunshine would do me good.

That, and food. Maybe I wasn't eating enough.

I finished frosting the cupcakes so they could go in the case, then told Beth I'd be out for about an hour. I'd get outside, take a short walk, and grab lunch. Hopefully that would energize me for the rest of my day.

After taking off my apron and hanging it on a hook, I grabbed my purse and went out the back door. It was June and the days were getting warmer. The sun felt great on my skin and the air was fresh. Perfect for a walk through town.

I glanced at my car in the back parking lot. No unexpected

packages. There hadn't been another once since the murder bear. Hopefully that meant it had been a mistake, or whoever had left it—whether it was Matt or someone else—had decided to stop.

That was a relief.

And the bear hadn't come to life and murdered anyone, so I had that going for me.

I went around to the front of the building and headed up the sidewalk. My body still felt oddly fatigued, even in the fresh air, so I picked up the pace to get my blood moving a little more. That had to help.

At the corner, a man in a faded flannel shirt and brown leather vest crouched in front of a wine barrel planter. A shaggy beard showed beneath his wide-brimmed hat, and he looked up at me with a smile that creased the skin around his eyes. Harvey Johnston. I'd met him once or twice and he'd always been friendly, if a little eccentric. Aunt Doris said he was a longtime Tilikum resident who was, in her words, not quite all there.

I figured Tilikum was just full of quirky people.

"Hi, Harvey." I paused next to him. "What are you up to?"

He stood and brushed the front of his vest, although it didn't look like he had dirt on his hands. "Good. Oh, no, that's not what you asked. What am I up to?"

It was hard to tell from his tone if he was just repeating the question or if he really wasn't sure. I waited to see if he wanted to answer.

"Oh!" He held up a finger, his eyes widening with excitement. "I know what I'm up to. I made these." He picked up what looked like a small picnic table with attached benches. Instead of a flat tabletop, it had a container filled with nuts and seeds.

"That's so cute. Is it for the squirrels?"

"Someone's been making squirrel-proof bird feeders and selling them all over town. I know our squirrels can be a nuisance, but the birds do just fine on their own. And since so many feeders are flinging them off like slingshots, I thought I'd give the squirrels a nice place to eat." He set the picnic table down next to the planter.

"That's smart. Maybe if they have their own little tables, they'll leave the birdseed alone."

One eye squinted almost shut as he tapped his temple. "Yes, indeed. Thinking, I was. And what are you up to today, Miss Tilburn?"

"Just getting out for a walk and I'll probably grab some food."

"Good, good." He patted the pockets on his vest and his brow furrowed, as if he'd lost something. "You have a nice day, now." He turned in a circle, looking around. "What did I do with it?"

I pointed to a canvas drawstring bag on the ground next to the planter. "Is that what you're looking for?"

"Oh, yes, I think it is." He picked up the bag and tipped his hat to me. "Afternoon, Miss Tilburn."

"Afternoon, Harvey."

He walked out into the street without looking for traffic and the driver of a green pickup slammed on his brakes to keep from hitting him. I winced, but Harvey didn't seem to notice. Just kept walking, muttering something to himself that I couldn't hear. The driver didn't make a scene, either. He just waited for Harvey to cross and went on his way.

Tilikum was definitely an interesting place.

A pair of squirrels scurried over and sat on the picnic table benches, happily eating from the tray. It made me smile.

Good job, Harvey Johnston.

I kept walking past the shops and restaurants, enjoying the sunshine. Outside the Dame and Dapper Barber Shop stood Lola, a huge statue of a pinup girl. Someone had put what looked like a crocheted beard with little pink flowers on her.

At the next corner, Harvey had placed another squirrel picnic table between two planters. A single, rather round squirrel sat on the bench, enjoying its lunch. Another one scampered over and climbed onto the bench across from it, but the first squirrel wasn't happy. It made a noise that could only be described as a cross between a chirp and a bark, its fluffy gray tail flicking back and forth. The other squirrel dashed away, disappearing across the street.

"A little territorial, aren't we?"

It ignored me and went back to its feast.

I walked a bit longer, just to get my body moving, until I came to the Copper Kettle diner. I'd been there a few times and they had the best house-made chicken noodle soup. That sounded delicious, so I went in.

The clink of dishes and scent of buttery toast greeted me. My stomach growled at the smell of food.

"Welcome in. Just one today or are you waiting for someone?" the hostess asked. She had dark blond hair in a bouncy ponytail and her name tag said Heidi.

"Just me." I tried to sound chipper about that. "I'm alone for lunch, but not alone, alone, if you know what I mean."

Heidi hesitated with a menu in her hand, looking slightly confused. "Okay. Would you like a booth?"

I let out an awkward laugh. "A booth is great, thank you."

She led me to a booth and set the menu on the table. I slid into the bench seat and fixed my low ponytail, but didn't even look at the menu, already excited about the soup I was suddenly craving.

A few moments later, the server came to take my order.

"What can I get you?" she asked.

"Chicken noodle soup would be great."

"I'm sorry, we're out. We have a lentil soup or lemon chicken and rice."

My shoulders slumped a little. I'd really been looking forward to the chicken noodle. Bad luck strikes again.

"The chicken and rice is fine. And just water to drink."

She smiled. "I'll get that going for you."

"Thanks."

With a deep breath, I leaned back against the cushion. My eyes felt heavy again. It was so strange. I'd been working in bakeries for years. I was accustomed to the hours. Sure, I woke up early and was at the bakery by four—basically the middle of the night for most people—but I went to bed super early to make up for it. And I'd been living that way for so long, it didn't bother me at all. Why did I suddenly feel like I wasn't getting enough sleep?

The hum of activity in the restaurant was oddly soothing. The scent of food, the clink of dishes, the low buzz of conversation. I found myself staring at nothing, my head resting against the cushion. The booths in the Copper Kettle were awfully comfortable.

I wondered what Garrett was doing.

"Harper?"

The female voice startled me, and I opened my eyes.

Wait, when did I close my eyes? Sugar cookies, I'd fallen asleep.

I blinked a couple of times and Marigold Haven's face came into focus. She stood at the side of the booth in a lavender flutter-sleeve blouse with a cream-colored skirt, and she smiled at me with concern in her eyes.

"Hi. Oh my gosh, were my eyes closed?"

She nodded. "Sorry to bother you. We noticed you sitting here when we came in and I thought I should make sure you're okay."

Another woman stood next to her, dressed in a white blouse and gray pencil skirt. She had long brown hair in a ponytail and the friendliest smile.

"This is my sister-in-law, Audrey," Marigold said. "Have you met?"

"I don't think so," I said. "I'm Harper Tilburn."

"Audrey Haven," she said. "I'm married to Josiah, one of Garrett's brothers. It's so nice to finally meet you. I keep thinking I should stop at Angel Cakes sometime and say hello, but I didn't want to make it weird."

"Why would that be weird?" Marigold asked.

"I don't know. I'm good at making things weird."

"Me too." I liked her already. "Do you want to join me?"

"Do you mind?" Marigold asked.

"Not at all. I'd love the company."

The two of them slid onto the seat across from me.

"This is so serendipitous," Marigold said. "Audrey texted to see if I could get away for lunch today, and here you are."

The server came with my soup and set it in front of me. "That's hot, so you might want to give it a minute. Do you two need menus?"

"Yes, please," Marigold said with a smile.

She brought menus for Marigold and Audrey as I idly stirred my soup, not sure I liked the way it smelled. They perused the menus for a few minutes until the server came back.

"Do you need more time, or are you ready to order?" she asked.

"I'm ready," Marigold said. "Harper's soup looks good. I'll have a bowl and a side salad with the huckleberry vinaigrette."

The server wrote down Marigold's order and turned to Audrey. "And what can I get started for you?"

"I'll have the chop salad with chicken. And a side of waffle fries."

Marigold laughed softly.

"What?" Audrey asked as she handed the server her menu. "It's called balance."

"Waffle fries do sound good," I said.

"I'll share if you want some."

"Thanks." I blew on a spoonful of soup and tried a sip. It

probably wasn't bad, objectively speaking, but somehow, it wasn't doing it for me.

Apparently I'd really wanted that chicken noodle.

"So how are things at Angel Cakes?" Marigold asked.

"Good. Busy, which is great. I appreciate the job security."

"I hear that," Audrey said.

"What do you do?"

"I work for the local newspaper, the Tilikum Tribune. I know, you're probably thinking, wait, newspapers still exist? Amazingly enough, ours does."

"That's because you're brilliant and full of good ideas," Marigold said.

"You're so encouraging," Audrey said, leaning her head on Marigold's shoulder. "Everyone needs a Mari in her life."

Marigold smiled and gave her a side hug. "Thank you."

Watching them share a brief sister-in-law moment—one so clearly filled with love—made my heart ache. I thought about my recent conversation with Holly. She was definitely not the encouraging type.

But what if—

No. I needed to stop that kind of thinking. I hadn't been seeing Garrett long enough to think about what it might be like to join his family.

But sugar cookies, having Audrey and Marigold as sisters-in-law? Could you blame me for the tug of longing? I'd liked Marigold from the first time we'd met. And I'd known Audrey for all of five minutes, and I wanted to be her best friend so bad I was about to suggest we all get matching T-shirts.

That said Haven on the back, like jerseys.

Thankfully, I had to stifle a yawn before I could actually verbalize that awkward idea.

"Are you okay?" Marigold asked. The concern in her expression was back.

"Yeah, just tired today." I paused, because that wasn't

quite accurate. "Actually, I've been tired for the last week or so. It's weird. At first I thought I was coming down with something, but I feel fine. Just like I'm not sleeping well, except I am."

"Is it your schedule at the bakery?" Audrey asked. "You must be up early."

"I do get up early, but I've been doing it for years. I don't know what's changed."

"Maybe it's a nutrient deficiency," Audrey said.

"Could be."

"Or hormones," Marigold said. "Personal question, but is your period due?"

"Yeah, it probably is. I bet that's the problem."

"Do you usually get sleepy before your period?" Audrey asked.

I thought about it for a second. "Not really. I've never had a lot of PMS symptoms. I got an IUD placed about five years ago and it didn't change anything either."

"And you still have it in?" Marigold asked.

I nodded.

She raised her eyebrows. "Are you sure?"

"Yeah. Why?"

"Oh," Audrey said. "That could be it. Or it could be if, you know…"

My eyes moved between the two of them. "Why do I feel like you just communicated telepathically?"

"I just think I know what she's getting at," Audrey said.

"What are you getting at?"

"Well," Marigold said, her voice halting. "It's just that you shared something with me and sometimes that particular thing results in a condition that can make a woman very tired."

I blinked at her a few times, my brain not wanting to make the connection she was suggesting. Or maybe it was my heart.

Or my entire mind and body.

Because if she was implying what I thought she was implying, and she was right, I was in big, big trouble.

"Sugar cookies," I breathed. "You think maybe I'm…"

Marigold bit her lip. "Maybe?"

My heart started to race. "I mean, we did… But I have a… Or I did have… I haven't checked it in a long time. I told him… I thought I… Oh no."

"It might not be," Marigold said. "The thought just popped into my head when you said you've been unusually tired. I'm so sorry, I shouldn't have said anything."

"Harper, your face is getting very pale," Audrey said.

Marigold took my hands. "Do you think you might pass out?"

I did feel a little dizzy, but I didn't think I'd faint. I just couldn't believe what she was saying.

Except I kind of could.

In fact, as soon as the word had entered my mind, I'd had the distinct feeling she was right.

I had a feeling I was pregnant.

"No, I'm not going to faint. But I am freaking out."

"Here's what we should do." Marigold squeezed my hands. "Let's go find out for sure. Audrey and I will come with you."

"But you just ordered."

"We'll get it to go," Audrey said, her voice cheerful. "I can be a little late getting back from lunch."

"I have a client at one, but I can have Stacey call her and let her know I'll be a little bit late."

"I don't want to make you late for work."

"How about we do it at the bakery?" Audrey asked. "That would save time, since it's close. I'd suggest my office, but as much as I adore Sandra, she can't keep a secret to save her life. Oh, and I have tests in my purse, so we don't even have to go to the store."

Marigold's eyes widened. "Why do you have tests in your purse?"

Audrey's cheeks flushed. "You know, in case I need one. I figured I'd be prepared." Excitement lit up her features. "Ooh, let's all take one!"

"Do you think you're pregnant?" Marigold asked.

"Probably not, but that way Harper won't feel so alone."

I bit the inside of my lip—hard—to keep from crying. Were they for real? They barely knew me and they were willing to be late for work so they could take a pregnancy test with me?

"What do you think?" Marigold asked, her voice soft. "Do you want to find out for sure?"

Still chewing on my lip so the tears wouldn't spill, I nodded. I didn't know what to say.

I'd never been so terrified in my entire life.

CHAPTER 22

Harper

THREE MINUTES.

I stepped out of the restroom and nodded. Marigold set the timer on her phone.

Audrey and Marigold had both taken pregnancy tests too. They'd gone first, leaving them on the counter in the restroom. Marigold had put a red lipstick next to hers, and Audrey had used a hair tie from her purse to mark her test. Mine sat next to them.

I'd glanced at them all when I set mine down, and I was pretty sure theirs were both negative. The three minutes hadn't elapsed, but unless a very faint second line was about to show up, two out of the three of us weren't pregnant.

Was I?

Beth had peeked into the kitchen when we'd arrived. I hadn't told her what we were up to, just that I'd run into some friends at lunch and they'd come back to the bakery with me. That explanation seemed to have worked. Plus a customer had walked in, so she'd gone back to the front to take care of them.

"My tummy is nervous," Marigold said. "I don't even

think I'm pregnant, it's too early in my cycle. But I've never taken a pregnancy test before."

"I wasted one when I first bought these," Audrey said. "I knew I wasn't pregnant then, but I couldn't resist."

"Are you and Josiah trying?" Marigold asked.

Audrey pressed her lips together in a smile and nodded. "Are you?"

"We're not preventing," Marigold said.

"Oh my gosh, this is so exciting." Audrey clutched her hands to her chest. "We could all be pregnant together. Even if we're not now, we could be soon."

My eyes widened. "Um…"

"Sorry," Audrey said. "I got a little overly excited for a second."

"It's okay. You're both married and ready for this. And I'm really, really not." I sighed. "I never sleep with a guy right away. It's not my thing. But there he was and he just… And I couldn't help but… It was like…"

"Trying to fight gravity?" Marigold asked.

"Yeah, exactly. Is that a Haven thing?"

"Yes," they said in unison.

I sank onto the stool next to the island and picked up one of the pregnancy test boxes. "This is so surreal."

Marigold put a gentle hand on my arm. "Either way, you're going to be fine. Garrett is a good man. If you are, I know you two will figure this out. And if you're not, this will be a really funny story to tell him someday."

"Emphasis on someday." I set the box down. "I'm not about to run down to the sheriff's office to tell him I had a pregnancy scare. He'd probably never see me again."

"Of course he would," Marigold said.

I raised my eyebrows in disbelief. "That would totally scare him off."

"I don't think so. He likes you too much."

A little flutter of hope mixed with all the nervousness. "How do you know?"

"For one, he doesn't sleep with someone right away either. Not even when he was young. I've known Garrett for most of my life, and I've never seen him like this. He keeps his cards close, but this isn't just sexual attraction. Not for him."

"It isn't for me, either. That's part of why I'm so scared. What if we were meant to be and this screws everything up?"

"It won't," Marigold reassured me.

"I agree," Audrey said. "It might seem like the end of the world, but it won't be."

"You guys don't understand. I have really bad luck. That's probably what this is. My bad luck curse coming in full force to take me down."

When the timer on Marigold's phone chimed, the knot in my stomach twisted and my heart jumped.

"We'll go in together." Marigold reached for my hand.

I clasped Marigold's hand on one side, Audrey's on the other, and we wedged ourselves into the bathroom. It wasn't large, but it was big enough for us to stand in front of the sink. I kept my eyes mostly closed so I couldn't see the test clearly. Not yet.

I took a deep breath, and looked.

"Mine's negative," Marigold said.

Audrey let out a sigh. "Mine too."

"Oh, Harper," Marigold whispered.

Sitting there on the counter, right where I'd left it, was the pregnancy test I'd taken.

It had two lines.

Theirs each had one.

I was pregnant.

My hand trembled as I reached out to pick it up. I lifted it closer, as if looking from six inches away was going to change the result. Marigold rubbed my back, but didn't say anything. Neither did Audrey.

In shared silence, we walked out of the bathroom. I still had the test in my hand, but I wasn't really looking at it. I stared straight ahead, not quite seeing anything, while my mind reeled. Pregnant. I was pregnant with Garrett Haven's baby.

"Sugar cookies," I breathed.

"Hey, Harper."

My body went stiff and my eyes widened. Perhaps if I'd been in a clearer state of mind, I would have softened my expression as I turned my head toward the voice. But I wasn't, so I probably looked like I was shocked out of my mind.

Because I was.

Owen stood in the doorway to the kitchen. "Are you okay?"

I opened my mouth, but nothing came out. It took me that long to remember I was holding a positive pregnancy test in plain sight.

My pregnancy test, announcing the baby I was going to have with Owen's dad.

I hid it behind my back and sputtered for a second before actual words would come out. "Hi. What are you... What's going... Hey."

"Hi, Owen," Marigold said.

"Hey, Aunt Mari. Aunt Audrey. What are you doing here?"

Audrey started to say something but Marigold put a hand on her arm and spoke first. "We had lunch with Harper."

"Cool." He turned his gaze back to me. His brow furrowed and the fact that he looked exactly like his father when he did that did not make me less jumpy. "What's going on?"

"Nothing." The word shot out of my mouth.

His furrow deepened. "That's super sus, you know that, right?"

I let out an awkward laugh, hoping Marigold would step closer and take the pregnancy test out of my hand. "What? There's nothing sus."

"Okay, but you're acting weird. Did you get another murder bear or something?"

"No, no. No more murder bears."

"Murder bear?" Audrey asked.

"Long story," I said.

"What are you up to?" Marigold asked. "It's too early for school to be out, isn't it?"

"Half day," he said. "Dad's at work, so I thought I'd see if Harper needs help."

Marigold and Audrey's gazes swung to me.

So cute, Audrey mouthed.

I nodded, still about to die of nervousness. Or maybe it was terror. The empty pregnancy test box was sitting right in the open. Any second, Owen could look, and it would only take a moment for him to read it.

He'd know.

"So…" Owen took a step. "Do you need help today?"

The three of us spoke simultaneously, and unfortunately none of us said the same thing.

"Not today."

"Sure!"

"I don't know."

Owen looked more confused than ever. My stomach turned. I hoped I wouldn't vomit, but with my luck I was probably going to hurl all over the kitchen and we'd have to close just to clean it up.

His shoulders slumped a little and his dejected expression made my heart ache more than my stomach hurt.

"Wait, Owen."

As he looked up to meet my eyes, something seemed to catch his attention. His brow furrowed again.

Why had I left that box just sitting there, out in the open?

He glanced at me, then at Marigold and Audrey. "I think I should go."

"No!" I said, too fast and too loud. Marigold and Audrey looked at me like I was crazy. "I mean, you don't have to. We just need to… I don't know. Do something. Can you wait out front?"

"Is that yours?" He pointed at the box.

I let out a very fake laugh. "That? No. Of course not. That would be crazy. Audrey had them in her purse. Which is totally appropriate for the season of life she's in."

"Then why are you holding one?"

I'd been talking with my hands without realizing it, waving the test around. I looked at it like I'd just discovered I was holding a snake. With a yelp, I let go and it clattered to the floor.

"Harper." Owen's voice was earnest. "Don't lie to me."

My breath caught in my throat and my heart felt like it might burst. I stared at him for a few heartbeats. "I'm pregnant."

"It's Dad's."

"Yes."

"He doesn't know. Like, you just found out?"

"Just now. It's only one test, but it's positive."

For a second, no one moved. I could barely breathe. Owen's eyes were locked on the pregnancy test, his mouth slightly open.

What was he going to say? What could possibly be going through his mind?

He slowly lifted his gaze to meet mine and his mouth turned up in a grin. "Whoa. Can I have permission to swear?"

That almost made me smile. "Yeah."

"Holy shit," he said on a laugh. "You and Dad are going to have a baby? Do you know what that means?"

I shook my head in disbelief. "It means a lot of things, but I'm not sure what you're getting at."

His smile grew. "I'm going to be a big brother."

The dam broke. Tears flooded my eyes and I ran to him, throwing my arms around him. He hugged me back, his embrace tight and intentional.

"Owen, I'm so sorry," I sobbed. "I didn't mean for this to happen."

He patted my back. "It's okay. Don't be sad."

Sniffling, I pulled away. "I'm basically losing it right now. This is very unexpected. And sugar cookies, I'm setting the worst example. Let's pretend I've been dating your dad for a long time or we're married or something. And don't ask for details. I'm not telling you how this happened."

"Wasn't going to. And it's okay, you're not setting a bad example."

I took a deep breath, trying to get a hold of myself. "I don't know what this means right now. Obviously I need to tell your dad. And maybe stop freaking out first."

"Don't freak out. Dad's going to be fine."

I raised my eyebrows. "Fine?"

"Okay, he might freak out too. But only at first."

"Why are you so calm? Wait, because you're fourteen and you have no idea how much this is going to change our lives."

He chuckled. "Maybe. But I think it's pretty cool."

"You do?"

"Yeah. Being an only child is boring."

"Owen, you're so awesome," Audrey said.

He grinned again. "Thanks."

"See?" Marigold put an arm around my shoulders and squeezed. "You've got this. It's going to be okay."

I clutched my stomach. I didn't think I'd vomit, but I couldn't completely rule it out, either. "Okay, this is happening."

"Can you promise me something?" Owen asked, his voice softening.

"What?"

He hesitated, a flash of emotion crossing his features. It almost looked like he was holding back tears. "Just don't leave."

"Oh, Owen." I brought him in for another hug. "I'm not going anywhere."

He hugged me back.

I pulled away, keeping my hands on his shoulders as I looked him in the eyes. "I don't know how this is all going to work. But whatever happens, your dad and I are in this together. That means you too. Promise."

He nodded and I stepped back a little.

"What time does your dad get off work today? Do you remember?"

"Six, I think."

I glanced at the time. That gave me a little less than five hours to figure out how to tell the man I'd just started dating I was pregnant with his child.

CHAPTER 23

Garrett

THE HOUSE WAS QUIET, but my mind was not.

Owen had texted earlier in the afternoon to let me know he'd be at my parents' place. They'd offered to bring him home later, so I didn't have to worry about picking him up. That had freed up my evening, so when Harper had texted to see if I wanted to get together, it had been an easy yes. I'd invited her to my place so we could decide what we wanted to do from there.

I should have been thinking about where to take her, but I was stuck in an endless loop. Frustration ate at me. I'd never had disciplinary issues at work. I took my job, and the ethics required to do it well, very seriously. I didn't use my position to harass or bully people. I strove to treat people with respect, no matter who they were.

Maybe it was just bad timing. A coincidence. Matt had a personal issue, but it wasn't actually related to my job. He was just trying to get me in trouble. His call happened to come on the heels of a guy who would have complained about any deputy who'd talked to him that day. And the anonymous complaint was obviously bogus.

But why? Why had someone called in with a fabricated

complaint about me? It wasn't just that it was anonymous, it hadn't happened. The caller had said I'd pulled him over, made him exit his vehicle, and frisked him without cause. But I couldn't recall a recent traffic stop that followed that scenario.

My gut was telling me something was wrong, but I couldn't put the pieces together. Did the pieces even fit? Was there an explanation that tied the complaints together? Or was I starting to tread into conspiracy theory weeds.

Maybe I was just being paranoid.

I went to a cupboard in the kitchen and took out a bottle of bourbon. I didn't drink very often, but I wanted something to take the edge off. Especially because Harper was on her way. I didn't want to be so wound up.

Although maybe what I needed was her.

I poured two fingers into a glass and took a sip. It slid down my throat, warming me from the inside. I couldn't deny that just the thought of Harper coming over was already calming me down. There was a tug of desire, sure, but even more than that, the anticipation of relief. As if the moment she walked in the door—as soon as I touched her—the tension would melt from my shoulders and back.

She had that effect on me.

I was moving too fast with her. I couldn't deny that, either. And not just because we'd been sleeping together. The physical connection was only a part of it. I craved her. And instead of trying to maintain control, I was giving in.

It wasn't responsible. I had a son to think about. Sure, he liked Harper, but that didn't mean he was ready for me to bring someone into our lives. I wasn't sure if *I* was ready for that.

Would she be interested in something long term? Or was this just a temporary stop for her. Could she see herself with a man with a son—a teenager who still had a lot of growing up to do?

The problem was, I didn't know. And I didn't want to put that kind of pressure on her.

I pinched the bridge of my nose against the beginnings of a headache. I had trust issues. I knew that about myself. Harper hadn't done anything to make me doubt her. But trust didn't come easy, and I was letting this get out ahead of me before I could be sure it was right.

It was possible I was careening headlong toward a cliff and I was going to go down. Hard.

The sound of a car in my driveway got my attention. It stirred something in my chest, sent a pulse of anticipation through me. She was here, and I absolutely ached to touch her.

I was in so much trouble.

A moment later, there was a knock on the door. I tossed back the rest of the bourbon and went to answer it.

She stood on my doorstep, wearing a pink dress with a beige cardigan. Her long hair was down in soft waves around her shoulders and her lips looked so kissable, I almost devoured her right there.

But I didn't. I held back.

"Hi." She tucked her hair behind her ear.

"Hey." I stepped aside so she could come in and shut the door behind her. Although I could sense the cliff looming, I couldn't resist her. I slipped my hands around her waist and brought her in for a kiss.

The feel of her lips against mine was almost too good. The knots in my back loosened and the blissful relief of an addict getting a hit poured through me. I'd missed her.

Too much.

She pulled away and rested her hands on my chest. "It's good to see you."

"It's good to see you, too."

"I know we don't really have plans tonight, but I thought maybe we could… um… I don't know… Just hang out?"

"Honestly, after the last couple of days, that sounds great. Do you want a drink or anything?"

"I'm fine for now. But what happened? Did you have a bad day?"

I thought about pouring myself another bourbon, but she was taking the edge off more than a drink would. I took her hand and led her to the living room so we could get comfortable.

"Today wasn't terrible, but yesterday, not so much."

"I'm sorry. What happened?"

I sat on the couch and drew her in next to me. She smelled like vanilla and sugar and her body was soft and warm.

"It's kind of a long story, but I'm sort of in trouble at work."

"For what?"

"There have been several complaints lodged about me. One was anonymous and it's clearly bullshit. Another one I'm not sure about. Seems like a guy who's disgruntled over something. He claims I harassed him, but I don't know what he's talking about. The third was that guy, Matt. He says I threatened him that day at the bakery when he was creeping you out."

"What? You didn't threaten him."

"I know I didn't. And Jack probably would have just asked me to explain the situation and that would have been that. Except it was one of three. Now he has concerns. He's worried it's a pattern."

"But if none of them are actual problems, it's just coincidence right? Maybe even…" She paused. "Maybe bad luck?"

"It could be."

"Bad things often happen in threes. Except…"

"Except what?"

"Nothing. Three makes sense. You had three complaints, so maybe that's it."

"I hope that's it." I took a deep breath, relishing her scent, and rested my cheek against her head. "I've had enough."

She didn't reply and there was a stiffness to her body that caught my attention. I'd been so focused on myself and my day, I hadn't noticed it at first. But when I thought about it, she seemed a little off. There'd been something in her expression when I'd first opened the door. And when I'd kissed her, she'd felt as if she were holding back, not sinking into it the way she usually did.

"Is everything okay?" I tucked her in closer and caressed her arm. "How was your day?"

"It was… interesting."

"Interesting? What does that mean?" A hint of alarm made my shoulders tighten. "Did Matt come back? Did he do something?"

"No, nothing like that. I ran into Marigold and Audrey at lunch."

"Oh. That's… nice?"

"Yeah, it was."

"Have you met Audrey before?"

"No, but I basically wanted to be her best friend after knowing her for about ten seconds."

"Sounds about right. Most people like her. She and Josiah are such a contrast, it's almost funny."

"Really?"

"Yeah. Josiah's a good guy, but he's like our dad. Doesn't exactly show his feelings. And Audrey's, you know, Audrey."

"She was really sweet. So is Marigold. You must have such a great family."

Her voice broke a little on the last word, and I shifted so I could see her face. "Hey. What's wrong?"

Sniffling, she shook her head. "Nothing."

"Are you sure?"

"No."

"Then what is it? I can't help you fix it if you don't tell me."

"I don't think this is the kind of thing that can be fixed."

"What are you talking about? Harper, just tell me what's wrong."

Her eyes lifted to meet mine and they brimmed with tears. My chest tightened with panic. Who'd hurt her? What had they done? I'd—

"I'm pregnant."

I froze, my eyes wide, mouth slightly open. Had I heard her correctly? Had she just said—

"You're what?"

"Pregnant. I took a test. It was very clear."

My mind reeled. It was like waking up from a nap to find you're not in your bed, but at the high point of a roller coaster and the car just started down the track, leaving your stomach behind.

I couldn't seem to remember how to use words. I got up, as if moving would help, and walked a few steps, then turned around. "You're sure?"

She nodded. The tears hadn't fallen yet and she bit her lip like she was trying to hold them back. "I took a couple more tests just to be sure. And by a couple, I mean eight."

I rubbed the back of my neck, trying to get my head together. Harper was pregnant. It was mine. I'd let my animal instincts have their way, taken her up against a wall, and gotten her fucking pregnant.

"Please don't ask," she whispered.

"Ask what?"

"If it's yours."

"What? No. I know it's mine. I just wasn't expecting this."

"Neither was I."

I was screwing this up. I could feel it happening as she watched me process what she'd said. She wanted me to hold her. Gather her in my arms and tell her everything was going to be okay.

But was it?

This wasn't like me. None of it was. I didn't take sex lightly; I never had. I didn't sleep with a woman right away. I was careful. I wasn't spontaneous. I was organized, responsible, accountable.

Until I wasn't.

She stood and smoothed down her dress. "I think maybe I should leave you alone so you can get your head around this. I know it's a lot. I've been freaking out for half the day."

"Harper."

"No, it's okay. I don't blame you. You didn't want this. You didn't want a relationship at all. I remember."

"I didn't mean that."

"Yes, you did." She walked toward the front door, but stopped and looked over her shoulder. "By the way, Owen knows. He came to the bakery after school and saw the box of tests. I told him the truth. I had to."

It was like being hit in the gut when I was already out of breath. "Owen knows?"

"Yeah. So do Audrey and Marigold. They were with me when I took the first test. But they won't tell anyone yet."

I blew out a breath. "You don't have to leave."

"I think I should. I think you need some time."

I did, although I didn't want her to walk away. But I couldn't seem to make myself do anything about it. All I had to do was walk over there and grab her. Wrap my arms around her and tell her not to go.

Instead, I stood frozen to the spot, shocked into immovability.

"Take your time." Her voice was soft. "I'll talk to you tomorrow."

And with that, she left.

CHAPTER 24

Garrett

PREGNANT. Harper was pregnant.

I stood in my living room, staring at nothing, while those words ran through my head. I repeated them, over and over, as if I needed the repetition to wrap my mind around what she'd said.

How the fuck had that happened?

Obviously I knew exactly how it had happened. But I still couldn't believe it. Having a baby hadn't been anywhere near my radar. It had been clear my ex didn't want more kids, and I hadn't pushed it with her. After my divorce, I'd convinced myself I didn't want another relationship, so a bigger family was out of the question. I hadn't even thought about it.

The conversation with Jack had left me reeling, but this was on another level. I was so shocked, it was hard to think straight.

I shouldn't have let her leave.

She hadn't seemed angry. It wasn't as if she'd stormed out and slammed the door behind her. Her willingness to give me what she thought I needed—space to process this news—hit me square in the chest. That had been a sacrifice on her part. A big one.

Shaking myself out of my stupor, I went to the kitchen to grab my phone and called her.

Straight to voicemail. She must have turned it off.

Damn it.

Maybe she was right. Maybe I needed time to process this. If she'd answered, what would I have said?

I didn't know what to say. What to think. How to react.

The walls felt like they were closing in on me. I raked a hand through my hair and, without really thinking about it, grabbed my keys and headed out the door.

―――――

The next ten or fifteen minutes were something of a blur. I drove by Harper's house, but her car wasn't there. After that, I found myself at the Timberbeast Tavern without any clear memory of how I'd gotten there. Autopilot, apparently.

I got out of my car, wandered inside, and parked myself at the bar.

Rocco came over, drawing his thick eyebrows together. "Hey, Garrett. You all right?"

"Not really."

He grunted and poured me a bourbon. He wasn't the type of bartender to listen to your problems, but he was the type who remembered your drink of choice. I appreciated that.

"Thanks."

It was early evening and there were only a handful of people in the bar. Classic rock played low in the background and Rocco disappeared into the back. I took a sip of my drink and set it down, hunching over my glass like the grizzled old-timer down the bar from me.

Pregnant. Harper was pregnant.

My phone buzzed and I almost fumbled it onto the floor. But it wasn't her. It was my brother, Luke.

Luke: *Dropping off Owen at home. Where are you?*

Me: *Timberbeast*

Luke: *He just said that tracks. What's going on?*

Me: *Long story*

Luke: *He says he's fine by himself. Going to do homework. Good with you?*

Me: *Yeah, that's fine. Tell him I'll be home in a little bit. He can text me if he needs anything.*

Luke: *Got it.*

I was about to set my phone down, when I decided to try Harper again. As expected, it went to voicemail, but this time I decided to leave a message. "Hey, Harper. I'm sorry. I messed up before. I shouldn't have let you leave. Call me when you get this, okay?"

I sat in silence for a while, taking idle sips of my bourbon, not really tasting it. That cliff I'd been anticipating had been a hell of a lot closer than I'd thought. It still felt as if I were free-falling, hurling through the air with no idea how far it was to the bottom.

Or how much it was going to hurt when I hit.

What were we going to do? How was this going to work? What did Owen think about it? There I was, trying to set a good example for my kid, and I go and get my very new girlfriend pregnant. What kind of a father did that?

A hand clapped on my back, jolting me from my thoughts. Someone did the same thing on the other side.

"Hey, man," Luke said and took the stool to my right.

Theo sat on my left.

"What are you guys doing here? I thought you were dropping off Owen."

"I did. Then I came here."

I blinked, trying to clear the haze in my mind. It felt like he'd texted me ten seconds ago, but I'd probably been sitting there brooding for a while.

"Why are you here?" I asked, turning to Theo.

"He called me. Said he might need brother reinforcements."

Rocco wandered over and tipped his chin. "Drink?"

"We'll take a round of whatever he's having," Luke said. "Thanks, Rocco."

He poured their drinks and slid them across the bar, then poured me another.

"So what's going on?" Luke asked. "Owen was suspiciously not surprised that you're here, but he claimed he didn't know anything."

"Is Harper okay?" Theo asked.

"Yes. And no." I took a deep breath. "She's pregnant."

"Whoa," Luke and Theo said simultaneously.

"Hold up," Luke said. "Are you serious?"

I nodded.

"Pregnant?" asked Theo.

"That's what I said."

They both leaned back. Probably exchanging a look behind me.

"What happened to just seeing if you're compatible?" Luke asked.

"They were seeing if they're compatible all right." Theo made a circle with his thumb and forefinger and moved his other finger in and out of it.

Luke snickered.

I elbowed Theo in the ribs.

"What?" Theo did it again. "It's the universal symbol for discovering compatibility."

I glared at him.

He patted me on the back. "I'm just giving you shit."

"You forgot, Garrett doesn't have a sense of humor," Luke said.

"Yes, I do. But this isn't funny."

"I mean, it's kinda funny," Theo said.

I glared at him again.

"I'm not saying it isn't a big deal. This is huge. But if any of us were going to unintentionally get a girl pregnant, it's funny that it's you."

"Why is that funny to you?"

"Isn't it obvious? You're the boy scout. Always prepared, always responsible."

"You say that like it's a bad thing."

"It's not. This is just… I don't know, an amusing reminder that you're human."

Blowing out a breath, I shook my head. "I'm an asshole. That's what I am. I knew I was moving too fast with her. I knew I needed to hold back. And what did I do?"

Theo made the "compatibility" motion again.

I elbowed him. Harder.

He laughed. "Sorry."

"Unlike football brain over there, I think this is serious," Luke said.

My gaze shifted to him.

"Don't look so skeptical. I'm not going to make a joke."

I lifted my eyebrows.

"But I am wondering when you had time to make a baby with your busy crime fighting schedule."

"Crime fighting? I'm not a comic book character."

"You could be. You've got that Captain America thing going on."

"Except I don't think Cap got anyone pregnant," Theo said.

"True."

"You two are so helpful," I deadpanned. "I'm glad you stopped in."

"Hey, jerks," a voice said behind me. "What's going on?"

I glanced over my shoulder at my brother, Zachary. He strolled over to the bar looking entirely too full of himself. I smirked at the smudge of what looked like red lipstick on his upper lip.

"What's on your face?" Theo asked.

Zachary swiped his nose. "Where? Did I get it?"

Theo mimicked wiping his upper lip. "There. It's either Marigold's lipstick, or you should probably see a doctor."

Grinning, Zachary rubbed his thumb across his lip. "What can I say, my wifey is hot."

"What are you doing here all by yourself?" Luke asked.

"There's a bunch of girl stuff going on at home. I figured I'd give them space."

That got my attention. "Girl stuff? Is Harper there?"

"Yeah. Audrey, too. Wouldn't be surprised if Josiah shows up here."

Some of the panic hovering in the back of my mind eased. At least I knew where she was.

As if on cue, Josiah walked through the door, his red flannel and jeans covered in splotches of paint. He had wide shoulders and a thick beard—looked a lot like a younger version of our dad.

"See?" Zachary jerked a thumb over his shoulder. "Told you."

Josiah studied us through narrowed eyes, as if deciding whether or not he wanted to stay. He wasn't the most social of the Haven brothers.

"Audrey doing girl stuff?" Luke asked.

Josiah grunted. "She's with Mari."

"Come on." Luke nudged me with his elbow. "Let's get a table."

We moved to a table and Zachary bought drinks for himself and Josiah. He also bought me another. I was pretty sure that was a bad idea, but I finished off my other glass in one swallow and took it.

Theo and Luke exchanged a look and Luke shrugged his shoulders.

"What's that about?" Zachary asked.

"Nothing," Luke and Theo said simultaneously.

Zachary's gaze moved around the table. "Why do I feel like we missed something?"

"Why do you care if we missed something?" Josiah asked.

"Because I want to know what's going on."

Luke and Theo both turned toward me. Zachary raised his eyebrows at me, as if to say, go ahead. Even Josiah looked mildly interested.

I was surprised they didn't already know. They would soon enough. This wasn't going to stay quiet, and I didn't expect their wives to keep it from them.

"Harper's pregnant."

Josiah's eyes widened slightly, but Zachary looked like he might fall out of his chair. He slammed his palms on the table and leaned forward. "What?"

"Exactly," Luke said.

"That explains Audrey," Josiah said. "I knew there was something going on."

A big grin stole over Zachary's face. "Congratulations."

I stared at him. "Excuse me?"

"Congratulations, man. I'm happy for you."

My other brothers looked at him with similar expressions of confusion.

"What?" he asked. "I get it, this probably wasn't planned, but it's still kind of awesome. Finish that drink, we need another round."

"We just got this round," Josiah said.

He stood up. "I know, but we need to celebrate. Rocco! Another round for the table."

My brothers tossed back their drinks, so I went ahead and swallowed mine. It burned going down, but I was starting to feel better. Warm, loose, calm. Maybe even a little bit happy?

Zachary was happy for me. Could I be happy too?

That was probably the bourbon, but I couldn't help the half smile on my lips.

Theo got up to help Zachary bring the drinks over from the bar. They sat and Zachary lifted his glass.

"To Garrett and Harper. And to the crazy fucking curve balls life throws at us."

I could drink to that. I lifted my glass, then drank it in one swallow.

That one didn't even burn.

"Lissen," I said, vaguely noticing my speech was a little off. "Don't tell Dad and Mom yet. Or anyone."

"We got you, bro," Luke said.

"This wasn't supposed to happen," I continued. "I'm a cop and responsible father. Or I thought I was."

"That's why this isn't the worst news," Zachary said. "You're a great father."

I had the most insane urge to get up and hug him. That was definitely the bourbon. Instead, I lifted my empty glass, as if to toast again. "Thanks, Z."

"Need another?" he asked.

"Sure, why the hell not?"

"Rocco, my good man," Zachary called as he stood. "Another round."

My head was getting increasingly fuzzy, but I couldn't seem to make myself worry about it. There was a part of me, buried beneath the alcohol, trying to remind me that drinking lowered inhibitions and led to poor decision making. That while another drink sounded like a great idea, it was anything but.

Unfortunately, I was already too drunk to listen.

Another drink turned into two. Or maybe three. I lost track. We gave each other shit, like we always did, and laughed our asses off. I had no idea which one of us was staying sober or how we were all getting home.

Or maybe I was the only drunk one. That was a solid possibility.

They gave me crap about Harper, repeating the "compatibility symbol" with their hands. We teased Josiah and Zachary about going soft for their wives, but we didn't really mean it. There was something unexpected and a little bit awesome about seeing Josiah and Zachary both happily married.

If I was being completely honest, I was jealous.

I'd never had what they did, even when I *was* married. Was that what Harper wanted? Was I crazy for thinking about it?

Probably.

But she did something to me. Filled a void I didn't like to acknowledge. I'd fallen hard and fast for that woman, and maybe it wasn't the worst thing in the world that we were having a baby together. Maybe it was meant to be.

I picked my head up, realizing I'd put it down on the table.

"Come on, my dude." Zachary and Luke hoisted me up between them.

"I this got." I shook my head, trying to clear it. "I got this."

"Yeah, you do." Zachary draped my arm around his shoulders. "Let's go. Time for bed."

"Drank too much," I muttered. "Blood alcohol above limit legal. No, above legal limit. Too high."

"Definitely too high," Z said as we started to walk out of the bar. "That's probably my fault. Don't worry, bro, you're not driving."

For some reason, that made me laugh. "Harper's pregnant."

Luke held the door for us, and Zachary led me to his truck.

"I know, man. You can crash on the couch at my place, okay?"

"You got him?" Luke asked.

"Yeah. I figure we should spare Owen the sight of his dad

blind drunk. And if he passes out in the truck, he can sleep it off there. It'll be a warm night, he'll be fine.

"Sounds good. I'll crash at his house so Owen isn't alone all night."

"Good call. Night, Luke."

I lifted my hand, trying to wave goodbye, but it threw off my balance and I stumbled into Zachary. "Oh, shit."

"One foot in front of the other, my dude," Zachary said. "There we go, in the truck."

Somehow I ended up in the passenger's seat of his truck. I ignored the fact that my car was in the parking lot and that I had to work in the morning. Problems for future Garrett.

Although future Garrett was going to be pissed.

CHAPTER 25

Harper

MARIGOLD HAD A LOVELY KITCHEN. She didn't have
a stand-mixer, but that wasn't a problem. She had plenty of
ingredients, and mixing by hand was part of the therapeutic
nature of stress-baking.

After leaving Garrett's house, I'd intended to go home and
do exactly what I was doing at Marigold's—bake entirely too
many sugary treats. Which was fine. It wouldn't have been
the first time.

But Marigold had texted to see how things were going
and wound up inviting me over. Audrey had arrived just
after me, but instead of curling up on the couch and spilling
all my feelings over cups of tea—which had probably been
Marigold's intent—I'd asked if I could mess up her kitchen.

I'd promised to clean up.

I wasn't great at sitting still under the best of circumstances. Even less so when I was stressed. And right then, I
was a big ball of chaotic stress energy. My hair was twisted
into a messy bun and I wore a pink apron with a ruffle hem
that I'd found in the pantry. It was so pristine, I had a feeling
Marigold had never worn it, let alone splattered it with eggs
and flour.

The air was filled with the scent of the double chocolate brownies I'd already put in the oven, and I was busy scooping peanut butter cookies onto a baking sheet.

"Are you sure there's nothing we can do to help?" Marigold asked.

She and Audrey sat on counter-height stools, watching me work. I had no idea what I'd done to deserve them. They barely knew me and there they were, giving up their evenings with their husbands to hang out with me.

The least I could do was feed them dessert.

"No, I've got it. If I stop moving, I'll... you know, stop moving. Can't have that."

"I'm not even hungry, and those brownies smell so good I could probably eat the entire pan," Audrey said. "And then have some of those cookies for dessert."

"You really do have a gift," Marigold said.

"Thank you." I dropped another scoop of dough onto the baking sheet, my mind already contemplating what I might make next.

Or whether I should stop using up all Marigold's ingredients and get out of her kitchen.

I hadn't said a lot since I'd arrived, and they hadn't asked. I got the sense they were waiting for me to share, and if I didn't, they weren't going to push.

It made me want to trust them, even more than I already did.

That was a little scary. I was already feeling a vulnerability hangover coming on, the fear that I'd shared too much—and trusted too much—making me want to retreat into my own little bubble. As I worked, I kept having to remind myself they weren't my mom or sister. I wasn't going to get an *I told you so*, or a *now you're stuck in a dead-end life with that small-town guy* from them.

I checked the oven timer again. I'd only set the one, so I needed to be careful. I'd turned my phone off. Not so much to avoid Garrett as to try to avoid my bad luck cutting in. The last thing I'd needed was a phone call from my mom or sister, and with my luck, that's exactly what would have happened.

Better not to chance it. I'd talk to Garrett in the morning.

I finished placing the balls of dough and started pressing them with a fork to make the classic peanut butter cookie impression on the tops. Marigold and Audrey chatted while I worked. Something about the normalcy of their conversation and the repetitive motion of pressing a fork into cookie dough helped calm me down. I felt a little less frantic.

"Obviously I told Garrett," I said out of the blue. "He wasn't angry or anything. Just shocked. And of course he would be. I am too."

"I can't imagine him getting mad," Marigold said.

"No, he wasn't." I went to the oven and peeked at the brownies. They needed more time. "But the timing could have been better. He'd just finished telling me all about his work troubles. I kept thinking I should wait. It's not like I'm going to be less pregnant tomorrow, and maybe not dumping this on him when he was already stressed would be better."

"I wouldn't say you're dumping anything on him," Audrey said.

"Still. I was going to wait, except he could tell something was wrong. He kept asking what was going on and I just blurted it out. It was like he could see right through me."

"What did he say?" Marigold asked, her voice gentle.

"I don't remember, exactly. Mostly he was shocked. I didn't stay long after that. I figured he needed space to process everything. I'd already had half a day to start coming to terms with it. I thought I should give him some time. Although now I'm wondering if that was the right thing."

"I bet it was," Marigold said. "Sometimes space to process is what we all need."

"And you can come back together tomorrow with clearer heads," Audrey said.

"That's true. I already feel a bit calmer than I did earlier, although baking always helps." I glanced at the mess. "Sorry I used so much stuff. I'll replace it."

Marigold waved a hand. "Don't even worry about it."

"I'm sorry if this is awkward," I said with a soft laugh. "You two hardly know me, and here I am dirtying up your kitchen and using all your flour while I pour out my problems to you."

"Sometimes friendships can be instant," Audrey said. "And you just need somebody."

"Absolutely," Marigold said.

My eyes stung with tears. "You're both too good to be true. I feel like my bad luck is going to come crashing in at any moment and, I don't know, start a kitchen fire or something."

"Bad luck?" Audrey asked.

I took a deep breath. "I realize this might sound a little out there, but I broke a mirror six years ago and I've had crazy bad luck ever since. The weirdest things happen to me and I'm sure it's because of the mirror curse. I don't know why it's surprising that my birth control failed. Of course it did. That's my luck."

"Maybe it won't turn out to be bad luck in the long run," Audrey said.

"I really want to believe that. But everything feels like chaos." The oven timer dinged, so I checked the brownies. They looked perfect. I took them out and set them on a cooling rack.

"That's totally valid," Marigold said. "Be gentle with yourself right now. You just found out something totally life changing and you're not sure what it means for your relationship."

"I think it's all going to work out," Audrey said. "Garrett will come around."

"Are you always this optimistic?" I asked.

She smiled. "Pretty much."

"I admire that. I just keep thinking about the night he stood me up. My aunt Doris set us up on a blind date and he missed it. And I thought, this is good. The bad luck curse is always lurking, so I should just wait to start dating until it's over. Then I won't have to worry about what the curse will do to sabotage me. And what did I do? The exact opposite of waiting. I jumped in head first. And look where that got me."

Audrey picked up her phone and her brows drew in. "Um…"

"Is something wrong?" Marigold asked.

"Josiah just texted. He says, 'Incoming.'"

"What does that mean?"

"That's Josiah speak for 'Garrett is coming here.'"

A twinge of nervousness pinged through me. "Why would he come here?"

"I bet he's with Zachary," Marigold said. "He must know you're here and wants to see you."

I bit my bottom lip. Was I ready to see him? I felt like a mess. My hair was in disarray, I probably had flour on my face. I needed to put the cookies in the oven, but I had a feeling if I did, I'd wind up burning them. So I left them on the counter and turned off the oven. I didn't want to tempt my bad luck into striking again, especially in someone else's house.

A moment later, we heard the sound of a car outside. My heart sped up and my stomach felt jumpy. I had the urge to shove a bunch of peanut butter cookie dough into my mouth, but I stopped myself.

Marigold got up and went to the door, then paused. "Is that singing?"

Audrey and I shared a glance. After a second, I heard it too. Men's voices, almost chanting, as if they were singing an old-fashioned drinking song.

The door flew open and Zachary came in. Garrett had his

arm draped over Zachary's shoulders and he leaned against him, as if he were having trouble standing on his own.

"Squirrel, oh squirrel, high up in the tree," they sang together, "bury them nuts, but save some for me. Have a whiskey, have a bourbon, a scotch or a beer. But don't kick the squirrel, make sure the way's clear."

They both laughed hysterically, as if that was the funniest thing they'd ever heard. Garrett especially.

I met Audrey's eyes, confusion plain on my face.

"Old Tilikum drinking song." She shrugged. "I guess drunk lumberjacks don't make sense."

"Oh boy." Marigold ushered them in and shut the door behind them. "Scale of one to ten, honey. How drunk are you?"

"Zero," Zachary said, enunciating the word. "I can't say as much for this guy, though."

"I'm not drunk." Garrett stumbled. "Much."

"This is definitely my fault." Zachary patted Garrett's chest. "Sorry, gorgeous."

"It's okay," Marigold said. "Should we get him to the guest room?"

"I think couch is our best bet." Zachary's gaze moved to me. "Sorry, Harper. Didn't want him going home to Owen like this."

"Is Owen alone?"

"Nah, Luke's over there. He'll spend the night."

"Where we are?" Garrett asked, blinking hard.

"My house, bro," Zachary said. "Your girl's here, by the way. I know you're drunk, but maybe don't say anything stupid."

Garrett narrowed his eyes at me. "Harper?"

It was hard not to laugh. The straight-backed sheriff's deputy was nowhere to be seen. This Garrett had a lazy smile and looked like he might fall over.

He was so endearing, I could hardly stand it.

"Yeah, I'm here. Why don't you go lie down. You don't look like you're going to be able to stay on your feet much longer."

"Too much drank," he mumbled. "No. Drank too much."

"I can see that."

"His fault." He attempted to elbow Zachary in the ribs, but it didn't look like there was much force behind it.

I took off the apron and set it on the counter while Zachary led a stumbling Garrett into the living room. He collapsed onto the couch and Zachary picked up his legs, turning him so he was lying down.

"There you go, my dude," Zachary said. "Feeling pukey or anything?"

"No. I've got this."

"Yeah." Zachary winked at me. "You definitely do."

Audrey gave me a quick hug goodbye and I went into the living room. I lowered myself onto the edge of the couch and ran my fingers through his hair. Zachary and Marigold quietly went into another room, leaving us alone.

"Hi, beautiful," he said, his eyes half-closed.

"Hey, there."

"Didn't mean to drink so much."

"I know. It's okay."

"Tried to call you."

"Oh, I'm sorry." I didn't know if touching him was the best idea right then, but I couldn't help myself. I caressed his stubbly jaw. "I turned my phone off."

His eyes drifted closed, then opened again. "Worried about you."

"I'm okay. Are you?"

He gave me a very lopsided grin. "Yeah. Good bourbon."

I laughed. "I can see that."

"Harper." He opened his eyes wider, as if he were trying to focus on my face. "I think I'm in love with you."

Those words hurt. Not because I didn't want to hear them. My heart wanted to soar with happiness.

But I had no idea if he meant it. Or if he'd regret all of this in the morning. If he even remembered.

I put my finger to his lips. "Shh. Not right now."

"No." He grabbed my wrist in a gentle grip. "That's what's so hard. I shouldn't love you yet. Aren't people supposed to take it slow? Doesn't it take time to know for sure?"

"I honestly don't know."

His gaze locked with mine and his eyes were suddenly clear. "I think I've loved you since the first time I saw you."

A single tear broke free and trailed down my cheek. "You're not going to remember this tomorrow."

"I will. I mean it, Harper. I love you."

I leaned down and pressed my lips to his. I wanted to believe him. I really, really did.

But I didn't know if I could.

CHAPTER 26

Garrett

I WOKE up with no idea where I was.

Gingerly, I cracked my eyes open. My temples throbbed with a headache and my neck felt like I'd slept in a weird position.

Too much bourbon. Way too much bourbon.

I glanced around, my vision slowly coming into focus, and shifted with a groan. Zachary and Marigold's house. I was on the couch in their living room.

How had I gotten there?

Oh, shit.

I'd been drunk the night before, but not so drunk that I didn't remember. Zachary had brought me to his place and deposited my drunk ass on his couch. But that wasn't what had me groaning again. Harper had been there.

Not only had she seen me drunk—which, honestly, wasn't the worst thing in the world, I could admit that—but I'd told her I loved her.

I remembered every word of our conversation. How insistent I'd been that I was in love with her.

The tear that trailed down her cheek.

She didn't believe me.

What a fucking mess.

Oh, no. Owen.

My phone was on the coffee table next to me. I fumbled for it, almost dropping it on my face, and checked my messages. I had a string of texts from Luke.

Going to your house to stay with Owen.

He's good. Even did his homework already.

Morning, sunshine. Don't stress, Owen got to school. He's fine.

I let out a relieved breath. Thank goodness for my brother. He got a pass for his hand in getting me drunk last night. Plus, it had mostly been Zachary. Married or not, he was still a troublemaker.

I glanced at the coffee table again. Someone—probably Marigold—had left me a glass of water and a couple of ibuprofen. I sat up and took the painkillers, gulping down the entire glass.

Trying to ignore the pain attempting to split my head open, I got up. If I didn't get moving, I was going to be late for work.

I groaned. Again. My car was at the Timberbeast.

"Oh hey, man." Zachary came down the hallway, buttoning his blue flannel. "Glad you're up. Do you have to work?"

"Yeah." My voice sounded like gravel.

"Bummer. I can give you a ride to your car."

"Thanks."

He grinned at me as he rolled the sleeves of his flannel up to his elbows. "No problem."

"I should be mad at you."

"Yeah, probably. But we had fun, didn't we?"

I rubbed my temples. "How are you in such a good mood? Aren't you hungover?"

"I only had two drinks."

"Seriously? You just sat there and got me shit-faced?"

There was that grin again. "Yeah. It was great."

I rolled my eyes and hoped the ibuprofen would kick in soon.

"Do you have time for food, or are you in a hurry?" he asked.

My stomach growled, as if trying to answer for me. "I have time if it's quick."

"Good. I know exactly what you need."

"What?"

"Zany Zebra."

Okay, he was right, that actually sounded great.

The Zany Zebra was a burger and ice cream place in a building with, you guessed it, black and white zebra stripes. Back in the days of the feud, it had been Bailey territory. But their burgers were famous for being the best hangover food, so we'd found ways to sneak over there and get them without being seen.

Nowadays, the feud was over, and we didn't have to disguise ourselves just to get greasy burgers. Which was a good thing. I didn't have the energy for that nonsense. I just wanted some food—and at least a pitcher of coffee—so I could survive the day.

As I climbed into Zachary's truck, he handed me a spare set of sunglasses, which cut down on the stabbing pain in my head. We drove over to Zany Zebra and got our food. Not only were they famous for their greasy burgers, they were open early and you could order said greasy burgers any time of day. I insisted on paying, although one could argue he owed me for all the bourbon he'd plied me with.

I inhaled two double cheeseburgers on the way to the Timberbeast. Zachary dropped me off, telling me to have a great day and make good choices as I got out of his truck. He was such an asshole.

Have a great day? Who was that guy, and what had he done with my brother?

It was probably the wife-effect. He was so happy all the

time, his snark had been cut at least in half. It had happened to Josiah, too. He grunted less and smiled more since he'd married Audrey.

It made my chest ache. That had not been my experience when I was married.

Our side trip to the Zany Zebra had left me just enough time to swing by my house to change before going into work. I probably looked like hell, but there wasn't anything I could do about that. At least I wasn't late. I looked bad enough as it was. I didn't need another knock against me.

My aviators cut out some of the glaring sunlight as I drove to work and my headache was starting to ease. Thankfully I had an iron stomach, so that wasn't a problem.

What I was going to do about Harper was another issue.

I almost took the left that would have taken me past the bakery. Maybe if that wouldn't have made me late, I would have. But what was I going to say to her? As the pain in my head receded, the tide of overwhelm washed over me.

She was pregnant.

I'd told her I was in love with her.

And she didn't believe me.

Did I believe me?

I knew the answer to that but I couldn't deal with it right then. I pulled into work and parked. I needed to focus. Compartmentalize. I was good at that. Do my job while I was on duty. Put aside my personal issues until I was off the clock.

———

I did just that for most of the day. But walking out to my car after I got off work brought my personal life crashing over me. I needed to talk to my son. See Harper. Figure out what I was going to say to her—what the hell we were going to do.

I slipped on my aviators, got in my car, and headed home to see Owen.

This was going to be interesting.

When I walked into the house, I almost tripped over Owen's backpack. With a roll of my eyes, I pushed it aside with my foot. We'd been over this a million times. There was a hook for him to hang his things. But it was a battle for another day.

Or maybe I felt guilty.

He sat sideways on the couch with a mug of hot chocolate on the coffee table. A drip trailed down the side of the mug, but he'd used a coaster, so I didn't worry about it.

There I went with the coasters again. Where had I gotten that? From my mom?

He glanced up from the game on his phone and pushed his headphones off his head as I walked in. "Hey, Dad."

"Hey." I'd never felt as awkward around my own son as I did right then. "Sorry about last night."

"Don't worry about it. Uncle Luke said you were too drunk to come home and went to sleep it off at Uncle Z and Aunt Marigold's."

Closing my eyes, I pinched the bridge of my nose. *Thanks for that, Luke.* "Yeah. I had too much to drink last night. It was irresponsible of me."

"How bad is the hangover?"

"You're fourteen. How do you know about hangovers?"

"From movies and stuff. And Uncle Z."

Figured. "I'm fine. But we need to talk."

"About what? I got my homework done already. I did it last night too, even before Uncle Luke came over."

I walked around to the other side of the couch, moved his feet, and sat down. "Not about your homework. About me and Harper."

His mouth turned up in a grin. "I already know."

"Yeah, I'm aware that she told you."

"That's why you got drunk last night, huh?"

"Yeah, but... No. Owen."

"What?"

I groaned. "Just listen. Finding out Harper's pregnant might be freaking you out, and that's totally fine. It's unexpected for all of us and you can take your time getting used to the idea."

"I'm not freaking out."

"You're not?"

"No. Why would I be freaking out? This is awesome."

I stared at him. Was he serious? "It's awesome?"

"Yeah, it's great. I'm going to be a big brother. Harper thought I'd freak out too and I don't know why. I hope it's a boy. No, then he might be like Will. Then again, if it's a girl, she might be like the twins. Do you think it's twins?"

"No. I don't—I hope not."

"You have to admit, that would be cool. Emma and Juliet are fun."

His cousins were fun. The sudden image of a tiny baby girl in my arms almost sucked the air from my lungs. But this conversation was starting to go sideways. "I don't think twins are likely. And that's not what I'm concerned about right now."

"What are you concerned about?"

He had no idea. I had a list a mile long. "You, first of all. I don't know how this is all going to work out, but our lives are going to change."

"Are you going to get married? You should."

"Slow down, kid."

"I'm just saying, it would be cool."

I looked at him for a moment. He really was okay with this. There wasn't a hint of sullenness in his posture or expression. He wasn't worried, he wasn't concerned. He was just… happy.

"I'm really glad you like Harper so much," I said, my voice soft.

"Yeah, she's great. You did good, Dad."

Something about that almost brought the sting of tears to my eyes. "Thanks, son." I took a deep breath. "Speaking of, I need to go talk to her. Are you good for a while?"

"Yeah, fine. If you're going to be late, I can make a frozen pizza."

I shook my head. That kid. He was something else. I patted his leg. "Love you."

His brow furrowed—the look he gave me when he thought I was being weird. "Love you too."

I went back to my bedroom to change, then left again to talk to my newly pregnant girlfriend.

———

A zing of nerves swept through me as I walked up to her door and knocked. I wished I'd handled it better when she'd first told me about the baby, but there wasn't anything I could do about that now.

Except grovel and hope she accepted my apology.

She opened the door and I almost asked what the hell had happened to her. She had smudges of flour on her face and smears of something chocolatey on her apron. Her low pony-tail did little to contain the flyaways around her face. It looked as if she'd been caught in a windstorm.

But her green eyes were so big and hopeful, the ache in my chest almost took me down.

"Hi."

"Can I come in?" I asked.

She nodded and I followed her back to her kitchen. Suddenly, I could see why she looked like a mess. Dirty mixing bowls were piled in the sink and empty sacks of sugar and flour had fallen on the floor. What looked like a couple dozen cupcakes sat on the island, and a glob of chocolate frosting oozed out of a piping bag.

"How are you feeling?" she asked.

"Shitty, but I deserve it."

"You had a few too many. We've all been there."

"Harper—"

"Oh, no." She pressed her hands to her cheeks and looked around, as if just seeing the disarray. "I'm covered in flour, aren't I? I don't even know what I'm doing. Stress baking on steroids. What am I going to do with these?"

"Harper." I moved closer to her and just like that, I knew. How I felt. What to say. I touched her cheek and my confidence grew, my resolve solidifying. "Just listen to me for a minute."

She pressed her lips together and nodded.

"I'm so sorry for how I handled it when you told me about the baby. I was surprised, but that's no excuse. I shouldn't have let you leave. And I'm sorry I didn't call you today. I was hungover and I had to work. But really, I wasn't sure what to say."

"It's okay, I understand. I—"

"Shh." I put a finger to her soft lips. "I know what to say now."

Her eyebrows lifted.

"I love you. I meant what I said last night. I've loved you since the first time I saw you. And that's crazy. It's totally unlike me. I'm not a jump in head-first, be spontaneous guy. I'm a take it slow, be responsible and careful guy. Except when I'm not."

She smiled, and I took my finger off her lips and caressed her cheek.

"When I'm with you, I feel whole in a way I've never felt before. I can't explain it. Maybe it's crazy and maybe it's too fast, but I don't care. I love you."

Her lower lip trembled.

"It's okay if you can't say it back yet. I just needed you to know."

"I love you too," she burst out, talking fast. "Sugar cookies, it's so crazy, but I do. I love you so much I'm afraid I'm going to explode."

I slid my hands around her and hauled her against me. Our mouths met in a kiss, slow and deep.

"So we're doing this?" I asked when I pulled back. "We're having a baby?"

She nodded. "We're having a baby."

This time I didn't react in shock or, like an idiot, let her walk away. I let her words sink in. Really heard them.

And I smiled.

She giggled, a few tears breaking free from the corners of her eyes. I leaned down and kissed her again. I loved her. I really did. I loved her so fucking much, I would have died for her.

And she was having my baby.

Nothing was going according to plan. But for once in my life, I didn't want the plan.

I just wanted her.

CHAPTER 27

Harper

IT FELT good to be off my feet, even just for the short drive home. After another long day at the bakery, and my body busy diverting energy to growing the tiny one, I was wiped.

However, I did feel better than I had in a while. At least I was no longer freaking out. It wasn't that I was completely chill about being pregnant—that was going to take a while to sink in—but it no longer felt like an emergency.

Garrett loved me. That was all I needed.

I'd slept at his place the previous night, which had been wonderful. The only downside was having to peel myself out of bed at three in the morning so I could get to the bakery. That was considerably harder when I had a warm Garrett next to me.

Small price to pay for the best sleep of my life.

I pulled up to my house, making a mental note that I had a package at the front door, and parked in my garage. When I got out of my car, I cast a quick glance at the box still sitting on top of the murder bear. I probably needed to just throw it away. Obviously it was a harmless stuffed animal—no sign that it was coming to life at night—but it creeped me out every time I saw it.

The door to the garage led into the kitchen, and I flicked on the lights when I went in. I didn't want to forget the package outside, so I made sure to grab it. It didn't seem like porch pirates were a huge problem in Tilikum, but why take the chance? I wasn't even sure what the package was. I didn't remember ordering anything recently, but you never knew what late night shopping I might have done and promptly forgotten about. Especially recently.

I brought the package into the kitchen and left it there. I wanted to get out of my clothes. Garrett and I didn't have plans, which meant I was probably sleeping at my own house. That was mildly disappointing. I had a feeling we were heading toward a more permanent—and shared—living arrangement, but I didn't want to just move myself in. And now that I knew he was in love with me and I was in love with him, I wasn't worried about all that. We'd figure it out.

After changing into a set of silky pajamas—so comfortable —I debated whether hunger or fatigue was going to win. Flopping on the couch for a while sounded nice, but I was discovering that if I went too long without eating, I got a bit nauseated. I headed for the kitchen to throw together a small dinner.

I thought about Garrett and Owen while I browned some ground beef and added a jar of sauce, imagining what it would be like to be making dinner for the three of us—eventually four. It gave me a little burst of happiness, a bounce in my step despite my tired feet. Maybe Garrett would be prepping steaks while Owen chopped vegetables and laid them out on a pan. I'd be putting the finishing touches on dessert— that was my specialty, after all—and we'd wind up eating it first, just for fun.

Tears stung my eyes, but not tears of sadness, stress, or confusion. They were tears of possibility. Of the joy of a new season of life that I'd never even thought to wish for. Who would have guessed I'd fall for a man with a teenage son?

That I'd wind up pregnant with his baby and be dancing around my kitchen, daydreaming about making us into a family.

I did a twirl and managed to stub my toe on the bottom of the refrigerator door.

"Ouch!"

My toe throbbed as I limped over to a stool and sat. How had I managed to kick the refrigerator door? Who did that?

Dang bad luck curse.

My hand strayed to my still-flat belly. Despite the copious amount of pregnancy tests I'd taken—and confirmation by my new doctor that all was well—it was hard to believe there really was a baby in there. Other than being tired, and the need-to-eat-or-get-nauseated-thing, I didn't feel much of anything. I'd read that was normal, but I was starting to look forward to the growing belly, the flutters and kicks, all the things that would make this baby's presence known.

Garrett's parents.

Why they flew into my head at that particular moment, I had no idea. I hadn't met them yet. But that was the point—I was having a baby with their son, and we'd never even met.

What were they going to think of me? Would they like me? Accept me? Would they hate me for getting knocked up? Did they want me around their grandson?

Okay, so maybe fatigue and mild nausea weren't the only pregnancy symptoms I was experiencing. That wasn't the first time my mood had flipped like a light switch. Dancing in the kitchen in a blissful daydream one moment, panicking about meeting my baby's grandparents the next. Hormones were wild.

I got up to stir my meat sauce without the spaghetti. What can I say, it sounded good. It needed to simmer for a few more minutes, so I grabbed the package and a pair of scissors to slice open the packing tape.

It was a small box, maybe nine by six inches or so. The

label had my name and address, but there wasn't a return address at all. Where had this come from? Usually things I bought online had some indication on the box as to what store they were from.

Weird.

I slid the scissors through the tape and opened the box. It was filled with crumpled brown packing paper. I took it out and set it aside.

At the bottom was a pair of beige underwear.

Wrinkling my nose, I pinched a bit of the waistband to pick them up. They were sort of crumpled, as if they'd been wadded up and tossed in the box. That was so weird. It was just one pair, and although they didn't look dirty, they weren't in any sort of packaging.

What was weirder, they looked exactly like my underwear.

Same brand, same style, same size. I even had some in that color.

The scent of burning food wafted through the kitchen.

"Sugar cookies," I spat out.

My dinner was quickly getting overcooked. I dropped the underwear back in the box and hurried to the stove. Of course I'd been distracted enough to ruin my dinner.

Just my luck.

I turned off the stove and moved the pan from the burner, eying the package with suspicion. It was creeping me out. Why had someone sent me an unmarked box with a wadded-up pair of underwear?

They weren't sexy. In fact, they were so dangerously close to granny panties as to be embarrassing. If Garrett wanted to send me a pair of underwear, he wouldn't have picked those.

But why did they look so much like mine?

Wait. Were they mine?

Obviously, that was impossible. It wasn't like I'd ever left a pair of panties somewhere and a well-meaning townsperson had sent them back to me. And I was the first to admit I was superstitious, but that didn't extend to the belief that a pair of underwear could magically transport itself from my drawer and mail itself to me.

But the likeliest alternative was unthinkable.

Had someone been in my house?

My heart rate picked up as I walked to my bedroom. Nothing seemed amiss. There were a few items in my laundry hamper, including underwear. I opened the top drawer of my dresser and rifled through my bras and underwear.

Was anything missing?

I couldn't tell. There were a few other pairs of the same beige granny panties, but I didn't remember how many I had. Was it four? Or had it been five? Six? I had no idea.

Panic rose and my chest felt tight as I backed out of my room. Were those mine? Had someone broken into my house and stolen them? Why? And why send them back?

I was so not okay.

Hurrying back to the kitchen, I found my phone. I had the presence of mind to take a few deep breaths before calling Garrett. I didn't want to sound freaked out, especially if it turned out to be nothing. After all, I was super hormonal. Maybe this was just my imagination running away with me.

"Tiny one, are all these wild hormones messing with my brain?" I asked, looking down at my belly.

Talking to a baby that was probably the size of a pea? I was definitely not okay.

My hands still trembled as I brought up his number and hit send.

"Hi," he said, and just the sound of his voice took my panic down a notch.

"Hey. Are you at work?"

"Yeah, I'm leaving soon. Are you okay? You sound upset."

"No, no, I'm fine. A little hormonal is all. But do you think you could come over?"

"Absolutely. I miss you."

Oh my heart. "I miss you too."

"I'll be there in a bit."

"Okay. See you soon."

While I waited, I cleaned up the mess in the kitchen and nibbled on some cheese so my stomach wouldn't hurt. I didn't touch the box—just left it sitting on the counter. There had to be a rational explanation. I just wasn't thinking of it.

I heard his car pull up outside and went to answer the door before he had a chance to knock. He was still in uniform, looking deliciously strong and protective. The way he swiped his aviators off his face and smiled made my insides melt.

Despite the disturbing package on my kitchen counter, I couldn't help but smile as he drew me against him and covered my mouth with his. The gentle pressure of his lips and the brush of his tongue sent a wave of desire flooding through me.

No wonder we were having a baby.

With my hands on his chest, I pulled away, trying to unscramble my brain as he shut the door behind him.

"It's so good to see you," I breathed.

"You too."

He moved closer again, and as much as I wanted him to devour me, I shifted back a little. "I got a weird package today. Can you look at it?"

His brow furrowed with concern. And why was that expression so sexy?

"Where is it?"

"In the kitchen."

I recognized the change in his demeanor as he went from Garrett my boyfriend to Garrett the cop. "Where was it when you found it?"

"It was by the front door when I got home."

"Show me."

I led him into the kitchen and pointed to it. "There."

He reached into a pocket and pulled out a pair of gloves, then began examining the box.

"No return address and no postage. Someone dropped this off."

That was disturbing. I hadn't even noticed the lack of postage.

He pinched the pair of underwear between his thumb and forefinger to pick them up. "This was all that was inside?"

"That and the packing material."

"Do you recognize them?"

"Um…" I so didn't want to admit I had underwear that looked like that. But lying about it to save myself from embarrassment wasn't going to help. "I have some just like them."

His gaze swung to mine and although his expression didn't change, there was an intensity in his eyes. "These are like the ones you have, or they're actually yours?"

"I don't know. I checked my drawer, but I don't remember how many pairs I have to know whether one is missing."

He pinched the waistband with his other hand, holding them up so the shape was visible in all its frumpy glory. "But these are the same? Brand, size, color, everything?"

"Yes. Can we maybe not analyze my embarrassing undergarments this closely? I know we're having a baby, but I don't think I'm ready for you to know about my ugly granny panties."

He dropped them in the box. "Let's check your bedroom."

I let him go first and he moved slowly, looking around like he was taking in every detail. He paused next to my dresser.

"Which drawer?"

"Top one."

"Is it okay if I look?"

"Yeah, go ahead."

He opened my top drawer and I only died inside a little bit as he quickly found every pair of beige granny panties I owned.

"Five. Are there any in your hamper or the laundry?"

"I don't think so."

"Could this have been a pack of six? Or two packs of three?"

"I honestly don't remember. But even if the ones in the box aren't mine, how did someone know I wear those? You're the only one in this town who's taken off my panties, and I certainly wasn't wearing those." I lowered my voice and muttered, "Thank goodness."

"And you're not wearing a pair like these now?"

"No," I said, as if I were shocked and insulted. Which was so dumb. Obviously I owned them. It wouldn't have been a leap to find that I wore them sometimes.

He put the underwear back in the drawer and closed it. "Have you accidentally left a door unlocked or come home to find anything out of place?"

"I don't think so."

"Have you noticed anything unusual? Maybe something on the floor and you didn't know how it got there or something moved from where it should have been?"

"Nothing I can remember."

He put his hands on his hips and let out a frustrated breath. "Damn it."

"What?"

"I'm concerned someone was in your house. Do you remember where you bought the underwear? Could you look it up to see if you should have five pairs or six?"

"We're getting very detailed."

"Love, it's my job."

Oh my goodness, he'd just called me love. My insides melted into a swirly puddle of sugary happiness.

"Okay. Of course I'll look it up."

We went back to the kitchen and I grabbed my phone. I searched my email for the underwear brand and sure enough, the order was still there.

It had been a pack of six. And we found five in my drawer.

Garrett asked if he could look again to confirm. We searched my bedroom top to bottom. Every drawer, all through my closet, even in the bathroom. He checked the laundry room to make sure they weren't there, even moving the washer and dryer to look behind them.

Nothing. No more granny panties.

We went back to the kitchen and he took off the gloves. "You should come to my place."

I wasn't about to argue—any excuse to stay at his place—but I wasn't sure what was going on. "Why?"

"Someone might have broken into your house." He gestured to the box. "And whoever did it, wants you to know. You can't stay here."

It felt as if all the color drained from my face and the awful sense of violation made my stomach churn. I put a hand over my mouth.

Garrett pulled me against him and wrapped his arms around me. "I'm not going to let anything happen to you. I swear."

I nodded against his chest. I didn't understand what was going on or why, but I knew Garrett would keep me safe.

CHAPTER 28

Garrett

TO SAY I was amped would have been an understatement.

After helping Harper pack some of her things, we left for my place. No way in hell was she staying at her house. Someone had been there. Had taken a pair of her underwear and sent it to her.

Just like Jasmine.

Taking a girl's panties had the whiff of a prank to it. It was so cliché, it was almost silly. But this wasn't just a stolen pair of underwear. The fact that whoever had taken them had then left them outside her house seemed like a message.

I couldn't ignore the possibility that someone was out to fuck with me, and that someone wasn't Jasmine's killer. It had been all over the Tilikum gossip line that I was investigating the case. A person with a sick sense of humor might have decided to mimic the events leading up to Jasmine's murder, targeting my girlfriend.

The problem was, the packages Jasmine had received weren't common knowledge. Because the original investigators had written them off as unrelated—without confirming, which was driving me nuts—they weren't part of the lore of her unsolved murder.

And my gut was telling me this was no prank. It was a taunt.

My shoulders and back were tense as I drove. Harper was quiet. I knew she was worried, and the sense of violation that accompanied a breaking and entering could run deep. Our homes are meant to be our safe places. Knowing someone with ill intent had been inside her home—in her bedroom—was bound to make her unsettled at best. Terrified at worst.

The whole thing pissed me off. No one fucked with my woman.

I reached over, clasping her hand in mine, and she gave me a weak smile.

"Everything will be fine," I said, willing it to be true. "Whatever is going on, it won't touch you at my place. You'll be safe."

"Thank you. I'm just so confused. Who would break into a woman's house just to take a pair of her underwear—and not even the cute ones—and send them back to her?"

"I don't know."

I hadn't told her about the similarities in Jasmine's case. I'd been trained not to share details of the cases I was working on with anyone. Plus, I didn't want to scare her. Maybe I was wrong and there wasn't a connection. She had enough on her mind already.

When we got to my house, I grabbed her things and brought them inside. Owen was on the couch playing a game on his phone, but he got up as soon as he saw Harper.

"What's going on?" he asked.

No way was I telling Owen about the package. "I thought it would be best if Harper stayed with us for a while."

"Cool."

"Don't worry, I'm not going to take over your room or anything," she teased.

"I wouldn't want you to. It's gross in there."

"Maybe you should clean it up," I said.

He shrugged, like it didn't matter. "Dad, I think she should pay rent, though."

I shot him a confused look. "What?"

"In the form of cookies."

She laughed. "That, I can do. Should we whip up some now?"

"You don't have to do that, love." I wasn't sure why I kept calling her that. It just slipped off my tongue so easily. "You bake all day at work."

"Yeah, but I love doing it. Besides, I'll make him do all the work." She gestured toward Owen.

Then it hit me what was happening. They were bonding. My son and my girlfriend wanted to spend time together.

My heart just about burst out of my chest.

"Great," I managed, and my voice was only slightly rough. "I'll bring your stuff upstairs. I need to make a call anyway."

"Thank you," she said.

I moved closer and leaned down to brush a soft kiss across her lips. Then I lowered my voice and spoke next to her ear. "Don't say anything about the box."

"Wasn't going to," she whispered.

I kissed her one last time, and she laughed when Owen groaned with mock disgust.

"Okay, bruh." She headed for the kitchen. "What do we have to work with?"

I left them to their baking and hauled her things up to my room. I'd never shared this bedroom with anyone—we'd lived in a different house when my ex and I had split up—and there was plenty of extra space. It helped that I didn't have a lot of stuff. I was a pretty simple guy.

With Harper busy with Owen downstairs, I decided to call Jack. I needed to know what he wanted me to do about that package she'd received, and fill him in on its possible connection to the Jasmine Joyner murder.

"Jack Cordero," he answered.

"It's Garrett."

"Yeah, Garrett. What's going on?"

"You have a minute? I need to walk you through something."

"Sure, go ahead."

"My girlfriend Harper found a box on her doorstep when she got home from work today. No return address, no postage. Inside was a pair of underwear. It's very likely that it's her underwear. Matches a set she has and there's a pair missing."

"Huh. That's disturbing. Any signs of a break in?"

"No. Whoever did this got in and out and didn't leave a trace."

"Where is she now?"

"My place."

"Good."

I lowered myself onto the edge of my bed. "There's more. Now, hear me out on this, because I know it might sound like a stretch. But you know the Jasmine Joyner case?"

"Yeah."

"Jasmine received a similar package shortly before she was murdered. A box with a pair of her underwear in it."

"Is that in the case file?"

"Sort of. When her sister was interviewed, she mentioned Jasmine had received a couple of strange packages shortly before she disappeared. But everyone assumed they were from an angry ex-boyfriend. He had a solid alibi for her murder—he was in Alaska—so the investigators at the time assumed the packages weren't related to the case."

"How do you know they were Jasmine's underwear?"

"It's not something I can prove, but that was what Jasmine and her sister believed at the time. They were an exact match."

"Was she also missing a pair?"

"They didn't know. That would be hard to determine anyway. Do you know how many pairs of underwear you own?"

"Good point. I doubt my wife does, either."

"Exactly. But Jack, Harper is missing a pair. We're sure of it. When she bought them, it was a set of six, and we could only find five. We looked everywhere. Not only was someone in her house, they're possibly mimicking one of the precursors to a murder I'm currently investigating."

"And you think it could be Jasmine's murderer." It wasn't a question.

"It's a possibility."

He paused for a moment and I heard his long exhale. "I'm going to have Spangler investigate the possible break in at Harper's house."

"Jack—"

"Don't argue. It's policy. You aren't working your girlfriend's case. But I'll let him know about the possible connection to the Joyner murder. If signs point to this being the same guy, we'll need all hands on deck anyway. You'll be involved."

My jaw hitched. She was my woman, I wanted to be the one to investigate. But he was right, it was department policy. There wasn't anything I could do. And Spangler was a good guy.

"Okay."

"And be careful. If this is really connected, and I'm not saying it is, you know what it means."

"Yeah, it means a lot of things. It means the killer is not only still out there, he's still in Tilikum. And he's very aware that someone is looking into his case."

"It also means he's good. Not a lot of guys can get in and out of a house without anyone knowing."

"He's evaded us for a decade. He's obviously good at a lot of things."

"Indeed," Jack said. "I'll pass this on to Spangler and he'll be in touch soon. Where's the package?"

"It's on her kitchen counter. Her prints will be all over it. Mine aren't."

"Got it. Listen, personal question for you."

"Yeah?"

"Is Harper uh… expecting?"

My brow furrowed. "How do you know about that?"

"Rumors. Figured if she is, you should know people are talking. And if she isn't, same thing. You should know people are talking."

I blew out a frustrated breath. "She is. It's new. Damn it, I haven't even told my family yet."

"No one will hear it from me."

"Thanks, Jack."

"Sure."

He ended the call, and I blew out another breath, trying to stay calm. But adrenaline coursed through my veins and my mind raced. How had someone gotten into Harper's house without her knowing?

Even more importantly, who was it? Was it the same person who'd killed Jasmine?

It might not have been my job to investigate the break-in at Harper's house, but it was absolutely my job to protect her.

I went downstairs to the sound of laughter in the kitchen and paused at the bottom of the steps. I could just see into the kitchen from where I was standing. Owen was mixing something in a bowl while Harper leaned against the counter. I didn't know what they were laughing at, but it was funny enough that Owen had to stop what he was doing for a second. Harper clutched her stomach and tears ran down her cheeks, she was laughing so hard.

I grabbed my chest, like a guy having a heart attack. I wanted this. I wanted it so much, my soul ached for it. The two people I loved more than anything, laughing while they baked cookies.

It looked like a future. It looked like a family.

I'd given up on that. Pushed it aside, because I'd thought my chance was over. I'd married the wrong woman and that was that. Owen was the best thing in my life, and I'd never regret him. But I'd truly believed single fatherhood was as good as it was going to get for me.

But maybe, just maybe, I'd been wrong.

And I dared to hope that the three of us—soon to be four—would actually be able to create a family.

CHAPTER 29

Harper

THAT WAS IT. I was going to die.

Okay, I was being dramatic. But as I walked up the front steps of Garrett's parents' house, I was seized with fear. My heart thumped so hard I wondered if the glance Owen cast over his shoulder meant he could hear it. My stomach churned and the sugary scent of the too many cookies I'd stress baked was making me queasy.

Garrett's hand on the small of my back provided comfort, but not enough to calm the raging storm of feelings that swept through me in time with the beat of my jumpy heart. Fear, hope, anxiety, excitement, anticipation, curiosity, all swirling around with a healthy dose of sheer terror.

But it was good. I wanted to meet Garrett's parents. Sugar cookies, I was pregnant with their grandchild.

I just hoped they liked me.

That voice inside me was so tiny, and yet so deep—the voice of the little girl who'd just wanted to be seen and understood.

Garrett knocked twice but didn't wait to be let in. He opened the door. "Hey Mom. Dad."

"They're probably in the kitchen." Owen walked in

without waiting for any acknowledgement from inside the house.

I shifted the box of cookies as Garrett stepped inside, and, for a second, it felt like I couldn't move. I knew it was silly. That I was overreacting. This didn't have to be such a big deal. But in that moment, my fears left me frozen.

Please don't let my bad luck show up tonight. Please.

Garrett glanced over his shoulder and his eyebrows drew in. He took the few steps back to the doorway and grabbed the cookies from me. "You okay?"

My eyes were probably too wide, my expression a mask of abject terror, as if I were faced with a seven-headed monster, not an introduction to my boyfriend's parents. My voice came out in a squeak. "Yes."

His features softened, the corners of his mouth turning up in a gentle smile. He took my hand in his and led me in. "Don't worry. They're going to love you. Just like I do."

I let out a long breath and a little bit of the tension in my body melted away. "I'm sorry. I don't know why I'm so nervous."

He placed a knuckle beneath my chin and lifted my face to his. "Don't be. I've got you."

As his lips brushed against mine, I felt a little more of the fear recede. I was still jumpy, and concerned about how the mirror curse might make itself known in front of his parents, but at least I had him.

And he was everything.

He took my hand and led me through the entryway and down a short hallway. Pictures adorned the walls, reminding me that Garrett was from a big family. There were kids everywhere—mostly boys. I didn't get a good look at every photo, but the image they painted made my heart ache a little. They looked so happy.

Owen was already in the kitchen, his hands shoved in the pockets of his hoodie, chatting with his grandma. Marlene

Haven didn't look as grandma-like as I'd been expecting. Her light brown hair had some gray and she wore it in a cute bob. She had beautiful blue eyes behind a pair of blue-rimmed glasses, and wore a navy T-shirt and jeans. A far cry from a little old lady, she looked vibrant.

"Well, hello," she said, turning to me and Garrett with a warm smile. "You must be Harper. I'm Marlene. It's so nice to meet you."

Oh my goodness, she really meant that.

"Hi. I'm Harper. Wait, you already said that. It's nice to meet you too. Sorry, I'm nervous."

Her smile widened. "Don't be. I promise, we don't bite."

"Most of the time." A burly man in a red flannel came into the kitchen. He sidled up next to Marlene and spoke into her ear, "But only when we're alone."

"Paul," she scolded, nudging him with her elbow.

His mouth turned up in a sly grin. He was clearly Garrett's father. The resemblance was obvious, although Paul had a thicker beard.

"I'll pretend I didn't hear that," Owen said.

"Dad, this is Harper." Garrett set the box on the counter. "She baked cookies for dessert."

"Several kinds. And brownies too."

Marlene's eyebrows lifted. "That's very generous of you."

"I bake when I'm stressed," I said, then wished I hadn't. "I mean, I love doing it anyway, so I don't mind."

Paul opened the box and leaned in, inhaling deeply. "Garrett, you should stress her out more often."

I laughed softly and it broke a bit of the tension I felt.

"Don't even think about it," Marlene said. "Those are for dessert."

He was already lifting a chocolate truffle cookie out of the box. With a slight grin at his wife, he took a bite. His eyes closed for a second and he groaned. "Damn. Son, she's a keeper."

Garrett slipped his hand around my waist and drew me closer. "I know."

"What kind are those?" Owen asked, crossing the kitchen to look in the box.

"Chocolate truffle cookies," I said. "They have a crispy exterior and a soft, truffle-like middle. Very rich, which is why they're small."

Marlene shook her head in defeat as Owen helped himself to a cookie and took a bite.

"Wow," Owen said around his bite. "I think I like these better than the brownies."

"Yeah? I'm glad. There are brownies in there, too. Some with walnuts, some without. And classic chocolate chip cookies. Also some apricot thumbprint cookies. Those are grain-free, but don't let that scare you. They taste delicious."

"That's quite the assortment of treats," Marlene said. "Thank you."

"You're welcome."

"I hope you like chili and cornbread. I asked Garrett if you have any allergies and he said he didn't think so."

"No, no allergies. And I like just about anything. I'm not picky."

"Good." She smiled again and every time she did, my nervousness eased a bit more. "I guess it's not a fancy meal, but we're not fancy people. It will fill you up and make you feel good."

"That sounds amazing. And it smells delicious."

"Owen, can you help set the table, please, honey?" she asked.

"Yeah, Grandma, I got it." He peeled off his hoodie and took it to the family room where he tossed it on the couch. "Do you want me to pour water too?"

Marlene didn't answer. She just stared at him with a puzzled expression on her face.

"What?" he asked.

Paul's brow furrowed. "What's going on?"

"Owen," Marlene said, then hesitated.

"Yeah?"

"What does your shirt say?"

He looked down and grinned. "I forgot I was wearing this."

My eyes locked on his shirt. It was crisp white—looked brand new. And in bold, block letters across the front, it read, *Big Brother*.

"Um..." Marlene slowly turned her gaze on me and Garrett.

I glanced up at him, my heart racing again. His mouth was slightly open.

"Whose shirt is that?" Paul asked.

Owen looked down at it again. "Mine. Who else's would it be?"

"But it says big brother."

"Yeah," he said with a grin. "Cool, huh? There's a shop downtown that has them. I didn't think they'd have my size because most of them were for little kids. But they had this one in a large. It's kind of big, but that's okay."

Paul shook his head. "I don't get the slang kids are using nowadays."

"Oh, is that what it is?" Marlene asked, turning back to Owen. "What does big brother mean?"

Owen looked confused. "What do you mean, what does it mean?"

Garrett cleared his throat. "Mom—"

"Does it mean you're cool or the best at something?" she asked. "That's all I can think of. What do you think it means, Paul?"

"Hell if I know. Half the time when he talks, I need a dictionary to understand him."

"What are you guys talking about?" Owen asked.

"I think he means the time you said dinner was, what was

it… bussin'?" Mom said. "There was some confusion over whether that was good or bad."

Paul grunted.

"Mom," Garrett tried again, but Marlene kept talking.

"It does roll off the tongue nicely. Bussin'. Tell me if I'm using it correctly. Those chocolate truffle cookies are bussin'."

Owen chuckled. "Yeah, Grandma. That's basically it. But it sounds weird when you say it."

"So what does the shirt mean?"

"Owen, they don't know," Garrett cut in before he could answer.

His eyes widened. "What? Why didn't you tell them?"

"That's why we're here."

"Dad, I thought they knew."

"Tell us what?" Paul asked. He seemed to realize what was going on about five seconds before Marlene. "Oh."

"Tell us—?" Marlene looked at Owen's shirt, then her gaze swung to me.

"Mom and Dad," Garrett said, pulling me closer. "Harper and I are having a baby."

I waited for it. The shock. The anger. The pointing fingers, blame throwing, and shaming.

How could you?

What were you thinking?

How could you be so irresponsible?

I was completely unprepared for what came next.

Marlene gasped, covering her mouth with both hands. "A baby?"

Paul tipped his chin to Garrett. "Congratulations, son."

"Oh my goodness, a baby?" Marlene said again, her eyes brimming with tears. She walked around the counter, reaching her hands toward me, and drew me in for a tight hug.

For a second, I was stiff in her embrace. What was happening? She was hugging me?

She was hugging me.

I softened into it, wrapping my arms around her. Tears stung my eyes, although I was still too shocked to properly cry.

"I know, I know." Marlene let go and took off her glasses to dab at her eyes. "I'm too emotional. This is just such beautiful news. I had no idea."

"It's um…" I hesitated. "A little bit of a surprise for us too."

"Life is funny that way, isn't it? Don't worry, I've been there. My Reese was a big surprise. And by big, I mean all ten pounds, two ounces of him."

My eyes widened. "Ten?"

"I'd say don't worry, since he's not biologically related to Garrett, but wasn't Garrett a big baby, Paul?"

He shrugged. "Am I supposed to remember?"

She laughed. "I'm pretty sure all three of Paul's boys were at least nine pounds. Runs in the family. But don't let that scare you. This baby won't necessarily be bigger than average."

"I think I was almost ten pounds," Owen said. "Wasn't I, Dad?"

"Ten pounds exactly," Garrett said.

I didn't know if I was more shocked at the sudden talk of ten-pound newborns and what that might mean for my body, or the fact that no one was lecturing me about how I'd ruined everyone's life.

They were happy about this?

Were they for real?

"Come on, let's eat." Marlene took my hands and led me toward the dining room. "How are you feeling? Are you sure chili is okay? If you're having heartburn, I can get you something else. It's not terribly spicy, but it might aggravate things."

"No, I feel fine. Just tired, mostly. No heartburn."

"If dinner doesn't smell good or taste good or anything, don't be afraid to speak up. I had food aversions with one of my pregnancies and it was terrible. Don't worry, I won't take it personally. I've been there." She pointed at a chair. "You can sit here."

"Thank you."

Owen was busy setting the table and Garrett stepped in to help. I felt weird sitting down before everyone was ready, but Marlene insisted they had everything under control. Paul brought in the chili, and if I was going to have any food aversions, I sure hoped it wouldn't be that night. It smelled fantastic.

Garrett sat beside me, with Owen across from us and Paul and Marlene at each end. We all dished up and started eating.

The topic of my pregnancy took a back seat. Owen had a lot to say about school. They were studying astronomy in science class and he was currently fascinated by black holes. We got quite the interesting explanation, and he was particularly excited to tell us about spaghettification. It sounded like something out of a horror movie to me, but apparently being stretched into a noodle shape was fascinating to his teenage-boy mind.

Owen might have been fascinated by black holes, but I was fascinated by Garrett's parents. By Paul's covert wink at his wife. By Marlene's knowing smile at her husband. The way they'd moved around the kitchen together, a subtle harmony of familiarity.

They were in love. You could see it, plain as day. They weren't putting on a show or trying to act differently because someone was watching. It was real.

It was so beautiful, it made my heart ache. I'd never seen anything like it. As far as I knew, my mother hadn't been in love with either of the men who'd fathered her daughters. And my aunt Doris had never been married. My grandfather had died when I was little, so I didn't remember seeing him with my grandmother.

Garrett's hand rested on my thigh while we ate. He gave me a little squeeze and when he turned to me, the corners of his mouth lifted. Our eyes locked and I searched his. We'd said it. We'd both admitted we were in love with each other. Was it that kind of love? The kind that survived all the craziness of life Paul and Marlene must have experienced?

I hoped so. I wanted it more than I'd ever wanted anything. Even more than I'd wanted the mirror curse to finally end.

I wanted this. I wanted Garrett, and Owen, and this baby. I had no idea what I was really in for—I had no experience with babies—but I knew I wanted it all anyway.

A little voice whispered in the back of my head, reminding me of the package. And the murder bear. About someone breaking into my house and going through my things. I was staying at Garrett's house, not because I was having his baby, but because something weird was going on and he didn't think I was safe.

And I started to worry that my mirror curse was going to show up in a big way and I'd be left grasping for a life I'd almost been able to touch.

CHAPTER 30

Garrett

NODDING ALONG, I listened to Mr. Bakerfield's story. He was a longtime Tilikum resident, in his seventies, and had cornered me in line at the Steaming Mug. Although it was my day off, I decided to give him my ear. He'd claimed to have information about the Joyner murder.

So did half the town. But so far, none of them actually did. Ever since word had gotten out that I was investigating the cold case, we'd been getting calls. Mostly they were people who wanted to recount their memories of the case or who had an insatiable urge to insert themselves into the drama by claiming to have information.

Part of my job was following up on every one of them.

"So that's how it happened," Mr. Bakerfield said. "They found her near that trail. Looked like she'd been strangled."

"Right." He'd just given me a loose overview of the case as most people had understood it, based on the reports in the local newspaper. "Is that all?"

He took a deep breath and gazed into the distance. "I think so. If memory serves."

"Got it. Okay, thanks for your time."

"Thank *you*, deputy. We appreciate you working on this case. It's high time the killer came to justice."

"Agreed."

With a solemn nod, he got up. I took a sip of my now lukewarm coffee, wishing I could get that last half hour back.

Since I'd already spent the morning recounting the public details of the case, I decided to go through with my plans for some off-duty investigating. I wanted to check out the area where I'd found the bracelet. I didn't think I'd necessarily uncover new evidence. But I wanted to walk the woods, see if I could make sense of why Jasmine might have been out there.

The door opened and my brother Luke wandered in. I hadn't seen him since the night at the Timberbeast. He tipped his chin and came over to take the now empty chair across from me.

"What are you up to?" I asked.

"Just grabbing some coffee. Day off or are you working undercover or something?" He gestured to my plain clothes.

"Day off."

A couple walked toward the door, arm in arm. I'd seen them around, but didn't remember their names off the top of my head.

"Good luck with your case, deputy," the man said.

I nodded to him. "Thanks."

"I guess you couldn't work undercover in this town," Luke observed. "Everybody knows you."

"Yeah. By the way, thanks again for staying with Owen the other night."

"No problem. Where is he today? Still in school?"

"Yeah, he has a few more days left before summer break."

"How'd you end up with such a good kid, anyway? If I ever have kids, I'm making you put me through your masterclass."

"Sometimes I think he's a good kid despite having me as a parent."

"Don't sell yourself short. You must have done something right. Let's be honest, we both know it wasn't his mother."

"No shit."

"Did you talk to Mom and Dad yet?"

"Yeah. They took it well."

"Sounds about right. I think Mom was starting to worry she wasn't going to get any more grandchildren."

"I don't think that's going to be a problem."

"Probably not."

The door opened and my aunt Louise came in, dressed in a pastel blue tracksuit with a string of pearls around her neck.

Luke twisted around to look and his head whipped back toward me. "That's my cue to go."

He stood, holding up his hand in an attempt to cover his face. But luck was not on his side. I smirked as Aunt Louise caught sight of him, her eyes lighting up and a broad smile crossing her face.

"Luke!" She held out her arms and moved toward him. "Honey, it's good to see you."

He gave her a quick hug. "Hi, Aunt Louise. I was just leaving."

"Don't be silly." Her eyes moved to me. "Well, look at this. Perfect. Come on, honey, sit down."

Aunt Louise helped herself to a chair from another table and pulled it over to mine. Luke looked defeated as he slumped into the seat across from me.

I watched with amusement. I knew the fear of being subjected to Aunt Louise's matchmaking scrutiny. But I was safe from all that now.

Luke, not so much.

"Hear me out," Louise said. "I know someone who's perfect for you. Absolutely perfect."

"Thanks, Aunt Louise, but you don't have to do that."

"Of course I do. It's my job. She's a teacher, very sweet. Just got out of a long-term relationship, so the timing is ideal."

Luke raised his eyebrows. "Ideal timing? Just out of a long-term relationship does not sound like ideal timing. It sounds like a rebound."

"Rebounds are a myth, dear. Many a couple has found love on the edge of heartbreak."

"That's very poetic, but I don't think so."

"C'mon, Luke," I said. "Fresh out of a breakup, maybe pining for her ex? Sounds like she's right up your alley."

He shot me a glare.

But I wasn't wrong. Luke had a tendency to only want women who were so obviously wrong for him, anyone could see it. Not that I had a lot of room to talk. But I'd only made that mistake once. Granted, I'd married her, and Luke had never gone that far.

Still, what guy would pass up the chance to give his brother shit, especially about women?

"Aunt Louise set me up with Harper," I said. "I think you should trust her."

His forehead tightened and he leaned forward. "Garrett, we're going to be late."

"Late for what?"

"You know, the thing I was going to help you with."

Aunt Louise smiled at us both.

I decided to have pity on Luke. Repay him for staying with Owen the other night when I was too drunk to go home.

"Oh yeah. I do need your help with that, and time is ticking. Good to see you, Aunt Louise. I'm sure Luke will think about it."

He shook his head as we both stood. "I'm not going to think about it."

Louise gathered up her handbag and wiggled her fingers at us. "See you later, boys. Luke, I'll be talking to you soon."

"Great, Aunt Louise, thanks," Luke said with a very fake smile.

I followed him out and he glanced back at the door, as if worried Aunt Louise wouldn't let him go.

"She's our aunt, and I love her, but no. Just, no."

I chuckled. "You didn't even get your coffee."

"Yeah, whatever."

Luke's get-out-of-there excuse got me thinking. Maybe I could use another set of eyes. Unofficially, of course.

"Are you busy?" I asked.

"I need to get back to the garage at some point. Why, what do you need?"

"I'm going to take a look at something. It's related to the cold case. Another set of eyes might not be a bad idea."

"Cop stuff? Hell yeah, let's do it."

We loaded into my SUV and I gave him the rundown on the way to the trailhead.

"I found a bracelet when I was investigating another crime. Turns out it matches the bracelet Jasmine Joyner was wearing when she disappeared. It's not much of a lead in and of itself, but it's how I got on the case in the first place."

"Got it."

"What's bugging me is the location. The original investigators assumed Jasmine had been abducted off the trail, pulled into the woods, killed, and left there. If that's the case, why was her bracelet somewhere else?"

"So what are we looking for? It's been ten years."

"I don't know. I don't think we're going to stumble on new evidence, I just want to get the lay of the land. See it for myself. It might spark something. And like I said, another set of eyes can't hurt."

"So I know I can't carry your gun, but what about a taser? You got an extra one of those?"

I gave him the side eye. "No."

"Why not? We're tracking a killer here."

"No tasers."

"You're no fun. You ever been hit by a taser?"

I nodded. "In training."

"Did it hurt?"

I glanced at him again. "Yes. It really fucking hurts."

"I almost made a bet with Evan Bailey that I could take a taser and not scream. He didn't believe me."

"Don't take that bet. Some of the toughest guys I know screamed."

"I said almost."

"Why would you even be talking about that?"

He shrugged. "I don't remember. There were a few beers involved."

"Sounds about right."

I pulled into the parking lot at the trailhead. There were quite a few cars, but I found a spot. We got out and started walking.

The air was still, the woods quiet except for the occasional bird call and the sound of our shoes. Squirrels darted out of the way, scurrying up tree trunks as we hiked off trail and made our way up a low rise.

I purposefully didn't tell Luke about the package Harper had received, or its possible connection to the Joyner case. Deputy Spangler had taken over investigating the break-in at her house, but so far, it looked like a dead end. She didn't have a doorbell camera and none of her neighbors had one that showed her driveway or front door. No one in the neighborhood remembered seeing someone drop off a package and there was no physical evidence of a break-in.

Whoever had done it was good. They hadn't left a shred of evidence.

Was it the same person who'd sent Jasmine a similar package? Had he then killed her?

I didn't know. But I was going to find him before this escalated.

Nothing was going to happen to Harper.

I stopped roughly where I found the bracelet. The stolen car was long gone. The bracelet itself was still in evidence, added to everything that had been collected in the case.

"This is it?" Luke asked.

"Yeah, the bracelet was over there." I pointed to the ground. "I don't know why she would have been here."

"Hiking off trail?"

"Maybe. But her body was found out that way." I pointed again. "Near a completely different trail."

"What if the bracelet wasn't hers?"

"That's possible. But my gut tells me it was. That she was here."

I pulled out my phone and opened a map. I'd already dropped a pin where Jasmine's body had been found and I marked the spot where Luke and I were standing for reference.

"Was she a hiker?" Luke asked.

"The case file says she liked to go for walks. But she wasn't described as a hiker. She was found wearing regular tennis shoes, not hiking boots. But the trail where she was found is pretty flat. Her shoes didn't raise any red flags at the time."

"But what do you think?"

"I think she was abducted somewhere else. The killer wasn't lurking in the woods, waiting to grab the first woman who was hiking alone. He chose her. There's evidence that he might have engaged in stalking behavior before he killed her. I think he grabbed her, subdued her, and brought her somewhere. Then he left her body near that trail. Made it look like it was a random attack."

"Which could be why her bracelet was here."

"Trent Jones got a stolen car out here. Allegedly," I added with a roll of my eyes. "But you wouldn't be able to see a vehicle from the parking area. The killer could have abducted her, driven her out here, then taken her somewhere. And her bracelet fell off in the process."

"Was this area searched at the time?"

"Not well. She was last seen at home, and like I said, no reason to think she'd have been in the woods. A hiker found her body." I checked my map and glanced around again. "Let's go that way. It's not a direct line to the location of her body, but we can always double back."

"Lead the way."

We started walking and it wasn't far before the pine trees got thicker. I scanned the area, not sure what I was looking for. Anything, really. Something the original investigators hadn't thought about or had missed.

"Her time of death is a question as well," I said as we walked. It wasn't that Luke needed all the details, but talking it out might help me put pieces together. "Determining time of death is as much an art as it is a science, so it's not always as accurate as we want."

"So you don't think it was accurate?"

"It just didn't have a lot of detail. Makes me wonder if something was missed. We don't even know for sure when she was abducted. She lived alone. Her sister reported her missing, but we don't actually know how long she'd been gone before that report."

"Which means the killer could have had her longer than they assumed."

"Exactly. The whole random act of violence on a hiking trail theory seems to work until you dig a little deeper."

A squirrel scampered down a tree trunk and stopped in front of us, as if hoping we were going to pause to give it a snack.

"Sorry, little guy." I patted my pockets as we walked by. "I don't have anything for you."

"He looks crushed," Luke said.

"I'm sure he'll be fine. I don't think any of the Tilikum squirrels are underfed."

We hiked up another rise and the trees opened up into a clearing, revealing the crumbling remains of an old barn. The wood panels were grayed with age and exposure to the weather and there was a tree growing in the middle of it, the branches reaching up through gaping holes in the roof. One wall was caved in, leaving the whole thing looking lopsided.

"I feel like I've been out here before." He pointed to a makeshift fire pit near the barn. It was mostly old coals with a few charred beer cans in the rubble. "Yep. We used to party out here sometimes."

"I thought you guys used to party down by the river."

"We did that too."

I kicked an old beer can as we walked around the barn. There were a few party spots local teenagers liked to use. They tended to rotate so guys like me wouldn't find them.

On the far side of the barn, the ground sloped up again and a faded wooden door was built right into the hillside.

"What's that?" Luke asked.

"Probably an old root cellar. They were common back in the day. Not many of them left."

"Who do you think owns it?"

"I don't know." I approached the door. It had an old padlock on it. "I thought this was all county land out here, but maybe it's private. I'll have to do some digging."

"Abandoned root cellar would be a good place to hide a victim."

"Yeah." I wiggled the lock, but it was on tight.

"We can't just open it, can we?"

"Nope. I need a warrant."

"That sucks. I mean, it doesn't. Property rights and all that. But I'd love to see what's inside."

"You and me both. Although for all we know, it's either

empty or just full of cigarettes and booze the high school kids stashed out here."

"Reminds me of that old hunter's cabin we used to use. Not for cigarettes and booze, but, you know…" He grinned.

I did know. The roof had leaked and one window had been broken, but we'd cleaned it up enough to make it a great spot to be alone with a girl. At least by our teenage standards. We'd put a lock on the door, too. Not because we kept anything there, but to keep our rivals, the Bailey brothers, out.

"If I get a judge to grant me a warrant and all I find in there is an expired box of condoms, I'm gonna be pissed."

Luke laughed. "I wouldn't be surprised."

We left the locked root cellar and continued our search, but didn't find anything. Just pine needles and a squirrel who yelled at us from its spot on a tree branch. Luke had to get back to his garage, so we called it a day and hiked back to my SUV.

———

The next day, I was back on patrol. And I was irritated. My morning had consisted of talking a guy out of setting his neighbor's hay bales on fire over the outcome of a poker game, responding to a noise complaint that turned out to be the guy's own TV on upstairs, and investigating a report of a stolen phone that I found under the passenger's seat of his car.

Yes, it was all my job. But I wanted to be working on the cold case.

On my way down the highway, I did stop and help a woman with a flat tire. That at least had felt worthwhile.

Brenna came on over the radio. "Squad seven."

"Go ahead, Bren."

"Can you take a trespassing call at 255 Wildrose Lane?"

I wasn't far from there. "10-4."

"Homeowner is out of town but someone drove by, I guess to check on it. Thinks they saw someone lurking around the outbuildings."

"That's the old Pine place, isn't it?"

"I believe so. Rich Pine?"

"Sounds right. It's probably just Harvey Johnston getting lost again, but I'll go check it out."

Rich Pine had been friends with my dad for years. He was a nice enough guy, but he had a thing for collecting old junk. His house was on the outskirts of town, on a plot of acreage that he'd managed to fill with stuff.

I drove down the long dirt road that led to his property. He didn't have any neighbors within sight, which was probably how he got away with his land looking like a junkyard. His house wasn't in bad shape and the front yard wasn't exactly clear of clutter, but it was mostly rusty odds and ends that he'd crafted into yard art.

Behind the house, however, were several outbuildings and a winding maze of junk. Rusted out cars that probably hadn't moved in decades, old farm equipment, tires, stacks of pallets and scrap wood, and an ancient fire truck that, cleaned up, probably belonged in a museum.

"Squad seven," I said into my radio.

"Go ahead, squad seven," Brenna answered.

"Put me at 255 Wildrose Lane. Going in to have a look around."

"10-4."

There wasn't a fence or anything to block my access, so I headed back into the mess. There was a vintage gas pump and a stack of old road signs. A pile of railroad ties and a collection of rusty bicycles. Some of it probably had value, especially for someone who would take the time to restore it, but most of the stuff looked like garbage.

Near the largest outbuilding was what looked like a late sixties Chevrolet truck. Luke was the car expert, not me, but I wondered if he knew Rich had it. Looked like the sort of thing my brother would have loved to get his hands on.

I walked carefully around the stacks and piles, the ground littered with random debris—screws, an old pencil, bits of string and other odds and ends. If someone had been there, they were probably long gone. I didn't hear anything. And it would be impossible to tell if someone had been there stealing things. I doubted Rich had an inventory of all the crap he owned.

Knowing Tilikum, it was just a squirrel colony, and whoever had called it in had just seen the movement of dozens of squirrels.

The hairs on the back of my neck suddenly stood on end. I hadn't heard anything. Not a creak of metal or the shifting of wood. Not even the sound of squirrels or other critters.

So what was setting me off?

With my senses on high alert, my body tense, I made my way around another outbuilding. I still didn't see or hear anything unusual, but my instincts were lit up like a patrol car in a high-speed chase.

Something was wrong.

Half expecting to come across an armed trespasser lying in wait—or maybe a wild predator stalking me—I turned the corner to the back side of the outbuilding.

Nothing.

I let out a breath. Maybe my instincts were off.

A creak was all the warning I had.

I turned in time to throw my arms up over my face as a pile of junk fell toward me. Trapped between a wall of stuff and the back of the outbuilding, I threw myself to one side, hoping I didn't get buried—or stabbed by something rusty.

My forearms took the brunt of it, but the weight of the pile knocked me to the ground. Searing pain tore across my upper arm and it felt like I was being pummeled with bricks.

A few seconds later, it was over. I lay on the ground,

covered in rubble, blood dripping from my arm. My eyes were gritty with dust and I could already feel the beginnings of about a dozen bruises.

Moving carefully so I didn't dislodge whatever had fallen on me and make things worse, I tested my arms and legs. I was going to be banged up, but nothing seemed to be broken. Thankfully, nothing had hit my head.

Grimacing, I worked my way out of the fallen pile. What the hell had happened? There was a lot of junk, but none of it had looked precarious enough to fall on its own.

I got to my feet and checked my arm. Something sharp had slashed a long gash across my biceps. It wasn't deep, but it was bleeding enough that I needed to at least get some gauze on it.

The sense that something was off didn't go away. Warily, I picked my way back around to the front of the property and went to my car. I didn't see anything. No sign of someone sneaking around the piles or taking off into the woods. No sound of a car, even in the distance.

But why had that pile fallen on me? No wind. No animals around, not even a squirrel. Was it just coincidence that I happened to walk by right at the moment gravity had its way with one of Rich's stacks of junk?

Was it the trespasser Rich Pine's friend had called about? Who would have been out there?

I got some gauze out of the first aid kit and mopped up the bleeding. Fortunately, I'd had my share of tetanus shots, so I wasn't worried about that. I checked in with dispatch and let her know I hadn't found anything unusual, but a pile of junk had fallen on me. Brenna made sure I was okay and said we might need to find some local help for Rich to make sure his property wasn't hazardous.

But that was the thing. It wasn't exactly organized, but it shouldn't have been dangerous. None of it had looked as if it were on the brink of falling over.

Another patrol car pulled up and Kade got out.

"You okay, man?" He gestured to the gauze I was holding on my arm.

"Yeah. Nothing serious. What are you doing here?"

"I was nearby. Heard the chatter on the radio, figured I'd swing by and see if you're okay."

"I'm all right." I glanced back at the property. "It was weird, though."

"What?"

"Seemed like someone was out there."

He shrugged. "Trespassing call."

"I know, but something feels off. Like it was more than just a random trespasser. I can't shake the feeling that it was intentional."

His forehead creased with concern. "What do you mean, someone lured you out here?"

It sounded half-crazy when he said it out loud. But that was exactly what I was thinking.

"Yeah."

"Maybe the trespasser was still there. Didn't want to get caught."

I glanced back at the property. Obviously that made sense. But that explanation didn't satisfy the sense of unease in my gut.

Kade still looked concerned. He pointed to my arm. "Should you get that looked at?"

"Nah. Just a scratch."

"Okay." He didn't sound convinced, but he went back to his car. "Careful out there."

"You too."

He got in and left, but I lingered for a moment, gazing at Rich Pine's property. I couldn't shake the feeling that something was going on. I just couldn't put my finger on what.

CHAPTER 31

Garrett

THE GLOW of my laptop provided the only light in my dining room. The sun had gone down, but I hardly noticed. My mind was feverishly fixed on the cold case. There was a ticking clock out there somewhere, I was convinced of it. The killer was going to strike again.

Whether or not my superiors believed it, I knew. That package on Harper's doorstep had been a taunt. He was still out there and he was going to kill again.

I couldn't let that happen.

Harper was upstairs asleep, and Owen had gone to a friend's house for the night. He hadn't been in trouble since the shoplifting incident, and I'd all but forgotten I'd threatened to ground him until he turned eighteen. He'd picked a good time to clean up his act. If I'd been dealing with a cold case murder, a pregnant girlfriend, and a wayward teenager, life would have been even more complicated than it already was.

Wincing slightly, I shifted my arm. The laceration wasn't serious. It had scabbed over in the several days since the visit to Rich Pine's property. The bruises were just that—bruises. They'd heal.

I still didn't know if the incident had been a coincidence. If I'd simply been in the wrong place at the wrong time. Harper was worried her bad luck was rubbing off on me. I'd told her not to worry about that—that even if it did, I'd handle it. I wasn't concerned about an amorphous concept like luck.

You can't arrest bad luck. A killer, though? I could arrest that. Lock it up and make sure it never hurt anyone again.

Especially my woman.

My eyes were tired with strain but I ignored the discomfort. I'd been poring over the old case files, rereading interviews, reports, and field notes. Looking for anything that would point me in the right direction. Anything that might give me the break I needed to find whoever had killed Jasmine.

Other than making sure I hadn't been seriously injured when the pile of junk toppled on me, my superiors weren't particularly concerned. Just an accident. I'd been lucky. When Rich Pine got back into town, they were going to reach out and see if he needed help cleaning up his property a bit so something like that didn't happen again.

I hadn't pushed the issue or tried to argue that someone had done it on purpose. I had no proof. No evidence. Just a hunch. And my instincts, sharp as they usually were, did not amount to a case.

Besides, I was slightly concerned they were going to start thinking I was paranoid.

And hell, maybe I was.

Thankfully, Harper hadn't received any more anonymous packages. If someone sent her flowers at this point, I'd probably lose my shit. Especially if they were white.

But it did make me wonder—could I find out who bought those flowers? It had been ten years, but that was still a lead I needed to follow up on. The flower shop in town had been open for twenty-five years and was still in business. If there was even a chance they had purchase records going back far enough, I needed to look into it. No stone unturned, as they said.

I pulled out a printed map of the trail system around Tilikum. I'd marked where Jasmine's body had been discovered, as well as where I'd found the bracelet and the location of the old barn and root cellar. They made a triangle, each about a mile apart.

There was no record of the barn or root cellar having been searched during the original investigation. It made sense. The assumption had been she'd been taken off the trail and killed where her body was later found. Beyond trying to find signs of the killer's escape, the investigators wouldn't have felt a need to search a wider area.

But he hadn't left anything behind.

I wanted in that cellar. According to county records, it was private property but held in a trust. There was quite a bit of land like that in the region—acreage once owned by old Tilikum families that had fallen into disuse over the decades as the town shrunk. It was too bad it wasn't part of the area my family had inherited back when my sister had gotten married. That would have made this a lot easier.

As it was, I needed a warrant to get in. And I wasn't sure how to write it so the judge would grant it.

Was proximity to the location of Jasmine's body enough? Although it would be hard for a man to carry a body that far, it wasn't impossible—especially for someone in good shape. For a second, I imagined talking Harper into letting me test it out on her.

Hey love, can we go out into the woods and you let me carry you as dead weight for about a mile?

Probably unnecessary, and slightly morbid, but tempting nonetheless.

I thought about calling Phillip Lancaster. I'd called him with questions about warrants before. He knew how to word them so a judge would be more amenable to granting them.

But it was late. I'd run it by Sergeant Denny, or maybe even Sheriff Jack, in the morning.

A pleasant tingle spread across the back of my neck and ran down my spine. I felt her, more than heard her, approach.

Harper slid her hands over my shoulders and wound her arms around me, leaning in to kiss my neck.

"What are you doing up?" I asked.

"I woke up and you weren't there."

My body stirred with desire. She was the only thing in the world that could tear me away from hunting a killer.

I shifted away from the table so I could draw her into my lap. She sat, dressed in a thin tank top and shorts, her legs straddling me. Her long hair was messy and loose, her eyes sleepy.

"It's not late." I rubbed my hands up and down her thighs. "Not for me, anyway."

"I know. But I missed you. You've been working since you got home."

I brushed her lips with a kiss. "Sorry. I've been preoccupied."

"It's okay. You have a lot on your mind." She gently touched the skin around the laceration. "How's this? Healing okay?"

"Don't worry, it's fine."

"I think worry is part of the deal. I had no idea what I was in for when I fell in love with a man in uniform."

I could hear the hint of humor in her voice, see the slight smile on her lips. But I knew she was still going to worry about me. My job was dangerous. There was no way around that.

"I take safety seriously. We're trained for it."

She leaned in and pressed her mouth to mine. "I know."

"What about you? How are you feeling? How's the tiny one?"

Her smile lit up her face. "The tiny one is fine. I feel okay. I definitely need to hire a second baker, but luckily we're busy enough for it. It's going to be hard to keep up as the tiny one becomes less tiny."

I traced a line between her breasts, down to her belly. She giggled softly, biting her lower lip.

"You should come to bed."

Work still tugged at me, but she was irresistible. Her warmth, her scent, her voice. She slipped off my lap and grabbed my hand. I got up and followed, leaving some of the weight of the burdens I carried behind.

As soon as we were in the bedroom, I tugged off my clothes and helped her out of hers, eager to feel her skin against mine. We climbed onto the bed and I took my time, kissing her, tasting her, as I worked my way down her body. She moaned beneath my touch, arching her back and writhing against the sheets.

I brought her to climax once, reveling in her pleasure, before moving to settle on top of her. Her eyelids fluttered, and even in the dim light, I could see the flush in her cheeks.

Our bodies joined with a burst of sensation. She was soft and warm, like silk against my rough edges. I lost myself in her heat, let go of all the tension and stress. There was nothing but her.

My woman. My love.

We moved, our rhythm quickening, until the intensity rose to a peak. I growled into her neck, thrusting hard, while her fingers dug into my back. I felt her come again and it was more than I could take. I unleashed, pouring myself into her.

Loving her with everything I had.

After we finished, she kept her arms around me. I held her and breathed her in.

"I love you," she whispered.

"I love you too." I picked myself up and braced myself so I could look at her. "Is everything okay?"

She nodded. "This was good."

One corner of my mouth lifted in a subtle grin. "Very good."

"I don't just mean that." She touched the side of my face. "I need this. Needed you."

"I'm always yours, love."

"I know. I just mean… sometimes I need you. This Garrett. Not deputy Haven."

"I'm sorry if I've been distant."

"You just work so hard. I don't want you to burn yourself out."

I didn't either, but she didn't understand. I had to keep her safe.

Leaning down, I brushed her lips with a soft kiss. "Things will calm down soon."

She smiled at me, her eyes so full of hope. "Yeah, they will."

I rolled off her and she settled against me. It wasn't long before her breathing evened. She was asleep.

The case tugged at me again. She was good for me, there was no doubt about that. But I had so much work to do. I needed to follow every lead and I just didn't have time.

So I waited until I was sure she was sound asleep and slipped out of bed. I had a killer to catch.

CHAPTER 32

Harper

THE BAKERY WAS HOPPING. We'd gone through all our cupcakes, but customers weren't deterred. Tourist season was in full swing in Tilikum, and that meant a steady stream of visitors looking for treats as they wandered around our little downtown. The pink lemonade cupcakes had been especially popular. I made a mental note to create a cookie version of the recipe.

Beth and I worked the line until it was manageable. She was such a rockstar. I was definitely giving her a raise. She was like a little Energizer bunny—never seemed to get tired no matter how busy we were.

Me, on the other hand? I was dragging.

Which was why, in the midst of my busy afternoon, it was so great that I had a potential new baker in the kitchen.

Mila had a dark brown pixie cut, dramatic eyeliner, and bold red lipstick. She lived in Wenatchee, a small-ish city not too far from Tilikum, and had been working in a bakery there for several years, but was looking for a change.

I was trying to decide what to make of her. She spoke in an odd monotone and her eye contact was intense. She had a whole Wednesday Addams vibe going on. But maybe she was just quirky. And what I really wanted to know was how well she could bake, especially under pressure.

I'd asked her to make chocolate chip cookies—a classic any baker needed to be able to make, and make well. I popped into the kitchen to check on her, and if the scent was anything to go by, she'd nailed it.

"How's it going back here?" I asked.

She checked her watch, then glanced at the timer. I approved of her double-timing tactic. "Excellent."

"It smells great."

"Thank you," she said, her voice completely expressionless.

"While we're waiting for the cookies, let's have you show me your cake decorating skills. I have a small cake in the fridge we can use."

"I can do that."

"Awesome." I went to the fridge and brought out a small layer cake that already had a crumb coat and put it on a rotating cake stand on the island. "Feel free to imagine this as anything you want. The top tier of a wedding cake, a baby shower cake, birthday cake. The sky's the limit."

She tilted her head to the side and a little groove formed between her eyes as she inspected the cake. "Baby shower," she declared definitively.

"Okay." My phone buzzed in my back pocket, so I pulled it out to check. Sugar cookies, it was my mother. "Go ahead and get started. I need to take this. I'll be right back."

I left her to it and headed out the back door. A prospective new employee did not need to be subjected to a conversation with my mother. Especially because I had yet to tell her I was pregnant.

This was going to be interesting.

"Hi, Mom. What's up?"

"Why do you insist on using that phrase?"

"What's up? I don't know. Habit, I guess."

She let out a frustrated sigh and I rolled my eyes. Lovely. This was already going so well.

"I have news," she said. "Your sister just accepted a promotion at work."

"Wow, that's great."

"It's more than great. It's extraordinary."

"Is she excited?"

"She's proud. As she should be."

"Awesome. Are you doing anything to celebrate?"

"I suppose I'll need to treat her to dinner."

"That would be nice." I scrunched my nose, dread making my stomach knot. Now was probably not the best time to tell her about the baby. But there was never going to be a good time. I needed to just rip the bandage off and be done with it. "So, Mom, I have some news as well."

"Oh?"

"I realize this is going to come as a surprise, but I want to first assure you that everything is fine. It's good news, okay?"

"That's quite the lead-in."

"I know, but I don't want you to hear what I'm going to say and immediately worry. Or judge me."

She groaned. "What did you do? You didn't burn down Doris's bakery, did you?"

"No." I took a deep breath. "I'm pregnant."

"I think I preferred a burned down bakery."

Okay, here it comes.

"You're pregnant? Harper, what on earth is wrong with you? How could you let this happen?"

"Well, it was a surprise, but we're both really excited about it."

"Tell me you're not going to marry him."

"What? I… I mean, we haven't really had that conversation. But why not?"

"If you're having the baby, and I assume by the way you

phrased it that you are, whatever you do, do not get married."

"Why?"

"Because then you're stuck with him. No one wants that. Not really. We've evolved. We don't need to be tethered to a caveman to meet our needs. We can meet our own needs quite well, financially and otherwise."

"Okay, but I'm in love with Garrett. If he wants to marry me, I'm absolutely going to say yes."

She groaned again. "I honestly don't know where you came from."

"Just because I want different things doesn't make me wrong, Mom. This baby was very unexpected, but it's turning out to be the best thing that's ever happened to me. So is Garrett. He's a wonderful man."

"I'm sure he seems that way, what with your hormones acting up."

"I don't think it's my hormones that are in love with him, but okay."

"You think that now, but wait ten years. When he's on the couch, scratching himself under his beer belly and keeping you awake at night with his snoring. Then we'll see how much you love him."

I had no idea why my mom was so cynical. She'd never been married. How did she have any idea what it was like? But fortunately, I was able to stop myself from asking her who'd hurt her so badly that she hated men so much.

It kind of made me grateful she'd never had a son. She hadn't been a terrible mother to me and my sister, but what would she have done with a boy? He would have perplexed her more than I did. And she had no idea what to do with me.

"How about this? I'll keep your advice in mind as I move forward. But I just wanted you to know that you're going to be a grandma and—"

"Stop."

"What?"

"I'm not a grandma."

"If I'm having a baby, that means you are."

"That child is not calling me grandma. It makes me sound old."

"That's fine. What should the baby call you?"

"I don't know. I'll have to give it some thought. But absolutely not grandma."

So maybe that was what this was about. She was feeling insecure about aging, and me having a baby reminded her that she wasn't in her twenties, or thirties, or forties anymore.

"You can let me know what you decide. There's plenty of time. It's still early and babies don't talk when they're newborns anyway."

"No, I suppose not."

"Tell Holly congratulations for me."

"I will. Do you have prenatal vitamins?"

That made me smile. She wasn't perfect, but she did care about me in her own way. "Yes. I have prenatal vitamins and a doctor and everything. I'm doing fine."

"Okay. Don't forget to take them. And eat a vegetable once in a while."

"I eat plenty. I bake for a living, but I don't live on pastries."

"I hope not. You'd never lose the baby weight."

"Sugar cookies, Mom. Sometimes you know the exact wrong thing to say."

"What did I say?"

"Nothing. It's fine. I'll talk to you later."

"Bye."

I ended the call. I could be mad, or at least annoyed, but for some reason, I wasn't. I hadn't expected her to be overjoyed about my pregnancy. And she wasn't. That was fine. I didn't need her to be. She'd come around, in her own way. And I'd make the best of it, like I always did.

Besides, this baby was going to have a set of grandparents here in Tilikum who loved him or her to pieces. And aunts, uncles, cousins. A big brother...

And just like that, I was crying.

"Hey, Harper. Are you okay?"

I jumped at the sound of Matt's voice and quickly wiped beneath my eyes. "Oh yeah. I'm fine. Just... nothing."

He was dressed in a faded gray T-shirt and basketball shorts and the poor guy really needed to learn how to trim his scraggly facial hair.

"Are you sure? You seem upset."

"I'm really fine. Happy tears, actually."

"Oh. That's good. Have you ever heard of the Garcia murder?"

His abrupt changes of subject into his fascination with true crime always left me slightly off kilter. "Um, no?"

He grinned. "It was really grisly. The killer kept the victim in a shed on his property for a while before he murdered her."

"That's terrible."

"They caught him, though. And he was dumb enough to have left DNA evidence. Got him for two other murders."

"Was that recent, or did it just pop into your head for some reason?"

"I was just doing some research."

"Oh. That's... nice."

"What did deputy Haven tell you about the Joyner case? Anything good?"

"He doesn't really talk to me about details. I don't think he's supposed to."

"Probably not. Do you think he's going to solve it?"

"I hope so. One less killer on the loose would be a good thing."

He glanced away, his eyes seemingly unfocused. "Yeah.

Shame no one's caught him yet. Who knows what else he could be up to."

There was an odd wistfulness in his voice that sent a chill down my spine. Did he know something?

Or was it worse than that?

He couldn't be the…

No.

He was just a guy who was a little strange and knew way too much about true crime stories.

Right?

"Do you think there are more victims?"

He slowly turned and met my eyes, his expression intense. He didn't say a word. Just nodded.

My heart sped up and I swallowed hard. "Well that's terrifying. I… I should go."

"Do you want to come over?"

"I'm sorry, what?"

"Do you want to come to my house?"

"Um…"

"I want you to meet Lily."

Sugar cookies, who was Lily? And why did I suddenly picture a soundproofed shed in Matt's backyard with a missing woman named Lily inside?

My voice shook slightly. "Who's Lily?"

"My pet."

This wasn't getting better. That made me picture a woman being held in a cage. "Pet?"

"Yeah, my bearded dragon. Do you want to come see her?"

I let out a breath. Okay, not a woman in a cage. But still. "Oh, no thank you. I shouldn't."

"She's very tame."

"That's great, Matt. I'm sure she's really cool. But I have to work."

"It wouldn't take long. I'm parked right there." He

pointed to a white van with the back doors open.

A. White. Van.

My eyes widened. Was this actually happening? All my childhood memories of stranger danger warnings had revolved around a creepy guy in a white van, and usually a pet. Granted, I'd been warned about not leaving with a stranger who claimed to have lost a puppy or something, not about saying no to going to some guy's house to see his bearded dragon.

And did he really mean bearded dragon, or was that some kind of weird euphemism?

I needed to get out of there before Matt started offering me candy.

"I can't, but thanks anyway." I backed away before turning decisively so my meaning would be clear. I was leaving. He said goodbye but I didn't answer. Just waved without looking.

My heart was still racing as I slipped into the bakery and locked the back door. It was just my luck I'd get a call from my mom then run into Matt outside.

Then I realized, of course. It was my luck.

I wasn't going to think too deeply about the physics of it all, but Matt seemed to be a product of my bad luck curse.

Or, at least, I hoped that was all he was. My gut had told me from the first time I'd met him that something was off. And every time I saw him, I felt the same way. I wanted to believe he was just a bit weird, but what if he wasn't? What if his fascination with true crime was more than it seemed.

A copycat, maybe? Did he fantasize about committing the crimes himself?

Had he ever acted out those fantasies?

My stomach turned over. Matt didn't seem like a killer. Did he?

I was probably letting my imagination run away with me. But I'd tell Garrett anyway, just in case.

CHAPTER 33

Harper

GOING HOME—EVEN though it technically wasn't my home—had never felt so good. Garrett's car was outside and Owen's bike leaned against the garage door. They were there. My love and my…

I wasn't quite sure what Owen and I were to each other yet. He was my baby's older brother and I liked to think we were friends.

Was I going to end up as his stepmom? Was that where this was going?

I hoped so.

Not that I had any clue how to be a stepmom, especially to a teenage boy. But Owen was so awesome. And if I was, that would mean we were all…

A family.

That was what I loved so much about seeing signs of them outside, knowing they were there. The idea of coming home to a family—a family where I actually belonged—was so tempting and beautiful, it made my heart ache.

I really needed to get myself together. Were my hormones acting up again? I swiped the tears from the corners of my eyes. I was so emotional.

I'd also had a weird day.

The good news was, Mila's baking audition had gone really well. Her chocolate chip cookies had come out perfectly —rich and gooey, with just the right amount of crispness around the edges. And she had an impressive set of cake decorating skills. Even better, when I'd offered her the job, she'd accepted on the spot. She still had some things to learn, but I thought of it as a good thing. She wasn't too set in her ways and could learn some of the Angel Cakes tricks.

Having another baker was going to take a lot of pressure off. And the timing was... I wasn't going to say lucky. But it was fortunate. She'd have plenty of time to get comfortable with our setup before I went on maternity leave.

I got out of my car and walked inside on tired feet. I didn't see Owen—he was probably upstairs in his room—but Garrett stood in the kitchen, his back to me. He'd already changed out of his uniform into a white T-shirt and gray joggers, and it looked like he was prepping something for dinner.

Making dinner. So simple, and yet so meaningful. I loved him so much.

I put my things down and by the way he shifted his head, I could tell he'd heard me. I went into the kitchen, sidled up behind him, and wrapped my arms around his waist. He was warm and solid and strong.

When he pulled me around to his front and put his arms around me, I sank into his embrace, resting my head on his chest. The tension of the day melted, and for a moment, I let myself get lost in him.

I shifted away and he moved in for a kiss. His lips were firm and soft, his kiss indulgent. How had I gotten so...

Nope. Not lucky. I didn't want to even think it, lest my bad luck swoop in and ruin everything.

He leaned in to speak low into my ear. "Hi, love. I missed you."

"I missed you too."

"How was your day?"

"Good. And also weird."

"Gross, you guys," Owen said. "Stop making out in the kitchen."

Garrett glanced over his shoulder, then turned back to me. With a subtle grin, he kissed me again while Owen groaned.

"If you don't stop, I'm going to Grandma and Grandpa's for dinner."

"Should we let him go?" Garrett asked, then brushed my lips with another kiss. "Then we could be alone."

"That's even worse," Owen said. "Is this what my life is going to be like now?"

I peeked around Garrett's shoulder and smiled at him. "Yes."

He was trying—and failing—to hide his grin. Turning away from us, he jumped over the back of the couch. "Tell me when it's safe to look up."

"He shouldn't hold his breath," Garrett whispered into my ear, then kissed his way down my neck.

With a soft giggle, I tilted my head. My body reacted to his lips on my skin, sending a burst of heat between my legs. But with Owen one room away, there wasn't anything I could do about it.

Which was fine. Maybe this meant I could coax Garrett into coming to bed early with me. He was working too much. I was surprised he was in the kitchen prepping dinner, although his laptop and paperwork were strewn over the dining table.

"How was your day weird?" Garrett asked finally.

I had to take a breath to clear my head. His kisses had that effect on me. "First of all, my mom called. I told her about the baby."

He swiped something off my cheek—probably flour—and kissed the spot. "What did she say?"

"Pretty much what I expected. 'What were you thinking? Why are you ruining your life?' You know, what every daughter longs to hear when she tells her mom she's making her a grandma. Oh, and she's declared she will not be called grandma. I told her to let me know what's acceptable."

His brow furrowed.

"Please don't be worried that I'm going to turn into my mother someday. That's definitely going to happen to my sister, but I've always been different."

He brushed my hair back from my face. "I'm not worried about that. I just don't understand."

"Understand what? My mom? Trust me, neither do I."

"How anyone could not see what a miracle you are."

Tears sprang to my eyes. "You're just saying that because you knocked me up."

He pressed another kiss to my lips. "No, I'm not. I'm saying that because I love you."

"Why are you so amazing?"

"I don't think I am. I'm just me. But I'm yours."

I wound my arms around his neck. "You're so amazing, I'm afraid you're too good to be true."

"Is everything else okay?"

"Yeah, it's just, you remember that guy Matt? The one who's kind of weird?"

His eyes narrowed and I felt tension creep into his shoulders. "Yes."

"I ran into him today, outside the bakery. I'm sure it was nothing, but I don't know."

"What did he do?"

"Mostly the usual. Brought up some weird true crime story out of nowhere. But then he asked if you've found anything on the Joyner case. That's the one you're working on, right?"

He nodded, his brow still furrowed with concern.

"I told him I didn't know. That you don't really talk about

your cases. And then he said something about it being a shame that a killer is on the loose and who knows what he's been up to all these years. It wasn't so much what he said as the way he said it. So then I asked if he thought there have been other victims. He looked right at me and his eyes got wider and he just nodded." I shivered. "It makes me cringe just thinking about it."

"He asked about the Joyner case?"

"Yeah."

"Did he ask specific questions?"

"He just asked if you'd found anything. Something like that. I don't remember his exact words."

He shifted away and rubbed his chin. "You said he brings up true crime stories?"

"Yeah. I think he's really into that. The first time he came into the bakery, he was wearing a true crime shirt, and he started telling me about a case. It was odd."

"Did you ever find out if he left the bear on your car?"

"No. I should ask him but I'm usually too busy trying to figure out how to get out of the conversation. Especially today. He tried to get me to go home with him."

His tone hardened. "He tried to what?"

"He asked if I'd go to his house to meet his pet bearded dragon. He has a white van, Garrett. An actual white van. That has to be too cliché to be real, right? He can't be an actual kidnapper with a white van."

"Did he try to force you inside?"

"No, nothing like that. I told him no thanks and went back into the bakery." Suddenly, dots connected. "Wait, didn't Matt file a complaint about you?"

"He was going to, but apparently didn't follow through."

"That's so strange. He didn't mention anything about it, not even when he was asking about the case you're working on. I don't get this guy."

I wasn't sure if Garrett was listening anymore. His eyes

were unfocused and he sat down at the table with his laptop. "Could he know?"

"Could he know what?"

"About the package," he said, almost under his breath, as he started scrolling through something on the screen.

"What package?"

He froze, his muscles tensing. "Never mind."

"No, what package? The one I got? Please tell me what's going on."

With a long exhale, he turned to look at me. "Not long before she was killed, Jasmine received a package from an unknown sender. It had a pair of her underwear in it."

The shock of what he'd just said reverberated through me like the sound of a gong. "What?"

"That doesn't mean there's a connection between her murder and the package on your porch."

"But it's the same. I got a package from an unknown sender with a pair of my own underwear. Which is just like the case you're trying to solve? How is that not a connection? Did she get a murder bear too?"

"No, she didn't get a bear."

"But what does this mean? Could Jasmine's killer be—" I stopped because I couldn't say it.

He glanced toward the couch, but Owen was wearing headphones. It didn't look like he could hear us.

"There are other possible explanations," Garrett said, lowering his voice. "Jasmine's murder was ten years ago, and as far as we know, he hasn't killed again. At least not with the same pattern. We don't even know if he's still in Tilikum. It's unlikely the same person would resurface now and start recreating the events leading to her death."

"But he might, especially since you're investigating the case."

"I know. Trust me, I'm looking at every scenario. But I'm also concerned about the fact that the town gossip line has been buzzing about the case. This might be someone who thinks they're funny playing a practical joke. Or it might be something worse."

"Like someone reenacting what happened back then?"

"Exactly. The police dismissed the package as being unrelated, so I don't know if the contents were ever public knowledge. But they could have been, especially when it was a missing persons case, before her body was found. I haven't had time to look up all the news coverage."

"So, you're saying someone could know about the package, especially if they were into true crime?"

"Yeah."

"We're talking about the same person, right? Matt?" My head spun and Garrett nodded. "I don't know. On the one hand, it kind of fits. The way he looked at me today made me wonder if he's more than just a true crime enthusiast. But on the other hand, unless he's hiding some serious thief skills, he doesn't seem like the type who could break into someone's house without getting caught."

"I agree, that's hard to imagine. But you never know."

"Maybe his awkward exterior is just a ruse."

"Honestly, it's possible. I've seen stranger things."

I put my hands on my churning stomach. "I don't like any of this."

He stood and gathered me in his arms. "I'm not going to let anything happen to you. I swear."

I took a deep breath, breathing him in. I believed him. But he couldn't stand guard over me all the time—couldn't always be there. And if this was someone's idea of a practical joke, it certainly wasn't funny.

But the alternatives were so much worse.

CHAPTER 34
Garrett

HARPER SHIFTED in her sleep and made a soft noise in her throat. I'd been staring at the ceiling for who knows how long, a million things running through my head. It felt like answers were just out of reach, veiled by the haze of time. If I could put all the pieces together, I could not only catch a killer, I could keep my woman safe.

And nothing mattered more than that.

I'd pored over what we had on Jasmine, looking for any similarities to Harper. Nothing stood out. Jasmine had been shorter, with different skin tone and darker hair. She'd been a massage therapist, not a baker. She'd been younger, too. Only twenty-four when she was killed.

But did that mean anything?

I needed to convince the judge to grant a warrant for that root cellar. It might not lead anywhere, but the need to act—to make some kind of progress—consumed me.

Harper moved again and her brow furrowed slightly. She seemed restless. I shifted closer so I could kiss her forehead—soothe whatever was troubling her as she slept.

I could do this forever.

The thought came out of nowhere. But it was simply the

truth. I didn't want to lose her—couldn't stand the thought. I wanted her next to me like this for the rest of my life.

No one was going to take her from me. No one.

I slid an arm around her waist and gently nudged her closer. She stirred, but didn't wake, settling against me. Her body was warm and soft, her closeness easing the tension in my muscles.

She was mine.

My eyes started to drift closed. Maybe I was finally going to get some rest. I took a slow, deep breath, inhaling her scent.

A slight creak caught my attention and my eyes shot open. Had that been the floor? Or was it just the house settling?

So much for sleep. My senses were alert, the hit of adrenaline chasing away my fatigue. Maybe it was Owen, getting up to use the bathroom or get some water. I needed to check. I wouldn't be able to relax until I was sure.

Reluctantly, I eased myself away from Harper's warm body, slipped out of bed, and tugged on a pair of boxer briefs. If Owen was up, I didn't want to traumatize him by walking out naked.

Then again, if someone was in the house, there was nothing like coming face to face with a big, naked cop who came from lumberjack stock.

Harper was still asleep, so I grabbed my firearm, crept out of the bedroom, and quietly shut the door behind me. My eyes were already adjusted to the darkness and there was a small nightlight in the hall, a holdover from when Owen was younger and had frequently found his way into my room at night.

Owen's door was closed, so I carefully turned the knob and peeked inside. He was in bed, sound asleep.

I shut the door and paused, listening. Nothing.

But I was still going to walk every inch of the house to make sure.

The spare bedroom was empty, as was the hall bathroom

—including the shower. My feet didn't make a sound as I crept down the stairs. I hesitated at the bottom, my ears straining.

Another creak made me freeze and the hairs on the back of my neck stood on end. A waft of cool air hit my skin.

Was someone there?

My training took over. There was no room for fear. I was calm, but ready. Whoever it was, they'd picked the wrong house.

I had a view of the entryway and front room. No sign of entry—forced or otherwise—and my doorbell camera hadn't alerted. There was another noise, coming from the back of the house, so I moved that way, my senses sharp.

Out of the corner of my eye, I saw a shadow move. A slight change of temperature as I made my way to the kitchen heightened my wariness. Had a window or door been opened and let in the night air? My heart beat harder as I took careful steps, pausing at the corner between the kitchen and the family room.

I turned the corner, weapon at the ready, but the room was empty. I hurried to the French doors that led out back. Locked. I flipped on the light, illuminating the porch, and peered into the darkness. Was that movement just inside the tree line?

My house backed up against a stretch of woods—no one lived behind me. I squinted into the night, straining to see. But if someone had been there, they were already gone.

For a second, I thought about following. But I hadn't checked the garage. I couldn't leave Harper and Owen alone in the house if there was even a chance someone was still there.

The door leading into the garage was locked and no one was inside.

I did another sweep of the house, checking every corner. I crisscrossed my way around, changing direction, opening doors, moving as softly as I could. No one was there and nothing seemed to be moved or missing.

Had someone been in the house? Had they slipped out just before I'd gone downstairs?

I went back to the French doors and crouched so I could see the lock at eye level. Those things weren't impossible to pick, if you knew what you were doing. And if someone was good at it, they could have locked it behind them when they left.

In and out without a trace.

Who the fuck was I dealing with?

I thought about calling it in and getting someone out there to start investigating. But I could already tell, there wasn't anything to investigate. If someone had been there, they were gone.

There might be some footprints outside, but in the dry weather I doubted it. I'd take a look when the sun was up, but I didn't hold out much hope I'd find anything conclusive.

The real problem was, if I called it in, I knew what they were going to think. I was being paranoid.

A few little noises in the night didn't warrant an all-out investigation. I knew that.

But someone had been there. I'd felt it.

They'd been in Harper's house, too. Hers had been the same thing, no sign of entry, no indication anyone had broken in. But someone had taken those underwear out of her drawer and put them in that box. I didn't care what my superiors said.

I just couldn't prove it. Yet.

Whoever was after my girl, I was going to find him before he could hurt her.

He was fucking with the wrong man.

CHAPTER 35

Garrett

I NEEDED MORE COFFEE. I hadn't slept the night before. A possible intruder tended to do that to a guy. One missed night of sleep wasn't going to kill me—I'd flipped between days and graveyard for a lot of my career, so I was used to it —but it hadn't done much for my mood.

I'd spent my morning on a half-day patrol shift, amped as all hell. I didn't want to be patrolling the county, I wanted to be catching a murderer. And figuring out who'd been in my house, if they weren't the same person.

The home invasion felt like another taunt. Someone sending a message that they could still get to Harper, even though she'd moved in with me. It made me fucking furious, both that someone had the audacity to do it, and that I hadn't caught them.

I would. They were messing with the wrong guy.

In the early afternoon, I was finally able to head back into town. I made a quick stop at the bakery to check on Harper. She was fine, just busy.

I'd also called in reinforcements. The Squirrel Protection Squad.

I didn't think a bunch of mostly retired townspeople were

going to be able to protect Harper from a killer. But at the very least, they'd hang around and make sure she was never alone. And they'd call me if they saw anything suspicious.

She sent me back to the office with a box of cookies. When I got there, I went in and took them to the break room, but I was too focused—or maybe too distracted—to grab one for myself. Not that I had a shortage of Harper's baked goods in my life. But I had a question I needed to investigate.

What was the deal with Matt Rudolph?

I hadn't run his background before, mostly because I didn't have good enough cause. A guy who seemed weird and appeared to like my girlfriend a little too much wasn't a justifiable reason to dig into his record—if he had one. And when he'd threatened to file a complaint against me, I had to keep out of it. Otherwise it would have looked like I was trying to dig up dirt on the guy to get myself out of trouble.

But at this point, I needed to know if he had a criminal history. It wouldn't tell me everything, but it could tell me something.

I ran his name and got a hit. Matt had been arrested seven years earlier. For breaking and entering.

Holy shit.

No conviction. There wasn't much information, but it looked like the case had been dropped. It was likely there hadn't been enough evidence to prosecute.

That didn't prove Matt had broken into Harper's house, or mine, but it definitely painted an interesting picture.

One arrest. No conviction. What did that mean? It might mean he'd been innocent—and according to the law, he was.

But it could also mean that he was just that good.

I needed to talk to him, preferably without spooking him so he wouldn't lawyer up too quickly. There was so much more I needed to know. Riled up as I was—that fucker was not going to hurt my woman—I knew I needed to stay calm and rational.

The original investigators in Jasmine's murder had made too many assumptions. It had cost us the case and a killer was still on the loose. I didn't want to make the same mistake.

But it would help if I had more to go on. I hadn't had an opportunity to talk to the florist yet. That was kind of a long shot, but what if it was the thing that connected the dots? If I could show there was even a possibility Matt had bought the flowers Jasmine had received, it would be enough to justify questioning him.

My gut told me that was where I needed to go next.

"Haven." Jack's voice cut through my concentration. He stood next to my desk with his arms crossed over his wide chest. "Can I see you for a minute?"

"Sure."

I got up and followed him to his office, my mind still reeling with possibilities. With next steps. I shut the door to Jack's office and took a seat while he did the same.

"What's going on with the Joyner case?" he asked.

I hesitated, debating how to answer his question. "I have some leads to pursue, but I don't have anything concrete."

He nodded slowly and I couldn't read his expression. "I have some concerns."

"About what?"

"Whether you should continue on this case."

I straightened. "Why? Are you still concerned about the complaints? I told you, those don't have any merit."

"I'm concerned because I'm seeing a pattern that I've seen before. I've been at this a long time, Garrett. I can tell when the job is getting to someone."

"The job isn't getting to me. And what pattern?"

"A guy starts to seem off. Slips up when he didn't used to. It might be breaks in protocol, evidence handling, badgering suspects—takes a lot of forms. Then comes paranoia."

"What makes you think I'm paranoid?"

"I've been to Rich Pine's place before. He has enough shit

to rebuild society if there's ever a zombie apocalypse. Something falling on you doesn't mean you were set up."

How the hell had he heard about that? "Nowhere in my report did I claim I'd been set up."

"No, but you told Sheehan you thought it was deliberate."

"Damn it, Kade. Did he seriously tell you that?"

"Because he's concerned. Said you sounded paranoid. Maybe even unhinged."

"I'm not paranoid, and I'm certainly not unhinged." I was about to say Kade had it out for me, but that was exactly what a paranoid person would say. "I realize I have no proof that someone tipped that pile onto me. But it was a trespassing call and I don't think it makes me crazy to speculate, especially when my gut tells me there was someone out there."

"Instincts are great when they prompt you to ask questions or consider different possibilities. But your gut feeling isn't evidence. And trust me, it can steer you wrong. This is what I'm talking about. I've seen plenty of guys start 'trusting their gut,'" he said, making air quotes, "when their gut is compromised by stress. The results aren't pretty."

"Jack—"

"Listen." He put a hand up. "I'm not ignoring the facts. Your girlfriend got a strange package and I agree that it's concerning, especially with the similarity to the Joyner case. You're taking extra care to keep her safe, and I applaud that. I never thought I'd say this, but I'm grateful for the SPS."

"You and me both."

"But you have a lot going on right now. This is a big case, and it can't be helping that the entire town is watching. Everyone wants to know if you're going to be the one to catch an elusive killer. Hell, people are taking bets as to who it is."

"You're kidding."

He rolled his eyes slightly. "I wish I were. In any case, you take that and add everything you've got going on in your personal life, and it's okay if things are getting to you. There's no shame in that. What is a problem is if you won't admit you're in over your head and at least need a break."

"Jack, I'm not in over my head. I'm telling you, I'm on the cusp of something."

"Don't make me put you on administrative leave."

Alarm shot through me and I sat forward in my chair. "No. Not now."

"I won't if you agree to take a few days off. Starting now."

I fought against the immediate urge to argue. *Stay calm. Be rational. Show him you're fine.*

"I'll take a few days off. But I have one lead I'd like to investigate first."

He raised his eyebrows.

"Jasmine received a second anonymous package before she was killed. Flowers, specifically white flowers with lilies. The original investigators assumed they were unrelated, like the first package, so they didn't look into it. I admit, this is a long shot, but I want to talk to the florist in town. They might not have purchase records going that far back, and whoever it was might have paid cash. I get it. Long shot. But this is a cold case. If the evidence was easy to find, they would have solved it ten years ago."

"All right. Talk to the florist. And then I don't want to see you for at least three days. Get some sleep. Don't spend your time poring over that case file."

"Yes, sir."

"And Garrett…"

I met his eyes.

"Law enforcement and paranoia are a bad combination. You start to think everyone's out to get you, it'll make you reckless and rash. I need you to keep your head on straight."

"I will."

By his expression, I could tell he wasn't sure if he believed me.

I got up and left, glad I hadn't called in the home invasion.

I heard a noise and my gut tells me someone got in and out of my house, but they didn't leave a trace. Paranoid? Yeah, that was exactly what he'd think.

Also, fuck you Kade for ratting me out. I shouldn't have said anything to him. To anyone.

I didn't know who I could trust anymore.

Except Harper. And if I were being honest, my brothers. There wasn't much any of them could do to help, but I knew they'd have my back no matter what.

I left and headed into town to Tilikum Blossoms and Blooms. Although I didn't know if that was where the flowers Jasmine had received had come from, it was the only florist in town, so a good place to start. If it proved to be a dead end, I'd still find an angle to use on Matt. One way or another, he and I were going to have a conversation.

The front of the store was basically covered in plants and flowers. Pots spilling with colorful blooms lined the sidewalk and bouquets filled the window. I went inside and was hit with the scent of roses.

I liked the way Angel Cakes smelled a lot better.

Margie Curtwright had owned Blossoms and Blooms since it opened, as far as I knew. She was in her sixties, with short silver hair and a friendly smile. Her beige apron had the store logo on the front, and she wore a little flower tucked behind her ear.

"Well, hello, officer." She tucked a flower into an arrangement-in-progress. "What can I do for you today? Something for your lady love?"

"Actually, I was hoping I could talk to you." Although while I was there, flowers weren't a bad idea.

She lifted her eyebrows. "About what? Surely I'm not in trouble."

"No, ma'am, not at all."

"That's a relief. What can I help you with?"

"I'm investigating—"

She gasped. "The Jasmine Joyner murder."

Of course she knew. Everyone did. "Yes. Not long before she was murdered, Ms. Joyner received flowers, but she didn't know who'd sent them. I'm wondering if there's a way to track down whether they might have come from your shop."

Her brow furrowed. "That's a tough one. What kind of flowers?"

"They were white, with lilies."

"And you don't know who sent them?"

"That's what I'm trying to find out. At the time, Jasmine assumed they were from her ex-boyfriend, but I suspect she was wrong."

She shook her head. "No, no, it wasn't a boyfriend."

"What makes you say that?"

"White lilies? Those aren't I love you flowers, or I'm sorry flowers. I suppose if he just waltzed in and chose an arrangement on his own he could have sent those. But if he had help, that isn't what he would have left with. Not for an ex-girlfriend. A white arrangement with lilies? Those are funeral flowers."

I stared at her for a second and she gasped again.

"Funeral flowers," she whispered. "Oh my."

That would certainly send a message. "I have an approximate date. Is there any way we could look to see if there's a purchase record?"

She tapped her lip. "Only if the customer paid with a credit card or check. If they paid with cash, I wouldn't have any information on them. But I'm afraid I don't keep credit card records that long. I don't have anything that goes that far back."

My shoulders tightened, but I tried not to let my frustration show. I knew it had been a long shot, but I was still pissed. I needed a damn break.

"Oh!" She held up a finger. "I wonder."

I hesitated, waiting for her to explain, but she just stared into the distance for a long moment.

"You wonder?"

"Sorry, I was thinking. Years ago, we suspected an employee was stealing from the till. We set up a camera. Sure enough, we were right. After that, we sort of forgot it was there. Just left it running."

I handed her the piece of paper where I'd made a note of the dates I wanted to check. "So you were recording this area on these dates?"

She slid it closer. "I'm pretty sure we were."

I almost hesitated to ask, half expecting her to cheerfully say they'd lost or deleted the files long ago. "Do you still have the footage?"

"I'm sure we do. Somewhere."

"Could I see it?"

Her face brightened. "Of course! I'd love to help catch a killer. You can have anything you need. If they make a show about the case, be sure to tell them my name. Give me a few minutes."

She disappeared into the back and I wandered around the store, eyeing the arrangements while I waited. Owen sent me a text, saying he was going to his grandparents' house for the evening. Uncle Theo was taking him. I let him know that was great and I'd see him later.

"That was easier than I thought!" Margie came out, waving a thumb drive. "My husband, God bless him, is so organized. I copied the files for you."

"Thank you, ma'am." I took the thumb drive. "I appreciate your help."

"My pleasure." She gestured to the flower arrangements. "See anything you like for your lady?"

"Actually..." I took a bouquet of red roses. "I'll take these."

"Classic." She nodded in approval. "I like it and she will too."

I went back to the counter and paid for the roses, then thanked Margie again.

Outside, the sun was bright, so I slipped on my aviators. As anxious as I was to get to the footage she'd given me, I decided to swing by the bakery first and give Harper her flowers. Angel Cakes was only a few streets away. Not that I needed a reason. Any excuse to see her.

The parking in front of the bakery was full, so I went around to the back, found a spot, grabbed the flowers, and got out.

As I walked by her car near the back entrance to the bakery, I did a double take. Something was tucked beneath the driver's side windshield wiper. It was a coaster from the Timberbeast Tavern. That was odd. Why would someone have put that on her car?

Wait.

I had a handful of Timberbeast coasters at home. Was that one from my house?

I set the bouquet on her hood and pulled a pair of gloves out of my pocket. The coaster was cardboard, white with the Timberbeast Tavern logo. This one had a chocolate brown splotch on it, just like the spots Owen left on the coasters when he had hot chocolate. The kid always made a mess. It was why I insisted he use a coaster.

Someone *had* been in my house. And they'd taken that coaster to prove it.

I looked up, my eyes sweeping the parking lot. Whoever they were, they were taunting Harper again—showing her they could still get to her. Newsflash: They couldn't. Because I was going to catch them first.

CHAPTER 36

Harper

HAVING a second baker was saving my life. The tiny one was taking a lot of energy. Which made sense. I was growing a person. I'd read an article that described pregnancy as running a marathon every day. No wonder I was tired.

Mila seemed to be settling in. She definitely had a few quirks. She always wore headphones while she worked, and when she did talk to me, her face remained expressionless and her voice monotone. But I was getting used to it and she and Beth appeared to get along. And her baking skills were solid, which was what mattered.

She had a handle on cookies for the pastry case, so I got to work frosting the latest batch of salted caramel cupcakes.

I glanced up just as Garrett appeared in the kitchen doorway out of nowhere, holding a bouquet of red roses. He was in uniform, looking so authoritative and official. I felt like a bit of a hot mess by comparison, with my loose ponytail and Angel Cakes apron covered in flour.

The corners of his mouth turned up in a slow smile. I loved it when he looked at me like that.

"Hey." I put down the piping bag and walked over to him. "What are you doing here?"

He handed me the flowers and pulled me in for a quick kiss. I set them on the island—they were so beautiful—and by the time I turned back around his smile had disappeared, his expression going stony. This wasn't Garrett my boyfriend, this was Garrett the cop.

It made me nervous.

"Thank you for the flowers. They're beautiful. I think we have a vase around here somewhere."

"Jack's making me take a few days off."

"Oh. That's good." I ran my hands up his broad chest. "You need it. You've been working too hard."

He nodded absently, and I could tell he didn't agree. "He thinks the case might be getting to me."

"Is it?"

"No." His voice was soft but resolute. "It's not. But I'll do it if it gets him off my back."

The hollows beneath his eyes betrayed his lack of sleep. I was worried about him. "You look tired."

He glanced at Mila. "Can I talk to you outside?"

I didn't think she'd hear anything, but I nodded. We stepped out the back door into the summer sun.

"Someone was in our house last night," he said.

Our house?

Was that how he saw it? Did that mean he wanted me to stay, like, permanently?

Wait. The other part sank in as I blinked at him.

"Someone broke in?"

"I heard them, but by the time I got downstairs, they were gone."

"Are you sure?"

He nodded once.

"Who's going over there to investigate? Is it like the thing at my house and they'll assign someone else to the case?"

"I didn't call it in."

"Why?"

He glanced away and let out a breath. "They won't find anything."

"Are you sure? Shouldn't they look?"

"If I thought it would help, believe me, I'd ask for the entire forensics team to tear the house apart. But it won't."

"Do you think they took something? Like last time?" I almost didn't want to ask. "Is this like the cold case again?"

"I don't think so. The only other thing Jasmine got was a bouquet of flowers. But yes, they took something."

"How do you know?"

"They left it on your car."

My stomach turned over. "What was it?"

"One of the Timberbeast coasters. I have a bunch of them in the house."

"Yeah, I've seen them."

"This one has a drip of hot chocolate on it."

"Owen drinks hot chocolate." My voice kept getting weaker.

"Exactly. But the thing is, it could be argued it's not from our house. Those things are all over this town. Rocco gives them out like candy."

"So they won't believe you if you say the coaster you found on my car proves that someone broke into the house."

"Right."

My stomach turned over with worry. I didn't want to doubt him. I wanted to believe he knew what he was doing. That his instincts were right and his superiors were wrong—he wasn't letting the case get to him.

But what if he was?

What if everything was coming to a head. Being a cop and a single dad with a new girlfriend and a surprise pregnancy, plus a cold case murder and a series of what could have been unrelated events. Strange, but unrelated.

Unlucky, even.

Oh no.

Was this all the bad luck curse at work? And was it going to drive him crazy?

"Okay, so maybe someone was in the house and maybe they took a coaster. That seems like a weird thing to take, doesn't it? Underwear makes sense. It seems like the sort of thing a creepy stalker-type person would take from a woman's house. It's intimate and shows he was not just in my bedroom, but in my top drawer. But a coaster? What's the point of that?"

"He's taunting you. He's showing you he was inside and he wants you to believe he can still get to you, even though you're in my house now."

I rubbed my hands up and down his chest, as if I could help calm him down. He was so tense. "What did you do with it?"

"I bagged it and put it in my pocket."

"I still think maybe you should have someone look into it."

He lowered his forehead to mine and quieted his voice. "I don't know who I can trust right now. And I have a lead I need to follow up on. It might confirm that I'm going in the right direction."

"But Jack told you to take time off. He probably said get some rest."

"He did. But I need to do this first. I just wanted to stop here and make sure you're okay. That was when I saw the coaster on your car."

I glanced over my shoulder toward my car. It was definitely disconcerting. He was right, those coasters were all over the place. I remembered the night Garrett had missed our blind date, Rocco had given me one. But what were the chances someone would randomly stick one on my car? Especially one with a dribble of hot chocolate on it?

"I'm fine. There's always so many people here, I don't

think I'm in any danger. And the SPS walk by constantly. I have a batch of cookies in the oven just for them, actually."

"Good. I'll make sure they stay until you close. They'll walk you to your car. And I don't want you to come home after work. Go up to my parents'. Owen will be there."

"You really don't think it's safe to go home? Won't you be there?"

He touched the side of my face. "Please, love. Just go to my parents'. I'll meet you there."

"Promise?"

"I promise." He leaned in and brushed my lips with a soft kiss. "Everything is going to be fine."

I wrapped my arms around him and rested my head on his chest. Why was this happening to me?

But I already knew the answer.

My bad luck curse was close to running out. It was going to find a way to get me, and I had a feeling it would make it big.

I just hoped Garrett could find a way for us to outrun it.

CHAPTER 37

Garrett

LEAVING Harper at the bakery was hard, but I'd see her in a few hours. She wouldn't be alone at any point and the best thing I could do to keep her safe was figure out once and for all who was after her.

I needed evidence to back up my instincts. Then we could get this guy off the streets.

And away from Harper.

I searched my house thoroughly when I got home, checking every room, every corner. I didn't think someone would be there, but at that point, I wasn't taking any chances. Did it make me paranoid? I figured it made me careful.

A prickle of anticipation made the hair on the back of my neck stand on end as I sat down with my laptop and inserted the thumb drive from the florist.

"Come on," I muttered under my breath. "Show me something."

She'd given me about a week's worth of footage. I tried to relax and settle in to the task, but my back and shoulders rippled with tension. After a few deep breaths, my mind cleared and I was able to lean on my training. Compartmentalize. Focus on the task.

The recording was surprisingly clear. That gave me some hope. It wasn't like a lot of security cams that were so grainy and low-resolution, you could hardly make out what someone was wearing, let alone facial features. The camera they'd used had a tight view of the front counter, including the cash register and both the employee working and any customers.

I skipped forward from customer to customer. The first was a woman who seemed to be placing an order. Margie wrote something down on a notepad and the customer didn't leave with anything. Next came a guy who picked up a vase filled with colorful flowers. Definitely not white funeral flowers.

A few more people came and went throughout that day, buying various things or placing orders. Some just seemed to come in and talk to whoever was working and then leave. It was tedious, fast-forwarding through long stretches of nothing until someone once again appeared on the screen. Then checking to see what they were buying—if anything— and who they might be.

The first day produced nothing. No one bought a white flower arrangement. I moved on to the next.

Hope started to fade as I worked. I was sleep deprived and not as calm as I wanted to be for this type of work. I kept getting distracted, wondering if Harper was okay. I resisted the urge to text her every five minutes. It wasn't going to help. She was busy at Angel Cakes. And she wasn't alone. She'd be fine.

Day two didn't have anything either. No one buying white flowers.

The third day was the same, as was the fourth. By the time I got to the fifth, I was ready to crawl out of my own skin. My shoulders ached and I was afraid I'd just wasted hours of time I'd never get back.

Meanwhile, Harper was still in danger.

I got up to take a quick break, stretching my back and legs. I figured caffeine might help, so I made a pot of coffee and poured a cup. There were only a few more days of footage to review. If I didn't find anything, either whoever had bought those flowers had purchased them earlier than I'd estimated, or he'd gotten them from a different shop.

That was fine. I'd hunt down every damn florist in the Cascades if I had to. I was going to find this guy.

I sat down with my hot cup of coffee, took a sip, and started again.

For some reason, the sixth day had been busy. Lots of people coming and going. Maybe it had been a weekend. Or they'd been running a sale to bring in more customers. Whatever the reason, I had to slow the footage down over and over again to check what people were buying.

I went to take another sip of coffee and realized I'd finished the cup. I glanced at the coffee pot. Did I need more?

I let the footage keep going to check the next person and all thoughts of coffee fled.

A man with white flowers.

He'd clearly picked them out of the arrangements on display. It wasn't something he'd ordered ahead of time. I'd noticed Margie or one of her employees would often go to the back to bring things out—presumably flowers that had been ordered ahead of time. But this guy brought a vase filled with white flowers to the counter.

That tracked. If he didn't want a record of his purchase, he wouldn't have special ordered something.

But who was it? It was a man, that was clear. But he was wearing a baseball cap. I couldn't see his face.

Damn it.

Come on, man, look up.

Margie rang him up. I could see him hand her cash. That also tracked. He wouldn't have used anything with his name on it.

She handed him some change and a receipt. He pocketed both and took the vase off the counter.

I still couldn't see his face.

My hands were on the desk, palms splayed, my face moving closer to the screen. Who was he? Was it Matt? The clothes were nondescript, just a T-shirt and jeans. Even his hat was plain gray, without a logo or anything identifying.

That had to be on purpose. He was making sure he didn't stand out. A guy who could blend in. Fly under the radar.

Was Matt that guy? Not really. But maybe he had a hidden side. Maybe the awkward true crime junkie was just for show.

I held my breath as he started to walk away. Nothing. Not even a glimpse of his face. I was about to go back and rewatch the entire exchange when he moved his face toward the camera and I finally got a look. I hit pause and increased the resolution.

And I couldn't believe what I was seeing.

It wasn't Matt Rudolph. Not even close. It wasn't any of our frequent fliers, a known criminal with a record. Not even someone I'd arrested before but had stayed out of trouble since.

It was Phillip Lancaster, the prosecuting attorney.

I sat back in my chair, dumbfounded. Phillip? He was a successful lawyer with a stellar reputation. Everybody loved him.

He couldn't have killed someone. That wasn't possible. He put bad guys away for a living.

I kept going through the footage to see if someone else had bought white flowers that day, or the next. Nothing. He was the only one. I went back to him so I could zoom in on the arrangement he bought. It was definitely white lilies. No question.

My stomach churned with a mix of anger and bewilderment. Was Phillip Jasmine's killer? This didn't prove it, but it meant he sure as hell might have been.

And I'd been sharing details of my investigation with him.

He had access to everything. Evidence, case files, all my reports, even my schedule. If he'd wanted to, he'd have no problem tracking my location at any time. He'd just have to ask dispatch. Wouldn't even need a reason. Everyone trusted him.

My gut was screaming at me that this was it. This was the answer.

It was him. Phillip Lancaster had killed Jasmine Joyner.

And he was going to try to kill Harper.

I flew out of my chair. This wasn't enough to question him, let alone enough for an arrest. The fact that he'd bought white flowers just before Jasmine went missing, and Jasmine's sister recalled her receiving similar flowers, was nothing but a coincidence in the eyes of the law.

But at that moment, I wasn't focused on Jasmine. I had to know if Phillip had been back to the florist to buy more white flowers.

Flowers that were going to end up on my doorstep—for Harper.

CHAPTER 38

Harper

GARRETT'S VISIT earlier in the day had left me jumpy. Did a coaster left on my car mean someone had been in the house? Or was it just a weird coincidence?

Did it mean I was in danger?

SPS members had been walking the block around the bakery, like soldiers on patrol. There were usually two, walking in opposite directions, and they'd stop in front of the bakery together, come in to check that all was well, then resume their circuit.

I felt a little bit ridiculous about it all. Was this necessary? Or was Sheriff Cordero right and Garrett was letting the case get to him?

Still, I was glad they were there. I didn't think they could stop my bad luck curse from striking—nothing could—but maybe they'd keep things from escalating. I could live with random bad luck. Burnt cookies, even if they did set off the fire alarm, were nothing compared to being targeted by a killer.

I went back to the kitchen to check the cookies I'd made for the SPS guys. They were cooling on a rack while Mila did some clean-up.

"Hey." I went to the island where my cookies were cooling and put my hand over them to feel how warm they were. "Are you about ready to head home?"

She didn't answer. Just kept washing something in the sink.

"Mila?"

Turning around, she popped an earbud out of one ear. "Were you speaking?"

"Right, headphones. I was just wondering if you're ready to head home."

"Almost."

"Okay. Thanks for your help today." I pointed to her headphones. "What are you listening to? I don't mean to be nosy, I'm just curious."

"True crime podcast," she answered in that odd monotone voice she had.

"Huh. We have a customer who's really into true crime." And might actually be a serial killer. "He likes to tell people about the cases."

"Oh."

She turned back to the sink.

She wasn't much of a conversationalist, but at least she was a good baker.

"To each her own," I mumbled to myself.

The cookies were cool enough to box up, so I grabbed a couple of to-go boxes and started packing them.

"What are those for?" she asked as she dried her hands.

"Oh, the SPS guys."

"Who are they and why are they continually pacing around the block?"

Sugar cookies, how did I answer that question? I didn't know Mila well enough to confide in her, and 'my boyfriend thinks a killer might be after me and wants to make sure I'm never alone' sounded... a little off.

"Well, they like to keep an eye on the squirrel population.

I guess they're focusing their efforts on our block for now." I shrugged. "I don't know, they're super sweet, so I like it when they're around."

Her expression—or lack thereof—didn't change, so I had no idea if that cleared anything up. "Oh."

"It's a Tilikum thing."

She finally—finally—cracked a little smile. "I like this town."

"Me too."

The smile disappeared as quickly as it had come. "I hope my work was satisfactory today."

"Yeah, it was great." Satisfactory? She was so weirdly cute. "You're doing a great job."

She gave me a crisp nod. "I will see you tomorrow."

"Have a nice evening, Mila."

Closing the lids on the boxes, I took them out front. I only had to wait a few minutes before this afternoon's SPS patrol members, Stan Albert and Russell Haven—apparently a distant Haven relative—appeared in the front window and came inside.

"Hello, gentlemen." I went around the counter with the boxes. "I have a little something for you to thank you for your time."

They each took a box. Stan opened his and his eyes widened. Russell brought his up to his nose and inhaled.

"What a treat," Russell said. "Thank you, Miss Harper."

"You're quite welcome. It's the very least I can do."

"We don't mind a bit. But I won't lie, fresh cookies make it an even more enjoyable task."

Those two were so delightful. "We're closing soon, and I won't need to stay late. So you can get back to your regular lives."

"No rush," Stan said. "Just let us know when you're leaving. Deputy Haven was very clear that we needed to see you all the way to your car."

"And make sure you leave safely."

"Thanks, guys. You're the best."

I went to the kitchen while they went back to their patrol, cookies in hand. That made me happy. At least I felt a little less guilty about them giving up their free time to watch the bakery.

"I'm out of here." Beth hung up her apron and took her purse down from a hook. "I'll see you in the morning."

"Bye, Beth. Have a good night."

There wasn't much time before closing, but I'd whipped up a couple of batches of experimental cookies that afternoon. Stress baking again? Probably. I had one in the oven—a dozen fig and feta cookies with honey. Maybe a little out there for my Tilikum customers, but they smelled good.

I'd just put the other batch—blackberry almond thumbprints—in the other oven when the front door opened. I set my two timers and went out to the front to greet my customer.

A man in a suit—jacket but no tie—was standing just inside the door. His shirt collar was unbuttoned and he had neatly trimmed salt and pepper hair.

"Hi, there. Can I help you?"

He gave me a friendly smile. "Harper?"

"Yes."

"It's nice to meet you. I'm Phillip. I know Garrett."

"Nice to meet you, too. Do you work in the sheriff's office?"

"I'm with the prosecuting attorney's office. But we work closely with the sheriff and his crew."

He kind of had a lawyer vibe. Sleek and professional. Well-spoken.

"So, Harper, I have a bit of a bone to pick with you." The corners of his mouth lifted slightly and there was a hint of humor in his voice.

Still, something made my stomach twinge a little.

"Oh?"

"People keep bringing goodies from your bakery into the sheriff's office. Half the time when I go in to meet with someone, I'm greeted by the scent of your cupcakes or cookies." He put his hands on his middle. "It's killing my waistline."

I smiled. "I guess, sorry not sorry?"

"That's fair. You're just doing your job. It's not your fault you do it so well."

"Thank you. At the risk of killing your waistline a bit more, do you want anything while you're here?"

His eyes held mine for a few seconds and that twinge in my stomach was back. Was that a pregnancy thing, or were my instincts telling me something?

I was so jumpy with everything that had been happening, I didn't know. It felt like anyone could make me nervous at that point.

"Yes, I'd absolutely like something." He broke eye contact and started perusing the pastry case.

The back of my neck tingled and the hair on my arms stood on end. A chill ran down my spine. Was it cold? Maybe the air conditioning had just turned on.

"So, how has Garrett been lately?" he asked, his gaze still on the case. "I talked to Sheriff Cordero a bit ago and he said Garrett is taking some leave."

"He's taking a few days off, yeah."

"Good. I'm glad to hear that. He's been working too hard."

"Yeah. Big case and everything."

"Right, the Joyner cold case. So much scrutiny. The whole town has been buzzing about it." He looked up. "Will the intrepid detective catch a killer?"

"Let's hope so."

"Indeed. A guy like that? We don't want him on the loose."

"No, definitely not."

He pointed to a row of double chocolate chunk cookies. "How about one of those."

"Is that going to be all, or would you like more than one? I'm just wondering if I should get you a box or not."

He put his hands on his middle again. "I'm afraid I need to pace myself. One will have to do. For today, at least."

I put a double chocolate chunk cookie in a bag and handed it to him, then rang him up. He gave me cash and as I was taking out his change, the door opened again. And in walked Matt.

My eyes widened and my already jumpy stomach did a leap. It was the weirdest thing. He looked so... nondescript. Not even that, he was almost bumbling. Maybe the contrast between him and Phillip was so stark—the sleek lawyer versus the rumpled awkward guy who drove a white van—it made it more apparent. But could I really believe Matt was a savvy thief? An expert at breaking and entering, and possibly responsible for much, much worse?

Phillip took his change and glanced over his shoulder. Was that a flicker of frustration in his eyes? Even anger?

Maybe I was the one who was getting paranoid.

He turned back to me. "Make sure Garrett takes those days off. I think he needs the break."

"Yeah," I said absently, looking toward the front window, hoping to see Stan and Russell circle around the block. "He was just going to follow up on a lead, then he'll go home. Take a break."

A timer went off in the kitchen. I'd set the one on my phone, but it wasn't chiming. Why did my bad luck love to mess with timers so much? I pulled my phone out of my pocket and checked. Sure enough, the timer wasn't even running.

Oh well, that was why I always used more than one. I set it on the counter. "Excuse me, I have to run back to get something out of the oven."

"No problem. It was nice to finally meet you. I'm sure I'll see you soon."

Another chill ran down my spine. I glanced between him and Matt, then out the window. Still no Stan or Russell.

"Be right with you," I said to Matt and ducked into the kitchen.

The scent of figs and honey filled the air and I hoped the feta would be a nice counterpoint to the sweetness. I took the perfectly browned cookies out of the oven and set them on the island. At least I hadn't burned them.

But I still had to deal with Matt.

Wishing Phillip hadn't left, or that Stan and Russell would come back, I went out front. Matt stood in front of the pastry case, hands shoved in the pockets of his baggy jeans. His beard was slightly less scraggly than usual, but his hair was matted down on top, like he'd been wearing headphones.

I pondered for a second while he looked over the selection. Garrett and I had wondered if Matt was behind everything. But him? Was he an expert lock-picker? A man with an uncanny ability to blend in, go unseen, and get in and out of someone's house without leaving a trace?

He scratched his backside. I was really starting to wonder.

Although, for all I knew, the guy I was seeing was an act, and all those true crime stories weren't things he'd heard on a podcast. They were stories of things he'd done.

"What are those?" He pointed to the case.

His voice startled me out of my thoughts. "Um, chewy pistachio cookies."

"Did you make them?"

"Actually, no."

He glanced up in surprise.

"We have a new baker. She made them earlier today."

His eyebrows drew together and he took a deep breath, as if this were a very difficult decision. "Okay. I'll try one."

I got one out and put it in a bag, then rang him up.

"I don't know if anything can be as good as the stuff you bake, but maybe."

"Trust me, she's very good."

Stan and Russell finally appeared in the window. They looked in and I tried to make a subtle get in here gesture. Fortunately, Matt didn't seem to notice. He was busy pulling out his cookie and inspecting it, like he'd never seen one before.

They came into the bakery and shared a glance, like they weren't sure what to do next. I mouthed, *it's okay, just wait here*. They nodded. Apparently they understood.

Because what did I really want them to do? Ask Matt to leave? He hadn't done anything. He was just taking his time, sampling his cookie. He hadn't tried to get me to leave with him in his van. He hadn't even told me any new crime stories.

That was a relief.

Hopefully, if Matt had anything nefarious in mind, just having other people around would be enough.

He took a bite of the cookie and as he chewed it, his expression brightened. "Wow. I'm sorry, Harper, but this might be my new favorite."

"That's great. No need to be sorry. We just want happy customers."

"This makes me very happy."

I couldn't help but smile. If I hadn't been concerned that he might be a secret serial killer out to murder me, I could have found him awkwardly endearing.

"See you later," Matt said out of the blue and turned around, still eating the rest of his cookie, and left.

That had been anticlimactic.

"That was him, right?" Russell asked. "The one we're supposed to look out for?"

I nodded. "Yeah, that's him."

"Don't worry, Miss Harper. We'll stick around in case he's lurking about."

A white van drove by the front window. "I think that was him leaving, but thank you."

They sat at one of the bistro tables by the window as I busied myself with getting ready to close. I'd be so relieved when I could finally go home.

Paul and Marlene's home, to be specific. Which I didn't mind. But it was a reminder that all was not well.

I just hoped whatever lead Garrett was following would give us some answers. Maybe even all the answers.

And that no one was waiting to ambush me when I went out to my car. Matt might not have looked like a cold-blooded killer, but he was a lot bigger than me. I glanced at Stan and Russell. They weren't exactly spring chickens. Maybe between the three of us, we could ward off an attacker.

But as I'd heard Garrett say before, whoever was behind all this was good. Very good. I had a feeling he couldn't be underestimated.

And it might take a lot more than a couple of sweet, good-hearted SPS volunteers to keep me safe.

CHAPTER 39

Garrett

I GRABBED my phone before heading out, trying to push down the undercurrent of desperation. The flowers were a ticking clock and an important clue. If Phillip had been back to buy another white arrangement, I'd know he was ready to make his move. And I could find a way to trap him.

And if not, I wasn't about to let my guard down. But at least it would tell me if I had more time to find what I needed to put a proper case together.

Either way, my priority was Harper. Yes, Jasmine deserved justice, and I'd do everything I could to make sure she, and her family, got it. But before I could do that, I had to make sure my woman was safe.

The florist wasn't far from the bakery. I'd check in there, then go pick up Harper myself. If my suspicions were correct, we needed a lot more than the well-meaning SPS patrols. I wanted the fucking secret service, but I'd have to make do. And I didn't know who I could trust at work. They already thought I was paranoid.

I couldn't tell them about Phillip. Not yet. Not until I had evidence. And I couldn't trust anyone else to keep Harper safe. The only people I did trust?

My family.

Thankfully, Owen was already at my parents' place. I'd take Harper there. It was perfect—only one way in or out. And I'd loop in my brothers. We'd fill the house, and it didn't matter how good he was, he'd never get through an entire family of Havens.

I stalked out of my house, amped with adrenaline. I tried to call Harper to let her know not to leave the bakery yet. She didn't pick up, so I left her a quick voicemail.

"Hey, love. I'm coming to pick you up. Don't go anywhere yet, just stay at the bakery. Love you."

I was about to get in my car when something caught my eye.

A package in front of the garage.

My heart almost stopped dead in my chest and a surge of dread spread through my gut.

No. It couldn't be.

Delivery people never left packages over there. They always brought them to the front door.

Which put them in sight of my doorbell camera.

This one was clearly outside the camera's field of vision.

I walked over and picked it up. No label. No return address. Nothing. Just a blank box. I tore off the tape, and although I knew exactly what I'd find inside, it still made my insides twist.

White funeral flowers.

No. Fuck that guy.

In a rage, I threw the box and rushed to my car. I turned on the engine and my phone rang. Harper.

"Hey, love," I said, my words coming out in a rush. "Don't leave the bakery. Stay where you are. I'm coming to get you right now."

She didn't reply. Had she butt dialed me?

"Harper?"

Still nothing.

I looked at the screen. The call was connected. Where was she?

"Harper, I can't hear you. Maybe you have a bad connection. Can you call me back?"

It wasn't her voice that answered. It was a man. "No."

Icy cold fear blasted through my chest. "Let me talk to her."

"I'm afraid not."

"Don't you fucking touch her."

"Can the heroic detective catch the killer before he claims another victim?" He was disguising his voice. It didn't sound like Phillip, but it had to be him.

"Do. Not. Touch. Her."

"Too late for that. But I will let you in on a secret. She's still alive. For now."

"Prove it. Let me talk to her."

The call went dead.

"Fuck!"

A second later, a text came through from Harper's phone.

I opened it to find a photo. It was dark and she wasn't looking straight at the camera, but that was her profile.

The bastard had her.

Where was she? The surroundings could have been anywhere. A room, a closet, a basement.

A root cellar?

I flew out of the car, ran to the house, and went into the garage. The bolt cutters were exactly where I thought they'd be. I grabbed them and raced back to the car.

Pulling out onto the street, my mind raced. Tracking her cell phone would be too slow. Even in an urgent case, there was always too much back and forth getting the cell companies to comply. It wouldn't get me to her fast enough.

Besides, all Phillip had to do was turn off her phone. The best we'd be able to do would be last known location. He was well aware of how that worked. He helped us write warrants for this kind of thing all the time.

And I didn't know who I could trust.

Jack? Kade? The other deputies? The department itself?

In that moment, I was no longer a deputy. No longer a cop. If saving her cost me my career, so be it. I'd do anything. Phillip was not going to kill her. Or our child.

Her phone didn't matter. I knew where she was. And I knew who I needed to call. I brought up Luke's number and hit send.

"Hey, man, what's up?" he answered. The connection sounded spotty.

"Don't talk for a second, just listen. I know who killed Jasmine Joyner. And he has Harper. Remember that old barn and root cellar?"

"What the fuck? Yeah, I remember."

"Meet me there. Now."

"I'm on the highway heading back to town, but I'll get there as fast as I can."

It was all coming together. He'd abducted Jasmine and driven her out into the woods. She'd lost her bracelet when he'd pulled her out of the car. He'd dragged or carried her to the root cellar where he'd killed her, then left her body near another trail.

Phillip was an outdoorsman. A hunter. He'd be accustomed to hauling elk, deer, whatever he was hunting, out of the woods. Moving a woman's body, even over a distance, wouldn't have been hard for him.

He was recreating his crime. Only this time, Harper was his intended victim. The packages, the flowers. The taunts, showing her he was watching her.

As for the rest, he'd been trying to get me out of the way. Get me in trouble at work so they'd take me off the case—off his case.

I hated that I'd made Harper his target. Would he have

chosen her as a victim if I hadn't started investigating the cold case? I didn't know, but I doubted it.

There was only one thing I could do. Catch the fucker.

Driven by single-minded determination, I flew out to the trailhead. Adrenaline pumped through my veins, burning away any remaining fatigue. He'd called to taunt me, and I knew it. I just had to hope this was part of his game. Part of the sick pleasure he got out of it. I had to believe she was breathing. That he'd wait, draw it out.

Time. Just a little more time.

Hang in there, Harper. I'm coming.

I pulled into the lot at the trailhead. Ignoring the cars already parked there, I went around them and drove into the woods. If someone could get a stolen car through the area, I could get through too. I'd drive as close as I could to the old barn and root cellar, saving precious minutes.

The trees grew thicker and I had to stop or risk hitting something. My heart thumped hard in my chest as I slammed the gear shift into park and jumped out of my car. Where was Luke? How far behind was he?

I called him again, but this time there was no answer. Voicemail.

Probably in a dead spot.

I trusted him. He was on his way. But could I afford to wait?

Shit.

Nope. Couldn't do it. If I was even a minute too late, I'd never forgive myself. I grabbed the bolt cutters and took off at a run. Luke would catch up. He knew the way.

The dilapidated barn came into view. I rushed past it and stopped in my tracks.

The root cellar door was wide open.

From where I was standing, I couldn't see into the dark interior. Was she there? Or was this just another taunt? Another attempt to make me think I was crazy.

I took in the surrounding area, wary of any sounds or movements. But I didn't see a thing. Approaching the cellar slowly, my senses on high alert, I looked around for the lock. Nothing. No lock. It was as if it had never been there.

"Harper?"

I heard the footsteps behind me just before the pain hit. Every muscle in my body went rigid and it felt like being battered with a hundred wooden clubs moving at lightning speed. I fell to the ground, unable to stay upright, the impact knocking the breath from my lungs.

A taser. It was a fucking taser.

Five seconds felt like an hour. But as soon as the electrical current stopped and my body started to regain movement, he hit the trigger again.

I needed to get the barbs out. But I couldn't move. My teeth ground together and the pain was unimaginable.

My arms were wrenched behind my back and fastened together. I couldn't tell if he used handcuffs or something else. The taser stopped and he lit it up again. I rode the lightning while he bound my ankles, every part of my body screaming in pain.

The taser stopped and my muscles unclenched, but as soon as I tried to move, I got a sharp kick in the ribs—right at my liver. It almost made me vomit.

"None of that," a male voice said.

"Phillip, you piece of shit," I ground out between gritted teeth, my face in the dirt.

"Swear at me all you want. It won't help."

"Fuck you."

"Good. I want you angry. It's going to make this so much more fun."

I didn't hear another word. For a split second, I felt the explosion of pain at the blow to my temple before everything went dark.

CHAPTER 40
Garrett

THE PAIN BROUGHT me back to consciousness.

Everything hurt. I'd been tased before, in training, so I knew what the aftermath felt like. But Phillip had hit the trigger multiple times, so this was worse. My muscles ached right down to my bones.

And my head. Fuck. He'd scored a perfect blow to my temple. Lights out.

Vaguely, I wondered if I had a concussion. The knock-out meant it was likely. Although, severe as a head injury could be, it was kind of the least of my problems.

Trying not to groan, I opened my eyes. I was on a floor, bound at the wrists and ankles. My head was on something hard—not the dirt of a root cellar. Metal. He'd moved me.

Which meant Luke wasn't going to find us.

"Are you waking up this time?"

I didn't answer. Just blinked, trying to get my head to clear. Trying to think through the pain.

"Welcome back."

Things started coming into focus. A small space with a metal floor and bare walls. And Phillip seated in a folding chair, one ankle crossed over his knee.

Where was Harper?

He tilted his head, regarding me with calculating eyes. "You're every bit as heavy as I thought you'd be. It wasn't easy to move you."

A coal of rage burned hot in my gut. "Where's Harper."

"She's fine."

"Tell me where she is."

He uncrossed his legs and leaned forward, resting his elbows on his knees. His hands were covered with supple leather gloves. He watched me for a long moment, like a predator toying with his prey. "You've been an interesting challenge, Haven. A worthy adversary. It's going to be an honor to kill you."

"What the fuck is that supposed to mean?"

He smiled. "I think I was clear."

"Why?"

"Why am I going to kill you?" He leaned back in his chair. "Because I can."

"That's it?"

"No, I suppose that's not it. It's been too long. I've been craving it. After a while, the craving becomes too strong and I have to give in. And once the idea came to me, I couldn't get it out of my head. Plus, I knew you'd never give up on a cold case."

"You did kill Jasmine."

He nodded slowly, his eyes unfocused, as if he were remembering the murder with pleasure. "She was my first."

"But not your last."

"No. Trust me, once you get a taste for it, there's no going back."

"Who else?"

"Sorry, Haven. You're not getting out of this alive, but I'm not stupid. Besides, none of them were in your jurisdiction. With the exception of Jasmine, and now you, I don't shit where I eat."

Hunting and fishing trips. Phillip Lancaster was known for going out of town on hunting and fishing trips.

My stomach turned at the implications. How many victims had he claimed?

"I do prefer women, though. We'll see how it feels to actually kill you. I might enjoy it more than I think."

Wait. My pain-addled brain was having a hard time keeping up. He was going to kill *me*. Had that been his plan all along?

"What did you do to Harper?"

A slow smile spread across his face. "Nothing. Yet."

I gritted my teeth and strained against my bonds.

"I don't have her." He pulled a phone out of his pocket. Harper's phone. "But I did manage to lift this when she wasn't looking."

"You sent a picture."

"I'd love to take credit, as it is a convincing picture. But AI software makes it all too easy."

The photo was fake. He didn't have her. But he'd said *yet*.

"Here's the part where I am going to let you in on a few things." He leaned forward again and looked me in the eyes. "Because I want you to know. I want you to know what I did to you. How I beat you."

He paused for a long moment, the dramatic bastard.

"I'd been thinking I needed a new challenge. Nothing was inspiring me. My last victim was so… unfulfilling. I wanted more. Something to really test me. And then you found Jasmine's bracelet." He shook his head slowly. "That fucking bracelet. I thought I'd attended to every detail, and there it was, all these years later, just waiting for some eager investigator to find it. That was when it hit me. You were my next challenge. And with you, I could recapture the magic I had with Jasmine."

"Magic?"

"Oh, yeah. Killing in my own town is, of course, incredibly risky. But it gave me a chance to play first. That's what I've been missing all these years. It's always so hurried. So rushed. I can't take my time. Get to know her first. Show her something's wrong, someone's watching. That was what I had with Jasmine. I watched her, tracked her, learned her schedule. And I was able to set the stage. Make sure that by the time I took her, she was already terrified."

"That's why you took her underwear."

"It's kind of a cliché, I know. But effective. It made it look like her ex was stalking her, but more importantly, it made her afraid. And I was the one who got to see her fear."

"You're a sick fuck."

"You have no idea."

"And funeral flowers?"

He waved a hand. "My attempt at being poetic, I guess. Until recently, I kind of regretted those. They were a bit too on the nose; not subtle. Of course, the idiot investigators had no clue. But as I was planning all this, I realized how much of a genius I really am. They gave me one more way to convince you your girlfriend was in danger."

Had it been me all along? He hadn't been targeting Harper. He'd been targeting me.

"How the fuck did you get in her house? And mine?"

"Easy. How do you think I put myself through law school? I've been breaking into houses since I was twelve."

"Was all this just to keep me from solving the Joyner case?"

"That's more like a bonus. You picking up that case gave me the inspiration I was craving. The challenge I've been wanting."

"Even if you kill me, someone else will pick up the pieces. You're going to get caught."

"Will I, though? Your department is strapped for resources. No one has time. Not many are as dedicated and single-minded as you are. Besides, in the aftermath of your death, they're going to discover just how disorganized you were. How much evidence you misplaced. The entire case is going to look like such a mess, no one's going to touch it. It'll be unsolvable. Kind of like the issues with the Trent Jones arrest, only on a bigger scale."

That bastard. He'd set me up.

"And that pristine, good guy reputation of yours? That'll be gone too. I've already started. A few complaints, unfounded or not, to sow the seeds of doubt. Then convince you someone's reenacting the Joyner murder with your girl-friend as the target, but without enough evidence to trigger a full-on investigation. Make it look like maybe you're a little off, and a lot paranoid."

"You piece of shit."

"That's not all, Haven." His voice hardened. "Jack shouldn't have just sent you home. I already told him that. I told him earlier I saw you in town and you didn't look good. There was something in your eyes. He should have ordered a mental health evaluation. But he didn't, did he? And now look what Garrett Haven did. He snapped. He murdered his lovely girlfriend, then killed himself."

I struggled against my bonds, itching to rip his face off.

"I don't have Harper, yet. But that's the next step. And it doesn't matter where she is right now. I'll get her. You're going to wait here and, trust me, no one is going to find you." He got off the chair and knelt next to me. "Then I'm going to bring her here and make you watch while I kill her. That's what I want. What I've been craving. Not just to kill someone stronger and more powerful than me. I want someone to watch. You get to witness something special, Haven. Some-thing glorious. The power of life and death. I'm going to break you before I kill you."

He paused again. My heart hammered against my chest and the bonds chafed against my skin. Rage burned in my veins like fire.

"Everyone is going to think you did it. You killed her. All the evidence will point to you, and you'll be dead too, so you won't be able to defend yourself. And I get to stand by and watch it all unfold, knowing that it was me. I'm the genius. I made this happen."

He stood and looked down at me. "I wanted you to know that before I go so you can picture it happening. I want you to sit with it until I get back. I'm going to kill you both and I'm going to love every second of it."

My control was on the verge of snapping. I strained against the bonds, teeth gritted, pain exploding through my entire body. He was not going to hurt her. I was not going to let it happen.

"Fuck!"

He took the chair, stepped over me, and I heard the sound of metal creaking. A heavy door? I craned my head but couldn't quite see where he went. It creaked again and the door shut.

I was alone.

Bound. Captured. Helpless.

For a second, a wave of despair crashed over me. It was my fault Harper and our child were in danger. I'd failed.

No. This was not how it ended.

Hot anger swept through me, burning away the doubt, the despair, the failure. I didn't know how I was going to do it, but I was going to save her. She was not going to die.

Phillip Lancaster had made a fatal mistake. He'd picked the wrong fucking man.

CHAPTER 41

Harper

I COULDN'T FIND my phone.

It was just my luck. Of course on a day when it felt like things were spiraling out of control, I'd lose my phone.

Stupid mirror curse.

Although I shouldn't have been surprised. I'd lost my phone approximately eight hundred thirty-four times since I'd broken that dang mirror.

I'd decided to stop looking and just head to Paul and Marlene's house. The SPS guys had waited long enough, and I could go back to the bakery with Garrett later to find it. No sense in making them hang around while I searched. I was so frazzled.

Besides, I had a feeling it would be sitting out in plain sight the next day. Things like that happened to me sometimes. I figured the bad luck curse had a dark sense of humor.

Stan and Russell walked me to my car after I locked up. Even with them there, I felt weirdly exposed. Like someone was watching.

"Thanks for everything." I opened my car door and tossed my purse inside.

"It's not a problem," Russell said. "Thanks for all the goodies."

"Of course. It's the least I could do."

In addition to the boxes I'd prepared just for them, I'd loaded them up with the day's leftover cookies and cupcakes for the SPS meeting they were having that evening.

"You sure you'll be okay getting home?" Stan asked.

"Oh yeah. I'm heading up to Paul and Marlene Haven's. Garrett is meeting me there."

"All right. Night, Harper."

"Have a great evening."

I got in my car and immediately locked the doors. Twisting around, I checked the back seat, just to make sure.

Sugar cookies, I really was being paranoid. No one was hiding in my car.

I was pretty sure I remembered the way to Paul and Marlene's, but I missed having my GPS. Stupid lost phone. I left the bakery and drove through town, my eyes flicking to the rearview mirror over and over. Tension made the back of my neck prickle. I didn't see anyone back there, even at a distance. Just a handful of other cars coming and going, like a normal evening in Tilikum. Nothing suss, as Owen would say.

But I was still nervous.

Had someone really broken into the house and taken a coaster? What a weird thing to do. But what if Garrett was right, and someone was taunting me?

He was overworked. Hadn't been sleeping enough. Worried about his job, about me, the baby, Owen, probably a million other things he hadn't shared with me. He carried the weight of the world on his broad shoulders.

Was it getting to him? Did he need more than a few days off?

Or was he right and something was happening to us? Something that was starting to spiral out of control?

I didn't know what to think.

My stomach gurgled. That had been happening off and on for the past several days, as if my body couldn't decide if it was hungry or not. At least I hadn't been plagued with morning sickness. That was something.

A disturbing thought crept into my mind as I drove. Had I left an oven on?

I'd been so distracted looking for my phone, I hadn't triple checked everything the way I usually did before I locked up for the night. Stan and Russell had been waiting for me, and I'd felt pressured to hurry. In my rush to leave, had I left it on?

In fact, had I left the blackberry almond thumbprints in the oven?

Sugar cookies, my entire afternoon felt like a blur. I distinctly remembered putting the batch of blackberry almond thumbprints into the oven. But I couldn't remember if I'd taken them out.

I had to have. Maybe I'd wrapped them to save for the next day when I'd add the blackberry filling.

I found my way to the turn up Paul and Marlene's long driveway. The log home was so cozy, even from the outside. The sight of it was comforting. I parked next to a truck, but Garrett wasn't there yet. That was mildly disappointing. I was craving the warmth and safety of his embrace.

Feeling slightly less nervous than I'd been the first time I visited Garrett's parents, I went to the front door and knocked. He'd just walked right in, but I didn't feel like I had come-in-without-knocking privileges.

Owen opened the door dressed in a gray hoodie, the basketball shorts his only concession to the summer weather.

His smile warmed my heart. "Hey. I didn't know you were coming over."

"Your dad asked me to meet him here."

"Cool." He stepped aside so I could go in. "I was just getting a snack with Uncle Theo."

I followed him inside. "A snack sounds good."

He paused and glanced at me over his shoulder. "You aren't going to tell me I'll spoil my dinner?"

"Didn't even occur to me. But I'm pregnant. I can snack all day and still eat a full meal."

He chuckled. "Cool."

"Has your dad called or anything? I lost my phone, so I don't know if he's tried to call me."

"No, but I can text him and let him know you're here." He pulled his phone out of his pocket and started typing.

"Thanks."

Eyes on his phone, he walked into the dining room. The table was strewn with a random assortment of snack foods—healthy and unhealthy alike. Bags of chips, a bowl of nuts, bananas—plus several discarded banana peels—oranges, a plate of cookies, a block of cheese with a knife sticking out of the top, pepperoni slices, and an open bag of beef jerky.

Theo stood next to the table and I got the impression he'd been wandering around the perimeter, grazing as he went.

"Hey, Harper," he said.

"A snack? This is a feast."

Owen pocketed his phone. "We were doing football drills."

"I guess you worked up an appetite."

"He's in a bulking phase," Theo said around a mouthful of food.

"What do you know." I put my hands on my belly. "Me too."

"Help yourself," Theo said.

Marlene came in and greeted me with a warm smile and a hug. She started to say something, then did a double take at the snack smorgasbord.

"What's all this?"

"Don't worry, Mom, I brought most of it." Theo grabbed a bag of chips and tore it open. "Well, some of it. I think we ate most of your bananas."

"You'll spoil his dinner," she said, gesturing toward Owen.

Owen looked at me as if to say, see?

"He's a growing boy," Theo said. "Besides, I kicked his butt outside. He'll be a bottomless pit for the rest of the day. Trust me."

"Boys," she said on a sigh. "They never quite grow up."

"Who doesn't grow up?" Paul shouldered his way in and nudged Theo out of the way so he could grab the beef jerky.

"Boys."

He grunted and grabbed the knife holding the block of cheese. He held it up for a second, scrutinizing it, then took the entire thing with him into another room.

"Paul," Marlene said, following him.

Owen took out his phone again, looked, and stuck it back in a pocket.

"No answer?"

He shook his head. "He's probably just busy. Happens a lot when he's working."

That was true. Although he wasn't supposed to be working.

"The good news is, he's taking a few days off." I grabbed an orange and started peeling, releasing the scent of citrus into the air. "So that will be nice."

"Why? Is he okay?"

"I think he's pretty tired."

Owen shoved his hands in his front pocket, but didn't say anything. I knew what that meant. He was worried about his dad.

Theo met my eyes and we seemed to understand each other. He grabbed a second bag of chips and slipped out of the room.

"Hey." I moved closer and rubbed a few circles across Owen's back. "Are you okay?"

"He thinks I'm still too young to understand what's going on. But I'm not. I hear what people say."

"What have you heard?"

"That he's losing it."

"He's not losing it. Who said that?"

He shrugged. "I don't know. People."

"It's probably hard to have a dad who's a cop, isn't it?"

"When I was little, I just thought it was cool. But what if something happens to him?" He turned toward me, meeting my eyes. "I don't have anyone else."

Tears sprang to my eyes and a lump rose in my throat. "I don't want to even think about something happening to him either. But you're not alone. You have this big, amazing family. And, you know, you maybe have me?"

He practically dove at me, wrapping his arms around me in a tight hug. It was one of the most beautiful, overwhelming, heart-melting things I'd ever experienced. I held him for a long moment, cherishing every second.

I loved this kid so much.

Sugar cookies, I really did. I loved him.

He let go and stepped back. I tried to play it as cool as I could, but I couldn't hide the fact that my eyes were misty.

"I'm glad it's you." His voice was quiet and he kept his eyes on the table. "Dad could have ended up with someone like... well, like my mom. I don't think he would have, but it would have sucked. You don't suck."

I burst out laughing and a few tears trailed down my cheeks. "I'm glad you don't think I suck." I swiped beneath my eyes.

A sense of unease was growing in the pit of my stomach. I wanted to believe what I'd said. That Garrett wasn't losing it and he was going to be fine. But the prickle on the back of my neck wouldn't go away.

Still, I felt like I needed to be reassuring. "I'm sure he's okay. He knows what he's doing."

"Yeah."

Theo popped his head back in the room. I gave him a quick nod and he grabbed an orange.

"Chips and fruit?" I asked. "Are you bulking too?"

"It's called balance, Harper."

I laughed.

And chips did sound good.

"Harper, would you like something a little healthier?" Marlene came in with a bowl of blackberries. "I guess they did put out some fruit, but I have these from Gram Bailey's garden. They're early for the season, but still delicious."

"Blackberries," I said under my breath. The cookies. Were they burning in the oven, about to set the entire building on fire? How quickly could the fire department get there if the alarm went off? It had been so fast last time, but that had been *un*lucky. We hadn't needed them and it had been so embarrassing.

The bad luck curse meant I probably had left the cookies in there. I'd locked the bakery with a batch of cookies in a hot oven, ready to burn. And if the curse was going to go out with a bang, that would definitely be one way to do it. Burning down my aunt's bakery would certainly be the worst bad luck the curse had dealt me so far.

Garrett wanted me to stay at his parents'. But I had to make sure.

"Owen, do you want to run to the bakery with me?"

"Sure. Why?"

"I have a terrible feeling I left an oven on. With cookies in it."

"That's not good."

"No, it's not." I turned to Marlene. "Those look delicious, but I need to go make sure I didn't make a terrible mistake before I left. It's been a very weird day and I kind of have a problem with bad luck. I wouldn't be surprised if the entire place is filled with smoke and the alarm short-circuited and won't go off. Or something. If Garrett gets here before we're back, tell him we're on our way. In and out, it should only take a few minutes."

"Unless it's on fire. Then we might be longer," Owen said.

"Right. That's going to be a bigger problem. Make sure you have your phone. If we see smoke in the distance, we're calling it in."

He patted his pocket. "Got it."

"All right," Marlene said. "But drive careful."

"I will. Thank you!"

Owen and I headed out to my car. As I drove, I crossed my fingers and toes, hoping I wasn't about to walk into a disaster.

CHAPTER 42

Garrett

BLINDING anger seared through my veins, flooding me with fire. A voice in the back of my head told me to calm down and think. Losing myself to rage and panic wasn't going to help. I needed to get out and get to Harper before he did.

As my mind snapped into focus, I noticed a humming sound and felt cold air blowing against my face. I wrenched myself to a sitting position and looked around, taking stock of my surroundings in the dim light. Where was I?

It looked like a walk-in freezer. And Phillip had turned it on.

Fuck.

He wanted to kill me himself, so he probably wouldn't leave me to freeze to death. I didn't know how long a big commercial freezer would take to get to temperature, but I would have guessed at least twelve hours, if not more. Apparently he intended to make me even more miserable while I waited. What a prick.

Still, I had a feeling the cold wasn't my biggest problem. I didn't know how long the oxygen would last. Worse than that, without a source of fresh air, I was at risk for carbon dioxide poisoning just from my own breathing.

If I'd been expecting a rescue, I'd have hunkered down, tried to stay warm, and moved as little as possible to keep my breathing slow and minimize exhalations.

But no one knew I was there. I had to get out. I had to save Harper.

Which meant I had to risk it.

But first, I had to get my arms and legs free. He'd used zip ties. Made sense. They were common and easy to obtain, and they wouldn't be traceable back to him.

He had to know I'd be able to get out of them, so I wasn't about to celebrate once I was unbound. Getting out of the freezer was going to be a much bigger challenge.

The fucker had taken my shoes. Probably making sure I didn't have any weapons or tools hidden in them. Getting to my feet with my hands behind my back and a massive amount of adrenaline pumping through my veins proved to be awkward, but I managed. Positioning my feet in a V-shape, I dropped into a hard squat as fast as I could, snapping the zip tie around my ankles.

With my legs free, I could move my feet apart for balance. Lifting my arms as far back as I could, I thrust them down. The zip tie held, and although I could feel it chafe and dig into my skin, I ignored the pain.

One more try and that zip tie snapped too.

Urgency gripped me. I had to get out. Had to get to Harper. But I couldn't barrel my way through the door.

I remembered seeing somewhere that commercial freezers had safety mechanisms to open the door in case someone accidentally locked themselves in. Phillip had probably broken it, but it would have been stupid not to try. There was a knob on the door, below the handle. I pushed it, but sure enough, it didn't do anything.

No surprise there. He wouldn't have made that mistake.

Frustrated, I grabbed the door handle and shook it. Barely even moved. He'd locked it tight.

I'd been unconscious when he'd dragged me in, so I hadn't seen what the freezer was made of. I ran my hands along the cold interior walls. How thick were they? I tried to remember the freezer at Harper's bakery. Sheet metal, maybe stainless steel or aluminum.

Where would it be the weakest?

Not the front. The door would be strong, designed to open and close thousands of times without the seals breaking.

That left the sides, back, or top.

Ceiling wasn't an option. It might very well be the weakest point, but whatever type of shelving had been in there, it was gone. And Phillip had taken the folding chair. I was tall, but not tall enough to reach the top and get any kind of leverage to pop or pry it open.

The back was probably up against a wall. Which meant I needed to break out one of the sides.

Was I strong enough?

Phillip didn't think so.

I was about to prove him wrong.

The temperature continued to drop as I tapped my knuckles along the wall, listening for any sign of a thinner or weaker area. It was hard to tell. I figured the walls had to be mostly insulation with a thin layer of metal on the outside.

One way to find out.

I kicked and my foot hit the wall, leaving nothing but a small dent.

Fuck.

I kicked it again, aiming for the same spot. Again. And again. The dent grew with each strike. My body screamed at me, my muscles still protesting from the effects of the taser. I ignored it.

Adrenaline and sheer will kept me going. Harper had no idea she was in danger. For all she knew, I was out following up on a lead, still unsure if everything was a big coincidence, or if someone meant her harm.

She had no idea Phillip was coming for her.

I wasn't going to let that sick fuck touch her. I'd beat myself bloody to get out of the fucking freezer.

Anything to save her.

My vision hazed over with rage as I rammed the wall with my shoulder. I had to get out. That fucker was not going to touch my woman.

Finally, I broke through the insulation and could see the outer layer. Silver metal. My breathing was ragged, filling the freezer with carbon dioxide, and my body ached with every move I made.

A vision of Harper filled my mind. Her mesmerizing eyes. That smile that had almost knocked me on my ass.

And I attacked the outer wall.

I had no idea where my strength came from. I was a big guy, and kept myself strong, but I went supernova. I beat the aluminum sheeting with everything I had until I finally broke through.

The metal was jagged where I'd torn through it, so I peeled off my shirt and used it to grip. I wrenched it open, widening the gap.

Before I was even out, I could see I had another problem. There was shit stacked against the side of the freezer.

Didn't matter. I'd get through somehow.

It was hard to tell in the dim light, but it looked like cardboard. Maybe a stack of boxes. I kicked through the hole I'd made. There was weight behind it, but it moved. That was all the encouragement I needed. I kicked again, shoving the box —or boxes, I couldn't tell yet—out of the way.

Finally, there was room for me to squeeze through the hole. I wedged myself out, heedless of the way the metal scraped, tearing into my skin.

Ignoring the hot bloom of blood across my back, I got out

and surveyed the space. It was surrounded by stacks of moving boxes, plastic storage totes, wooden crates, and other random shit I didn't bother to identify. I shoved my way through, heedless of the danger of the entire stack falling on me. I was half out of my mind, fueled by relentless determination to save her.

Nothing fell, and when I finally emerged from the stacks of crap, I found myself in a metal sided pole barn.

Where the fuck was I?

I ran to the door. Of course it was locked, but that wasn't going to stop me. Not even close.

Amped as I was, it only took a few tries to kick the door down.

The daylight was blinding, and I squinted against the brightness as I rushed outside and tried to orient myself.

There was shit everywhere out there, too.

Then it hit me. I'd been there before. It was Rich Pine's property, where the pile of junk had fallen on me.

My detective brain tried to turn on, running through the possibilities. Was Rich Pine just out of town and his property was convenient? Or was there a connection between him and Phillip?

I had a feeling Phillip was using it without his knowledge, but I'd deal with that later. First, I had to find Harper.

Racing through the maze of junk, and ignoring the rocks and other shit digging into my feet, I made my way toward the front of the property. There were cars parked among the debris, but I doubted any of them ran. And hot wiring a car wasn't in my skill set. Luke would probably know how, but—

Luke. I needed to call my brother.

Rich's house looked empty. No lights inside, no cars parked in the driveway. And I was running out of time.

Could he have a landline?

There was one way to find out.

It had been years since I'd picked a lock, but I didn't want to kick the guy's door in. Plus, my body had already taken a beating. I gave myself sixty seconds to find something I could use to pick the lock. If I came up short, I was busting my way in.

Focusing on my breathing, I kept myself calm despite the rising panic. I hunted around, looking for something small. A paper clip had been my tool of choice when Reese and I had been up to no good as kids. But what were the chances—

In the trodden down grass, I found one. I actually found a fucking paper clip.

About time I got lucky.

I ran to the front door and it was just like riding a bike. In seconds, I was in.

"Hello? Tilikum sheriff's department."

No one answered, and no one would have believed I was a deputy, given my lack of uniform, badge, gun, and the fact that I was beat up, bleeding, shirtless, and barefoot.

The house wasn't as cluttered as the yard, but close. Where would a guy like Rich keep a landline?

Kitchen.

Bingo. There was an old black phone, not even a cordless, on the kitchen counter, perched on a stack of old newspapers.

I picked it up and breathed out a sigh of relief. Dial tone. It was connected. I punched in Luke's number and waited.

"Hello?"

"Luke, it's Garrett."

"Holy shit, where are you? I've been looking everywhere."

"Don't talk for a second. Just listen."

"You said that last time."

"Luke," I barked at him. "Phillip Lancaster is on his way to abduct Harper. He ambushed me at the root cellar and locked me in a freezer in an outbuilding on Rich Pine's property."

"What?!"

"I know, it all sounds crazy. But he's planning on killing her and framing me, making it look like a murder suicide."

"Where's Harper?"

"I don't know. Phillip has her phone. She was supposed to go to Mom and Dad's after work."

"Where are you? Rich Pine's?"

"Yeah. Do you know where that is?"

"I'm like two minutes from there. On my way."

Two minutes were going to feel like an eternity. How long had Phillip been gone? I had no way of knowing.

"Don't hang up, though," Luke said. "You've had me scared shitless. I went out to that barn and root cellar and there was nothing there. Less than nothing. The door was wide open, but there wasn't shit inside. And you were nowhere."

"Phillip fucking tased me, then clocked me in the head to knock me out."

"Holy shit. Have you called this in or did you call me first?"

"I called you. I don't know who I can trust. I just have to get to Harper."

"Got it. Don't worry, bro. We'll get her." His voice lowered, as if he were talking to himself. "And if I don't get a ticket, it's going to be a miracle."

I stayed on the line, waiting for him to show up. As soon as I heard his car, I slammed the phone down and ran out.

"Call Theo," I said as soon as I'd shut the car door. "He drove Owen up there and Mom never answers her phone."

"True story." He made the call and put it on speaker. "Theo, are you at Mom and Dad's and is Harper there?"

"I'm here, but she left."

"Where did she go?"

"The bakery. Something about an oven being on. She took Owen with her. Said they'd be back. Where are you?"

My eyes widened with horror. Harper and Owen were together, and not in the safety of my parents' house.

I didn't have to say a word. Luke was already driving, pedal to the metal, heading for town.

"Harper's in trouble," Luke said. "I've got Garrett. We're heading to the bakery."

"In trouble how?"

"I'll explain later. Just don't tell Mom."

Luke ended the call and put his phone in the center console. He glanced at me. "You look terrible. Why aren't you wearing a shirt? Never mind, are you bleeding?'

"Probably."

"Did he really lock you in a freezer?"

"Yeah."

"Holy shit," he muttered.

"Call Owen."

He tried Owen's number. No answer.

I was not going to think about what that meant. "Just drive."

"On it."

We raced toward the bakery and I was filled with single-minded determination.

Save them. They were all that mattered.

CHAPTER 43

Harper

THE BAKERY DIDN'T APPEAR to be on fire, so at least I had that going for me.

There also weren't any fire engines or other emergency vehicles, so maybe that meant I hadn't left cookies in the oven to burn.

I parked in the back and Owen and I got out. Garrett still hadn't called, which was bothering me more than I wanted to admit to Owen. That sense of unease that had been growing in the pit of my stomach had only intensified on the drive into town. I was worried about the bakery, but more than that, I was worried about Garrett.

Something was telling me he wasn't okay.

We went to the back door and I unlocked it. Maybe I'd find my phone and there would be a message from Garrett, telling me where he was. It would explain why he hadn't answered Owen, and we'd know when to expect him back at his parents' house.

Smoke didn't billow out of the kitchen when I opened the door. That was a good sign.

"Maybe I didn't leave the oven on after all." I stepped

inside and Owen followed. Then I locked the door behind us, just in case.

Without the SPS patrolling, I felt vulnerable.

I didn't miss the furrow in his brow as I flipped on the lights.

He was worried too.

I wouldn't lie to him and say everything was going to be okay. I hoped that was true, but I didn't know what was going on with his dad any more than he did. It seemed disingenuous to offer empty platitudes, even in an attempt to make him feel better.

He was a kid, but too grown up for that.

Instead, I patted him on the arm, then went to check the oven.

Off.

I let out a breath. "Sorry. It's not on. We didn't need to rush down here."

He shrugged. "That's okay."

I could have sworn I put cookies in, though. Had I imagined that? I opened the oven and sure enough, there they were. My blackberry almond thumbprints, sitting in a cold oven, not baking.

"Sugar cookies, what did I do?"

I pulled the baking sheet out and set it on the island. Apparently I hadn't turned the oven on at all.

Or maybe I'd tried to turn it on and my bad luck had intervened. It was probably broken.

"Are those just dough?" Owen asked.

I put my hands on my hips and shook my head sadly. "Yeah. I don't know what's up with me today, but apparently I stuck those in a cold oven and then forgot all about them. That's better than leaving an oven on, but still. What's up with my brain?"

"Pregnancy brain."

"You're probably right. But how do you know about that?"

"My math teacher last year was pregnant. She complained about it all the time."

I put a hand on my belly. Not that there was any outward sign of the baby, but the tiny one was still making him-or-herself known. "I actually like the idea of it being pregnancy brain, and not another manifestation of my bad luck curse."

"What do you want to do with these?"

"I'll toss them. I don't want to take the time to bake them. I feel like we should get back."

The hairs on the back of my neck stood on end and a chill ran down my spine. I was about to ask Owen if it was just me when I realized we weren't alone.

A man stood just inside the back door. He was dressed in black, including black gloves on his hands. How had he gotten in? I'd locked it. Pregnancy brain or not, I'd absolutely locked it.

Then it hit me. Someone had broken into my house, and Garrett's. Locks wouldn't mean much to someone like that.

"Don't scream." The man pulled a gun and pointed it at Owen. "Phone. On the counter."

"Do what he says," I whispered.

Owen took his phone out of his pocket and set it next to the sheet of unbaked cookies.

My mind reeled, fear and confusion swirling in a haze. Who was he? He looked familiar.

Wait. Phillip, from the prosecutor's office. He'd been in the bakery earlier that day.

"I didn't count on two of you." He narrowed his eyes at Owen. "But I can make this work. It's going to make for quite a story when all is said and done. The whole family."

Owen inched toward me. Phillip didn't say anything, so I reached out and grabbed his arm, pulling him next to me. His phone buzzed on the island, but I couldn't see the screen. Not that it mattered. We couldn't answer it.

"What do you want?" Owen asked.

"No questions. Do what you're told, and I won't have to shoot you."

"You can't shoot her," Owen said. "She's pregnant."

Phillip rolled his eyes. "Like I care. Here's what's going to happen. My car is parked just outside. You're going to walk out the door and get in the back seat. The door's already open. Cooperate and you live."

Owen leaned closer. "He's not going to shoot us in the middle of town."

"No?" Phillip asked. "Don't test me, kid. I've done far worse and gotten away with it."

"Where are you going to take us?" Owen asked.

"Owen, I think you should be quiet now."

"She's a smart woman," Phillip said. "Let's go."

"We're not going with you," Owen said, a note of defiance in his voice.

My heart beat furiously. Could we get out the front before he shot us? A moving target was harder to hit, but we'd have to navigate through the kitchen, out the doorway, and around the counter and pastry case. Then get out the locked front door, all without getting shot in the back.

He'd shoot Owen first. I could see it in his eyes.

Owen twitched. He wanted to try to run.

"Don't," I whispered. "He'll kill you."

"No he won't," he whispered back.

Phillip let out a frustrated sigh. He kept the gun trained on Owen and pulled something from his belt. It looked like another gun, only it was black and yellow.

He pointed the second weapon right at me. "He's right, I don't want to shoot you here. But you are coming with me."

"No!" Owen shouted, twisting so his body moved in front of me.

He yelled in pain and fell to the floor.

A taser. Phillip had just hit him with a taser.

"Stop!" I screamed.

Owen groaned, his teeth clenched, and his rigid body convulsed.

"Please stop!"

His body went still, but only for half a second. The convulsing began again and Owen cried out.

"No! Stop it!"

"Listen, you little shit." The taser stopped but Phillip pulled the trigger yet again. "I can do this all day."

I had to stop him. But what could I do? I couldn't overpower him. And he was watching me. It wasn't like I could throw flour in his eyes. The only thing close enough for me to grab was the baking sheet with cold cookie dough on it. That wasn't going to help.

"Out the back," Phillip said. "Now."

I heard the slightest noise, coming from the front of the bakery. The wind outside? Was it even windy out there? Owen groaned, curling up in pain.

Phillip narrowed his eyes and took slow steps toward the doorway. He still had the gun, and I knew if I moved, he'd pull the trigger on the taser again. Or maybe just shoot us both and be done with it.

"We're leaving." Phillip looked down at Owen. "Get up and don't fuck around."

Out of nowhere, a hulking figure appeared in the doorway. Phillip's eyes went wide with shock as Garrett barreled toward him.

It was as if everything moved in slow motion. Phillip's face turning toward me, his eyes blazing with malice. The gun centering on my chest. Garrett's roar of rage and Owen's shout.

Garrett smashed into Phillip right as the gun went off. I hit the floor next to Owen and he yanked me against him.

No pain. He'd missed.

The next few seconds were a blur as Garrett and Phillip wrestled for control of the gun. I held onto Owen, trying to shield him while he tried to do the same for me. Someone else appeared in the doorway, but before I could make sense of who it was, the gun fired again, the sharp pop so loud it rang in my ears.

Everything froze and it felt as if my heart stopped. Garrett was on the floor. Was he shot?

"Dad!" Owen yelled.

Phillip slumped over, falling to the floor.

Garrett rose, his face hard as he got to his feet. He was covered in sweat, dirt, and blood. He didn't have a shirt or shoes on. Vaguely I was aware that the other man was Luke. He was on his phone, talking to someone. Probably 911.

But I only had eyes for Garrett.

Breathing hard, he walked over to us and dropped to his knees. He scooped us both into his arms and held us tight.

Relief washed over me and I couldn't have stopped the tears if I'd tried. I clung to him, and to Owen, sobbing. Phillip had come to kill us. He'd been ready to kill us all.

But Garrett had saved us.

He'd saved his family.

CHAPTER 44

Garrett

THE COUCH in the small hospital waiting room was hard and uncomfortable. But I didn't care. I had one arm around Harper, the other around Owen. My injuries, aches, and pains, the mountains of paperwork I'd have waiting for me when I went back to work. None of it mattered.

They were alive, and we were together.

When Luke and I had arrived at Angel Cakes, we'd found it closed and locked—but the kitchen lights on. I'd known, without a shadow of a doubt, that Phillip was in there with them. I'd picked the lock as quietly as I could—with the rusty paperclip I was keeping forever—Luke and I had slipped inside, and seconds later, chaos had ensued.

And yet, I remembered every detail, as sharp as if I'd been moving in slow motion.

Crawling across the floor to get behind the pastry case. The sound of Phillip's voice. And then the look on his face when I popped up in the doorway. My son on the floor, the gun moving toward Harper.

I'd lost it.

Become driven by rage.

I'd tackled him. Wrestled for control of the weapon.

Time stopped at the sound of it firing, stalling in the split second when I'd wondered which one of us had been hit.

Harper nestled against me. The warmth of her body kept me centered and calm. Owen leaned into me on my other side, his poor body exhausted and sore.

But it was over. I'd gotten to them in time.

Luke had been right behind me, but everything had happened so fast. And with the first gunshot, he'd instinctively dropped to the floor. About to dive in and help when it had all ended, he'd kept his head and called 911.

I didn't know how to thank him. He'd had my back, no questions asked, no wasted time. And he'd helped save my family.

Paramedics had arrived first, followed moments later by several of my fellow deputies. I did my best to shield Owen and Harper from the grisly scene and took them outside.

We'd been taken directly to the hospital where Owen had the barbs from the taser removed. Fortunately, he hadn't sustained any major injuries. He was just going to feel like he'd been hit by a truck for a while. And to my enormous relief, Harper was unharmed.

She'd told me what Owen had done. The taser had been meant for her.

I was so proud of my son it made my chest feel like it might burst.

They'd patched me up—my injuries were superficial—and brought the three of us to the waiting room so we could be together. I figured whoever was being assigned the case would be in soon to ask follow-up questions, then we'd be released to go home.

Home. That sounded like heaven.

The door opened and Jack came in, dressed in uniform. Harper sat up a little, but I kept my arm around her.

Jack grabbed an ottoman and pulled it in front of the

couch, then took a seat. He shook his head slowly. "Holy shit."

That made me chuckle. "You can say that again."

"Sorry, Owen." He let out a long breath. "Garrett, I owe you an apology. I should have trusted you when you said something was going on."

"I don't blame you. You have to follow protocol."

"Yeah, but I also need to know my people. Your instincts rarely steer you wrong. I should have given you more support."

"Thanks, Jack."

"I'd ask how you are, but I'd imagine you're exhausted, sore, and probably hungry. So I'll try not to take up too much of your time. I was just out at Rich Pine's property. I don't know how the hell you beat your way out of that freezer. You're lucky it was a pretty thin sheet of aluminum on the outside."

"I knew what he was going to do. Getting out was my only option."

He shook his head again, his expression slightly bewildered. "Adrenaline can make a man capable of a lot of things. But that was something else."

"Have you started searching Phillip's residence?"

"We've secured it. We're working on processing the scene at Angel Cakes first." His eyes moved to Harper. "It's going to take us a few days, but we'll also make sure there's no sign of what happened in there."

"Thank you," she said.

"You three have been through a very traumatic ordeal. We've already got several therapists lined up. You can reach out and choose who you feel comfortable with, or we can do it for you. Either way, we're going to make sure you get the support you need. And Garrett, you're on administrative leave. Don't argue, it's protocol."

I wasn't about to argue. I knew I needed it, so I just nodded.

"Phillip didn't just kill Jasmine," I said. "He told me he's killed more. He wouldn't give me any details, but who knows how many other victims are out there."

"We'll reach out to the FBI. Hopefully we can track them all down. Give their families some closure."

"I know I can't investigate this case, but I want to see what you find. He has to have something. A guy like him would keep trophies."

"We can keep you in the loop." He turned to Owen. "You were more than brave today. The whole department is proud of you."

"Thanks, Sheriff."

"You'll make a great deputy someday, if you decide to follow in your dad's footsteps."

"I was just doing what my dad would have done," Owen said quietly.

I tightened my arm around him and cleared the lump from my throat. Jack met my eyes and nodded.

The door opened again and Kade walked in, carrying three greasy bags from the Zany Zebra.

Jack grinned. "I did need to talk to you, but I was also stalling for time. We figured you guys needed food."

Nothing had ever smelled so good.

That wasn't quite true. Harper's cookies always smelled like the best thing I could imagine.

But my stomach growled at the scent of burgers and fries.

"Thanks, Jack." I took the bags from Kade and handed them to Harper and Owen. "Thanks, man."

"No problem. It's the least we can do after the day you've had."

Jack stood and I got up so I could properly shake his hand.

As Jack left, and Owen dove into the food like he'd been starving for weeks, I stepped aside so I could talk to Kade.

His lip curled in a smirk. "Glad you didn't die."

"Thanks, man." My brow furrowed. I hated that I still had to wonder. Kade couldn't have been involved, could he? Working with Phillip somehow? My instincts said no, and it didn't add up. Phillip would have been a lone wolf. He wasn't the type to have an accomplice. Too much risk, and he'd have to share in his sick version of glory.

But something had been up with Kade.

"Can I ask you something?"

"Sure," he said.

"Is everything okay? It seems like something might be going on. I know, I'm one to talk. But what's up?"

He glanced away and let out a breath.

"I don't mean to pry if it's personal."

"It is, but I should have just said something. My wife has been dealing with some health problems. It's been pretty frustrating, but I think she finally has a diagnosis. We should be getting somewhere."

"I'm sorry, man. That's rough."

"Yeah." He looked down. "Sorry if I've been a dick lately. Perpetual bad mood, you know?"

"Yeah, I get it."

He held out his hand and I took it. "You were the right man for the investigator spot. No hard feelings."

"Thanks, Sheehan. And thanks for the burgers."

"Sure. I'll let you get to it. I've got dinner out in my car, so I better get it home to Erin before it gets cold."

"Sounds good. I'll see you later."

I went back to the couch and sat between Harper and Owen. Zany Zebra burgers had never tasted so good—not even when I was hungover. We inhaled our food, signed our discharge paperwork, and then it was time to go home.

Josiah and Zachary had retrieved my SUV and brought it to the hospital. We climbed in just as fatigue started setting in. Fortunately, it was a short drive home.

The flowers were still where I'd thrown them, off in the side yard next to the driveway. I ignored them. They didn't matter anymore.

It was over. We were safe. And I'd never been so grateful for the people I loved.

CHAPTER 45

Harper

ANGEL CAKES DIDN'T LOOK different.

It was so strange. The most horrifying day of my life had gone down right in that very kitchen. But you'd never know any of it had happened.

I was grateful for that. Not to be morbid, but if there'd been a big bloodstain on the floor, I would have had to convince Aunt Doris to sell the place and move.

Fortunately, Sheriff Jack's people had made it look like nothing had happened. And interestingly, being there didn't bring back a flood of unwanted memories. I knew what we'd been through. But it wasn't as painful as I'd thought it might be.

Garrett, Owen, and I had already met with a therapist together, to help us start processing the incident. We'd be able to meet with her individually as needed, too. Owen was adorably humble about his heroics, once again saying he'd just done what his dad would do and that he'd been worried a taser would hurt his baby sibling. He had strong protector instincts, just like his father.

He was going to be the best big brother to the tiny one. I couldn't wait.

Garrett had been gradually unwinding, his tension unraveling. The more time he spent at home with us, the more he relaxed. His smile came easily and he was sleeping well at night.

After several weeks of administrative leave, it was his first day back at work, so I'd decided it was time to reopen Angel Cakes.

It felt awesome to be back.

I'd spent the early morning in my happy place—baking dozens of delicious, sugary treats. Horatio, our illustrious bread baking genius, had stocked us up with bread and dinner rolls, and I'd filled the pastry case with my most popular cookies and cupcakes.

Mila had arrived around six to help and she'd been busy decorating the backlog of custom cake orders. And when Beth had come in to work the front counter when we opened for business, we'd shared a big, teary hug.

But something was bothering me. Things were almost too good. It was like the bad luck curse had gone dormant.

It wasn't over. I still had months before the seven years were up. But since the day after the incident, I'd been—dare I say it—lucky.

Mostly, it had been little things. I'd found twenty dollars in the pocket of one of my zip-up hoodies. Lemons had been on sale, so I'd been able to stock up for all the lemon-flavored goodies I wanted to make. I'd been craving pepperoni pizza like crazy and won a free one in a drawing at Home Slice Pizza.

But a few things felt... bigger. Okay, the free pizza had been a huge one, because pregnancy cravings were no joke. But the sheriff's office had also recovered my phone and it was undamaged, so I didn't have to buy a new one. And my landlord had offered to let me break my lease if I wanted to officially move in with Garrett. I hadn't even asked.

And the biggest one of all? My mom and sister had both

asked—separately—if I was having a baby shower and if they could be invited. And neither of them had criticized me for the pregnancy, or Garrett, or Tilikum, or any of my life choices.

What was even happening?

"How's it going over there?" I asked Mila.

She didn't look up from the cake she was decorating. It was for a bridal shower and looking spectacular. It was rose gold with pink flowers and little white and gold pearls.

Pausing for a second, I gazed at it. So pretty. So… bridal.

Mila glanced up and pulled an earbud out of her ear. "Sorry. Did you say something?"

"Oh, nothing. Just asking how you're doing. I forgot you had your earbuds in. True crime again?"

"Yes, always," she said, her voice typically monotone. "I suppose you aren't interested in hearing what it's about."

"You know, I could live without it."

"Fair." She put her earbud back in and continued with her work.

I heard a familiar voice up front. Aunt Doris. I was surprised she hadn't come in through the kitchen. Beth poked her head in the back to get my attention.

"Yep, I'm coming." My timer dinged—just in time, and I'd only set one. Was that lucky or just a coincidence? I took the batch of lemon cupcakes out of the oven and set them on the island to cool, then went out front to see my aunt.

Wearing a simple blue dress, Doris stood at the pastry case with Louise Haven, who wore a bright yellow tracksuit.

"Hi, ladies."

I'd visited Aunt Doris a few days after the incident—that wasn't the sort of story you could tell your slightly fragile aunt over the phone. She looked at me like she wanted to feed me chicken soup.

"Honey, how are you?" Doris reached across the counter

to take my hands. "Are you sure you didn't reopen too soon?"

"Oh, Doris, she's fine." Louise waved her hand, like she was batting away a fly. "Look at her. Tough as nails and sweet as sugar. Perfect for my Garrett."

I smiled and squeezed Doris's hands before letting go. "Thanks, Louise. Not so sure about the tough as nails part, but I appreciate the compliment."

"I still can't believe it," Doris said. "That monster was living among us all those years."

"I always thought he was shifty," Louise said.

"Did you?" Doris asked. "I thought you said he was an asset to the community."

"If I did, I was wrong. Besides, thanks to Garrett, he can't hurt another soul. I'd put a check in the Haven column, but I guess we don't keep score against the Baileys anymore."

Doris rolled her eyes. "Oh, Louise."

"Sorry, Doris. I'm glad the feud ended. But you can't blame me for my family loyalty."

"Of course not, dear," Doris said. "And you're right. If there's ever another serial killer on the loose, Garrett Haven would be the one to call. But I will say, if the bakery catches fire, you know it's the Baileys who'll save the day."

"Fair enough. We all have our place in this town. Anyway, Harper, dear, we're here to place a special order."

"Absolutely." I grabbed a notepad and a pen. "What can I do for you?"

"The SPS is having a big meeting this Sunday. We'd like to surprise them with dessert. I'm open to your suggestions."

"But they should have nuts," Doris said.

That made me laugh a little. "Nuts would be appropriate. How many do you think will be there?"

"That's a good question." Louise tapped her chin. "Let's just assume a hundred and that should be close enough."

"Sounds about right," Doris said.

"A hundred SPS members? Wow. They've really grown."

"It's a big job," Doris said. "We just want to support them the best we can."

"All right." I scribbled a few notes. "Nut-filled goodies for about a hundred by Sunday. And I'll include a box of nut-free goodies too, in case anyone is allergic or just doesn't like them."

"Such a good heart," Doris said. "Thank you."

"Do you want anything before you go?"

"Yes, but pick for me," Louise said. "I'll turn around so I won't see. I want to be surprised."

Doris's eyes brightened. "Good idea. Me too."

The door opened and another customer walked in.

But not just any customer. It was Matt Rudolph.

Well, at least I knew he wasn't a serial killer.

While Doris and Louise stood with their backs turned, I chose a strawberry cream cheese cupcake for Doris and a sugared lemon cupcake for Louise. I packed them up in small to-go boxes and slid them across the counter.

"All right, ladies. Surprises are in the boxes."

"What do we owe you?" Louise asked.

"You know your money's no good here. Go on, go cause some trouble."

They both smiled and took their cupcakes. Matt inched up behind them, standing slightly too close. Louise turned around and startled, almost dropping her box.

"Oh my goodness, young man. I didn't see you there."

"Sorry," Matt said and took an overly large step backward.

"Bye, honey." Doris waved as she and Louise left.

My familiar smile at Doris turned into my customer service smile. "Hi there, Matt. What can I do for you?"

"Hi, Harper." He was wearing his true crime T-shirt again. "I'm happy you're here. I didn't know if you were going to reopen the bakery."

"Yeah, we had to close for a little bit."

"I heard."

Surprisingly, he didn't launch into questions about the ordeal. With his passion for true crime stories, I thought he'd want to hear the whole thing straight from me. Word had gone around town about what had happened, so there was no way he didn't know at least some of the awful details.

Maybe he was actually reading the room on this one.

Although I knew he wasn't behind everything that had happened, I still had one unanswered question.

"Matt, can I ask you something?"

"Sure."

"Did you leave a teddy bear in a gift bag on my car a while ago?"

He sighed. "Yeah, that was me."

"You didn't leave a note."

"I know. I forgot about that part."

"Was it supposed to be… a gift?"

"Yeah, I thought you were nice and pretty. But then I found out you were with Garrett Haven, so I backed off."

"Oh." I smiled at him, not quite sure what to say. He still gave me the weirds a little bit, but not in the same way anymore. "Well, thank you for the gift. Is there any chance you'd like it back?"

"That's okay. You can keep it."

"That's very nice of you. Thank you, Matt. How about I give you a little gift in return?" I swept my hand over the pastry case. "Pick anything you'd like. It's on me."

"Yeah? Thanks, Harper. But I still want you to come over and meet my bearded dragon. I know she'd like you." He pulled out his phone and held it up. Sure enough, his lockscreen had a picture of a lizard. "See?"

I nodded slowly. "She's really cool. Thanks for the invitation."

"I have a question." Mila came through the doorway. She

paused and looked at Matt for what felt like too long to not be considered staring. "Nice shirt."

Matt looked up from the pastry case and his eyes widened. "Thanks. I love true crime."

She gazed at him, her lips parted. "Me too."

"Do you listen to podcasts?"

"All day long," she said, her usually monotone voice going a little dreamy.

Sugar cookies, I had a feeling I was witnessing a real-life case of love at first sight. There might as well have been little red hearts and fireworks and birds singing around them.

"Matt, this is Mila. She's our new baker. And Mila, this is Matt. He loves true crime and also has a bearded dragon."

"That's my favorite animal," she said.

"Mine too."

Neither of them were looking at me. They stared into each other's eyes, as if they'd hypnotized each other.

"Okay, so Matt, take your time. Mila, you just… keep doing what you're doing. You can ask me your question later."

She nodded slowly, but her eyes didn't leave Matt.

I had a feeling they were just going to stand there, staring at each other, so I decided to intervene. I stood behind Mila, so I was in Matt's line of vision, and waved to get his attention. Then I mouthed, *ask her out.*

He blinked, like he was coming out of a trance. "Mila, do you want to go out with me?"

"Yes, so much."

"Can you go right now?"

She looked at me and, although I could hardly detect any change in her usual blank expression, I had to imagine there was some excitement in her heavily lined eyes.

The whole thing was so weird, but also adorable. "Yeah, go ahead. Have fun talking true crime and stuff. I'll see you tomorrow."

"Thank you." She gave me a quick nod before heading back to the kitchen to retrieve her belongings.

Matt caught my eye and, with a wide smile, gave me a very obvious thumbs up. Not subtle, that one.

Mila walked out and tucked her hand under Matt's arm. She hadn't even taken her apron off.

"Bye, you two. Have a nice date."

They left without another word to me.

Beth came back out front. "What was that about?"

"I think I just witnessed insta-love."

"Mila?" she asked. "How do you know? Did she smile?"

"No." I shook my head, gazing the way they'd gone. "But he asked her out and she said yes on the spot. They both love true crime, and bearded dragons, so I guess they have that going for them."

"Huh." She shook her head. "Only in Tilikum."

I went back to the kitchen to see where Mila had left off with the cake. It was almost done, so I started putting on the final touches. It occurred to me that what I'd just seen might have been considered good luck. Matt had come in at a good time to meet Mila. It wasn't crowded. And Mila had gone up front—which she almost never did—at exactly the right moment.

Was that Mila's luck? Matt's? Maybe both?

Did it have anything to do with mine?

I was probably overthinking again. Not everything had to do with luck.

Stepping back to look at my work, I sighed, admiring the bridal shower cake. My stomach gurgled, as if the tiny one was reminding me that he or she was there.

I wasn't going to be sad. Yes, there was a little lump in my throat and a not-so-little longing in my heart. But what more did I want?

I was in love with the best man I'd ever known and he loved me back. We were having a baby together. We'd been through a harrowing ordeal and survived. If anything, it had brought us closer. Owen, too. We shared a bond that no one could ever break.

And yet, I couldn't deny that longing. It was there, deep in my heart. It wasn't about cakes or showers or parties or dresses or even rings.

It was about becoming Garrett's wife. I really, really wanted that.

I just hoped he did too.

CHAPTER 46

Garrett

IT WAS hard to believe what I was seeing.

Our forensics team had searched Phillip Lancaster's residence. They'd combed every inch of his house and property and, in the end, brought back numerous boxes filled with potential evidence.

There was a lot that was going to help investigators track down his additional victims. Maps, hunting and fishing guides, local souvenirs. He had a pin collection that we all hoped didn't indicate the number of women he'd killed. There were dozens.

But the real story was in a stack of unsent letters.

Phillip had been writing to someone named Al Bisbee for years. Since before he'd killed Jasmine Joyner.

It turned out, Bisbee was in prison in California. He'd been convicted of several murders of young women. The last one had been about a year before Phillip had killed Jasmine. Then Bisbee had been caught by authorities.

And apparently, Phillip's fascination had been born.

His early letters read like fan mail. It made my stomach turn. As they moved on, they provided details of his murders. Like a protégé boasting to a mentor.

It was fucking weird. He'd clearly known he'd never be able to send them. Prisoners' mail wasn't private and Bisbee was never getting out. Yet, he'd kept writing to this guy, bragging about his murders and how he was never going to get caught.

When I got to the letters about me, I had to sit down.

Jack had warned me. Told me I didn't need to read them—that maybe I shouldn't.

In a way, it was helpful. It showed me I hadn't been losing my mind. He'd recorded everything he did, step by step. In fact, he'd documented much more than any of his previous crimes.

It was as if he'd been building this up in his mind to the point that he considered it his masterpiece. Killing me and Harper and framing it as a murder-suicide was clearly the most elaborate crime he'd ever attempted. And he'd fantasized about it to a shocking degree.

There weren't just the letters. He'd sketched it out—literally. He wasn't exactly a skilled artist, but he wasn't terrible. And the pictures he'd drawn were harrowing.

Let's just say they depicted what he'd planned, complete with law enforcement discovering the grisly scene.

I'd never wanted to take the life of another person in the line of duty. But this guy? I had no regrets. The world was a better—and safer—place without him in it.

And he really had been behind it all. Or at least, most of it. He'd paid people to file the complaints, although the one from Matt Rudolph had just been bad timing. He'd never actually filed his and had apologized later. I'd told him no hard feelings.

Phillip had tampered with evidence and with my reports and recommended against prosecuting Trent Jones. Just another way to make me look bad—cast doubt in the minds of my superiors.

He'd also written about his break-in at Harper's house.

How he'd decided to reenact the events of his first murder to make me believe she was his intended victim. He'd wanted me scared, panicked that someone was after her. And he'd watched it all from afar, gloating the entire time.

It was no surprise to read that he'd been behind the incident at Rich Pine's. Nor that Rich had no idea someone would use an old freezer in one of his outbuildings to hold a victim hostage. Phillip had simply seen an opportunity—Rich was often out of town and his property was fairly isolated.

I'd been right about Jasmine and the root cellar. He had killed her there. According to his letters, he'd originally planned to kill me there, but changed his mind when he decided to kill Harper too. He'd wanted more space, and a place he thought would hold me while he enacted the rest of his sick plan.

Reading his words was as vindicating as it was disturbing. And the rest of his letters would help the FBI in their investigations of his other crimes.

But really, I was just glad the ordeal was over. I was ready to move on.

I left the evidence and walked away from it, literally and symbolically leaving Phillip Lancaster and all his evil behind.

Besides, I still had a job to do. The people of our town still counted on me and my entire agency to ensure their safety.

I went back to my desk and found a white envelope with my name handwritten on the outside. That was odd. No stamp, so someone must have dropped it off. Inside was a short letter in the same handwriting. My brow furrowed as I read it.

Deputy Haven,

. . .

I just wanted you to know, I get it. It wasn't personal. You were just doing your job.

I checked in to treatment. My girlfriend is having a baby and I don't want my kid growing up like I did.

Thanks for not breaking my nose or something last time you arrested me.

Trent Jones

I stared at the letter for a long moment. It was short, but profound. I really hoped Trent completed his treatment program and started getting his life together. Despite our history, I'd be the first one to cheer him on. And not just for his sake. For his child.

Looked like impending fatherhood was doing a lot of good for Trent. That made me smile.

———

My first day back on the job wound up being pleasantly normal. I'd assisted on a squirrel call—they were getting into the Timberbeast again—had a good informal chat with some members of the SPS, and literally helped a little old lady cross a street.

Life wasn't always simpler in a small town, but I'd never take it for granted when it was.

I went home and found Owen on the couch—mostly his knees sticking up. He was wearing headphones and, by the look of it, playing a game on his phone. Hesitating in the hallway, I watched him for a moment. I loved that kid so much.

Not for the first time, I wondered if I had it in me to be a father to another child. Could I love the tiny one with this same intensity? With my whole heart?

Time would tell. But if loving Harper had taught me anything, it was that I tended to underestimate love. Before her, I wouldn't have thought I had it in me to love a woman as much as I loved Harper.

But love had smacked me upside the head. And thank goodness it had. So maybe I didn't need to worry that my heart wouldn't be big enough for another child. It always made room.

Seemed like love wanted to grow.

Owen looked up and noticed me. He pulled off his headphones and sat up straighter. "Hi, Dad."

"Hey, bud."

"Done with work?"

"Yeah. I actually wanted to talk to you about something." I sat on the other side of the couch.

"Am I in trouble?"

"Should you be?"

He tried to hide a grin. "No. I don't think so. No shoplifting at least."

That wasn't what I'd meant to bring up, but since he had. "Can we talk about that?"

"I did my time, Dad. It's over."

"I know, I don't mean punishment. Why did you do it?"

The corners of his mouth lifted. "I wanted cookies?"

"C'mon. Why did you really do it?"

His brow furrowed and he glanced away. "It's stupid."

"Son, you can tell me."

"I was mad."

"At who?"

"I don't even know. At Mom, I guess. And kind of at you."

"Mad at me because Mom didn't stay?"

"Yeah. I know it isn't your fault. I'm not a grown-up, but I get that adults make their own choices and have to take responsibility for them."

"It's a big deal that you understand that. I guess I haven't completely failed."

He grinned again. "You're actually a really good dad. I have some friends who aren't as lucky as I am."

That hit me square in the chest. "Thanks. I've done my best."

"Let's be honest. I'm pretty awesome, so you can take some of the credit."

I nudged his leg. "You are awesome. But don't go too Uncle Z on me."

"Why not? He's awesome too. Maybe I get some of my awesomeness from him."

"Let's just say it runs in the family and call it good."

"Fair."

"Can I ask you another question?"

"Sure."

"Are you still mad?"

"At Mom? A little bit, yeah. I just don't get it. But I also think things are better without her. She wasn't good at being a mom, even when she was here. It's less confusing this way."

"For what it's worth, I'm sorry."

"It's okay. It's not your fault. Except you picked her, so that part is. But if you hadn't, I wouldn't exist, so I can't be too upset about it."

I nodded in acknowledgment. "I'll never regret it, because I got you."

"And you redeemed yourself with Harper, so you have that."

A broad smile crept over my face. "That's actually what I wanted to talk to you about."

"About Harper? She's okay, right?"

I hated that my son had to bear the burden of trauma. He was handling it well, especially with help from his therapist. But still. As a father, I wanted to protect him—from everything. Even though I knew I couldn't. I patted his knee. "She's fine. I have something that I want to ask her, but it impacts you too, so I didn't want to do it before I talked to you."

He sat up straighter, his eyes widening with excitement. "Are you gonna marry her?"

"I'd like to ask her."

His head dropped back against the cushion. "Finally. Geez Dad, it took you long enough."

"Long enough? Our relationship has moved alarmingly fast."

"Whatever. You love her and she loves you. And you're having a baby together. It's not like you don't know you're going to get married. Just do it, already."

"I take it you don't have any concerns about this."

"My only concern is you waiting too long, and she starts to think you're never going to ask, and then there's a pointless miscommunication that leads to drama. No one needs that."

I couldn't help but laugh. "Where do you get this stuff?"

He shrugged. "I don't know. So how are you going to propose? Do you have a ring? Can I be in the wedding? Do I get to wear a suit?"

"I don't know. I picked it out but haven't picked it up yet. Yes, of course you can. And absolutely you'll wear a suit."

"Okay, but you should let me help you propose. You're not going to do it right on your own."

"Excuse me?"

"What's your plan?"

I hesitated. "I thought I'd take her out to dinner."

Groaning, he rolled his eyes. "Boring."

"What's boring about that? I was going to take her to the restaurant where we had our first date. That's romantic."

"It's okay. But c'mon, Dad, we're Havens. We can do better. Uncle Josiah remodeled a house for Audrey. And Uncle Z threw Mari a costume ball. We have big shoes to fill."

"We?"

"I'm in on this too, Mr. Single Dad. You're stuck with me. So is Harper, but if she says no, it's definitely you, not me."

I laughed again—harder this time. "You're killin' me, kid. So what's your big idea?"

"Okay, hear me out…"

CHAPTER 47

Harper

THE CINNAMON SUGAR swirl cupcakes smelled amazing.

Cinnamon had sounded good, so I'd decided Angel Cakes needed a batch of them for the pastry case. It was usually more of a fall flavor, but hey, I was pregnant and in charge. That meant we had cinnamony goodness in the summer.

I had a feeling customers weren't going to mind.

As delicious as the cinnamon smelled, my mind drifted to the pepperoni pizza I had waiting at home. My pepperoni craving was in full force. I probably needed to eat a vegetable once in a while, but apparently the tiny one wanted pizza. Who was I to argue?

My hand drifted to my belly. The tiny one was still, well, tiny. But my pants were getting snug. And okay, that might have been due to the pizza. My bras didn't fit, either, but that wasn't pepperoni's fault.

And Garrett certainly wasn't complaining.

I started on a batch of blackberry almond thumbprints. They'd been a surprise hit—once I'd finally had a chance to bake a batch, instead of forgetting them in a cold oven. Customers were loving my new selection of grain-free treats.

We still offered lots of our favorites, but so many customers had commented that they loved having alternative choices. And I'd been having fun experimenting, so it was a definite win-win.

The noise of a siren caught my attention. I wondered if the fire engine was about to race by. Wouldn't have been the first time. At least it wasn't coming to the bakery. We hadn't had any more burnt baked goods setting off the fire alarm incidents.

In fact, my luck seemed to be holding.

The sound grew, so I went out front to see what was going on. A sheriff's department patrol car came screeching down the street and stopped at an angle in front of the bakery. A second later, another one did the same thing, creating a V-shape with the first.

"Um, should we be worried?" Beth asked.

"I don't know."

Another patrol car arrived, lights flashing and siren blaring.

It was starting to make me nervous. If there'd been a bank across the street, I would have wondered if it was being robbed.

"Harper Tilburn," a voice on a loudspeaker boomed. "Please exit the building."

Beth and I looked at each other with wide eyes.

"Was that Garrett?" she asked.

"It didn't sound like him."

"Harper Tilburn," the voice said again. "Please exit the building with your hands in the air."

"Okay, this has to be a joke," I said. "Are pranks on girl-friends a Tilikum thing? I thought it was just the old feud."

"I think you should do what he says. It's the cops."

I laughed. This had to be a joke.

Although why would Garrett be pulling a prank on me?

"Okay, I'll see what they want."

I went to the front of the bakery and poked my head out. "Hi?"

The sirens had stopped but the blue and red lights still flashed. It was quite the sight.

"That's it, ma'am. Come outside and keep your hands where we can see them."

There seemed to be an abundance of law enforcement officers, although none of them were pointing weapons at me like you might see in a movie. They were standing outside their cars, most with sunglasses and crossed arms.

I stepped out and held my hands at shoulder height, palms out. "What's going on?"

"Keep walking, ma'am. Hands up."

I laughed a little, but I didn't see Garrett. What was happening? This couldn't be real.

Tourist season was in full swing and the spectacle was generating a small crowd. Some of the deputies moved to keep people from getting closer, blocking the sidewalks on both sides of the street.

"Step into the street, ma'am," the voice said, still using the loudspeaker.

I couldn't tell who it was. The rest of them just stood there, watching me. I glanced up the road and saw Marigold and Audrey, along with Annika and her husband. I wanted to wave, but I'd also been instructed by law enforcement to stand in the street. So I decided to do what I'd been told.

"Is everything okay?" I asked. "This is weird, you guys."

The door of one of the patrol cars opened and I had to do a double take. It was Owen. But without his hoodie, I almost didn't recognize him. He wore a crisp white button-down shirt, slacks, and a pair of aviator sunglasses. He reached back into the car and took out a big bouquet of red roses.

I clasped my hands to my chest.

"Hands up, ma'am."

I laughed again and put my hands up. "Sorry."

Owen grinned as he walked over to me. Had he grown? He'd always been taller than me, but he seemed to keep getting bigger.

He held out the flowers.

"Can I lower my hands to take them?" I asked.

"Yeah, it's fine," Owen said.

I tucked them in the crook of my elbow. They smelled wonderful. "What's going on?"

He didn't answer, but his smile grew.

The driver's side of the same patrol car opened and Garrett got out.

His big, muscular body gave his uniform a workout and his aviators were so sexy, I could hardly stand it. With a slight smirk on his lips, he walked toward me.

"What is happening?" I asked. "I feel like I'm in trouble but also not because of the flowers."

He took my hand in his and brought it to his lips. Then he did the most incredible thing I'd ever seen.

He dropped to one knee.

Sugar cookies. He was going to…

This was…

Oh my goodness.

"Harper, will you do me the honor of becoming my wife?"

My mouth opened but I'd completely forgotten how to use words. I stared at him, frozen in place, while the blue and red lights flashed around me.

Owen leaned closer to his dad. "I told you we need the pizza."

"What do you think, love?" He took a box out of his pocket and opened it, revealing a beautiful blue topaz surrounded by a halo of tiny diamonds. "Will you marry me?"

"Pizza, Dad," Owen whispered.

"Yes!" I squealed. "Yes, yes, yes. Sorry, I forgot how to talk for a second. Yes, please. I want to marry you so much."

He took out the ring and slipped it on my finger, then rose and scooped me into his arms. My feet left the ground and he twirled me around while the sirens blared in a cacophony of chaotic noise.

Vaguely, I was aware of people clapping and cheering all around us. He set me down on my feet and brought his mouth to mine for a kiss.

He pulled away for a second, but kissed me again, as if he couldn't get enough. I was laughing and crying and kissing him all at the same time. It was a big, beautiful whirlwind.

Finally, he pulled back. Owen stood next to us, now holding a pizza box from Home Slice.

"Open it," he said.

I lifted the lid and the tantalizing scent of pepperoni pizza almost made my eyes roll back. "That smells so good. I've been dreaming about pizza all day."

"But look," Owen said.

I looked into the box and the words Marry Me were spelled out in pepperoni.

"Oh my gosh, you have a proposal pizza too?"

"Owen insisted," Garrett said with a shrug. "Although most of this was his idea."

"Dad was just going to take you out to dinner." He rolled his eyes. "Boring."

"This was amazing. Thank you."

To my surprise, that wasn't the only thing Owen had suggested. There wasn't just one pizza, there were enough pizzas to feed half the town. The patrol cars blocked off the street and people began milling around as someone set up folding tables to serve all the food. Paper plates and coolers of drinks appeared, as if by magic. And someone had even brought peanut butter cookies from Nature's Basket Grocery to treat the squirrels.

In minutes, we were at the center of an impromptu engagement party.

I had Beth bring out treats, emptying the pastry case. It felt kind of amazing. The bakery was doing so well, I didn't have to worry about what losing one afternoon of business would cost. I could just give and celebrate with my friends and neighbors.

And the pizza was so satisfying. Nothing had ever tasted so good as indulging my pregnancy craving.

I got hugs from everyone I knew in town, and a lot of people I didn't. Matt and Mila were there, holding hands, looking like the strangest couple I'd ever seen—the awkward guy and the goth girl. Marigold teared up when she hugged me, as did Audrey. Annika and her family were there, Paul and Marlene seemed to appear out of nowhere, and there were so many Haven brothers, I pretty much lost track.

Owen came over with a plate of pizza and held it out to me. "Did you get enough?"

I put a hand on my stomach. "I'm so stuffed, I don't think I have room for both pizza and a baby."

He smiled. "Just wanted to make sure."

"You are such an amazing kid. You know that, right?"

"Cool, but don't make it weird."

"Oh, I'm gonna make it weird." I stepped in for a hug and wrapped my arms around him. He hugged me with one arm, the other still holding the paper plate.

Just before I let go, he spoke quietly. "I'm glad you said yes."

"I'm glad you wanted me to."

He stepped back. "You make really good cookies, so…"

I laughed. "Thank you. I appreciate that."

Garrett slipped an arm around my waist and drew me against him. "Did you get enough pizza?"

Owen held up the plate. "Already asked."

Turning toward him, I looked up into his eyes. The way he smiled at me, like he'd never been happier, made my heart so warm and squishy, I thought I might melt right there.

"Hi, love," he said, his voice low.

"Hi."

"Happy engagement day."

"Thank you."

"Did I miss anything?"

"No. I can't imagine anything better."

"Good." He leaned down and kissed the tip of my nose. "Neither can I."

"I love you so much."

"I love you too."

He brought his lips to mine, and I fought a small smile as I ignored Owen's groan. It was our engagement day, he could live with it. And as Garrett kissed me, I realized something. It was like a flash of awareness, sparking through my brain with bright intensity.

My bad luck was gone.

The mirror curse shouldn't have been over for another several months. But I hadn't had a single incident of bad luck recently.

Garrett had broken the curse.

Okay sure, I'd gotten pregnant unexpectedly, but that wasn't bad luck. No, it was the best thing that had ever happened to me. And yes, we'd been targeted by a raving lunatic serial killer and could have been murdered. But we weren't. And now an evil man would never hurt another person again.

Plus, the bakery was thriving, the criminal who'd hated Garrett had gotten help, creepy Matt had found a love connection with stoic Mila, Aunt Doris was enjoying retirement, I had wonderful new friends, and was surrounded by a huge new family I loved like crazy.

That seemed like a lot of good, especially for a girl who'd gotten awfully used to the bad.

Garrett had definitely broken the curse.

And now I was going to be his wife.

He pulled away and gently touched my face. I loved him so much, I felt like my heart could burst. We were going to be a family, the three of us—soon to be four. I'd never imagined I could be so happy, so fulfilled, so in love and at peace.

My dreams were coming true, even the ones I'd been too afraid to dream. I couldn't have imagined a better happy ending to our story.

And really, we were just beginning.

Epilogue

HARPER

NEVER BEFORE HAD a red velvet cupcake tasted so good.

I closed my eyes, savoring the sweetness and texture. It felt like I hadn't eaten in days and my reward was a decadent feast of deliciousness.

With a contented sigh, I finished my treat. Mila had brought a dozen to the hospital for us to share, and with the craziness of the last twenty-four hours, I hadn't eaten mine yet. Garrett's sat in the box, the lone cupcake left, and I was more than a little bit tempted to devour his, too.

He slept in what we'd named the daddy chair—a wide, pink recliner that leaned almost all the way back. Why someone had chosen pink, I had no idea. But the color didn't really matter. His eyes were closed, his bare chest rising and falling with the slow rhythm of his breathing. And on his chest, dressed in nothing but a diaper with a blanket over her, was our daughter, Isla.

She'd come into the world after what had felt like an eternity of labor, but had only been about twelve hours from the time we'd arrived at the hospital. I'd never forget the experience of seeing the tiny one for the first time. Her round face, her eyes blinking in what was probably confusion, her sweet little mouth.

That perfect little face had bunched up and she'd started screaming. It had been a sight to behold.

I couldn't stop staring at her little elbows and knees, her fingers and toes. The wispy blond babyfuzz on her head. She'd cried a lot at first, only calming down when the nurse finished with her and put her in my arms.

My heart had just about burst. And looking at her, sound asleep on her daddy's bare chest, my love for her welled up, filling me with warmth and gratitude.

I loved them so much.

How could you love someone you'd only laid eyes on a few hours before? How could my entire body be so attuned to her, so intent on her well-being? If I'd been worried I didn't have enough love to give, those fears melted in the fire of mother's love that consumed me.

Her arrival in our lives had been a surprise, but she was the best gift I'd ever been given.

So was Garrett.

After our engagement day, we'd decided to get married right away. It had been a small ceremony without a lot of fanciness or fuss. Marigold had helped put it all together, and even on our shoestring budget and tight timeline, she'd made it beautiful. My mom and sister had been there, along with Garrett's entire big family. It had been simple, but incredibly meaningful, joining us together as a family.

Garrett stirred, taking a deep breath, and opened his eyes.

"Hi, sleepyhead."

He gave Isla a soft kiss on the head. "Hi. Sorry, I didn't mean to fall asleep."

"That's okay. She's not crying, so that's a win."

"She has a set of lungs on her, doesn't she?"

I smiled. She certainly did. "Did Owen cry a lot when he was born?"

His brow furrowed and he paused. "Actually, I don't think he did. He was a pretty easy newborn. It wasn't until he started walking that things got rough."

"I wonder what she has in store for us."

"She's a new adventure," he said.

There was a soft knock on the door and Owen peeked his head inside. "Is it safe to come in?"

My face lit up with a smile. "Yes, come in."

Owen was dressed in a black hoodie and jeans. His hair was getting a little long—the front was almost in his eyes. I made a mental note to make sure he got a haircut soon. If he wanted one. Maybe the hair in the eyes thing was what he was going for.

"Oh," he breathed as he approached his dad and new baby sister. "She's so small."

"Do you want to hold her?" Garrett asked.

Although I was usually struck by how grown-up Owen looked, in that moment, his face had all the wonder and innocence of a child.

"Yeah."

Garrett sat up and laid Isla on his lap to swaddle her in the blanket. Then he stood and placed her gently in Owen's arms.

"Wow," Owen whispered, gazing at her sleeping face. "Oh my gosh, I love her so much."

It was such a beautiful moment, deep emotion welled up inside me, bringing tears to my eyes. "Isn't she perfect?"

"Oh look, her eyes are opening a little." He shifted his weight back and forth, gently rocking her. "Hi, baby sister. I'm your big brother, Owen."

Garrett sat on the edge of the bed and put his arm around me. How had I gotten so—yes, I was going to say it —lucky? I was married to the man of my dreams, Owen had become the son of my heart, and now we had our sweet baby girl.

I was ready to burst with happiness.

Garrett kissed my temple. "I'm going to go find some food. I just realized I'm starving. Do you want anything?"

"I just had a cupcake, but I could still eat. Maybe something with protein to balance it out a little."

"Got it. Owen, are you hungry?"

"No, Grandma has been stuffing me with food pretty much constantly. Actually, yes, I could eat."

Garrett gave me another kiss, then left in search of… I couldn't remember what time it was. Lunch? Dinner? Who knew at that point.

"Is she awake?" I asked.

"No, she closed her eyes again." Owen lowered himself onto the edge of the bed. "Can I talk to you about something?"

"Of course."

"I was thinking." He paused for a moment. "My cousin Thomas has a stepdad."

"Yeah, I know Levi is his stepdad."

"But he just calls him Dad. And Grandma is Dad's stepmom, but he just calls her Mom. And you're Isla's mom, so she needs to learn to call you Mom, and I was thinking maybe I could…"

I held my breath, a lump forming in my throat.

He raised his eyes to meet mine. "Maybe I could call you Mom? I know I'm not a little kid like Thomas was when he met Levi, or like Dad when Grandma and Grandpa got married. But I keep thinking about it, and if it's okay with you…"

A single tear broke free from the corner of my eye. "I would love it if you called me Mom."

"Really?"

"Yes, really." I swiped the tear from my cheek. "I didn't

carry you as a baby and I wasn't there when you were born, but you're the son of my heart. You always will be."

I could see the tears forming in his eyes and I just about lost it. Sniffling a little, he glanced away. "Thanks. Mom."

For some reason, that made me laugh. Not because it was funny, but because I was so happy, I couldn't help myself.

Owen laughed too, and a few tears did sneak out of the corners of his eyes. I pretended not to notice as he wiped them away.

"I love you, kiddo," I said. "And look at you. You're already the best big brother."

He gazed at Isla. "She's pretty awesome. And I love you too."

As if she knew we needed a little dose of reality in the midst of our moment, Isla squirmed in Owen's arms and let out a cry.

"Uh-oh." Owen handed her to me. "I think she needs you."

"She's probably hungry. Being born is hard work."

"Do you need me to leave?"

"They're just boobs, Owen. It's not that big of a deal."

His face flushed and he turned his back to me. Isla got an arm free of her swaddle and stretched.

"There you go, sweet girl." I worked on situating her so I could get her to latch while Owen hilariously refused to look. Not that I blamed him. I wouldn't have wanted to see my mom's—or stepmom's, if I'd had one—boobs either. Even in the context of nursing a baby.

Garrett came back in and the smell of burgers wafted in with him. My stomach growled. The hospital's food wasn't half bad—or maybe I was just that hungry. The room had a small table where he set up our meal, but before he started on his, he brought mine over and fed me bites while I nursed our daughter.

He was such an amazing man.

And the best part? He was mine.

We belonged to each other, all four of us. We'd been through a lot to get to that moment. But we'd never given up. Garrett had risked everything for the people he loved—for his family.

He was, and always would be, my real-life hero.

Bonus Epilogue

SEVERAL YEARS LATER...

The house was deceptively quiet when I walked in. I took off my aviators and shut the door behind me. Where was everybody?

It had been a typical day keeping the citizens of my town safe. Kade and I had de-escalated a potential confrontation at Tilikum Hardware between a couple of guys arguing over a lawnmower. Harvey Johnston had gotten stuck on the roof of the library. No one was quite sure how he'd managed to get up there, and it had taken the fire department to help get him down. And Mrs. Greely had waved me down as I drove through town, complaining that a squirrel gang was targeting her chihuahua, Spanx. It was an ongoing problem. I managed to calm her down. Spanx, however, never stopped yipping.

The life of a small-town deputy.

But where were my babies?

I found them at the dining table, deeply engrossed in coloring. Four-year-old Isla had a little groove between her eyebrows and the tip of her tongue stuck out the corner of her mouth. She was working very hard to color within the lines of the flowers on her coloring page. Her light brown hair was braided and she wore what was probably her seventh outfit of the day—a blue dress with a little puppy on the front.

Our younger daughter, two-year-old Alana, sat across from her big sister. Her blond hair was in pigtails and she wasn't dressed at all. We had a hard time keeping anything but a diaper on her. Unlike her sister, she scribbled all over the page with reckless abandon.

They hadn't noticed me, so I watched them for a moment. Isla was so much like Owen—and like me. Calm, careful, meticulous. But Alana? She was the wild child of the bunch. She'd swept into our lives like a tiny tornado.

I loved them so much, I ached with it.

A plate of cookies sat in the center of the table and crumbs trailed around the crayons and coloring pages—mostly around Alana's. Isla's place was fairly neat.

"Hi, girls."

Two precious faces looked up at me, their eyes wide, mouths smiling.

"Hi, Daddy." Isla immediately went back to her coloring. I could tell it was very important to her.

Alana jumped down from her chair and I scooped her up. She threw her arms around my neck and gave me a noisy kiss on the cheek before bending at the waist and practically diving out of my arms.

"Wuv you, Daddy." She scrambled back up into her chair, grabbed a green crayon, and attacked her coloring page with fervent determination.

I laughed. "Where's Mommy?"

In answer, Harper's arms wound around my waist. I shifted and pulled her in front of me. It was the best part of my day, the hours spent apart making me crave her, and the sweet relief of her presence was a balm to my soul.

Leaning in, I kissed her softly. "Hi, love."

"Hi. How was your day?"

"Good. Normal. How was yours?"

"Good. Busy."

I kissed her again, savoring her soft lips. Over the last several years, we'd settled into our life as a family. We welcomed our girls, survived the sleepless nights of the newborn phase, watched them grow into the unique, amazing kids they were becoming with a sense of awe. This was really our life.

The biggest change, however, wasn't having babies. It was watching Owen grow up and start the next season of his life.

After playing varsity for Tilikum High School, he'd earned a full-ride football scholarship to UW. No one had prepared me for how hard it would be to drop him off in that dorm room, hours from home. How could the little guy who'd once needed my help to tie his shoes be eighteen, and ready to conquer the world?

Harper had kept it all in during move-in day until we'd gone back to our SUV. Then the tears had come in a flood. They had such a special bond. And in some ways, it was harder for her than it was for me. I'd experienced the fullness of his childhood—all eighteen years. She felt like she had to let go too soon.

But we'd adjusted, as families do. We missed him, but we were so proud of the young man he was becoming.

And he was due to be home for spring break any time. A friend from high school was giving him a ride back to town. I couldn't wait to see him.

"Have you heard from Owen yet?" I asked, keeping my arms around Harper.

"Not yet. He texted me when he left Seattle and I haven't heard from him since. But he should be here any minute."

I glanced at the girls. They were both still hard at work on their pictures. "They're awfully focused."

"I know, it's amazing. I wish they'd be this into coloring

every day. I actually got to go to the bathroom by myself just now. It was heaven."

I kissed her forehead. "You're such a good mommy."

She smiled. "Thanks."

The front door opened and the girls looked up. Alana's crayon fell from her hand and clattered to the floor.

Owen's voice came from the front of the house. "Dad? Mom?"

"Owen!" the girls shouted in unison and jumped down from their seats.

They ran past me and Harper, thundering down the hallway, their feet making a surprising amount of noise for how small they were. Harper and I followed, stopping to watch while Owen crouched down and caught his baby sisters in his outstretched arms.

"Why aren't they this excited to see me?" I asked idly.

"They see you every day," Harper said, winding an arm around my waist.

And to be fair, the sight of them clinging to Owen with squeals of joy and laughter made my chest ache with love yet again.

He hoisted them both up, one in each arm. "Hi, babies."

"We're not babies!" Alana drummed her fist on his chest a few times.

"Yes, you are. You're my babies."

"We colored pictures for you," Isla said. "Come see!"

He set them down and they stampeded back to the dining room. Owen left his duffel bag near the door and wrapped Harper in a hug.

"Hi, Mom."

"Hi, kiddo. It's so good to see you."

He let her go and I drew him in for a hug. He might have been a freshman in college, but he was still my boy. "Hey, Son."

"Hi, Dad."

Harper dabbed her eyes. "Sugar cookies, we missed you so much. How was the drive?"

"It was fine."

"Are you hungry?"

He grinned. "I snacked most of the way, but yeah, I'm always hungry."

Not for the first time, it struck me how big he'd gotten. He was as tall as I was, with an athletic frame. And he looked so damn grown up. He was a far cry from the hoodie-wearing middle schooler who'd shoplifted cookies from Angel Cakes Bakery.

"Owen!" Alana shouted from the dining room. "Lookie!"

"I better go see," he said.

We followed him into the dining room and I put my arm around Harper, holding her close while the girls showed him their artwork. Isla had one carefully colored picture with flowers and bees and a yellow sun. Alana had at least a dozen pages of randomly colored scribbles, but she was every bit as proud of her work.

He sat in one of the dining chairs and both girls managed to scramble into his lap. He held them, one on each knee, and helped himself to a cookie.

Harper blew out a breath. "I'm not crying, you're crying."

I pulled her in tighter, wrapping my arms around her, and kissed her head. "It's going to be a great week."

"Yeah it is. So good to have us all under one roof. Even just for a little while."

The girls were content to sit in Owen's lap for a few minutes, so Harper and I got out enough snacks to serve as dinner. Isla and Alana thought they were getting something special, with string cheese, crackers, and apple slices as their meal. Little did they know it was easier for their parents to toss a bunch of snack food on the table and call it good.

If Owen was tired after the drive, he didn't let it slow him down. He patiently sat with his sisters, then played tea party with them after dinner. Isla showed him how to lift his pinkie when he held his plastic teacup, and he dutifully played his part.

When it was time for the girls to go to bed, he read them their stories and tucked them in. Alana only got up six times for "one more hug," so it was a pretty typical night. Finally, the pitter patter of sneaky little feet subsided and my baby girls went to sleep.

Harper brought out the chocolate truffle cookies she'd baked for Owen—they were his favorite. We settled on the couch in the quiet of post-bedtime-for-the-littles bliss.

"So is there anything special you want to do this week while you're home?" Harper asked. "Or maybe just sleep."

Owen smiled. "Sleep sounds good. Mostly I want to hang out. I figure I'll take the girls up to Grandma and Grandpa's at some point."

"They'd love that."

"Maybe I can even convince Alana to wear clothes."

"Good luck. She undressed in the grocery store while I was waiting to check out the other day."

Owen's eyebrows drew together. "She better outgrow that."

I laughed. "She will. You went through a naked phase when you were two."

"Did I?"

"Yeah, and an only pees outside phase." I glanced at Harper. "Alana doesn't pee outside, right?"

"No, she's still blissfully unaware that peeing is a thing until her diaper is wet. But she's only two. She'll get there." She held out the plate of cookies and Owen took another one. "How did your biology test go?"

"I can confidently say I passed." He took a triumphant bite of his cookie.

I shook my head and laughed a little. His grades were fine, I wasn't worried about it. He was managing to juggle a demanding sport with a full load of classes. I couldn't have been more proud of him.

"And…" She paused, giving him a conspiratorial eyebrow raise. "Anything else new?"

"No. Not really."

"Nothing?" she asked.

He shook his head.

My lips turned up in a subtle grin. I knew what she was getting at, but it was cute watching him miss her meaning. And watching her try to ask him about girls, without actually asking him about girls.

"So that's all that's going on?" she asked. "Biology test. Classes. Nothing else is new?"

He shrugged. "I guess not."

"But is there anything else we might want to know about?"

"Mom, what are you talking about?"

"She's trying to ask if there's a girl in your life," I said.

"Oh. Why didn't you just say that?"

She let out an exasperated breath. "I was trying to be subtle."

"Mom, I'm a guy. We don't always get subtle. And no, there's not a girl. I was talking to this one girl in my history class a little bit, but it didn't go anywhere."

"Why not?" she asked.

"I don't know." He glanced away. "I think she was more interested in the fact that I'm a football player than in me. Like it didn't matter who I was, she just wanted to be dating a guy on the team."

Harper wrinkled her nose. "That's not good."

"Yeah, I don't need that nonsense," Owen said.

I pulled Harper against me. "Give it time. When you meet the right one for you, she'll be worth the wait."

Harper tilted her face up to me and smiled.

"Please don't start making out," Owen said.

Obviously I couldn't let that challenge go unanswered. With a grin at my son, I kissed my wife. She giggled into my mouth. Owen groaned.

"I'm gonna take my stuff up to my room." He grabbed another cookie and stood. "Plus, I have a reading assignment I have to finish before I go back."

"Okay," Harper said. "Your bed has clean sheets and everything. I'll be at the bakery tomorrow, so if you want to stop by, everyone would love to see you."

"I will. Thanks, Mom."

"Night, Son," I said.

"Night, Dad."

He grabbed his duffel bag and hauled it upstairs. Harper nestled against me, her cheek resting on my chest. Holding her close, I took a deep breath, savoring the moment. My family was whole again, and the older Owen got, the more I appreciated those times.

Harper had come into my life when I least expected it. And nothing had ever been the same. She liked to say I'd saved her, but really, it was the other way around. She'd saved me, and I hadn't even realized how much I'd needed saving.

She was my wife, my love, my everything.

———

Dear reader

Dear reader,

Once upon a time, when I was a brand-new baby author, I thought writing would get easier someday. Surely by the time I'd written nearly forty books, writing the next one wouldn't be so hard. There must come a point when I'd have this whole writing thing all figured out and I could just sail on through each new book while my fingers moved effortlessly across the keyboard, producing word magic.

That's not how it works. At all.

In fact, I've found that most of my writer friends agree, it only gets harder.

I think a lot of that has to do with expectations—not just from readers, but from ourselves. We know what we're capable of, and we're always striving to get better.

In any case, this book was hard.

What makes each book a challenge often varies, and in this case, it was the deputy himself, Garrett Haven. Write a brother who's in law enforcement, I thought. It'll be fun, I thought.

You don't realize how much you don't know about a profession until you find yourself in the position of having to write convincingly about it. And as I began this book I realized I know nothing about law enforcement.

I didn't want to rely on cop shows or movies. Those aren't necessarily true to life, and I wouldn't know what's realistic and what isn't. Of course it's all fiction, but even in fiction, I want to do my best to portray things that do exist in real life as accurately as possible.

So what's a girl to do? Listen to true crime podcasts, obviously.

Someone turned me on to Small Town Dicks, a true crime podcast hosted by retired detectives. Listening to those episodes helped me to sink into the profession a little bit and immerse myself in their lingo. I also found a Facebook group dedicated to providing a place for writers to ask questions about law enforcement. That led me to the book *Cops and Writers*, which had a ton of information aimed at helping writers depict law enforcement accurately.

Armed with that info, and a lot more research besides, I dove into this book. It still wasn't easy, but I'm grateful for the help that was available.

Aside from the cop lingo, protocol, and cold case info, I had a romance to write! I have to say, I loved this take on an insta-love story. Maybe it wasn't quite instant, but Garrett and Harper were head over heels for each other pretty fast.

It was fun to push Garrett out of his comfort zone and draw Harper into the family she so deeply longed for. And Owen. Oh, sweet Owen Haven. He was the surprise of the story for me as I wrote. He took the spotlight more than I anticipated, and I loved every second of it.

I hope you did too.

Love,

Claire

Acknowledgments

Thank you to my team for kicking butt behind the scenes so I can write. Nikki, Alex, and Stacey, you're a dream team!

To Lori for your creativity and brilliance in cover design. And for putting up with all the times we asked for a little more green, but also less green, and maybe blue, but less blue too.

To Michelle for being marvelous to work with and cleaning up the story so my errant commas don't trip anyone.

To Erma for lending your time and your sharp eye to hunt down pesky typos.

To the lovely folks in Cops and Writers on Facebook, and to Patrick J. O'Donnell, author of *Cops and Writers: From the Academy to the Street,* for lending your professional expertise and answering questions.

To my family, for your love, support, and (sometimes dark and mildly inappropriate) humor. You're the reason I do what I do.

And to my readers. Thank you for continuing on this journey with me. I hope you're loving this family as much as I am!

Also by Claire Kingsley

For a full and up-to-date listing of Claire Kingsley books visit
www.clairekingsleybooks.com/books/

For comprehensive reading order, visit

www.clairekingsleybooks.com/reading-order/

––––––––

The Haven Brothers

Small-town romantic suspense with CK's signature endearing characters and heartwarming happily ever afters. Can be read as stand-alones.

Obsession Falls (Josiah and Audrey)

Storms and Secrets (Zachary and Marigold)

Temptation Trails (Garrett and Harper)

The rest of the Haven brothers will be getting their own happily ever afters!

––––––––

How the Grump Saved Christmas (Elias and Isabelle)

A stand-alone, small-town Christmas romance.

––––––––

The Bailey Brothers

Steamy, small-town family series with a dash of suspense. Five unruly brothers. Epic pranks. A quirky, feuding town. Big HEAs. Best read in order.

Protecting You (Asher and Grace part 1)

Fighting for Us (Asher and Grace part 2)

Unraveling Him (Evan and Fiona)

Rushing In (Gavin and Skylar)

Chasing Her Fire (Logan and Cara)

Rewriting the Stars (Levi and Annika)

————

The Miles Family

Sexy, sweet, funny, and heartfelt family series with a dash of suspense. Messy family. Epic bromance. Super romantic. Best read in order.

Broken Miles (Roland and Zoe)

Forbidden Miles (Brynn and Chase)

Reckless Miles (Cooper and Amelia)

Hidden Miles (Leo and Hannah)

Gaining Miles: A Miles Family Novella (Ben and Shannon)

————

Dirty Martini Running Club

Sexy, fun, feel-good romantic comedies with huge… hearts. Can be read as stand-alones.

Everly Dalton's Dating Disasters (Prequel with Everly, Hazel, and Nora)

Faking Ms. Right (Everly and Shepherd)

Falling for My Enemy (Hazel and Corban)

Marrying Mr. Wrong (Sophie and Cox)

Flirting with Forever (Nora and Dex)

————

Bluewater Billionaires

Hot romantic comedies. Lady billionaire BFFs and the badass heroes who love them. Can be read as stand-alones.

The Mogul and the Muscle (Cameron and Jude)

The Price of Scandal, Wild Open Hearts, and Crazy for Loving You

More Bluewater Billionaire shared-world romantic comedies by Lucy Score, Kathryn Nolan, and Pippa Grant

————

Bootleg Springs

by Claire Kingsley and Lucy Score

Hot and hilarious small-town romcom series with a dash of mystery and suspense. Best read in order.

Whiskey Chaser (Scarlett and Devlin)

Sidecar Crush (Jameson and Leah Mae)

Moonshine Kiss (Bowie and Cassidy)

Bourbon Bliss (June and George)

Gin Fling (Jonah and Shelby)

Highball Rush (Gibson and I can't tell you)

————

Book Boyfriends

Hot romcoms that will make you laugh and make you swoon. Can be read as stand-alones.

Book Boyfriend (Alex and Mia)

Cocky Roommate (Weston and Kendra)

Hot Single Dad (Caleb and Linnea)

————

Finding Ivy (William and Ivy)

A unique contemporary romance with a hint of mystery. Stand-alone.

His Heart (Sebastian and Brooke)

A poignant and emotionally intense story about grief, loss, and the transcendent power of love. Stand-alone.

The Always Series

Smoking hot, dirty talking bad boys with some angsty intensity. Can be read as stand-alones.

Always Have (Braxton and Kylie)

Always Will (Selene and Ronan)

Always Ever After (Braxton and Kylie)

The Jetty Beach Series

Sexy small-town romance series with swoony heroes, romantic HEAs, and lots of big feels. Can be read as stand-alones.

Behind His Eyes (Ryan and Nicole)

One Crazy Week (Melissa and Jackson)

Messy Perfect Love (Cody and Clover)

Operation Get Her Back (Hunter and Emma)

Weekend Fling (Finn and Juliet)

Good Girl Next Door (Lucas and Becca)

The Path to You (Gabriel and Sadie)

About the Author

Claire Kingsley is a #1 Amazon bestselling author of sexy, heartwarming contemporary romance, romantic comedies, and small-town romantic suspense. She writes sassy, quirky heroines, swoony heroes who love big, romantic happily ever afters, and all the big feels.

She can't imagine life without coffee, great books, and the characters who inhabit her imagination. She lives in the inland Pacific Northwest with her three kids.

www.clairekingsleybooks.com

Printed in the USA
CPSIA information can be obtained
at www.ICGtesting.com
LVHW090818200924
791520LV00005B/496